Voyager Classics

OUT OF THE
SILENT PLANET

PERELANDRA

C S LEWIS

HarperCollinsPublishers

Voyager Classics
An Imprint of HarperCollins*Publishers*
77–85 Fulham Palace Road,
Hammersmith, London W6 8JB

www.voyager-books.com

This paperback edition 2001
1 3 5 7 9 8 6 4 2

Out of the Silent Planet previously published in paperback by
Voyager 2000
First published in Great Britain by
John Lane (The Bodley Head) Ltd 1938

Perelandra previously published in paperback by
Voyager 2000
First published in Great Britain by
John Lane (The Bodley Head) Ltd 1943

Out of the Silent Planet Copyright © C. S. Lewis Pte Ltd 1938
Perelandra Copyright © C.S. Lewis Pte Ltd 1943

ISBN 0 00 711793 0

Set in Stempel Garamond

Printed and bound in Great Britain by
Biddles Limited, Surrey

Out of the Silent Planet

VOYAGER CLASSICS

To celebra... greatest wor... f s...
V...
resp... ... th...
the very best in imagi... ...tive n... ...ney have not only given enjoyment to millions of readers around the world but have challenged and changed perceptions of the genre.

Authors as varied as J R R Tolkien, C S Lewis, Ray Bradbury, Aldous Huxley, Isaac Asimov, Clive Barker and William Gibson have inspired generations of new writers and film-makers around the world. This highly-collectable series of essential reads is a must-have for all book lovers.

TO MY BROTHER W.H.L.

A lifelong critic of the
space-and-time story

NOTE Certain slighting references to earlier stories of this type which will be found in the following pages have been put there for purely dramatic purposes. The author would be sorry if any reader supposed he was too stupid to have enjoyed Mr H. G. Wells's fantasies or too ungrateful to acknowledge his debt to them.

1

The last drops of the thundershower had hardly ceased falling when the Pedestrian stuffed his map into his pocket, settled his pack more comfortably on his tired shoulders, and stepped out from the shelter of a large chestnut tree into the middle of the road. A violent yellow sunset was pouring through a rift in the clouds to westward, but straight ahead over the hills the sky was the colour of dark slate. Every tree and blade of grass was dripping, and the road shone like a river. The Pedestrian wasted no time on the landscape but set out at once with the determined stride of a good walker who has lately realised that he will have to walk farther than he intended. That, indeed, was his situation. If he had chosen to look back, which he did not, he could have seen the spire of Much Nadderby, and, seeing it, might have uttered a malediction on the inhospitable little hotel which, though obviously empty, had refused him a bed. The place had changed hands since he last went for a walking tour in these parts. The kindly old landlord on whom he had reckoned had been replaced by someone whom the barmaid referred to as 'the lady', and the lady was apparently a British innkeeper of that orthodox school who regard guests as a nuisance. His only chance now was Sterk, on the far side of the hills, and a good six miles away. The map marked an inn at Sterk. The Pedestrian was too experienced to build any very sanguine hopes on this, but there seemed nothing else within range.

He walked fairly fast, and doggedly, without looking much about him, like a man trying to shorten the way with some interesting train of thought. He was tall, but a little round-shouldered, about thirty-five to forty years of age, and dressed with that particular kind of shabbiness which marks a member of the intelligentsia on a holiday. He might easily have been mistaken for a doctor or a schoolmaster at first sight, though he had not the man-of-the-world air of the one or the indefinable breeziness of the other. In fact, he was a philologist, and fellow of a Cambridge college. His name was Ransom.

He had hoped when he left Nadderby that he might find a night's lodging at some friendly farm before he had walked as far as Sterk. But the land this side of the hills seemed almost uninhabited. It was a desolate, featureless sort of country mainly devoted to cabbage and turnip, with poor hedges and few trees. It attracted no visitors like the richer country south of Nadderby and it was protected by the hills from the industrial areas beyond Sterk. As the evening drew in and the noise of the birds came to an end it grew more silent than an English landscape usually is. The noise of his own feet on the metalled road became irritating.

He had walked thus for a matter of two miles when he became aware of a light ahead. He was close under the hills by now and it was nearly dark, so that he still cherished hopes of a substantial farmhouse until he was quite close to the real origin of the light, which proved to be a very small cottage of ugly nineteenth-century brick. A woman darted out of the open doorway as he approached it and almost collided with him.

'I beg your pardon, sir,' she said. 'I thought it was my Harry.'

Ransom asked her if there was any place nearer than Sterk where he might possibly get a bed.

'No, sir,' said the woman. 'Not nearer than Sterk. I dare say as they might fix you up at Nadderby.'

She spoke in a humbly fretful voice as if her mind were intent on something else. Ransom explained that he had already tried Nadderby.

'Then I don't know, I'm sure, sir,' she replied. 'There isn't hardly any house before Sterk, not what you want. There's only The Rise, where my Harry works, and I thought you was coming from that way, sir, and that's why I come out when I heard you, think-ing it might be him. He ought to be home this long time.'

'The Rise,' said Ransom. 'What's that? A farm? Would they put me up?'

'Oh no, sir. You see there's no one there now except the Professor and the gentleman from London, not since Miss Alice died. They wouldn't do anything like that, sir. They don't even keep any servants, except my Harry for doing the furnace like, and he's not in the house.'

'What's this professor's name?' asked Ransom with a faint hope.

'I don't know, I'm sure, sir,' said the woman. 'The other gentle-man's Mr Devine, he is, and Harry says the *other* gentleman is a professor. He don't know much about it, you see, being a little simple, and that's why I don't like him coming home so late, and they said they'd always send him home at six o'clock. It isn't as if he didn't do a good day's work, either.'

The monotonous voice and the limited range of the woman's vocabulary did not express much emotion, but Ransom was stand-ing sufficiently near to perceive that she was trembling and nearly crying. It occurred to him that he ought to call on the mysterious professor and ask for the boy to be sent home: and it occurred to him just a fraction of a second later that once he were inside the house – among men of his own profession – he might very rea-sonably accept the offer of a night's hospitality. Whatever the process of thought may have been, he found that the mental pic-ture of himself calling at The Rise had assumed all the solidity of a thing determined upon. He told the woman what he intended to do.

'Thank you very much, sir, I'm sure,' she said. 'And if you would be so kind as to see him out of the gate and on the road before you leave, if you see what I mean, sir. He's that frightened of the Professor and he wouldn't come away once your back was turned, sir, not if they hadn't sent him home themselves like.'

Ransom reassured the woman as well as he could and bade her goodbye, after ascertaining that he would find The Rise on his left in about five minutes. Stiffness had grown upon him while he was standing still, and he proceeded slowly and painfully on his way.

There was no sign of any lights on the left of the road – nothing but the flat fields and a mass of darkness which he took to be a copse. It seemed more than five minutes before he reached it and found that he had been mistaken. It was divided from the road by a good hedge and in the hedge was a white gate: and the trees which rose above him as he examined the gate were not the first line of a copse but only a belt, and the sky showed through them. He felt sure now that this must be the gate of The Rise and that these trees surrounded a house and garden. He tried the gate and found it locked. He stood for a moment undecided, discouraged by the silence and the growing darkness. His first inclination, tired as he felt, was to continue his journey to Sterk: but he had committed himself to a troublesome duty on behalf of the old woman. He knew that it would be possible, if one really wanted, to force a way through the hedge. He did not want to. A nice fool he would look, blundering in upon some retired eccentric – the sort of a man who kept his gates locked in the country – with this silly story of a hysterical mother in tears because her idiot boy had been kept half an hour late at his work! Yet it was perfectly clear that he would have to get in, and since one cannot crawl through a hedge with a pack on, he slipped his pack off and flung it over the gate. The moment he had done so, it seemed to him that he had not till now fully made up his mind – now that he must break into the garden if only in order to recover the pack. He became very angry with the woman, and with himself, but he got down on his hands and knees and began to worm his way into the hedge.

The operation proved more difficult than he had expected and it was several minutes before he stood up in the wet darkness on the inner side of the hedge smarting from his contact with thorns and nettles. He groped his way to the gate, picked up his pack, and then for the first time turned to take stock of his surroundings. It was lighter on the drive than it had been under the trees and he had no difficulty in making out a large stone house divided from him by a width of untidy and neglected lawn. The drive branched into two a little way ahead of him – the right-hand path leading in a gentle sweep to the front door, while the left ran straight ahead, doubtless to the back premises of the house. He noticed that this path was churned up into deep ruts – now full of water – as if it were used to carrying a traffic of heavy lorries. The other, on which he now began to approach the house, was overgrown with moss. The house itself showed no light: some of the windows were shuttered, some gaped blank without shutter or curtain, but all were lifeless and inhospitable. The only sign of occupation was a column of smoke that rose from behind the house with a density which suggested the chimney of a factory, or at least of a laundry, rather than that of a kitchen. The Rise was clearly the last place in the world where a stranger was likely to be asked to stay the night, and Ransom, who had already wasted some time in exploring it, would certainly have turned away if he had not been bound by his unfortunate promise to the old woman.

He mounted the three steps which led into the deep porch; rang the bell, and waited. After a time he rang the bell again and sat down on a wooden bench which ran along one side of the porch. He sat so long that though the night was warm and starlit the sweat began to dry on his face and a faint chilliness crept over his shoulders. He was very tired by now, and it was perhaps this which prevented him from rising and ringing the third time: this, and the soothing stillness of the garden, the beauty of the summer sky, and the occasional hooting of an owl somewhere in the neighbourhood which seemed only to emphasise the underlying tranquillity of his surroundings. Something like drowsiness had already descended upon him when he found himself startled into vigilance. A peculiar noise was going on – a scuffling, irregular noise, vaguely reminiscent of a football scrum. He stood up. The noise was unmistakable by now. People in boots were fighting or wrestling or playing some game. They were shouting too. He could not make out the words but he heard the monosyllabic barking ejaculations of men who are angry and out of breath. The last thing Ransom wanted was an adventure, but a conviction that he ought to investigate the matter was already growing upon him when a much louder cry rang out in which he could distinguish the words, 'Let me go. Let me go,' and then, a second later, 'I'm not going in there. Let me go home.'

Throwing off his pack, Ransom sprang down the steps of the porch, and ran round to the back of the house as quickly as his stiff and footsore condition allowed him. The ruts and pools of the muddy path led him to what seemed to be a yard, but a yard surrounded with an unusual number of outhouses. He had a momentary vision of a tall chimney, a low door filled with red firelight, and a huge round shape that rose black against the stars, which he took for the dome of a small observatory: then all this was blotted out of his mind by the figures of three men who were struggling together so close to him that he almost cannoned into them. From the very first Ransom felt no doubt that the central figure, whom the two others seemed to be detaining in spite of his struggles, was the old woman's Harry. He would like to have thundered out, 'What are you doing to that boy?' but the words that actually came – in rather an unimpressive voice – were, 'Here! I say! …'

The three combatants fell suddenly apart, the boy blubbering. 'May I ask,' said the thicker and taller of the two men, 'who the devil you may be and what you are doing here?' His voice had all the qualities which Ransom's had so regrettably lacked.

'I'm on a walking tour,' said Ransom, 'and I promised a poor woman –'

'Poor woman be damned,' said the other. 'How did you get in?'

'Through the hedge,' said Ransom, who felt a little ill-temper coming to his assistance. 'I don't know what you're doing to that boy, but –'

'We ought to have a dog in this place,' said the thick man to his companion, ignoring Ransom.

'You mean we should have a dog if you hadn't insisted on using Tartar for an experiment,' said the man who had not yet spoken.

6

He was nearly as tall as the other, but slender, and apparently the younger of the two, and his voice sounded vaguely familiar to Ransom.

The latter made a fresh beginning. 'Look here,' he said, 'I don't know what you are doing to that boy, but it's long after hours and it is high time you sent him home. I haven't the least wish to interfere in your private affairs, but –'

'Who are you?' bawled the thick man.

'My name is Ransom, if that is what you mean. And –'

'By Jove,' said the slender man, 'not Ransom who used to be at Wedenshaw?'

'I was at school at Wedenshaw,' said Ransom.

'I thought I knew you as soon as you spoke,' said the slender man. 'I'm Devine. Don't you remember me?'

'Of course. I should think I do!' said Ransom as the two men shook hands with the rather laboured cordiality which is traditional in such meetings. In actual fact Ransom had disliked Devine at school as much as anyone he could remember.

'Touching, isn't it?' said Devine. 'The far-flung line even in the wilds of Sterk and Nadderby. This is where we get a lump in our throats and remember Sunday evening Chapel in the DOP. You don't know Weston, perhaps?' Devine indicated his massive and loud-voiced companion. '*The* Weston,' he added. 'You know. The great physicist. Has Einstein on toast and drinks a pint of Schrödinger's blood for breakfast. Weston, allow me to introduce my old schoolfellow, Ransom. Dr Elwin Ransom. *The* Ransom, you know. The great philologist. Has Jespersen on toast and drinks a pint –'

'I know nothing about it,' said Weston, who was still holding the unfortunate Harry by the collar. 'And if you expect me to say that I am pleased to see this person who has just broken into my garden, you will be disappointed. I don't care twopence what school he was at nor on what unscientific foolery he is at present wasting money that ought to go to research. I want to know what he's doing here: and after that I want to see the last of him.'

'Don't be an ass, Weston,' said Devine in a more serious voice. 'His dropping in is delightfully apropos. You mustn't mind Weston's little way, Ransom. Conceals a generous heart beneath a grim exterior, you know. You'll come in and have a drink and something to eat, of course?'

'That's very kind of you,' said Ransom. 'But about the boy –'

Devine drew Ransom aside. 'Barmy,' he said in a low voice. 'Works like a beaver as a rule but gets these fits. We are only trying to get him into the wash-house and keep him quiet for an hour or so till he's normal again. Can't let him go home in his present state. All done by kindness. You can take him home yourself presently if you like – and come back and sleep here.'

Ransom was very much perplexed. There was something about the whole scene suspicious enough and disagreeable enough to convince him that he had blundered on something criminal, while on the other hand he had all the deep, irrational conviction of his age and class that such things could never cross the path of an ordinary person except in fiction and could least of all be associated with professors and old schoolfellows. Even if they had been ill-treating the boy, Ransom did not see much chance of getting him from them by force.

While these thoughts were passing through his head, Devine had been speaking to Weston, in a low voice, but no lower than was to be expected of a man discussing hospitable arrangements in the presence of a guest. It ended with a grunt of assent from Weston. Ransom, to whose other difficulties a merely social embarrassment was now being added, turned with the idea of making some remark. But Weston was now speaking to the boy.

'You have given enough trouble for one night, Harry,' he said. 'And in a properly governed country I'd know how to deal with you. Hold your tongue and stop snivelling. You needn't go into the wash-house if you don't want –'

'It weren't the wash-house,' sobbed the halfwit, 'you know it weren't. I don't want to go in *that* thing again.'

'He means the laboratory,' interrupted Devine. 'He got in there and was shut in by accident for a few hours once. It put the wind up him for some reason. Lo, the poor Indian, you know.' He turned to the boy. 'Listen, Harry,' he said. 'This kind gentleman is going to take you home as soon as he's had a rest. If you'll come in and sit down quietly in the hall I'll give you something you like.' He imitated the noise of a cork being drawn from a bottle – Ransom remembered it had been one of Devine's tricks at school – and a guffaw of infantile knowingness broke from Harry's lips.

'Bring him in,' said Weston as he turned away and disappeared into the house. Ransom hesitated to follow, but Devine assured him that Weston would be very glad to see him. The lie was barefaced, but Ransom's desire for a rest and a drink were rapidly overcoming his social scruples. Preceded by Devine and Harry, he entered the house and found himself a moment later seated in an armchair and awaiting the return of Devine, who had gone to fetch refreshments.

2

The room into which he had been shown revealed a strange mixture of luxury and squalor. The windows were shuttered and curtainless, the floor was uncarpeted and strewn with packing cases, shavings, newspapers and books, and the wallpaper showed the stains left by the pictures and furniture of the previous occupants. On the other hand, the only two armchairs were of the costliest type, and in the litter which covered the tables, cigars, oyster shells and empty champagne bottles jostled with tins of condensed milk and opened sardine tins, with cheap crockery, broken bread, teacups a quarter full of tea and cigarette ends.

His hosts seemed to be a long time away, and Ransom fell to thinking of Devine. He felt for him that sort of distaste we feel for someone whom we have admired in boyhood for a very brief period and then outgrown. Devine had learned just half a term earlier than anyone else that kind of humour which consists in a perpetual parody of the sentimental or idealistic cliché's of one's elders. For a few weeks his references to the Dear Old Place and to Playing the Game, to the White Man's Burden and a Straight Bat, had swept everyone, Ransom included, off their feet. But before he left Wedenshaw Ransom had already begun to find Devine a bore, and at Cambridge he had avoided him, wondering from afar how anyone so flashy and, as it were, ready-made could be so successful. Then had come the mystery of Devine's election to the Leicester fellowship, and the further mystery of his increasing wealth. He had long since abandoned Cambridge for London, and was presumably something 'in the city'. One heard of him occasionally and one's informant usually ended either by saying, 'A damn clever chap, Devine, in his own way', or else by observing plaintively, 'It's a mystery to me how that man has got where he is.' As far as Ransom could gather from the brief conversation in the yard, his old schoolfellow had altered very little.

He was interrupted by the opening of the door. Devine entered alone, carrying a bottle of whiskey on a tray with glass, and a syphon.

'Weston is looking out something to eat,' he said as he placed the tray on the floor beside Ransom's chair, and addressed himself to opening the bottle. Ransom, who was very thirsty indeed by now, observed that his host was one of those irritating people who forget to use their hands when they begin talking. Devine started to prise up the silver paper which covered the cork with the point of a corkscrew, and then stopped to ask:

'How do you come to be in this benighted part of the country?'

'I'm on a walking tour,' said Ransom; 'slept at Stoke Underwood last night and had hoped to end at Nadderby tonight. They wouldn't put me up, so I was going on to Sterk.'

'God!' exclaimed Devine, his corkscrew still idle. 'Do you do it for money, or is it sheer masochism?'

'Pleasure, of course,' said Ransom, keeping his eye immovably on the still unopened bottle.

'Can the attraction of it be explained to the uninitiate?' asked Devine, remembering himself sufficiently to rip up a small portion of the silver paper.

'I hardly know. To begin with, I like the actual walking –'

'God! You must have enjoyed the army. Jogging along to Thingummy, eh?'

'No, no. It's just the opposite of the army. The whole point about the army is that you are never alone for a moment and can never choose where you're going or even what part of the road you're walking on. On a walking tour you are absolutely detached. You stop where you like and go on when you like. As long as it lasts you need consider no one and consult no one but yourself.'

'Until one night you find a wire waiting at your hotel saying, "Come back at once",' replied Devine, at last removing the silver paper.

'Only if you were fool enough to leave a list of addresses and go to them! The worst that could happen to me would be that man on the wireless saying, "Will Dr Elwin Ransom, believed to be walking somewhere in the Midlands –" '

'I begin to see the idea,' said Devine, pausing in the very act of drawing the cork. 'It wouldn't do if you were in business. You are a lucky devil! But can even you just disappear like that? No wife, no young, no aged but honest parent or anything of that sort?'

'Only a married sister in India. And then, you see, I'm a don. And a don in the middle of long vacation is almost a non-existent creature, as you ought to remember. College neither knows nor cares where he is, and certainly no one else does.'

The cork at last came out of the bottle with a heart-cheering noise.

'Say when,' said Devine, as Ransom held out his glass. 'But I feel sure there's a catch somewhere. Do you really mean to say that no one knows where you are or when you ought to get back, and no one can get hold of you?'

Ransom was nodding in reply when Devine, who had picked up the syphon, suddenly swore. 'I'm afraid this is empty,' he said. 'Do you mind having water? I'll have to get some from the scullery. How much do you like?'

'Fill it up, please,' said Ransom.

A few minutes later Devine returned and handed Ransom his long delayed drink. The latter remarked, as he put down the half-emptied tumbler with a sigh of satisfaction that Devine's choice of residence was at least as odd as his own choice of a holiday.

'Quite,' said Devine. 'But if you knew Weston you'd realise that it's much less trouble to go where he wants than to argue the matter. What you call a strong colleague.'

'Colleague?' said Ransom inquiringly.

'In a sense.' Devine glanced at the door, drew his chair closer to Ransom's, and continued in a more confidential tone. 'He's the goods all right, though. Between ourselves, I am putting a little money into some experiments he has on hand. It's all straight stuff – the march of progress and the good of humanity and all that, but it has an industrial side.'

While Devine was speaking something odd began to happen to Ransom. At first it merely seemed to him that Devine's words were no longer making sense. He appeared to be saying that he was industrial all down both sides but could never get an experiment to fit him in London. Then he realised that Devine was not so much unintelligible as inaudible, which was not surprising, since he was now so far away – about a mile away, though perfectly clear like something seen through the wrong end of a telescope. From that bright distance where he sat in his tiny chair he was gazing at Ransom with a new expression on his face. The gaze became disconcerting. Ransom tried to move in his chair but found that he had lost all power over his own body. He felt quite comfortable, but it was as if his legs and arms had been bandaged to the chair and his head gripped in a vice; a beautifully padded, but quite immovable, vice. He did not feel afraid, though he knew that he ought to be afraid and soon would be. Then, very gradually, the room faded from his sight.

Ransom could never be sure whether what followed had any bearing on the events recorded in this book or whether it was merely an irresponsible dream. It seemed to him that he and Weston and Devine were all standing in a little garden surrounded by a wall. The garden was bright and sunlit, but over the top of the wall you could see nothing but darkness. They were trying to climb over the wall and Weston asked them to give him a hoist up. Ransom kept on telling him not to go over the wall because it was so dark on the other side, but Weston insisted, and all three of them set about doing so. Ransom was the last. He got astride on the top of the wall, sitting on his coat because of the broken bottles. The other two had already dropped down on the outside into the darkness, but before he followed them a door in the wall – which none of them had noticed – was opened from without and the queerest people he had ever seen came into the garden bringing Weston and Devine back with them. They left them in the garden and retired into the darkness themselves, locking the door behind them. Ransom found it impossible to get down from the wall. He remained sitting there, not frightened but rather uncomfortable because his right leg, which was on the outside, felt so dark and his left leg felt so light. 'My leg will drop off if it gets much darker,' he said. Then he looked down into the darkness and asked, 'Who are you?' and the Queer People must still have been there for they all replied, 'Hoo – Hoo – Hoo?' just like owls.

He began to realise that his leg was not so much dark as cold and stiff, because he had been resting the other on it for so long: and also that he was in an armchair in a lighted room. A conversation was going on near him and had, he now realised being going on for some time. His head was clear. He realised that he had been drugged or hypnotised, or both, and he felt that some control over his own body was returning to him though he was still very weak. He listened intently without trying to move.

'I'm getting a little tired of this, Weston,' Devine was saying, 'and specially as it's my money that is being risked. I tell you he'll do quite as well as the boy, and in some ways better. Only, he'll be coming round very soon now and we must get him on board at once. We ought to have done it an hour ago.'

'The boy was ideal,' said Weston sulkily. 'Incapable of serving humanity and only too likely to propagate idiocy. He was the sort of boy who in a civilised community would be automatically handed over to a state laboratory for experimental purposes.'

'I dare say. But in England he is the sort of boy in whom Scotland Yard might conceivably feel an interest. This busybody, on the other hand, will not be missed for months, and even then no one will know where he was when he disappeared. He came alone. He left no address. He has no family. And finally he has poked his nose into the whole affair of his own accord.'

'Well, I confess I don't like it. He is, after all, human. The boy was really almost a – a preparation. Still, he's only an individual, and probably a quite useless one. We're risking our own lives, too. In a great cause –'

'For the Lord's sake don't start all that stuff now. We haven't time.'

'I dare say,' replied Weston, 'he would consent if he could be made to understand.'

'Take his feet and I'll take his head,' said Devine.

'If you really think he's coming round,' said Weston, 'you'd better give him another dose. We can't start till we get the sunlight. It wouldn't be pleasant to have him struggling in there for three hours or so. It would be better if he didn't wake up till we were under way.'

'True enough. Just keep an eye on him while I run upstairs and get another.'

Devine left the room. Ransom saw through his half-closed eyes that Weston was standing over him. He had no means of foretelling how his own body would respond, if it responded at all, to a sudden attempt at movement, but he saw at once that he must take his chance. Almost before Devine had closed the door he flung himself with all his force at Weston's feet. The scientist fell forward across the chair, and Ransom, flinging him off with an agonising effort, rose and dashed out into the hall. He was very weak and fell as he entered it: but terror was behind him and in a couple of seconds he had found the hall door and was working desperately to master the bolts. Darkness and his trembling hands were against him. Before he had drawn one bolt, booted feet were clattering over the carpetless floor behind him. He was gripped by the shoulders and the knees. Kicking, writhing, dripping with sweat, and bellowing as loud as he could in the faint hope of rescue, he prolonged the struggle with a violence of which he would have believed himself incapable. For one glorious moment the door was open, the fresh night air was in his face, he saw the reassuring stars and even his own pack lying in the porch. Then a heavy blow fell on his head. Consciousness faded, and the last thing of which he was aware was the grip of strong hands pulling him back into the dark passage, and the sound of a closing door.

3

When Ransom came to his senses he seemed to be in bed in a dark room. He had a pretty severe headache, and this, combined with a general lassitude, discouraged him at first from attempting to rise or to take stock of his surroundings. He noticed, drawing his hand across his forehead, that he was sweating freely, and this directed his attention to the fact that the room (if it was a room) was remarkably warm. Moving his arms to fling off the bedclothes, he touched a wall at the right side of the bed: it was not only warm, but hot. He moved his left hand to and fro in the emptiness on the other side and noticed that there the air was cooler – apparently the heat was coming from the wall. He felt his face and found a bruise over the left eye. This recalled to his mind the struggle with Weston and Devine, and he instantly concluded that they had put him in an outhouse behind their furnace. At the same time he looked up and recognised the source of the dim light in which, without noticing it, he had all along been able to see the movements of his own hands. There was some kind of skylight imme-diately over his head – a square of night sky filled with stars. It seemed to Ransom that he had never looked out on such a frosty night. Pulsing with brightness as with some unbearable pain or pleasure, clustered in pathless and countless multitudes, dreamlike in clarity, blazing in perfect blackness, the stars seized all his atten-tion, troubled him, excited him, and drew him up to a sitting posi-tion. At the same time they quickened the throb of his headache, and this reminded him that he had been drugged. He was just for-mulating to himself the theory that the stuff they had given him might have some effect on the pupil and that this would explain the unnatural splendour and fullness of the sky, when a disturbance of silver light, almost a pale and miniature sunrise, at one corner of the skylight, drew his eyes upward again. Some minutes later the orb of the full moon was pushing its way into the field of vision. Ransom sat still and watched. He had never seen such a moon – so white, so blinding and so large. 'Like a great football just outside the glass,' he thought, and then, a moment later, 'No – it's bigger than that.' By this time he was quite certain that something was seriously wrong with his eyes: no moon could possibly be the size of the thing he was seeing.

The light of the huge moon – if it was a moon – had by now illuminated his surroundings almost as clearly as if it were day. It was a very strange room. The floor was so small that the bed and a table beside it occupied the whole width of it: the ceiling seemed to be nearly twice as wide and the walls sloped outward as they rose, so that Ransom had the impression of lying at the bottom of a deep and narrow wheelbarrow. This confirmed his belief that his sight was either temporarily or permanently injured. In other respects, however, he was recovering rapidly and even beginning to feel an unnatural lightness of heart and a not disagreeable excitement. The heat was still oppressive, and he stripped off everything but his shirt and trousers before rising to explore. His rising was disastrous and raised graver apprehensions in his mind about the effects of being drugged. Although he had been conscious of no unusual muscular effort, he found himself leaping from the bed with an energy which brought his head into sharp contact with the skylight and flung him down again in a heap on the floor. He found himself on the other side against the wall – the wall that ought to have sloped outwards like the side of a wheelbarrow, according to his previous reconnaissance. But it didn't. He felt it and looked at it; it was unmistakably at right angles to the floor. More cautiously this time, he rose again to his feet. He felt an extraordinary lightness of body: it was with difficulty that he kept his feet on the floor. For the first time a suspicion that he might be dead and already in the ghost-life crossed his mind. He was trembling, but a hundred mental habits forbade him to consider this possibility. Instead, he explored his prison. The result was beyond doubt: all the walls looked as if they sloped outwards so as to make the room wider at the ceiling than it was at the floor, but each wall as you stood beside it turned out to be perfectly perpendicular – not only to sight but to touch also if one stooped down and examined with one's fingers the angle between it and the floor. The same examination revealed two other curious facts. The room was walled and floored with metal, and was in a state of continuous faint vibration – a silent vibration with a strangely lifelike and unmechanical quality about it. But if the vibration was silent, there was plenty of noise going on – a series of musical raps or percussions at quite irregular intervals which seemed to come from the ceiling. It was as if the metal chamber in which he found himself was being bombarded with small, tinkling missiles. Ransom was by now thoroughly frightened – not with the prosaic fright that a man suffers in a war, but with a heady, bounding kind of fear that was hardly distinguishable from his general excitement: he was poised on a sort of emotional watershed from which, he felt, he might at any moment pass either into delirious terror or into an ecstasy of joy. He knew now that he was not in a submarine: and the infinitesimal quivering of the metal did not suggest the motion of any wheeled vehicle. A ship, then, he supposed, or some kind of airship ... but there was an oddity in all his sensations for which neither supposition accounted. Puzzled, he sat down again on the bed, and stared at the portentous moon.

An airship, some kind of flying machine ... but why did the moon look so big? It was larger than he had thought at first. No moon could really be that size; and he realised now that he had known this from the first but had repressed the knowledge through terror. At the same moment a thought came into his head which stopped his breath – there could be no full moon at all that night. He remembered distinctly that he had walked from Nadderby on a moonless night. Even if the thin crescent of a new moon had escaped his notice, it could not have grown to this in a few hours. It could not have grown to this at all – this megalomaniac disc, far larger than the football he had at first compared it to, larger than a child's hoop, filling almost half the sky. And where was the old 'man in the moon' – the familiar face that had looked down on all the generations of men? The thing wasn't the Moon at all; and he felt his hair move on his scalp.

At that moment the sound of an opening door made him turn his head. An oblong of dazzling light appeared behind him and instantly vanished as the door closed again, having admitted the bulky form of a naked man whom Ransom recognised as Weston. No reproach, no demand for an explanation, rose to Ransom's lips or even to his mind; not with that monstrous orb above them. The mere presence of a human being, with its offer of at least some companionship, broke down the tension in which his nerves had long been resisting a bottomless dismay. He found, when he spoke, that he was sobbing.

'Weston! Weston!' he gasped. 'What is it? It's not the Moon, not that size. It can't be, can it?'

'No,' replied Weston, 'it's the Earth.'

4

Ransom's legs failed him, and he must have sunk back upon the bed, but he only became aware of this many minutes later. At the moment he was unconscious of everything except his fear. He did not even know what he was afraid of: the fear itself possessed his whole mind, a formless, infinite misgiving. He did not lose consciousness, though he greatly wished that he might do so. Any change – death or sleep, or, best of all, a waking which should show all this for a dream – would have been inexpressibly welcome. None came. Instead, the lifelong self-control of social man, the virtues which are half hypocrisy or the hypocrisy which is half a virtue, came back to him and soon he found himself answering Weston in a voice not shamefully tremulous.

'Do you mean that?' he asked.

'Certainly.'

'Then where are we?'

'Standing out from Earth about eighty-five thousand miles.'

'You mean we're – in space,' Ransom uttered the word with difficulty as a frightened child speaks of ghosts or a frightened man of cancer.

Weston nodded.

'What for?' said Ransom. 'And what on earth have you kidnapped me for? And how have you done it?'

For a moment Weston seemed disposed to give no answer; then, as if on a second thought, he sat down on the bed beside Ransom and spoke as follows:

'I suppose it will save trouble if I deal with these questions at once, instead of leaving you to pester us with them every hour for the next month. As to how we do it – I suppose you mean how the space-ship works – there's no good your asking that. Unless you were one of the four or five real physicists now living you couldn't understand: and if there were any chance of your understanding you certainly wouldn't be told. If it makes you happy to repeat words that don't mean anything – which is, in fact, what unscientific people want when they ask for an explanation – you may say we work by exploiting the less observed properties of solar radiation. As to why we are here, we are on our way to Malacandra …'

'Do you mean a star called Malacandra?'

'Even you can hardly suppose we are going out of the solar system. Malacandra is much nearer than that: we shall make it in about twenty-eight days.'

'There isn't a planet called Malacandra,' objected Ransom.

'I am giving it its real name, not the name invented by terrestrial astronomers,' said Weston.

'But surely this is nonsense,' said Ransom. 'How the deuce did you find out its real name, as you call it?'

'From the inhabitants.'

It took Ransom some time to digest this statement. 'Do you mean to tell me you claim to have been to this star before, or this planet, or whatever it is?'

'Yes.'

'You can't really ask me to believe that,' said Ransom. 'Damn it all, it's not an everyday affair. Why has no one heard of it? Why has it not been in all the papers?'

'Because we are not perfect idiots,' said Weston gruffly.

After a few moments' silence Ransom began again. 'Which planet is it in our terminology?' he asked.

'Once and for all,' said Weston, 'I am not going to tell you. If you know how to find out when we get there, you are welcome to do so: I don't think we have much to fear from your scientific attainments. In the meantime, there is no reason for you to know.'

'And you say this place is inhabited?' said Ransom.

Weston gave him a peculiar look and then nodded. The uneasiness which this produced in Ransom rapidly merged in an anger which he had almost lost sight of amidst the conflicting emotions that beset him.

'And what has all this to do with me?' he broke out. 'You have assaulted me, drugged me, and are apparently carrying me off as a prisoner in this infernal thing. What have I done to you? What do you say for yourself?'

'I might reply by asking you why you crept into my backyard like a thief. If you had minded your own business you would not be here. As it is, I admit that we have had to infringe your rights. My only defence is that small claims must give way to great. As far as we know, we are doing what has never been done in the history of man, perhaps never in the history of the universe. We have learned how to jump off the speck of matter on which our species began; infinity, and therefore perhaps eternity, is being put into the hands of the human race. You cannot be so small-minded as to think that the rights or the life of an individual or of a million individuals are of the slightest importance in comparison with this.'

'I happen to disagree,' said Ransom, 'and I always have disagreed, even about vivisection. But you haven't answered my question. What do you want me for? What good am I to do you on this – on Malacandra?'

'That I don't know,' said Weston. 'It was no idea of ours. We are only obeying orders.'

'Whose?'

There was another pause. 'Come,' said Weston at last. 'There is really no use in continuing this cross-examination. You keep on asking me questions I can't answer: in some cases because I don't know the answers, in others because you wouldn't understand them. It will make things very much pleasanter during the voyage if you can only resign your mind to your fate and stop bothering yourself and us. It would be easier if your philosophy of life were not so insufferably narrow and individualistic. I had thought no one could fail to be inspired by the role you are being asked to play: that even a worm, if it could understand, would rise to the sacrifice. I mean, of course, the sacrifice of time and liberty, and some little risk. Don't misunderstand me.'

'Well,' said Ransom, 'you hold all the cards, and I must make the best of it. I consider *your* philosophy of life raving lunacy. I suppose all that stuff about infinity and eternity means that you think you are justified in doing anything – absolutely anything – here and now, on the off chance that some creatures or other descended from man as we know him may crawl about a few centuries longer in some part of the universe.'

'Yes – anything whatever,' returned the scientist sternly, 'and all educated opinion – for I do not call classics and history and such trash education – is entirely on my side. I am glad you raised the point, and I advise you to remember my answer. In the meantime, if you will follow me into the next room, we will have breakfast. Be careful how you get up: your weight here is hardly appreciable compared with your weight on Earth.'

Ransom rose and his captor opened the door. Instantly the room was flooded with a dazzling golden light which completely eclipsed the pale earthlight behind him.

'I will give you darkened glasses in a moment,' said Weston as he preceded him into the chamber whence the radiance was pouring. It seemed to Ransom that Weston went up a hill towards the doorway and disappeared suddenly downwards when he had passed it. When he followed – which he did with caution – he had the curious impression that he was walking up to the edge of a precipice: the new room beyond the doorway seemed to be built on its side so that its farther wall lay almost in the same plane as the floor of the room he was leaving. When, however, he ventured to put forward his foot, he found that the floor continued flush and as he entered the second room the walls suddenly righted themselves and the rounded ceiling was over his head. Looking back, he perceived that the bedroom in its turn was now heeling over – its roof a wall and one of its walls a roof.

'You will soon get used to it,' said Weston, following his gaze. 'The ship is roughly spherical, and now that we are outside the gravitational field of the Earth "down" means – and feels – towards the centre of our own little metal world. This, of course, was fore-seen and we built her accordingly. The core of the ship is a hollow globe – we keep our stores inside it – and the surface of that globe is the floor we are walking on. The cabins are arranged all round this, their walls supporting an outer globe which from our point of view is the roof. As the centre is always "down", the piece of floor you are standing on always feels flat or horizontal and the wall you are standing against always seems vertical. On the other hand, the globe of floor is so small that you can always see over the edge of it – over what would be the horizon if you were a flea – and then you see the floor and walls of the next cabin in a different plane. It is just the same on Earth, of course, only we are not big enough to see it.'

After this explanation he made arrangements in his precise, ungracious way for the comfort of his guest or prisoner. Ransom, at his advice, removed all his clothes and substituted a little metal girdle hung with enormous weights to reduce, as far as possible, the unmanageable lightness of his body. He also assumed tinted glasses, and soon found himself seated opposite Weston at a small table laid for breakfast. He was both hungry and thirsty and eager-ly attacked the meal which consisted of tinned meat, biscuit, but-ter and coffee.

But all these actions he had performed mechanically. Stripping, eating and drinking passed almost unnoticed, and all he ever remembered of his first meal in the spaceship was the tyranny of heat and light. Both were present in a degree which would have been intolerable on Earth, but each had a new quality. The light was paler than any light of comparable intensity that he had ever seen; it was not pure white but the palest of all imaginable golds, and it cast shadows as sharp as a floodlight. The heat, utterly free from moisture, seemed to knead and stroke the skin like a gigantic masseur: it produced no tendency to drowsiness: rather, intense alacrity. His headache was gone: he felt vigilant, courageous and magnanimous as he had seldom felt on Earth. Gradually he dared to raise his eyes to the skylight. Steel shutters were drawn across all but a chink of the glass, and that chink was covered with blinds of some heavy and dark material; but still it was too bright to look at.

'I always thought space was dark and cold,' he remarked vaguely.

'Forgotten the sun?' said Weston contemptuously.

Ransom went on eating for some time. Then he began, 'If it's like this in the early morning,' and stopped, warned by the expression on Weston's face. Awe fell upon him: there were no mornings here, no evenings, and no night – nothing but the changeless noon which had filled for centuries beyond history so many millions of cubic miles. He glanced at Weston again, but the latter held up his hand.

'Don't talk,' he said. 'We have discussed all that is necessary. The ship does not carry oxygen enough for any unnecessary exertion; not even for talking.'

Shortly afterwards he rose, without inviting the other to follow him, and left the room by one of the many doors which Ransom had not yet seen opened.

5

The period spent in the space-ship ought to have been one of terror and anxiety for Ransom. He was separated by an astronomical distance from every member of the human race except two whom he had excellent reasons for distrusting. He was heading for an unknown destination, and was being brought thither for a purpose which his captors steadily refused to disclose. Devine and Weston relieved each other regularly in a room which Ransom was never allowed to enter and where he supposed the controls of their machine must be. Weston, during his watches off, was almost entirely silent. Devine was more loquacious and would often talk and guffaw with the prisoner until Weston rapped on the wall of the control room and warned them not to waste air. But Devine was secretive after a certain point. He was quite ready to laugh at Weston's solemn scientific idealism. He didn't give a damn, he said, for the future of the species or the meeting of two worlds.

'There's more to Malacandra than that,' he would add with a wink. But when Ransom asked him what more, he would lapse into satire and make ironical remarks about the white man's burden and the blessings of civilisation.

'It *is* inhabited, then?' Ransom would press.

'Ah – there's always a native question in these things,' Devine would answer. For the most part his conversation ran on the things he would do when he got back to Earth: oceangoing yachts, the most expensive women and a big place on the Riviera figured largely in his plans. 'I'm not running all these risks for fun.'

Direct questions about Ransom's own role were usually met

with silence. Only once, in reply to such a question, Devine, who was then in Ransom's opinion very far from sober, admitted that they were rather 'handing him the baby'.

'But I'm sure,' he added, 'you'll live up to the old school tie.'

All this, as I have said, was sufficiently disquieting. The odd thing was that it did not very greatly disquiet him. It is hard for a man to brood on the future when he is feeling so extremely well as Ransom now felt. There was an endless night on one side of the ship and an endless day on the other: each was marvellous and he moved from the one to the other at his will, delighted. In the nights, which he could create by turning the handle of a door, he lay for hours in contemplation of the skylight. The Earth's disk was nowhere to be seen, the stars, thick as daisies on an uncut lawn, reigned perpetually with no cloud, no moon, no sunrise, to dispute their sway. There were planets of unbelievable majesty, and constellations undreamed of: there were celestial sapphires, rubies, emeralds and pin-pricks of burning gold; far out on the left of the picture hung a comet, tiny and remote: and between all and behind all, far more emphatic and palpable than it showed on Earth, the undimensioned, enigmatic blackness. The lights trembled: they seemed to grow brighter as he looked. Stretched naked on his bed, a second Dana, he found it night by night more difficult to disbelieve in old astrology: almost he felt, wholly he imagined, 'sweet influence' pouring or even stabbing into his surrendered body. All was silence but for the irregular tinkling noises. He knew now that these were made by meteorites, small, drifting particles of the world-stuff that smote continually on their hollow drum of steel; and he guessed that at any moment they might meet something large enough to make meteorites of ship and all. But he could not fear. He now felt that Weston had justly called him little-minded in the moment of his first panic. The adventure was too high, its circumstance too solemn, for any emotion save a severe delight. But the days – that is, the hours spent in the sunward hemisphere of their microcosm – were the best of all. Often he rose after only a few hours sleep to return, drawn by an irresistible attraction, to the regions of light; he could not cease to wonder at the noon which always awaited you however early you were to seek it. There, totally immersed in a bath of pure ethereal colour and of unrelenting though unwounding brightness, stretched his full length and with eyes half closed in the strange chariot that bore them, faintly quivering, through depth after depth of tranquillity far above the reach of night, he felt his body and mind daily rubbed and scoured and filled with new vitality. Weston, in one of his brief, reluctant answers, admitted a scientific basis for these sensations: they were receiving, he said, many rays that never penetrated the terrestrial atmosphere.

But Ransom, as time wore on, became aware of another and more spiritual cause for his progressive lightening and exultation of heart. A nightmare, long engendered in the modern mind by the mythology that follows in the wake of science, was falling off him. He had read of 'Space': at the back of his thinking for years had lurked the dismal fancy of the black, cold vacuity, the utter deadness, which was supposed to separate the worlds. He had not known how much it affected him till now – now that the very name 'Space' seemed a blasphemous libel for this empyrean ocean of radiance in which they swam. He could not call it 'dead'; he felt life pouring into him from it every moment. How indeed should it be otherwise, since out of this ocean the worlds and all their life had come? He had thought it barren; he saw now that it was the womb of worlds, whose blazing and innumerable offspring looked down nightly even upon the Earth with so many eyes – and here, with how many more! No: Space was the wrong name. Older thinkers had been wiser when they named it simply the heavens – the heavens which declared the glory – the

> happy climes that ly
> Where day never shuts his eye
> Up in the broad fields of the sky.

He quoted Milton's words to himself lovingly, at this time and often.

He did not, of course, spend all his time in basking. He explored the ship (so far as he was allowed), passing from room to room with those slow movements which Weston enjoined upon them lest exertion should over tax their supply of air. From the necessity of its shape, the space-ship contained a good many more chambers than were in regular use; but Ransom was also inclined to think that its owners – or at least Devine intended these to be filled with cargo of some kind on the return voyage. He also became, by an insensible process, the steward and cook of the company; partly because he felt it natural to share the only labours he could share – he was never allowed into the control room – and partly in order to anticipate a tendency which Weston showed to make him a servant whether he would or not. He preferred to work as a volunteer rather than in admitted slavery: and he liked his own cooking a good deal more than that of his companions.

It was these duties that made him at first the unwilling, and then the alarmed, hearer of a conversation which occurred about a fortnight (he judged) after the beginning of their voyage. He had washed up the remains of their evening meal, basked in the sunlight, chatted with Devine – better company than Weston, though in Ransom's opinion much the more odious of the two – and retired to bed at his usual time. He was a little restless, and after an hour or so it occurred to him that he had forgotten one or two small arrangements in the galley which would facilitate his work in the morning. The galley opened off the saloon or day room, and its door was close to that of the control room. He rose and went there at once. His feet, like the rest of him, were bare.

The galley skylight was on the dark side of the ship, but Ransom did not turn on the light. To leave the door ajar was sufficient, as this admitted a stream of brilliant sunlight. As everyone who has 'kept house' will understand, he found that his preparations for the morning had been even more incomplete than he supposed. He did his work well, from practice, and therefore quietly. He had just finished and was drying his hands on the roller towel behind the galley door when he heard the door of the control room open and saw the silhouette of a man outside the galley – Devine's, he gathered. Devine did not come forward into the saloon, but remained standing and talking – apparently into the control room. It thus came about that while Ransom could hear distinctly what Devine said, he could not make out Weston's answers.

'I think it would be damn' silly,' said Devine. 'If you could be sure of meeting the brutes where we alight there might be something in it. But suppose we have to trek? All we'd gain by your plan would be having to carry a drugged man and his pack instead of letting a live man walk with us and do his share of the work.'

Weston apparently replied.

'But he *can't* find out,' returned Devine. 'Unless someone is fool enough to tell him. Anyway, even if he suspects, do you think a man like that would have the guts to run away on a strange planet? Without food? Without weapons? You'll find he'll eat out of your hand at the first sight of a *sorn*.'

Again Ransom heard the indistinct noise of Weston's voice.

'How should I know?' said Devine. 'It may be some sort of chief: much more likely a mumbo-jumbo.'

This time came a very short utterance from the control room: apparently a question. Devine answered at once.

'It would explain why he was wanted.'

Weston asked him something more.

'Human sacrifice, I suppose. At least it wouldn't be human from *their* point of view; you know what I mean.'

Weston had a good deal to say this time, and it elicited Devine's characteristic chuckle.

'Quite, quite,' he said. 'It is understood that you are doing it all from the highest motives. So long as they lead to the same actions as *my* motives, you are quite welcome to them.'

Weston continued; and this time Devine seemed to interrupt him.

'You're not losing your own nerve, are you?' he said. He was then silent for some time, as if listening. Finally, he replied:

'If you're so fond of the brutes as that you'd better stay and inter-breed – if they have sexes, which we don't yet know. Don't you worry. When the time comes for cleaning the place up we'll save one or two for you, and you can keep them as pets or vivisect them or sleep with them or all three – whichever way it takes you … Yes, I know. Perfectly loathsome. I was only joking. Good night.'

A moment later Devine closed the door of the control room, crossed the saloon and entered his own cabin. Ransom heard him bolt the door of it according to his invariable, though puzzling, custom. The tension with which he had been listening relaxed. He found that he had been holding his breath, and breathed deeply again. Then cautiously he stepped out into the saloon.

Though he knew that it would be prudent to return to his bed as quickly as possible, he found himself standing still in the now familiar glory of the light and viewing it with a new and poignant emotion. Out of this heaven, these happy climes, they were presently to descend – into *what*? *Sorns*, human sacrifice, loath-some sexless monsters. What was a *sorn*? His own role in the affair was now clear enough. Somebody or something had sent for him. It could hardly be for him personally. The somebody wanted a vic-tim – any victim – from Earth. He had been picked because Devine had done the picking; he realised for the first time – in all circum-stances a late and startling discovery – that Devine had hated him all these years as heartily as he hated Devine. But what was a *sorn*? When he saw them he would eat out of Weston's hands. His mind, like so many minds of his generation, was richly furnished with bogies. He had read his H. G. Wells and others. His universe was peopled with horrors such as ancient and medieval mythology could hardly rival. No insect-like, vermiculate or crustacean Abominable, no twitching feelers, rasping wings, slimy coils, curl-ing tentacles, no monstrous union of superhuman intelligence and insatiable cruelty seemed to him anything but likely on an alien world. The *sorns* would be … would be … he dared not think what the *sorns* would be. And he was to be given to them. Somehow this seemed more horrible than being caught by them. Given, handed over, offered. He saw in imagination various incompatible monstrosities – bulbous eyes, grinning jaws, horns, stings, mandibles. Loathing of insects, loathing of snakes, loathing of things that squashed and squelched, all played their horrible symphonies over his nerves. But the reality would be worse: it would be an extra-terrestrial Otherness – something one had never thought of, never could have thought of. In that moment Ransom made a decision. He could face death, but not the *sorns*. He must escape when they got to Malacandra, if there were any possibility. Starvation, or even to be chased by *sorns*, would be better than being handed over. If escape were impossible, then it must be suicide. Ransom was a pious man. He hoped he would be forgiven. It was no more in his power, he thought, to decide otherwise than to grow a new limb. Without hesitation he stole back into the galley and secured the sharpest knife: henceforward he determined never to be parted from it.

Such was the exhaustion produced by terror that when he regained his bed he fell instantly into stupefied and dreamless sleep.

6

He woke much refreshed, and even a little ashamed of his terror on the previous night. His situation was, no doubt, very serious: indeed the possibility of returning alive to Earth must be almost discounted. But death could be faced, and rational fear of death could be mastered. It was only the irrational, the biological, horror of monsters that was the real difficulty: and this he faced and came to terms with as well as he could while he lay in the sunlight after breakfast. He had the feeling that one sailing in the heavens, as he was doing, should not suffer abject dismay before any earth-bound creature. He even reflected that the knife could pierce other flesh as well as his own. The bellicose mood was a very rare one with Ransom. Like many men of his own age, he rather under-estimated than over-estimated his own courage; the gap between boyhood's dreams and his actual experience of the War had been startling, and his subsequent view of his own unheroic qualities had perhaps swung too far in the opposite direction. He had some anxiety lest the firmness of his present mood should prove a short-lived illusion; but he must make the best of it.

As hour followed hour and waking followed sleep in their eternal day, he became aware of a gradual change. The temperature was slowly falling. They resumed clothes. Later, they added warm underclothes. Later still, an electric heater was turned on in the centre of the ship. And it became certain, too – though the phenomenon was hard to seize – that the light was less overwhelming than it had been at the beginning of the voyage. It became certain to the comparing intellect, but it was difficult to *feel* what was happening as a diminution of light and impossible to think of it as 'darkening' because while the radiance changed in degree, its unearthly quality had remained exactly the same since the moment he first beheld it. It was not, like fading light upon the Earth, mixed with the increasing moisture and phantom colours of the air. You might halve its intensity, Ransom perceived, and the remaining half would still be what the whole had been – merely less, not other. Halve it again, and the residue would still be the same. As long as it was at all, it would be itself – out even to that unimagined distance where its last force was spent. He tried to explain what he meant to Devine.

'Like thingummy's soap!' grinned Devine. Pure soap to the last bubble, eh?'

Shortly after this the even tenor of their life in the space-ship began to be disturbed. Weston explained that they would soon begin to feel the gravitational pull of Malacandra.

'That means,' he said, 'that it will no longer be "down" to the centre of the ship. It will be "down" towards Malacandra – which from our point of view will be under the control room. As a consequence, the floors of most of the chambers will become wall or roof, and one of the walls a floor. You won't like it.'

The result of this announcement, so far as Ransom was concerned, was hours of heavy labour in which he worked shoulder to shoulder now with Devine and now with Weston as their alternating watches liberated them from the control room. Water tins, oxygen cylinders, guns, ammunition and foodstuffs had all to be piled on the floors alongside the appropriate walls and lying on their sides so as to be upright when the new 'downwards' came into play. Long before the work was finished disturbing sensations began. At first Ransom supposed that it was the toil itself which so weighted his limbs: but rest did not alleviate the symptom, and it was explained to him that their bodies, in response to the planet that had caught them in its field, were actually gaining weight every minute and doubling in weight with every twenty-four hours. They had the experiences of a pregnant woman, but magnified almost beyond endurance.

At the same time their sense of direction – never very confident on the space-ship – became continuously confused. From any room on board, the next room's floor had always looked downhill and felt level: now it looked downhill and felt a little, a very little, downhill as well. One found oneself running as one entered it. A cushion flung aside on the floor of the saloon would be found hours later to have moved an inch or so towards the wall. All of them were afflicted with vomiting, headache and palpitations of the heart. The conditions grew worse hour by hour. Soon one could only grope and crawl from cabin to cabin. All sense of direction disappeared in a sickening confusion. Parts of the ship were definitely below in the sense that their floors were upside down and only a fly could walk on them: but no part seemed to Ransom to be indisputably the right way up. Sensations of intolerable height and of falling – utterly absent in the heavens – recurred constantly. Cooking, of course, had long since been abandoned. Food was snatched as best they could, and drinking presented great difficulties: you could never be sure that you were really holding your mouth below, rather than beside, the bottle. Weston grew grimmer and more silent than ever. Devine, a flask of spirits ever in his hand, flung out strange blasphemies and coprologies and cursed Weston for bringing them. Ransom ached, licked his dry lips, nursed his bruised limbs and prayed for the end.

A time came when one side of the sphere was unmistakably down. Clamped beds and tables hung useless and ridiculous on what was now wall or roof. What had been doors became trap-doors, opened with difficulty. Their bodies seemed made of lead. There was no more work to be done when Devine had set out the clothes – their Malacandrian clothes – from their bundles and squatted down on the end wall of the saloon (now its floor) to watch the thermometer. The clothes, Ransom noticed, included heavy woollen underwear, sheepskin jerkins, fur gloves and eared caps. Devine made no reply to his questions. He was engaged in studying the thermometer and in shouting down to Weston in the control room.

'Slower, slower,' he kept shouting. 'Slower, you damned fool. You'll be in air in a minute or two.' Then sharply and angrily. 'Here! Let me get at it.'

Weston made no replies. It was unlike Devine to waste his advice: Ransom concluded that the man was almost out of his senses, whether with fear or excitement.

Suddenly the lights of the Universe seemed to be turned down. As if some demon had rubbed the heaven's face with a dirty sponge, the splendour in which they had lived for so long blenched to a pallid, cheerless and pitiable grey. It was impossible from where they sat to open the shutters or roll back the heavy blind. What had been a chariot gliding in the fields of heaven became a dark steel box dimly lighted by a slit of window, and falling. They were falling out of the heaven, into a world. Nothing in all his adventures bit so deeply into Ransom's mind as this. He wondered how he could ever have thought of planets, even of the Earth, as islands of life and reality floating in a deadly void. Now, with a certainty which never after deserted him, he saw the planets – the 'earths' he called them in his thought – as mere holes or gaps in the living heaven – excluded and rejected wastes of heavy matter and murky air, formed not by addition to, but by subtraction from, the surrounding brightness. And yet, he thought, beyond the solar system the brightness ends. Is that the real void, the real death? Unless ... he groped for the idea ... unless visible light is also a hole or gap, a mere diminution of something else. Something that is to bright unchanging heaven as heaven is to the dark, heavy earths ...

Things do not always happen as a man would expect. The moment of his arrival in an unknown world found Ransom wholly absorbed in a philosophical speculation.

7

'Having a doze?' said Devine. 'A bit blasé' about new planets by now?'

'Can you see anything?' interrupted Weston.

'I can't manage the shutters, damn them,' returned Devine. 'We may as well get to the manhole.'

Ransom awoke from his brown study. The two partners were working together close beside him in the semi-darkness. He was cold and his body, though in fact much lighter than on Earth, still felt intolerably heavy. But a vivid sense of his situation returned to him; some fear, but more curiosity. It might mean death, but what a scaffold! Already cold air was coming in from without, and light. He moved his head impatiently to catch some glimpse between the labouring shoulders of the two men. A moment later the last nut was unscrewed. He was looking out through the manhole.

Naturally enough all he saw was the ground – a circle of pale pink, almost of white; whether very close and short vegetation or very wrinkled and granulated rock or soil he could not say. Instantly the dark shape of Devine filled the aperture, and Ransom had no time to notice that he had a revolver in his hand – 'For me or for *sorns* or for both?' he wondered.

'You next,' said Weston curtly.

Ransom took a deep breath and his hand went to the knife beneath his belt. Then he got his head and shoulders through the manhole, his two hands on the soil of Malacandra. The pink stuff was soft and faintly resilient, like india-rubber: clearly vegetation. Instantly Ransom looked up. He saw a pale blue sky – a fine winter morning sky it would have been on Earth – a great billowy cumular mass of rose-colour lower down which he took for a cloud, and then 'Get out,' said Weston from behind him. He scrambled through and rose to his feet. The air was cold but not bitterly so, and it seemed a little rough at the back of his throat. He gazed about him, and the very intensity of his desire to take in the new world at a glance defeated itself. He saw nothing but colours – colours that refused to form themselves into things. Moreover, he knew nothing yet well enough to see it: you cannot see things till you know roughly what they are. His first impression was of a bright, pale world – a watercolour world out of a child's paint-box; a moment later he recognised the flat belt of light blue as a sheet of water, or of something like water, which came nearly to his feet. They were on the shore of a lake or river.

'Now then,' said Weston, brushing past him. He turned and saw to his surprise, a quite recognisable object in the immediate foreground – a hut of unmistakably terrestrial pattern though built of strange materials.

'They're human,' he gasped. 'They build houses?'

'*We* do,' said Devine. 'Guess again,' and, producing a key from his pocket, proceeded to unlock a very ordinary padlock on the door of the hut. With a not very clearly defined feeling of disappointment or relief Ransom realised that his captors were merely returning to their own camp. They behaved as one might have expected. They walked into the hut, let down the slats which served for windows, sniffed the close air, expressed surprise that they had left it so dirty, and presently re-emerged.

'We'd better see about the stores,' said Weston.

Ransom soon found that he was to have little leisure for observation and no opportunity of escape. The monotonous work of transferring food, clothes, weapons and many unidentifiable packages from the ship to the hut kept him vigorously occupied for the next hour or so, and in the closest contact with his kidnappers. But something he learned. Before anything else he learned that Malacandra was beautiful; and he even reflected how odd it was that this possibility had never entered into his speculations about it. The same peculiar twist of imagination which led him to people the universe with monsters had somehow taught him to expect nothing on a strange planet except rocky desolation or else a network of nightmare machines. He could not say why, now that he came to think of it. He also discovered that the blue water surrounded them on at least three sides: his view in the fourth direction was blotted out by the vast steel football in which they had come. The hut, in fact, was built either on the point of a peninsula or on the end of an island. He also came little by little to the conclusion that the water was not merely blue in certain lights like terrestrial water but 'really' blue. There was something about its behaviour under the gentle breeze which puzzled him – something wrong or unnatural about the waves. For one thing, they were too big for such a wind, but that was not the whole secret. They reminded him somehow of the water that he had seen shooting up under the impact of shells in pictures of naval battles. Then suddenly realisation came to him: they were the wrong shape, out of drawing, far too high for their length, too narrow at the base, too steep in the sides. He was reminded of something he had read in one of those modern poets about a sea rising in 'turreted walls'.

'Catch!' shouted Devine. Ransom caught and hurled the parcel on to Weston at the hut door.

On one side the water extended a long way – about a quarter of a mile, he thought, but perspective was still difficult in the strange world. On the other side it was much narrower, not wider than fifteen feet perhaps, and seemed to be flowing over a shallow – broken and swirling water that made a softer and more hissing sound than water on earth; and where it washed the hither bank – the pinkish-white vegetation went down to the very brink – there was a bubbling and sparkling which suggested effervescence. He tried hard, in such stolen glances as the work allowed him, to make out something of the farther shore. A mass of something purple, so huge that he took it for a heather-covered mountain, was his first impression: on the other side, beyond the larger water, there was something of the same kind. But there, he could see over the top of it. Beyond were strange upright shapes of whitish green; too jagged and irregular for buildings, too thin and steep for mountains. Beyond and above these again was the rose-coloured cloud-like mass. It might really be a cloud but it was very solid looking and did not seem to have moved since he first set eyes on it from the manhole. It looked like the top of a gigantic red cauliflower – or like a huge bowl of red soapsuds – and it was exquisitely beautiful in tint and shape.

Baffled by this, he turned his attention to the nearer shore beyond the shallows. The purple mass looked for a moment like a plump of organ-pipes, then like a stack of rolls of cloth set up on end, then like a forest of gigantic umbrellas blown inside out. It was in faint motion. Suddenly his eyes mastered the object. The purple stuff was vegetation: more precisely it was vegetables, vegetables about twice the height of English elms, but apparently soft and flimsy. The stalks – one could hardly call them trunks – rose smooth and round, and surprisingly thin, for about forty feet: above that, the huge plants opened into a sheaf-like development, not of branches but of leaves, leaves large as lifeboats but nearly transparent. The whole thing corresponded roughly to his idea of a submarine forest: the plants, at once so large and so frail, seemed to need water to support them, and he wondered that they could hang in the air. Lower down, between the stems, he saw the vivid purple twilight, mottled with paler sunshine, which made up the internal scenery of the wood.

'Time for lunch,' said Devine suddenly. Ransom straightened his back; in spite of the thinness and coldness of the air, his forehead was moist. They had been working hard and he was short of breath. Weston appeared from the door of the hut and muttered something about 'finishing first'. Devine, however, overruled him. A tin of beef and some biscuits were produced, and the men sat down on the various boxes which were still plentifully littered between the space-ship and the hut. Some whiskey – again at Devine's suggestion and against Weston's advice – was poured into the tin cups and mixed with water: the latter, Ransom noticed, was drawn from their own water tins and not from the blue lakes.

As often happens, the cessation of bodily activity drew Ransom's attention to the excitement under which he had been labouring ever since their landing. Eating seemed almost out of the question. Mindful, however, of a possible dash for liberty, he forced himself to eat very much more than usual, and appetite returned as he ate. He devoured all that he could lay hands on either of food or drink: and the taste of that first meal was ever after associated in his mind with the first unearthly strangeness (never fully recaptured) of the bright, still, sparkling unintelligible landscape – with needling shapes of pale green, thousands of feet high, with sheets of dazzling blue soda-water, and acres of rose-red soapsuds. He was a little afraid that his companions might notice, and suspect, his new achievements as a trencherman; but their attention was otherwise engaged. Their eyes never ceased roving the landscape; they spoke abstractedly and often changed position, and were ever looking over their shoulders. Ransom was just finishing his protracted meal when he saw Devine stiffen like a dog, and lay his hand in silence on Weston's shoulder. Both nodded. They rose. Ransom, gulping down the last of his whiskey, rose too. He found himself between his two captors. Both revolvers were out. They were edging him to the shore of the narrow water, and they were looking and pointing across it.

At first he could not see clearly what they were pointing at. There seemed to be some paler and slenderer plants than he had noticed before among the purple ones; he hardly attended to them, for his eyes were busy searching the ground – so obsessed was he with the reptile fears and insect fears of modern imagining. It was the reflections of the new white objects in the water that sent his eyes back to them: long, streaky, white reflections motionless in the running water – four or five, no, to be precise, six of them. He looked up. Six, white things *were* standing there. Spindly and flimsy things, twice or three times the height of a man. His first idea was that they were images of men, the work of savage artists; he had seen things like them in books of archaeology. But what could they be made of, and how could they stand? – so crazily thin and elongated in the leg, so top-heavily pouted in the chest, such stalky, flexible-looking distortions of earthly bipeds ... like something seen in one of those comic mirrors. They were certainly not made of stone or metal, for now they seemed to sway a little as he watched; now with a shock that chased the blood from his cheeks he saw that they were alive, that they were moving, that they were coming at him. He had a momentary, scared glimpse of their faces, thin and unnaturally long, with long, drooping noses and drooping mouths of half-spectral, half-idiotic solemnity. Then he turned wildly to fly and found himself gripped by Devine.

'Let me go,' he cried.

'Don't be a fool,' hissed Devine, offering the muzzle of his pistol. Then, as they struggled, one of the things sent its voice across the water to them: an enormous horn-like voice far above their heads.

'They want us to go across,' said Weston.

Both the men were forcing him to the water's edge. He planted his feet, bent his back and resisted donkey fashion. Now the other two were both in the water pulling him, and he was still on the land. He found that he was screaming. Suddenly a second, much louder and less articulate noise broke from the creatures on the far bank. Weston shouted, too, relaxed his grip on Ransom and suddenly fired his revolver not across the water but up it. Ransom saw why at the same moment.

A line of foam like the track of a torpedo was speeding towards them, and in the midst of it some large, shining beast. Devine shrieked a curse, slipped and collapsed into the water. Ransom saw a snapping jaw between them, and heard the deafening noise of Weston's revolver again and again beside him and, almost as loud, the clamour of the monsters on the far bank, who seemed to be taking to the water, too. He had had no need to make a decision. The moment he was free he had found himself automatically darting behind his captors, then behind the space-ship and on as fast as his legs could carry him into the utterly unknown beyond it. As he rounded the metal sphere a wild confusion of blue, purple and red met his eyes. He did not slacken his pace for a moment's inspection. He found himself splashing through water and crying out not with pain but with surprise because the water was warm. In less than a minute he was climbing out on to dry land again. He was running up a steep incline. And now he was running through purple shadow between the stems of another forest of the huge plants.

8

A month of inactivity, a heavy meal and an unknown world do not help a man to run. Half an hour later, Ransom was walking, not running, through the forest, with a hand pressed to his aching side and his ears strained for any noise of pursuit. The clamour of revolver shots and voices behind him (not all human voices) had been succeeded first by rifle shots and calls at long intervals and then by utter silence. As far as eye could reach he saw nothing but the stems of the great plants about him receding in the violet shade, and far overhead the multiple transparency of huge leaves filtering the sunshine to the solemn splendour of twilight in which he walked. Whenever he felt able he ran again; the ground continued soft and springy, covered with the same resilient weed which was the first thing his hands had touched in Malacandra. Once or twice a small red creature scuttled across his path, but otherwise there seemed to be no life stirring in the wood; nothing to fear – except the fact of wandering unprovisioned and alone in a forest of unknown vegetation thousands or millions of miles beyond the reach or knowledge of man.

But Ransom was thinking of *sorns* – for doubtless those were the *sorns*, those creatures they had tried to give him to. They were quite unlike the horrors his imagination had conjured up, and for that reason had taken him off his guard. They appealed away from the Wellsian fantasies to an earlier, almost an infantile, complex of fears. Giants ogres – ghosts – skeletons: those were its key words. Spooks on stilts, he said to himself; surrealistic bogy-men with their long faces. At the same time, the disabling panic of the first moments was ebbing away from him. The idea of suicide was now far from his mind; instead, he was determined to back his luck to the end. He prayed, and he felt his knife. He felt a strange emotion of confidence and affection towards himself – he checked himself on the point of saying, 'We'll stick to one another.'

The ground became worse and interrupted his meditation. He had been going gently upwards for some hours with steeper ground on his right, apparently half scaling, half skirting a hill. His path now began to cross a number of ridges, spurs doubtless of the higher ground on the right. He did not know why he should cross them, but for some reason he did; possibly a vague memory of earthly geography suggested that the lower ground would open out to bare places between wood and water where *sorns* would be more likely to catch him. As he continued crossing ridges and gullies he was struck with their extreme steepness; but somehow they were not very difficult to cross. He noticed, too, that even the smallest hummocks of earth were of an unearthly shape – too narrow, too pointed at the top and too small at the base. He remembered that the waves on the blue lakes had displayed a similar oddity. And glancing up at the purple leaves he saw the same theme of perpendicularity – the same rush to the sky – repeated there. They did not tip over at the ends; vast as they were, air was sufficient to support them so that the long aisles of the forest all rose to a kind of fan tracery. And the *sorns*, likewise – he shuddered as he thought it – they too were madly elongated.

He had sufficient science to guess that he must be on a world lighter than the Earth, where less strength was needed and nature was set free to follow her skyward impulse on a superterrestrial scale. This set him wondering where he was. He could not remember whether Venus was larger or smaller than Earth, and he had an idea that she would be hotter than this. Perhaps he was on Mars; perhaps even on the Moon. The latter he at first rejected on the ground that, if it were so, he ought to have seen the Earth in the sky when they landed; but later he remembered having been told that one face of the Moon was always turned away from the Earth.

For all he knew he was wandering on the Moon's outer side; and irrationally enough, this idea brought about him a bleaker sense of desolation than he had yet felt.

Many of the gullies which he crossed now carried streams, blue hissing streams, all hastening to the lower ground on his left. Like the lake they were warm, and the air was warm above them, so that as he climbed down and up the sides of the gullies he was continually changing temperatures. It was the contrast, as he crested the farther bank of one such small ravine, which first drew his attention to the growing chilliness of the forest; and as he looked about him he became certain that the light was failing, too. He had not taken night into his calculations. He had no means of guessing what night might be on Malacandra. As he stood gazing into the deepening gloom a sigh of cold wind crept through the purple stems and set them all swaying, revealing once again the startling contrast between their size and their apparent flexibility and lightness. Hunger and weariness, long kept at bay by the mingled fear and wonder of his situation, smote him suddenly. He shivered and forced himself to proceed. The wind increased. The mighty leaves danced and dipped above his head, admitting glimpses of a pale and then a paler sky; and then, discomfortingly, of a sky with one or two stars in it. The wood was no longer silent. His eyes darted hither and thither in search of an approaching enemy and discovered only how quickly the darkness grew upon him. He welcomed the streams now for their warmth.

It was this that first suggested to him a possible protection against the increasing cold. There was really no use in going farther; for all he knew he might as well be walking towards danger as away from it. All was danger; he was no safer travelling than resting. Beside some stream it might be warm enough to lie. He shuffled on to find another gully, and went so far that he began to think he had got out of the region of them. He had almost determined to turn back when the ground began falling steeply; he slipped, recovered and found himself on the bank of a torrent. The trees – for as 'trees' he could not help regarding them – did not quite meet overhead, and the water itself seemed to have some faintly phosphorescent quality, so that it was lighter here. The fall from right to left was steep. Guided by some vague picnicker's hankering for a 'better' place, he went a few yards upstream. The valley grew steeper, and he came to a little cataract. He noticed dully that the water seemed to be descending a little too slowly for the incline, but he was too tired to speculate about it. The water was apparently hotter than that of the lake – perhaps nearer its subterranean source of heat. What he really wanted to know was whether he dared drink it. He was very thirsty by now; but it looked very poisonous, very unwatery. He would try not to drink it; perhaps he was so tired that thirst would let him sleep. He sank on his knees and bathed his hands in the warm torrent; then he rolled over in a hollow close beside the fall, and yawned.

The sound of his own voice yawning – the old sound heard in night nurseries, school dormitories and in so many bedrooms – liberated a flood of self-pity. He drew his knees up and hugged himself; he felt a sort of physical, almost a filial, love for his own body. He put his wrist-watch to his ear and found that it had stopped. He wound it. Muttering, half whimpering to himself, he thought of men going to bed on the far-distant planet Earth – men in clubs, and liners, and hotels, married men, and small children who slept with nurses in the room, and warm, tobacco-smelling men tumbled together in forecastles and dug-outs. The tendency to talk to himself was irresistible ... 'We'll look after you, Ransom ... we'll stick together, old man.' It occurred to him that one of those creatures with snapping jaws might live in the stream. 'You're quite right, Ransom,' he answered mumblingly. 'It's not a safe place to spend the night. We'll just rest a bit till you feel better, then we'll go on again. Not now. Presently.'

9

It was thirst that woke him. He had slept warm, though his clothes were damp, and found himself lying in sunlight, the blue waterfall at his side dancing and coruscating with every transparent shade in the whole gamut of blue and flinging strange lights far up to the underside of the forest leaves. The realisation of his position, as it rolled heavily back upon consciousness, was unbearable. If only he hadn't lost his nerve the *sorns* would have killed him by now. Then he remembered with inexpressible relief that there was a man wandering in the wood – poor devil he'd be glad to see him. He would come up to him and say, 'Hullo, Ransom,' – he stopped, puzzled. No, it was only himself: he was Ransom. Or was he? Who was the man whom he had led to a hot stream and tucked up in bed, telling him not to drink the strange water? Obviously some newcomer who didn't know the place as well as he. But whatever Ransom had told him, he was going to drink now. He lay down on the bank and plunged his face in the warm rushing liquid. It was good to drink. It had a strong mineral flavour, but it was very good. He drank again and found himself greatly refreshed and steadied. All that about the other Ransom was nonsense. He was quite aware of the danger of madness, and applied himself vigorously to his devotions and his toilet. Not that madness mattered much. Perhaps he was mad already, and not really on Malacandra but safe in bed in an English asylum. If only it might be so! He would ask Ransom – curse it! there his mind went playing the same trick again. He rose and began walking briskly away.

The delusions recurred every few minutes as long as this stage of his journey lasted. He learned to stand still mentally, as it were, and let them roll over his mind. It was no good bothering about them. When they were gone you could resume sanity again. Far more important was the problem of food. He tried one of the 'trees' with his knife. As he expected, it was toughly soft like a vegetable, not hard like wood. He cut a little piece out of it, and under this operation the whole gigantic organism vibrated to its top – it was like being able to shake the mast of a full-rigged ship with one hand. When he put it in his mouth he found it almost tasteless but by no means disagreeable, and for some minutes he munched away contentedly. But he made no progress. The stuff was quite unswallowable and could only be used as a chewing-gum. As such he used it, and after it many other pieces; not without some comfort.

It was impossible to continue yesterday's flight as a flight – inevitably it degenerated into an endless ramble, vaguely motivated by the search for food. The search was necessarily vague, since he did not know whether Malacandra held food for him nor how to recognise it if it did. He had one bad fright in the course of the morning, when, passing through a somewhat more open glade, he became aware first of a huge, yellow object, then of two, and then of an indefinite multitude coming towards him. Before he could fly he found himself in the midst of a herd of enormous pale furry creatures more like giraffes than anything else he could think of, except that they could and did raise themselves on their hind legs and even progress several paces in that position. They were slenderer, and very much higher, than giraffes, and were eating the leaves off the tops of the purple plants. They saw him and stared at him with their big liquid eyes, snorting in *basso profondissimo*, but had apparently no hostile intentions. Their appetite was voracious. In five minutes they had mutilated the tops of a few hundred 'trees' and admitted a new flood of sunlight into the forest. Then they passed on.

This episode had an infinitely comforting effect on Ransom. The planet was not, as he had begun to fear, lifeless except for *sorns*. Here was a very presentable sort of animal, an animal which man could probably tame, and whose food man could possibly share. If only it were possible to climb the 'trees'! He was staring about him with some idea of attempting this feat, when he noticed that the devastation wrought by the leaf-eating animals had opened a vista overhead beyond the plant tops to a collection of the same greenish-white objects which he had seen across the lake at their first landing.

This time they were much closer. They were enormously high, so that he had to throw back his head to see the top of them. They were something like pylons in shape, but solid; irregular in height and grouped in an apparently haphazard and disorderly fashion. Some ended in points that looked from where he stood as sharp as needles, while others, after narrowing towards the summit, expanded again into knobs or platforms that seemed to his terrestrial eyes ready to fall at any moment. He noticed that the sides were rougher and more seamed with fissures than he had realised at first, and between two of them he saw a motionless line of twisting blue brightness – obviously a distant fall of water. It was this which finally convinced him that the things, in spite of their improbable shape, were mountains; and with that discovery the mere oddity of the prospect was swallowed up in the fantastic sublime. Here, he understood, was the full statement of that *perpendicular* theme which beast and plant and earth all played on Malacandra – here in this riot of rock, leaping and surging skyward like solid jets from some rock fountain, and hanging by their own lightness in the air, so shaped, so elongated, that all terrestrial mountains must ever after seem to him to be mountains lying on their sides. He felt a lift and lightening at the heart.

But next moment his heart stood still. Against the pallid background of the mountains and quite close to him – for the mountains themselves seemed but a quarter of a mile away – a moving shape appeared. He recognised it instantly as it moved slowly (and, he thought, stealthily) between two of the denuded plant tops – the giant stature, the cadaverous leanness, the long, drooping,

51

wizard-like profile of a *sorn*. The head appeared to be narrow and conical; the hands or paws with which it parted the stems before it as it moved were thin, mobile, spidery and almost transparent. He felt an immediate certainty that it was looking for him. All this he took in in an infinitesimal time. The ineffaceable image was hardly stamped on his brain before he was running as hard as he could into the thickest of the forest.

He had no plan save to put as many miles as he could between himself and the *sorn*. He prayed fervently that there might be only one; perhaps the wood was full of them – perhaps they had the intelligence to make a circle round him. No matter – there was nothing for it now but sheer running, running, knife in hand. The fear had all gone into action; emotionally he was cool and alert, and ready – as ready as he ever would be – for the last trial. His flight led him downhill at an ever-increasing speed; soon the incline was so steep that if his body had had terrestrial gravity he would have been compelled to take to his hands and knees and clamber down. Then he saw something gleaming ahead of him. A minute later he had emerged from the wood altogether; he was standing, blinking in the light of sun and water, on the shore of a broad river, and looking out on a flat landscape of intermingled river, lake, island and promontory – the same sort of country on which his eyes had first rested in Malacandra.

There was no sound of pursuit. Ransom dropped down on his stomach and drank, cursing a world where *cold* water appeared to be unobtainable. Then he lay still to listen and to recover his breath. His eyes were upon the blue water. It was agitated. Circles shuddered and bubbles danced ten yards away from his face. Suddenly the water heaved and a round, shining, black thing like a cannonball came into sight. Then he saw eyes and mouth – a puffing mouth bearded with bubbles. More of the thing came up out of the water. It was gleaming black. Finally it splashed and wallowed to the shore and rose, steaming, on its hind legs – six or seven feet high and too thin for its height, like everything in Malacandra. It had a coat of thick black hair, lucid as sealskin, very short legs with webbed feet, a broad beaver-like or fish-like tail, strong fore-limbs with webbed claws or fingers, and some complication halfway up the belly which Ransom took to be its genitals. It was something like a penguin, something like an otter, something like a seal; the slenderness and flexibility of the body suggested a giant stoat. The great round head, heavily whiskered, was mainly responsible for the suggestion of seal; but it was higher in the forehead than a seal's and the mouth was smaller.

There comes a point at which the actions of fear and precaution are purely conventional, no longer felt as terror or hope by the fugitive. Ransom lay perfectly still, pressing his body as well down into the weed as he could, in obedience to a wholly theoretical idea that he might thus pass unobserved. He felt little emotion. He noted in a dry, objective way that this was apparently to be the end of his story – caught between a *sorn* from the land and a big, black animal from the water. He had, it is true, a vague notion that the jaws and mouth of the beast were not those of a carnivore; but he knew that he was too ignorant of zoology to do more than guess.

Then something happened which completely altered his state of mind. The creature, which was still steaming and shaking itself on the bank and had obviously not seen him, opened its mouth and began to make noises. This in itself was not remarkable; but a lifetime of linguistic study assured Ransom almost at once that these were articulate noises. The creature was *talking*. It had language. If you are not yourself a philologist, I am afraid you must take on trust the prodigious emotional consequences of this realisation in Ransom's mind. A new world he had already seen – but a new, an extra-terrestrial, a non-human language was a different matter. Somehow he had not thought of this in connexion with the *sorns*; now, it flashed upon him like a revelation. The love of knowledge is a kind of madness. In the fraction of a second which it took Ransom to decide that the creature was really talking, and while he still knew that he might be facing instant death, his imagination had leaped over every fear and hope and probability of his situation to follow the dazzling project of making a Malacandrian grammar. *An Introduction to the Malacandrian Language – The Lunar Verb – A Concise Martian-English Dictionary* ... the titles flitted through his mind. And what might one not discover from the speech of a non-human race? The very form of language itself, the principle behind all possible languages, might fall into his hands. Unconsciously he raised himself on his elbow and stared at the black beast. It became silent. The huge bullet head swung round and lustrous amber eyes fixed him. There was no wind on the lake or in the wood. Minute after minute in utter silence the representatives of two so far-divided species stared each into the other's face.

Ransom rose to his knees. The creature leaped back, watching him intently, and they became motionless again. Then it came a pace nearer, and Ransom jumped up and retreated, but not far; curiosity held him. He summoned up his courage and advanced holding out his hand; the beast misunderstood the gesture. It backed into the shallows of the lake and he could see the muscles tightened under its sleek pelt, ready for sudden movement. But there it stopped; it, too, was in the grip of curiosity. Neither dared let the other approach, yet each repeatedly felt the impulse to do so himself, and yielded to it. It was foolish, frightening, ecstatic and unbearable all in one moment. It was more than curiosity. It was like a courtship – like the meeting of the first man and the first woman in the world; it was like something beyond that; so natural is the contact of sexes, so limited the strangeness, so shallow the reticence, so mild the repugnance to be overcome, compared with the first tingling intercourse of two different, but rational, species.

The creature suddenly turned and began walking away. A disappointment like despair smote Ransom.

'Come back,' he shouted in English. The thing turned, spread out its arms and spoke again in its unintelligible language; then it resumed its progress. It had not gone more than twenty yards away when Ransom saw it stoop down and pick something up. It returned. In its hand (he was already thinking of its webbed forepaw as a hand) it was carrying what appeared to be a shell – the shell of some oyster-like creature, but rounder and more deeply domed. It dipped the shell in the lake and raised it full of water. Then it held the shell to its own middle and seemed to be pouring something into the water. Ransom thought with disgust that it was urinating in the shell. Then he realised that the protuberances on the creature's belly were not genital organs nor organs at all; it was wearing a kind of girdle hung with various pouch-like objects, and it was adding a few drops of liquid from one of these to the water in the shell. This done it raised the shell to its black lips and drank – not throwing back its head like a man but bowing it and sucking like a horse. When it had finished it refilled the shell and once again added a few drops from the receptacle – it seemed to be some kind of skin bottle – at its waist. Supporting the shell in its two arms, it extended them towards Ransom. The intention was unmistakable. Hesitantly, almost shyly, he advanced and took the cup. His fingertips touched the webbed membrane of the creature's paws and an indescribable thrill of mingled attraction and repulsion ran through him; then he drank. Whatever had been added to the water was plainly alcoholic; he had never enjoyed a drink so much.

'Thank you,' he said in English. 'Thank you very much.'

The creature struck itself on the chest and made a noise. Ransom did not at first realise what it meant. Then he saw that it was trying to teach him its name – presumably the name of the species.

'*Hross*,' it said, '*hross*,' and flapped itself.

'*Hross*,' repeated Ransom, and pointed at it; then 'Man,' and struck his own chest.

'*Hma – h a – hman*,' imitated the *hross*. It picked up a handful of earth, where earth appeared between weed and water at the bank of the lake.

'*Handra*,' it said. Ransom repeated the word. Then an idea occurred to him.

'*Malacandra*?' he said in an inquiring voice. The *hross* rolled its eyes and waved its arms, obviously in an effort to indicate the whole landscape. Ransom was getting on well. *Handra* was earth the element; *Malacandra* the 'earth' or planet as a whole. Soon he would find out what *Malac* meant. In the meantime 'H disappears after C' he noted, and made his first step in Malacandrian phonetics. The *hross* was now trying to teach him the meaning of *handramit*. He recognised the root *handra-* again (and noted 'They have suffixes as well as prefixes'), but this time he could make nothing of the *hross*'s gestures, and remained ignorant what a *handramit* might be. He took the initiative by opening his mouth, pointing to it and going through the pantomime of eating. The Malacandrian word for *food* or *eat* which he got in return proved to contain consonants unreproducible by a human mouth, and Ransom, continuing the pantomime, tried to explain that his interest was practical as well as philological. The *hross* understood him, though he took some time to understand from its gestures that it was inviting him to follow it. In the end, he did so.

It took him only as far as where it had got the shell, and here, to his not very reasonable astonishment, Ransom found that a kind of boat was moored. Man-like, when he saw the artefact he felt more certain of the *hross*'s rationality. He even valued the creature the more because the boat, allowing for the usual Malacandrian height and flimsiness, was really very like an earthly boat; only later did he set himself the question, 'What else could a boat be like?' The *hross* produced an oval platter of some tough but slightly flexible material, covered it with strips of a spongy, orange-coloured substance and gave it to Ransom. He cut a convenient length off with his knife and began to eat; doubtfully at first and then ravenously. It had a bean-like taste but sweeter; good enough for a starving man. Then, as his hunger ebbed, the sense of his situation returned with dismaying force. The huge, seal-like creature seated beside him became unbearably ominous. It seemed friendly; but it was very big, very black, and he knew nothing at all about it. What were its relations to the *sorns*? And was it really as rational as it appeared?

It was only many days later that Ransom discovered how to deal with these sudden losses of confidence. They arose when the rationality of the *hross* tempted you to think of it as a man. Then it became abominable – a man seven feet high, with a snaky body, covered, face and all, with thick black animal hair, and whiskered like a cat. But starting from the other end you had an animal with everything an animal ought to have – glossy coat, liquid eye, sweet breath and whitest teeth – and added to all these, as though Paradise had never been lost and earliest dreams were true, the charm of speech and reason. Nothing could be more disgusting than the one impression; nothing more delightful than the other. It all depended on the point of view.

· 10 ·

When Ransom had finished his meal and drunk again of the strong waters of Malacandra, his host rose and entered the boat. He did this head-first like an animal, his sinuous body allowing him to rest his hands on the bottom of the boat while his feet were still planted on the land. He completed the operation by flinging rump, tail and hind legs all together about five feet into the air and then whisking them neatly on board with an agility which would have been quite impossible to an animal of his bulk on Earth.

Having got into the boat, he proceeded to get out again and then pointed to it. Ransom understood that he was being invited to follow his example. The question which he wanted to ask above all others could not, of course, be put. Were the *hrossa* (he discovered later that this was the plural of *hross*) the dominant species on Malacandra, and the *sorns*, despite their more man-like shape, merely a semi-intelligent kind of cattle? Fervently he hoped that it might be so. On the other hand, the *hrossa* might be the domestic animals of the *sorns*, in which case the latter would be super-intelligent. His whole imaginative training somehow encouraged him to associate superhuman intelligence with monstrosity of form and ruthlessness of will. To step on board the *hross*'s boat might mean surrendering himself to *sorns* at the other end of the journey. On the other hand, the *hross*'s invitation might be a golden opportunity of leaving the *sorn*-haunted forests for ever. And by this time the *hross* itself was becoming puzzled at his apparent inability to understand it. The urgency of its signs finally determined him. The thought of parting from the *hross* could not be seriously entertained; its animality shocked him in a dozen ways, but his longing to learn its language, and, deeper still, the shy, ineluctable fascination of unlike for unlike, the sense that the key to prodigious adventure was being put in his hands – all this had really attached him to it by bonds stronger than he knew. He stepped into the boat.

The boat was without seats. It had a very high prow, an enormous expanse of free-board, and what seemed to Ransom an impossibly shallow draught. Indeed, very little of it even rested on the water; he was reminded of a modern European speed-boat. It was moored by something that looked at first like rope; but the *hross* cast off not by untying but by simply pulling the apparent rope in two as one might pull in two a piece of soft toffee or a roll of plasticine. It then squatted down on its rump in the stern-sheets and took up a paddle – a paddle of such enormous blade that Ransom wondered how the creature could wield it, till he again remembered how light a planet they were on. The length of the *hross*'s body enabled him to work freely in the squatting position despite the high gunwale. It paddled quickly.

For the first few minutes they passed between banks wooded with the purple trees, upon a waterway not more than a hundred yards in width. Then they doubled a promontory, and Ransom saw that they were emerging on to a much larger sheet of water – a great lake, almost a sea. The *hross*, now taking great care and often changing direction and looking about it, paddled well out from the shore. The dazzling blue expanse grew moment by moment wider around them; Ransom could not look steadily at it. The warmth from the water was oppressive; he removed his cap and jerkin, and by so doing surprised the *hross* very much.

He rose cautiously to a standing position and surveyed the Malacandrian prospect which had opened on every side. Before and behind them lay the glittering lake, here studded with islands, and there smiling uninterruptedly at the pale blue sky; the sun, he noticed, was almost immediately overhead – they were in the Malacandrian tropics. At each end the lake vanished into more complicated groupings of land and water, softly, featherily embossed in the purple giant weed. But this marshy land or chain of archipelagoes, as he now beheld it, was bordered on each side with jagged walls of the pale green mountains, which he could still hardly call mountains, so tall they were, so gaunt, sharp, narrow and seemingly unbalanced. On the starboard they were not more than a mile away and seemed divided from the water only by a narrow strip of forest; to the left they were far more distant, though still impressive – perhaps seven miles from the boat. They ran on each side of the watered country as far as he could see, both onwards and behind them; he was sailing, in fact, on the flooded floor of a majestic canyon nearly ten miles wide and of unknown length. Behind and sometimes above the mountain peaks he could make out in many places great billowy piles of the rose-red substance which he had yesterday mistaken for cloud. The mountains, in fact, seemed to have no fall of ground behind them; they were rather the serrated bastion of immeasurable tablelands, higher in many places than themselves, which made the Malacandrian horizon left and right as far as eye could reach. Only straight ahead and straight astern was the planet cut with the vast gorge, which now appeared to him only as a rut or crack in the tableland.

He wondered what the cloud-like red masses were and endeavoured to ask by signs. The question was, however, too particular for sign-language. The *hross*, with a wealth of gesticulation – its arms or fore-limbs were more flexible than his and in quick motion almost whip-like – made it clear that it supposed him to be asking about the high ground in general. It named this *harandra*. The low, watered country, the gorge or canyon, appeared to be *handramit*. Ransom grasped the implications, *handra* earth, *harandra* high earth, mountain, *handramit*, low earth, valley. Highland and lowland, in fact. The peculiar importance of the distinction in Malacandrian geography he learned later.

By this time the *hross* had attained the end of its careful navigation. They were a couple of miles from land when it suddenly ceased paddling and sat tense with its paddle poised in the air; at the same moment the boat quivered and shot forward as if from a catapult. They had apparently availed themselves of some current. In a few seconds they were racing forward at some fifteen miles an hour and rising and falling on the strange, sharp, perpendicular waves of Malacandra with a jerky motion quite unlike that of the choppiest sea that Ransom had ever met on Earth. It reminded him of disastrous experiences on a trotting horse in the army; and it was intensely disagreeable. He gripped the gunwale with his left hand and mopped his brow with his right – the damp warmth from the water had become very troublesome. He wondered if the Malacandrian food, and still more the Malacandrian drink, were really digestible by a human stomach. Thank heaven he was a good sailor! At least a fairly good sailor. At least –

Hastily he leaned over the side. Heat from blue water smote up to his face; in the depth he thought he saw eels playing: long, silver eels. The worst happened not once but many times. In his misery he remembered vividly the shame of being sick at a children's party … long ago in the star where he was born. He felt a similar shame now. It was not thus that the first representative of humanity would choose to appear before a new species. Did *hrossa* vomit too? Would it know what he was doing? Shaking and groaning, he turned back into the boat. The creature was keeping an eye on him, but its face seemed to him expressionless; it was only long after that he learned to read the Malacandrian face.

The current meanwhile seemed to be gathering speed. In a huge curve they swung across the lake to within a furlong of the farther shore, then back again, and once more onward, in giddy spirals and figures of eight, while purple wood and jagged mountain raced backwards and Ransom loathingly associated their sinuous course with the nauseous curling of the silver eels. He was rapidly losing all interest in Malacandra: the distinction between Earth and other planets seemed of no importance compared with the awful distinction of earth and water. He wondered despairingly whether the *hross* habitually lived on water. Perhaps they were going to spend the night in this detestable boat …

His sufferings did not, in fact, last long. There came a blessed cessation of the choppy movement and a slackening of speed, and he saw that the *hross* was backing water rapidly. They were still afloat, with shores close on each side; between them a narrow channel in which the water hissed furiously – apparently a shallow. The *hross* jumped overboard, splashing abundance of warm water into the ship; Ransom, more cautiously and shakily, clambered after it. He was about up to his knees. To his astonishment, the *hross*, without any appearance of effort, lifted the boat bodily on to the top of its head, steadied it with one fore-paw, and proceeded, erect as a Grecian caryatid, to the land. They walked forward – if the swinging movements of the *hross*'s short legs from its flexible hips could be called walking – beside the channel. In a few minutes Ransom saw a new landscape.

The channel was not only a shallow but a rapid – the first, indeed, of a series of rapids by which the water descended steeply for the next half mile. The ground fell away before them and the canyon – or *handramit* – continued at a very much lower level. Its walls, however, did not sink with it, and from his present position Ransom got a clearer notion of the lie of the land. Far more of the highlands to left and right were visible, sometimes covered with the cloud-like red swellings, but more often level, pale and barren to where the smooth line of their horizon marched with the sky. The mountain peaks now appeared only as the fringe or border of the true highland, surrounding it as the lower teeth surround the tongue. He was struck by the vivid contrast between *harandra* and *handramit*. Like a rope of jewels the gorge spread beneath him, purple, sapphire blue, yellow and pinkish white, a rich and variegated inlay of wooded land and disappearing, reappearing, ubiquitous water. Malacandra was less like earth than he had been beginning to suppose. The *handramit* was no true valley rising and falling with the mountain chain it belonged to. Indeed, it did not belong to a mountain chain. It was only an enormous crack or ditch, of varying depth, running through the high and level *harandra*; the latter, he now began to suspect, was the true 'surface' of the planet – certainly would appear as surface to a terrestrial astronomer. To the *handramit* itself there seemed no end; uninterrupted and very nearly straight, it ran before him, a narrowing line of colour, to where it clove the horizon with a V-shaped indenture. There must be a hundred miles of it in view, he thought; and he reckoned that he had put some thirty or forty miles of it behind him since yesterday.

All this time they were descending beside the rapids to where the water was level again and the *hross* could relaunch its skiff. During this walk Ransom learned the words for boat, rapid, water, sun and carry; the latter, as his first verb, interested him particularly. The *hross* was also at some pains to impress upon him an association or relation which it tried to convey by repeating the contrasted pairs of words *hrossa-handramit* and *séroni-harondra*. Ransom understood him to mean that the *hrossa* lived down in the *handramit* and the *séroni* up on the *harandra*. What the deuce were *séroni*, he wondered. The open reaches of the *harandra* did not look as if anything lived up there. Perhaps the *hrossa* had a mythology – he took it for granted they were on a low cultural level – and the *séroni* were gods or demons.

The journey continued, with frequent, though decreasing, recurrences of nausea for Ransom. Hours later he realised that *séroni* might very well be the plural of *sorn*.

The sun declined, on their right. It dropped quicker, than on Earth, or at least on those parts of Earth that Ransom knew, and in the cloudless sky it had little sunset pomp about it. In some other queer way which he could not specify it differed from the sun he knew; but even while he speculated the needle-like mountain tops stood out black against it and the *handramit* grew dark, though eastward (to their left) the high country of the *harandra* still shone pale rose, remote and smooth and tranquil, like another and more spiritual world.

Soon he became aware that they were landing again, that they were treading solid ground, were making for the depth of the purple forest. The motion of the boat still worked in his fantasy and the earth seemed to sway beneath him; this, with weariness and twilight, made the rest of the journey dream-like. Light began to glare in his eyes. A fire was burning. It illuminated the huge leaves overhead, and he saw stars beyond them. Dozens of *hrossa* seemed to have surrounded him; more animal, less human, in their multitude and their close neighbourhood to him, than his solitary guide had seemed. He felt some fear, but more a ghastly inappropriateness. He wanted men – any men, even Weston and Devine. He was too tired to do anything about these meaningless bullet heads and furry faces – could make no response at all. And then, lower down, closer to him, more mobile, came in throngs the whelps, the puppies, the cubs, whatever you called them. Suddenly his mood changed. They were jolly little things. He laid his hand on one black head and smiled; the creature scurried away.

He never could remember much of that evening. There was more eating and drinking, there was continual coming and going of black forms, there were strange eyes luminous in the firelight; finally, there was sleep in some dark, apparently covered place.

Ever since he awoke on the space-ship Ransom had been thinking about the amazing adventure of going to another planet, and about his chances of returning from it. What he had not thought about was *being* on it. It was with a kind of stupefaction each morning that he found himself neither arriving in, nor escaping from, but simply living on, Malacandra; waking, sleeping, eating, swimming, and even, as the days passed, talking. The wonder of it smote him most strongly when he found himself, about three weeks after his arrival, actually going for a walk. A few weeks later he had his favourite walks, and his favourite foods; he was beginning to develop habits. He knew a male from a female *hross* at sight, and even individual differences were becoming plain. Hyoi who had first found him – miles away to the north – was a very different person from the grey-muzzled, venerable Hnohra who was daily teaching him the language; and the young of the species were different again. They were delightful. You could forget all about the rationality of *hrossa* in dealing with them. Too young to trouble him with the baffling enigma of reason in an inhuman form, they solaced his loneliness, as if he had been allowed to bring a few dogs with him from the Earth. The cubs, on their part, felt the liveliest interest in the hairless goblin which had appeared among them. With them, and therefore indirectly with their dams, he was a brilliant success.

Of the community in general his earlier impressions were all gradually being corrected. His first diagnosis of their culture was what he called 'old stone age'. The few cutting instruments they possessed were made of stone. They seemed to have no pottery but a few clumsy vessels used for boiling, and boiling was the only cookery they attempted. Their common drinking vessel, dish and ladle all in one was the oyster-like shell in which he had first tasted *hross* hospitality; the fish which it contained was their only animal food. Vegetable fare they had in great plenty and variety; some of it delicious. Even the pinkish-white weed which covered the whole *handramit* was edible at a pinch, so that if he had starved before Hyoi found him he would have starved amidst abundance. No *hross*, however, ate the weed (*honodraskrud*) for choice, though it might be used *faute de mieux* on a journey. Their dwellings were beehive-shaped huts of stiff leaf and the villages – there were several in the neighbourhood – were always built beside rivers for warmth and well upstream towards the walls of the *handramit* where the water was hottest. They slept on the ground.

They seemed to have no arts except a kind of poetry and music which was practised almost every evening by a team or troupe of four *hrossa*. One recited half chanting at great length while the other three, sometimes singly and sometimes antiphonally, interrupted him from time to time with song. Ransom could not find out whether these interruptions were simply lyrical interludes or dramatic dialogue arising out of the leaders' narrative. He could make nothing of the music. The Voices were not disagreeable and the scale seemed adapted to human ears, but the time pattern was meaningless to his sense of rhythm. The occupations of the tribe or family were at first mysterious. People were always disappearing for a few days and reappearing again. There was a little fishing and much journeying in boats of which he never discovered the object. Then one day he saw a kind of caravan of *hrossa* setting out by land each with a load of vegetable food on its head. Apparently there was some kind of trade in Malacandra.

He discovered their agriculture in the first week. About a mile down the *handramit* one came to broad lands free of forest and clothed for many miles together in low pulpy vegetation in which yellow, orange and blue predominated. Later on, there were lettuce-like plants about the height of a terrestrial birch tree. Where one of these overhung the warmth of water you could step into one of the lower leaves and lie deliciously as in a gently moving, fragrant hammock. Elsewhere it was not warm enough to sit still for long out of doors; the general temperature of the *handramit* was that of a fine winter's morning on Earth. These food-producing areas were worked communally by the surrounding villages, and division of labour had been carried to a higher point than he expected. Cutting, drying, storing, transport and something like manuring were all carried on, and he suspected that some at least of the water channels were artificial.

But the real revolution in his understanding of the *hrossa* began when he had learned enough of their language to attempt some satisfaction of their curiosity about himself. In answer to their questions he began by saying that he had come out of the sky. Hnohra immediately asked from which planet or earth (*handra*). Ransom, who had deliberately given a childish version of the truth in order to adapt it to the supposed ignorance of his audience, was a little annoyed to find Hnohra painfully explaining to him that he could not live in the sky because there was no air in it; he might have come through the sky but he must have come from a *handra*. He was quite unable to point Earth out to them in the night sky. They seemed surprised at his inability, and repeatedly pointed out to him a bright planet low on the western horizon – a little south of where the sun had gone down. He was surprised that they selected a planet instead of a mere star and stuck to their choice; could it be possible that they understood astronomy? Unfortunately he still knew too little of the language to explore their knowledge. He turned the conversation by asking them the name of the bright southern planet, and was told that it was Thulcandra – the silent world or planet.

'Why do you call it *Thulc*?' he asked. 'Why silent?' No one knew.

'The *séroni* know,' said Hnohra. 'That is the sort of thing they know.'

Then he was asked how he had come, and made a very poor attempt at describing the space-ship – but again:

'The *séroni* would know.'

Had he come alone? No, he had come with two others of his kind – bad men ('bent' men was the nearest *hrossian* equivalent) who tried to kill him, but he had run away from them. The *hrossa* found this very difficult, but all finally agreed that he ought to go to Oyarsa. Oyarsa would protect him. Ransom asked who Oyarsa was. Slowly, and with many misunderstandings, he hammered out the information that Oyarsa (1) lived in Meldilorn; (2) knew everything and ruled everyone; (3) had always been there; and (4) was not a *hross*, nor one of the *séroni*. Then Ransom, following his own idea, asked if Oyarsa had made the world. The *hrossa* almost barked in the fervour of their denial. Did people in Thulcandra not know that Maleldil the Young had made and still ruled the world? Even a child knew that. Where did Maleldil live, Ransom asked.

'With the Old One.'

And who was the Old One? Ransom did not understand the answer. He tried again.

'Where was the Old One?'

'He is not that sort,' said Hnohra, 'that he has to live anywhere,' and proceeded to a good deal which Ransom did not follow. But he followed enough to feel once more a certain irritation. Ever since he had discovered the rationality of the *hrossa* he had been haunted by a conscientious scruple as to whether it might not be his duty to undertake their religious instruction; now, as a result of his tentative efforts, he found himself being treated as if *he* were the savage and being given a first sketch of civilised religion – a sort of *hrossian* equivalent of the shorter catechism. It became plain that Maleldil was a spirit without body, parts or passions.

'He is not a *hnau*,' said the *hrossa*.

'What is *hnau*?' asked Ransom.

'You are *hnau*. I am *hnau*. The *séroni* are *hnau*. The *pfifltriggi* are *hnau*.'

'*Pfifltriggi*?' said Ransom.

'More than ten days' journey to the west,' said Hnohra. 'The *harandra* sinks down not into the *handramit* but into a broad place, an open place, spreading every way. Five days' journey from the north to the south of it; ten days' journey from the east to the west. The forests are of other colours there than here, they are blue and green. It is very deep there, it goes to the roots of the world. The best things that can be dug out of the earth are there. The *pfifltriggi* live there. They delight in digging. What they dig they soften with fire and make things of it. They are little people, smaller than you, long in the snout, pale, busy. They have long limbs in front. No *hnau* can match them in making and shaping things as none can match us in singing. But let *Hmān* see.

He turned and spoke to one of the younger *hrossa* and presently, passed from hand to hand, there came to him a little bowl. He held it close to the firelight and examined it. It was certainly of gold, and Ransom realised the meaning of Devine's interest in Malacandra.

'Is there much of this thing?' he asked.

Yes, he was told, it was washed down in most of the rivers; but the best and most was among the *pfifltriggi*, and it was they who were skilled in it. *Arbol hru*, they called it – Sun's blood. He looked at the bowl again. It was covered with fine etching. He saw pictures of *hrossa* and of smaller, almost frog-like animals; and then, of *sorns*. He pointed to the latter inquiringly.

'*Séroni*,' said the *hrossa*, confirming his suspicions. 'They live up almost on the *harandra*. In the big caves.' The frog-like animals – or tapir-headed, frog-bodied animals – were *pfifltriggi*. Ransom turned it over in his mind. On Malacandra, apparently, three distinct species had reached rationality, and none of them had yet exterminated the other two. It concerned him intensely to find out which was the real master.

'Which of the *hnau* rule?' he asked.

'Oyarsa rules,' was the reply.

'Is he *hnau*?'

This puzzled them a little. The *séroni*, they thought, would be better at that kind of question. Perhaps Oyarsa was *hnau*, but a very different *hnau*. He had no death and no young.

'These *séroni* know more than the *hrossa*?' asked Ransom.

This produced more a debate than an answer. What emerged finally was that the *séroni* or sorns were perfectly helpless in a boat, and could not fish to save their lives, could hardly swim, could make no poetry, and even when *hrossa* had made it for them could understand only the inferior sorts; but they were admittedly good at finding out things about the stars and understanding the darker utterances of Oyarsa and telling what happened in Malacandra long ago – longer ago than anyone could remember.

'Ah – the intelligentsia,' thought Ransom. 'They must be the real rulers, however it is disguised.'

He tried to ask what would happen if the *sorns* used their wisdom to make the *hrossa* do things – this was as far as he could get in his halting Malacandrian. The question did not sound nearly so urgent in this form as it would have done if he had been able to say 'used their scientific resources for the exploitation of their uncivilised neighbours'. But he might have spared his pains. The mention of the *sorns*' inadequate appreciation of poetry had diverted the whole conversation into literary channels. Of the heated, and apparently technical, discussion which followed he understood not a syllable.

Naturally his conversations with the *hrossa* did not all turn on Malacandra. He had to repay them with information about Earth. He was hampered in this both by the humiliating discoveries which he was constantly making of his own ignorance about his native planet, and partly by his determination to conceal some of the truth. He did not want to tell them too much of our human wars and industrialisms. He remembered how H. G. Wells's Cavor had met his end on the Moon; also he felt shy. A sensation akin to that of physical nakedness came over him whenever they questioned him too closely about men – the *hmāna* as they called them. Moreover, he was determined not to let them know that he had been brought there to be given to the *sorns*; for he was becoming daily more certain that these were the dominant species. What he did tell them fired the imagination of the *hrossa*: they all began making poems about the strange *handra* where the plants were hard like stone and the earth-weed green like rock and the waters cold and salt, and *hmāna*, lived out on top, on the *harandra*.

They were even more interested in what he had to tell them of the aquatic animal with snapping jaws which he had fled from in their own world and even in their own *handramit*. It was a *hnakra*, they all agreed. They were intensely excited. There had not been a *hnakra* in the valley for many years. The youth of the *hrossa* got out their weapons – primitive harpoons with points of bone – and the very cubs began playing at *hnakra*-hunting in the shallows. Some of the mothers showed signs of anxiety and wanted the cubs to be kept out of the water, but in general the news of the *hnakra* seemed to be immensely popular. Hyoi set off at once to do something to his boat and Ransom accompanied him. He wished to make himself useful, and was already beginning to have some vague capacity with the primitive *hrossian* tools. They walked together to Hyoi's creek, a stone's throw through the forest.

On the way, where the path was single and Ransom was following Hyoi, they passed a little she-*hross*, not much more than a cub. She spoke as they passed, but not to them: her eyes were on a spot about five yards away.

'Who do you speak to, Hrikki?' said Ransom.

'To the *eldil*.'

'Where?'

'Did you not see him?'

'I saw nothing.'

'There! There!' she cried suddenly. 'Ah! He is gone. Did you not see him?'

'I saw no one.'

'Hyoi,' said the cub, 'the *hmān* cannot see the *eldil*!'

But Hyoi, continuing steadily on his way, was already out of earshot, and had apparently noticed nothing. Ransom concluded that Hrikki was 'pretending' like the young of his own species. In a few moments he rejoined his companion.

·⟨12⟩·

They worked hard at Hyoi's boat till noon and then spread themselves on the weed close to the warmth of the creek, and began their midday meal. The war-like nature of their preparations suggested many questions to Ransom. He knew no word for war, but he managed to make Hyoi understand what he wanted to know. Did *séroni* and *hrossa* and *pfifltriggi* ever go out like this, with weapons, against each other?

'What for?' asked Hyoi.

It was difficult to explain. 'If both wanted one thing and neither would give it,' said Ransom, 'would the other at last come with force? Would they say, give it or we kill you?'

'What sort of thing?'

'Well – food, perhaps.'

'If the other *hnau* wanted food, why should we not give it to them? We often do.'

'But how if we had not enough for ourselves?'

'But Maleldil will not stop the plants growing.'

'Hyoi, if you had more and more young, would Maleldil broaden the *handramit* and make enough plants for them all?'

'The *séroni* know that sort of thing. But why should we have more young?'

Ransom found this difficult. At last he said:

'Is the begetting of young not a pleasure among the *hrossa*?'

'A very great one, *Hmān*. This is what we call love.'

'If a thing is a pleasure, a *hmān* wants it again. He might want the pleasure more often than the number of young that could be fed.'

It took Hyoi a long time to get the point.

'You mean,' he said slowly, 'that he might do it not only in one or two years of his life but again?'

'Yes.'

'But why? Would he want his dinner all day or want to sleep after he had slept? I do not understand.'

'But a dinner comes every day. This love, you say, comes only once while the *hross* lives?'

'But it takes his whole life. When he is young he has to look for his mate; and then he has to court her; then he begets young; then he rears them; then he remembers all this, and boils it inside him and makes it into poems and wisdom.'

'But the pleasure he must be content only to remember?'

'That is like saying, "My food I must be content only to eat."'

'I do not understand.'

'A pleasure is full grown only when it is remembered. You are speaking, *Hmān*, as if the pleasure were one thing and the memory another. It is all one thing. The *séroni* could say it better than I say it now. Not better than I could say it in a poem. What you call remembering is the last part of the pleasure, as the *crah* is the last part of a poem. When you and I met, the meeting was over very shortly, it was nothing. Now it is growing something as we remember it. But still we know very little about it. What it will be when I remember it as I lie down to die, what it makes in me all my days till then – that is the real meeting. The other is only the beginning of it. You say you have poets in your world. Do they not teach you this?'

'Perhaps some of them do,' said Ransom. "But even in a poem does a *hross* never long to hear one splendid line over again?'

Hyoi's reply unfortunately turned on one of those points in their language which Ransom had not mastered. There were two verbs which both, as far as he could see, meant *to long* or *yearn*; but the *hrossa* drew sharp distinction, even an opposition, between them. Hyoi seemed to him merely to be saying that everyone would long for it (*wondelone*) but no one in his senses could long for it (*hluntheline*).

'And indeed,' he continued, 'the poem is a good example. For the most splendid line becomes fully splendid only by means of all the lines after it; if you went back to it you would find it less splendid than you thought. You would kill it. I mean in a good poem.

'But in a bent poem, Hyoi?'

'A bent poem is not listened to, *Hmān*.'

'And how of love in a bent life?'

'How could the life of a *hnau* be bent?'

'Do you say, Hyoi, that there are no bent *hrossa*?'

Hyoi reflected. 'I have heard,' he said at last, 'of something like what you mean. It is said that sometimes here and there a cub at a certain age gets strange twists in him. I have heard of one that wanted to eat earth; there might, perhaps, be somewhere a *hross* likewise that wanted to have the years of love prolonged. I have not heard of it, but it might be. I have heard of something stranger. There is a poem about a *hross* who lived long ago, in another *handramit*, who saw things all made two – two suns in the sky, two heads on a neck; and last of all they say that he fell into such a frenzy that he desired two mates. I do not ask you to believe it, but that is the story: that he loved two *hressni*.'

Ransom pondered this. Here, unless Hyoi was deceiving him, was a species naturally continent, naturally monogamous. And yet, was it so strange? Some animals, he knew, had regular breeding seasons; and if nature could perform the miracle of turning the sexual impulse outward at all, why could she not go further and fix it, not morally but instinctively, to a single object? He even remembered dimly having heard that some terrestrial animals, some of the 'lower' animals, were naturally monogamous. Among the *hrossa*, anyway, it was obvious that unlimited breeding and promiscuity were as rare as the rarest perversions. At last it dawned upon him that it was not they, but his own species, that were the puzzle. That the *hrossa* should have such instincts was mildly surprising; but how came it that the instincts of the *hrossa* so closely resembled the unattained ideals of that far-divided species Man whose instincts were so deplorably different? What was the history of Man? But Hyoi was speaking again.

'Undoubtedly,' he said. 'Maleldil made us so. How could there ever be enough to eat if everyone had twenty young? And how could we endure to live and let time pass if we were always crying for one day or one year to come back – if we did not know that every day in a life fills the whole life with expectation and memory and that these are that day?'

'All the same,' said Ransom, unconsciously nettled on behalf of his own world, 'Maleldil has let in the *hnakra*.'

'Oh, but that is so different. I long to kill this *hnakra* as he also longs to kill me. I hope that my ship will be the first and I first in my ship with my straight spear when the blackjaws snap. And if he kills me, my people will mourn and my brothers will desire still more to kill him. But they will not wish that there were no *hnéraki*; nor do I. How can I make you understand, when you do not understand the poets? The *hnakra* is our enemy, but he is also our beloved. We feel in our hearts his joy as he looks down from the mountain of water in the north where he was born; we leap with him when he jumps the falls; and when winter comes, and the lake smokes higher than our heads, it is with his eyes that we see it and know that his roaming time is come. We hang images of him in our houses, and the sign of all the *hrossa* is a *hnakra*. In him the spirit of the valley lives; and our young play at being *hnéraki* as soon as they can splash in the shallows.'

'And then he kills them?'

'Not often them. The *hrossa* would be bent *hrossa* if they let him get so near. Long before he had come down so far we should have sought him out. No, *Hmān*, it is not a few deaths roving the world around him that make a *hnau* miserable. It is a bent *hnau* that would blacken the world. And I say also this. I do not think the forest would be so bright, nor the water so warm, nor love so sweet, if there were no danger in the lakes. I will tell you a day in my life that has shaped me; such a day as comes only once, like love, or serving Oyarsa in Meldilorn. Then I was young, not much

76

more than a cub, when I went far, far up the *handramit* to the land where stars shine at midday and even water is cold. A great waterfall I climbed. I stood on the shore of Balki the pool, which is the place of most awe in all worlds. The walls of it go up for ever and ever and huge and holy images are cut in them, the work of old times. There is the fall called the Mountain of Water. Because I have stood there alone, Maleldil and I, for even Oyarsa sent me no word, my heart has been higher, my song deeper, all my days. But do you think it would have been so unless I had known that in Balki *hnéraki* dwelled? There I drank life because death was in the pool. That was the best of drinks save one.'

'What one?' asked Ransom.

'Death itself in the day I drink it and go to Maleldil.'

Shortly after that they rose and resumed their work. The sun was declining as they came back through the wood. It occurred to Ransom to ask Hyoi a question.

'Hyoi,' he said, 'it comes into my head that when I first saw you and before you saw me, you were already speaking. That was how I knew that you were *hnau*, for otherwise I should have thought you a beast, and run away. But who were you speaking to?'

'To an *eldil*.'

'What is that? I saw no one.'

'Are there no *eldila* in your world, *Hmān*? That must be strange.'

'But what are they?'

'They come from Oyarsa – they are, I suppose, a kind of *hnau*.'

'As we came out today I passed a child who said she was taking to an *eldil*, but I could see nothing.'

'One can see by looking at your eyes, *Hmān*, that they are different from ours. But *eldila* are hard to see. They are not like us. Light goes through them. You must be looking in the right place and the right time; and that is not likely to come about unless the *eldil* wishes to be seen. Sometimes you can mistake them for a sunbeam or even a moving of the leaves; but when you look again you see that it was an *eldil* and that it is gone. But whether your eyes can ever see them I do not know. The *séroni* would know that.'

13

The whole village was astir next morning before the sunlight – already visible on the *harandra* – had penetrated the forest. By the light of the cooking fires Ransom saw an incessant activity of *hrossa*. The females were pouring out steaming food from clumsy pots; Hnohra was directing the transportation of piles of spears to the boats; Hyoi, in the midst of a group of the most experienced hunters, was talking too rapidly and too technically for Ransom to follow; parties were arriving from the neighbouring villages; and the cubs, squealing with excitement, were running hither and thither among their elders.

He found that his own share in the hunt had been taken for granted. He was to be in Hyoi's boat, with Hyoi and Whin. The two *hrossa* would take it in turns to paddle, while Ransom and the disengaged *hross* would be in the bows. He understood the *hrossa* well enough to know that they were making him the noblest offer in their power, and that Hyoi and Whin were each tormented by the fear lest he should be paddling when the *hnakra* appeared. A short time ago, in England, nothing would have seemed more impossible to Ransom than to accept the post of honour and danger in an attack upon an unknown but certainly deadly aquatic monster. Even more recently, when he had first fled from the *sorns* or when he had lain pitying himself in the forest by night, it would hardly have been in his power to do what he was intending to do today. For his intention was clear. Whatever happened, he must show that the human species also were *hnau*. He was only too well aware that such resolutions might look very different when the moment came, but he felt an unwonted assurance that somehow or other he would be able to go through with it. It was necessary, and the necessary was always possible. Perhaps, too, there was something in the air he now breathed, or in the society of the *hrossa*, which had begun to work a change in him.

The lake was just giving back the first rays of the sun when he found himself kneeling side by side with Whin, as he had been told to, in the bows of Hyoi's ship, with a little pile of throwing-spears between his knees and one in his right hand, stiffening his body against the motion as Hyoi paddled them out into their place. At least a hundred boats were taking part in the hunt. They were in three parties. The central, and far the smallest, was to work its way up the current by which Hyoi and Ransom had descended after their first meeting. Longer ships than he had yet seen, eight-paddled ships, were used for this. The habit of the *hnakra* was to float down the current whenever he could; meeting the ships, he would presumably dart out of it into the still water to left or right. Hence while the central party slowly beat up the current, the light ships, paddling far faster, would cruise at will up and down either side of it to receive the quarry as soon as he broke what might be called his 'cover'. In this game numbers and intelligence were on the side of the *hrossa*; the *hnakra* had speed on his side, and also invisibility, for he could swim under water. He was nearly invulnerable except through his open mouth. If the two hunters in the bows of the boat he made for muffed their shots, this was usually the last of them and of their boat.

In the light skirmishing parties there were two things a brave hunter could aim at. He could keep well back and close to the long ships where the *hnakra* was most likely to break out, or he could get as far forward as possible in the hope of meeting the *hnakra* going at its full speed and yet untroubled by the hunt, and of inducing it, by a well-aimed spear, to leave the current then and there. One could thus anticipate the beaters and kill the beast – if that was how the matter ended – on one's own. This was the desire of Hyoi and Whin; and almost – so strongly they infected him – of

Ransom. Hence, hardly had the heavy craft of the beaters begun their slow progress up-current amid a wall of foam when he found his own ship speeding northward as fast as Hyoi could drive her, already passing boat after boat and making for the freest water. The speed was exhilarating. In the cold morning the warmth of the blue expanse they were clearing was not unpleasant. Behind them arose, re-echoed from the remote rock pinnacles on either side of the valley, the bell-like, deep-mouthed voices of more than two hundred *hrossa*, more musical than a cry of hounds but closely akin to it in quality as in purport. Something long sleeping in the blood awoke in Ransom. It did not seem impossible at this moment that even he might be the *hnakra*-slayer; that the fame of *Hmān hnakrapunt* might be handed down to posterity in this world that knew no other man. But he had had such dreams before, and knew how they ended. Imposing humility on the newly risen riot of his feelings, he turned his eyes to the troubled water of the current which they were skirting, without entering, and watched intently.

For a long time nothing happened. He became conscious of the stiffness of his attitude and deliberately relaxed his muscles. Presently Whin reluctantly went aft to paddle, and Hyoi came forward to take his place. Almost as soon as the change had been effected, Hyoi spoke softly to him and said, without taking his eyes off the current:

'There is an *eldil* coming to us over the water.'

Ransom could see nothing – or nothing that he could distinguish from imagination and the dance of sunlight on the lake. A moment later Hyoi spoke again, but not to him.

'What is it, sky-born?'

What happened next was the most uncanny experience Ransom had yet had on Malacandra. He heard the voice. It seemed to come out of the air, about a yard above his head, and it was almost an octave higher than the *hross*'s – higher even than his own. He realised that a very little difference in his ear would have made the *eldil* as inaudible to him as it was invisible.

'It is the Man with you, Hyoi,' said the voice. 'He ought not to be there. He ought to be going to Oyarsa. Bent *hnau* of his own kind from Thulcandra are following him; he should go to Oyarsa. If they find him anywhere else there will be evil.'

'He hears you, sky-born,' said Hyoi. 'And have you no message for my wife? You know what she wishes to be told.'

'I have a message for Hleri,' said the *eldil*. 'But you will not be able to take it. I go to her now myself. All that is well. Only – let the Man go to Oyarsa.'

There was a moment's silence.

'He is gone,' said Whin. 'And we have lost our share in the hunt.'

'Yes,' said Hyoi with a sigh. 'We must put *Hmān* ashore and teach him the way to Meldilorn.'

Ransom was not so sure of his courage but that one part of him felt an instant relief at the idea of any diversion from their present business. But the other part of him urged him to hold on to his new-found manhood; now or never – with such companions or with none – he must leave a deed on his memory instead of one more broken dream. It was in obedience to something like conscience that he exclaimed:

'No, no. There is time for that after the hunt. We must kill the *hnakra* first.'

'Once an *eldil* has spoken,' began Hyoi, when suddenly Whin gave a great cry (a 'bark' Ransom would have called it three weeks ago) and pointed. There, not a furlong away, was the torpedo-like track of foam; and now, visible through a wall of foam, they caught the metallic glint of the monster's sides. Whin was paddling furiously. Hyoi threw and missed. As his first spear smote the water his second was already in the air. This time it must have touched the *hnakra*. He wheeled right out of the current. Ransom saw the great black pit of his mouth twice open and twice shut with its snap of shark-like teeth. He himself had thrown now – hurriedly, excitedly, with unpractised hand.

'Back,' shouted Hyoi to Whin who was already backing water with every pound of his vast strength. Then all became confused.

He heard Whin shout 'Shore !' There came a shock that flung him forward almost into the *hnakra*'s jaws and he found himself at the same moment up to his waist in water. It was at him the teeth were snapping. Then as he flung shaft after shaft into the great cavern of the gaping brute he saw Hyoi perched incredibly on its back – on its nose – bending forward and hurling from there. Almost at once the *hross* was dislodged and fell with a wide splash nearly ten yards away. But the *hnakra* was killed. It was wallowing on its side, bubbling out its black life. The water around him was dark and stank.

When he recollected himself they were all on shore, wet, steaming, trembling with exertion and embracing one another. It did not now seem strange to him to be clasped to a breast of wet fur. The breath of the *hrossa*, which, though sweet, was not human breath, did not offend him. He was one with them. That difficulty which they, accustomed to more than one rational species, had perhaps never felt, was now overcome. They were all *hnau*. They had stood shoulder to shoulder in the face of an enemy, and the shapes of their heads no longer mattered. And he, even Ransom, had come through it and not been disgraced. He had grown up.

They were on a little promontory free of forest, on which they had run aground in the confusion of the fight. The wreckage of the boat and the corpse of the monster lay confused together in the water beside them. No sound from the rest of the hunting party was audible; they had been almost a mile ahead when they met the *hnakra*. All three sat down to recover their breath.

'So,' said Hyoi, 'we are *hnakrapunti*. This is what I have wanted all my life.'

At that moment Ransom was deafened by a loud sound – a perfectly familiar sound which was the last thing he expected to hear. It was a terrestrial, human and civilised sound; it was even European. It was the crack of an English rifle; and Hyoi, at his feet, was struggling to rise and gasping. There was blood on the white weed where he struggled. Ransom dropped on his knees beside him. The huge body of the *hross* was too heavy for him to turn round. Whin helped him.

'Hyoi, can you hear me?' said Ransom with his face close to the round seal-like head. 'Hyoi, it is through me that this has happened. It is the other *hmāna* who have hit you, the bent two that brought me to Malacandra. They can throw death at a distance with a thing they have made. I should have told you. We are all a bent race. We have come here to bring evil on Malacandra. We are only half *hnau* – Hyoi …' His speech died away into the inarticulate. He did not know the words for 'forgive', or 'shame', or 'fault', hardly the word for 'sorry'. He could only stare into Hyoi's distorted face in speechless guilt. But the *hross* seemed to understand. It was trying to say something, and Ransom laid his ear close to the working mouth. Hyoi's dulling eyes were fixed on his own, but the expression of a *hross* was not even now perfectly intelligible to him.

'*Hnā – hmā*,' it muttered and then, at last, '*Hman hnakrapunt.*' Then there came a contortion of the whole body, a gush of blood and saliva from the mouth; his arms gave way under the sudden dead weight of the sagging head, and Hyoi's face became as alien and animal as it had seemed at their first meeting. The glazed eyes and the slowly stiffening, bedraggled fur, were like those of any dead beast found in an earthly wood.

Ransom resisted an infantile impulse to break out into imprecations on Weston and Devine. Instead he raised his eyes to meet those of Whin who was crouching – *hrossa* do not kneel – on the other side of the corpse.

'I am in the hands of your people, Whin,' he said. 'They must do as they will. But if they are wise They will kill me and certainly they will kill the other two.'

'One does not kill *hnau*,' said Whin. 'Only Oyarsa does that. But these other, where are they?'

Ransom glanced around. It was open on the promontory but thick wood came down to where it joined the mainland, perhaps two hundred yards away.

'Somewhere in the wood,' he said. 'Lie down, Whin, here where the ground is lowest. They may throw from their thing again.'

He had some difficulty in making Whin do as he suggested. When both were lying in dead ground, their feet almost in the water, the *hross* spoke again.

'Why did they kill him?' he asked.

'They would not know he was *hnau*,' said Ransom. 'I have told you that there is only one kind of *hnau* in our world. They would think he was a beast. If they thought that, they would kill him for pleasure, or in fear, or' (he hesitated) 'because they were hungry. But I must tell you the truth, Whin. They would kill even a *hnau*, knowing it to be *hnau*, if they thought its death would serve them.'

There was a short silence.

'I am wondering,' said Ransom, 'if they saw me. It is for me they are looking. Perhaps if I went to them they would be content and come no farther into your land. But why do they not come out of the wood to see what they have killed?'

'Our people are coming,' said Whin, turning his head. Ransom looked back and saw the lake black with boats. The main body of the hunt would be with them in a few minutes.

'They are afraid of the *hrossa*,' said Ransom. 'That is why they do not come out of the wood. I will go to them, Whin.'

'No,' said Whin. 'I have been thinking. All this has come from not obeying the *eldil*. He said you were to go to Oyarsa. You ought to have been already on the road. You must go now.'

'But that will leave the bent *hmāna* here. They may do more harm.'

'They will not set on the *hrossa*. You have said they are afraid. It is more likely that we will come upon them. Never fear – they will not see us or hear us. We will take them to Oyarsa. But you must go now, as the *eldil* said.'

'Your people will think I have run away because I am afraid to look in their faces after Hyoi's death.'

'It is not a question of thinking but of what an *eldil* says. This is cubs' talk. Now listen, and I will teach you the way.'

The *hross* explained to him that five days' journey to the south the *handramit* joined another *handramit*; and three days up this other *handramit* to west and north was Meldilorn and the seat of Oyarsa. But there was a shorter way, a mountain road, across the corner of the *harandra* between the two canyons, which would bring him down to Meldilorn on the second day. He must go into the wood before them and through it till he came to the mountain wall of the *handramit*; and he must work south along the roots of the mountains till he came to a road cut up between them. Up this he must go, and somewhere beyond the tops of the mountains he would come to the tower of Augray. Augray would help him. He could cut weed for his food before he left the forest and came into the rock country. Whin realised that Ransom might meet the other two *hmāna* as soon as he entered the wood.

'If they catch you,' he said, 'then it will be as you say, they will come no farther into our land. But it is better to be taken on your way to Oyarsa than to stay here. And once you are on the way to him, I do not think he will let the bent ones stop you.

Ransom was by no means convinced that this was the best plan either for himself or for the *hrossa*. But the stupor of humiliation in which he had lain ever since Hyoi fell forbade him to criticise. He was anxious only to do whatever they wanted him to do, to trouble them as little as was now possible, and above all to get away. It was impossible to find out how Whin felt; and Ransom sternly repressed an insistent, whining impulse to renewed protestations and regrets, self-accusations that might elicit some word of pardon. Hyoi with his last breath had called him *hnakra*-slayer; that was forgiveness generous enough and with that he must be content. As soon as he had mastered the details of his route he bade farewell to Whin and advanced alone towards the forest.

14

Until he reached the wood Ransom found it difficult to think of anything except the possibility of another rifle bullet from Weston or Devine. He thought that they probably still wanted him alive rather than dead, and this, combined with the knowledge that a *hross* was watching him, enabled him to proceed with at least external composure. Even when he had entered the forest he felt himself in considerable danger. The long branchless stems made 'cover' only if you were very far away from the enemy; and the enemy in this case might be very close. He became aware of a strong impulse to shout out to Weston and Devine and give himself up; it rationalised itself in the form that this would remove them from the district, as they would probably take him off to the *sorns* and leave the *hrossa* unmolested. But Ransom knew a little psychology and had heard of the hunted man's irrational instinct to give himself up – indeed, he had felt it himself in dreams. It was some such trick, he thought, that his nerves were now playing him. In any case he was determined henceforward to obey the *hrossa* or *eldila*. His efforts to rely on his own judgement in Malacandra had so far ended tragically enough. He made a strong resolution, defying in advance all changes of mood, that he would faithfully carry out the journey to Meldilorn if it could be done.

This resolution seemed to him all the more certainly right because he had the deepest misgivings about that journey. He understood that the *harandra*, which he had to cross, was the home of the *sorns*. In fact he was walking of his own free will into the very trap that he had been trying to avoid ever since his arrival on Malacandra. (Here the first change of mood tried to raise its head. He thrust it down.) And even if he got through the *sorns* and reached Meldilorn, who or what might Oyarsa be? Oyarsa, Whin had ominously observed, did not share the *hrossa*'s objection to shedding the blood of a *hnau*. And again, Oyarsa ruled *sorns* as well as *hrossa* and *pfifltriggi*. Perhaps he was simply the arch-*sorn*. And now came the second change of mood. Those old terrestrial fears of some alien, cold, intelligence, superhuman in power, sub-human in cruelty, which had utterly faded from his mind among the *hrossa*, rose clamouring for readmission. But he strode on. He was going to Meldilorn. It was not possible, he told himself, that the *hrossa* should obey any evil or monstrous creature; and they had told him – or had they? he was not quite sure – that Oyarsa was not a *sorn*. Was Oyarsa a god? – perhaps that very idol to whom the *sorns* wanted to sacrifice him. But the *hrossa*, though they said strange things about him, clearly denied that he was a god. There was one God, according to them, Maleldil the Young; nor was it possible to imagine Hyoi or Hnohra worshipping a bloodstained idol. Unless, of course, the *hrossa* were after all under the thumb of the *sorns*, superior to their masters in all the qualities that human beings value, but intellectually inferior to them and dependent on them. It would be a strange but not an inconceivable world; heroism and poetry at the bottom, cold scientific intellect above it, and overtopping all, some dark superstition which scientific intellect, helpless against the revenge of the emotional depths it had ignored, had neither will nor power to remove. A mumbo-jumbo … but Ransom pulled himself up. He knew too much now to talk that way. He and all his class would have called the *eldila* a superstition if they had been merely described to them, but now he had heard the voice himself. No, Oyarsa was a real person if he was a person at all.

He had now been walking for about an hour, and it was nearly midday. No difficulty about his direction had yet occurred; he had merely to keep going uphill and he was certain of coming out of the forest to the mountain wall sooner or later. Meanwhile he felt remarkably well, though greatly chastened in mind. The silent, purple half light of the woods spread all around him as it had spread on the first day he spent in Malacandra, but everything else was changed. He looked back on that time as on a nightmare, on his own mood at that time as a sort of sickness. Then all had been whimpering, unanalysed, self-nourishing, self-consuming dismay. Now, in the clear light of an accepted duty, he felt fear indeed, but with it a sober sense of confidence in himself and in the world, and even an element of pleasure. It was the difference between a landsman in a sinking ship and a horseman on a bolting horse: either may be killed, but the horseman is an agent as well as a patient.

About an hour after noon he suddenly came out of the wood into bright sunshine. He was only twenty yards from the almost perpendicular bases of the mountain spires, too close to them to see their tops. A sort of valley ran up in the re-entrant between two of them at the place where he had emerged: an unclimbable valley consisting of a single concave sweep of stone, which in its lower parts ascended steeply as the roof of a house and farther up seemed almost vertical. At the top it even looked as if it hung over a bit, like a tidal wave of stone at the very moment of breaking; but this, he thought, might be an illusion. He wondered what the *hrossa's* idea of a road might be.

He began to work his way southward along the narrow, broken ground between wood and mountain. Great spurs of the mountains had to be crossed every few moments, and even in that light-weight world it was intensely tiring. After about half an hour he came to a stream. Here he went a few paces into the forest, cut himself an ample supply of the ground weed, and sat down beside the water's edge for lunch. When he had finished he filled his pockets with what he had not eaten and proceeded.

He began soon to be anxious about his road, for if he could make the top at all he could do it only by daylight, and the middle of the afternoon was approaching. But his fears were unnecessary. When it came it was unmistakable. An open way through the wood appeared on the left – he must be somewhere behind the *hross* village now – and on the right he saw the road, a single ledge, or in places, a trench, cut sidewise and upwards across the sweep of such a valley as he had seen before. It took his breath away – the insanely steep, hideously narrow staircase without steps, leading up and up from where he stood to where it was an almost invisible thread on the pale green surface of the rock. But there was no time to stand and look at it. He was a poor judge of heights, but he had no doubt that the top of the road was removed from him by a more than Alpine distance. It would take him at least till sundown to reach it. Instantly he began the ascent.

Such a journey would have been impossible on earth; the first quarter of an hour would have reduced a man of Ransom's build and age to exhaustion. Here he was at first delighted with the ease of his movement, and then staggered by the gradient and length of the climb which, even under Malacandrian conditions, soon bowed his back and gave him an aching chest and trembling knees. But this was not the worst. He heard already a singing in his ears, and noticed that despite his labour there was no sweat on his forehead. The cold, increasing at every step, seemed to sap his vitality worse than any heat could have done. Already his lips were cracked; his breath, as he panted, showed like a cloud; his fingers were numb. He was cutting his way up into a silent arctic world, and had already passed from an English to a Lapland winter. It frightened him, and he decided that he must rest here or not at all; a hundred paces more and if he sat down he would sit for ever. He squatted on the road for a few minutes, slapping his body with his arms. The landscape was terrifying. Already the *handramit* which had made his world for so many weeks was only a thin purple cleft sunk amidst the boundless level desolation of the *harandra* which now, on the farther side, showed clearly between and above the mountain peaks. But long before he was rested he knew that he must go on or die.

The world grew stranger. Among the *hrossa* he had almost lost the feeling of being on a strange planet; here it returned upon him with desolating force. It was no longer 'the world', scarcely even 'a world': it was a planet, a star, a waste place in the universe, millions of miles from the world of men. It was impossible to recall what he had felt about Hyoi, or Whin, or the *eldila*, or Oyarsa. It seemed fantastic to have thought he had duties to such hobgoblins – if they were not hallucinations – met in the wilds of space. He had nothing to do with them: he was a man. Why had Weston and Devine left him alone like this?

But all the time the old resolution, taken when he could still think, was driving him up the road. Often he forgot where he was going, and why. The movement became a mechanical rhythm – from weariness to stillness, from stillness to unbearable cold, from cold to motion again. He noticed that the *handramit* – now an insignificant part of the landscape – was full of a sort of haze. He had never seen a fog while he was living there. Perhaps that was what the air of the *handramit* looked like from above; certainly it was different air from this. There was something more wrong with his lungs and heart than even the cold and the exertion accounted for. And though there was no snow, there was an extraordinary brightness. The light was increasing, sharpening and growing whiter and the sky was a much darker blue than he had ever seen on Malacandra. Indeed, it was darker than blue; it was almost black, and the jagged spines of rock standing against it were like his mental picture of a lunar land scape. Some stars were visible.

Suddenly he realised the meaning of these phenomena. There was very little air above him: he was near the end of it. The Malacandrian atmosphere lay chiefly in the *handramits*; the real surface of the planet was naked or thinly clad. The stabbing sunlight and the black sky above him were that 'heaven' out of which he had dropped into the Malacandrian world, already showing through the last thin veil of air. If the top were more than a hundred feet away, it would be where no man could breathe at all. He wondered whether the *hrossa* had different lungs and had sent him by a road that meant death for man. But even while he thought of this he took note that those jagged peaks blazing in sunlight against an almost black sky were level with him. He was no longer ascending. The road ran on before him in a kind of shallow ravine bounded on his left by the tops of the highest rock pinnacles and on his right by a smooth ascending swell of stone that ran up to the true *harandra*. And where he was he could still breathe, though gasping, dizzy and in pain. The blaze in his eyes was worse. The sun was setting. The *hrossa* must have foreseen this; they could not live, any more than he, on the *harandra* by night. Still staggering forward, he looked about him for any sign of Augray's tower, whatever Augray might be.

Doubtless he exaggerated the time during which he thus wandered and watched the shadows from the rocks lengthening towards him. It cannot really have been long before he saw a light ahead – a light which showed how dark the surrounding landscape had become. He tried to run but his body would not respond. Stumbling in haste and weakness, he made for the light; thought he had reached it and found that it was far farther off than he had supposed; almost despaired; staggered on again, and came at last to what seemed a cavern mouth. The light within was an unsteady one and a delicious wave of warmth smote on his face. It was firelight. He came into the mouth of the cave and then, unsteadily, round the fire and into the interior, and stood still blinking in the light. When at last he could see, he discerned a smooth chamber of green rock, very lofty. There were two things in it. One of them, dancing on the wall and roof, was the huge, angular shadow of a *sorn*: the other, crouched beneath it, was the *sorn* himself.

15

'Come in, Small One,' boomed the *sorn*. 'Come in and let me look at you.'

Now that he stood face to face with the spectre that had haunted him ever since he set foot on Malacandra, Ransom felt a surprising indifference. He had no idea what might be coming next, but he was determined to carry out his programme; and in the meantime the warmth and more breathable air were a heaven in themselves. He came in, well in past the fire, and answered the sorn. His own voice sounded to him a shrill treble.

'The *hrossa* have sent me to look for Oyarsa,' he said.

The *sorn* peered at him. 'You are not from this world,' it said suddenly.

'No,' replied Ransom, and sat down. He was too tired to explain.

'I think you are from Thulcandra, Small One,' said the *sorn*.

'Why?' said Ransom.

'You are small and thick and that is how the animals ought to be made in a heavier world. You cannot come from Glundandra, for it is so heavy that if any animals could live there they would be flat like plates – even you, Small One, would break if you stood up on that world. I do not think you are from Perelandra, for it must be very hot; if any came from there they would not live when they arrived here. So I conclude you are from Thulcandra.'

'The world I come from is called Earth by those who live there,' said Ransom. 'And it is much warmer than this. Before I came into your cave I was nearly dead with cold and thin air.'

The *sorn* made a sudden movement with one of its long fore-limbs. Ransom stiffened (though he did not allow himself to retreat), for the creature might be going to grab him. In fact, its intentions were kindly. Stretching back into the cave, it took from the wall what looked like a cup. Then Ransom saw that it was attached to a length of flexible tube. The *sorn* put it into his hands.

'Smell on this,' it said. 'The *hrossa* also need it when they pass this way.'

Ransom inhaled and was instantly refreshed. His painful short-ness of breath was eased and the tension of chest and temples was relaxed. The *sorn* and the lighted cavern, hitherto vague and dream-like to his eyes, took on a new reality.

'Oxygen?' he asked; but naturally the English word meant nothing to the *sorn*.

'Are you called Augray?' he asked.

'Yes,' said the *sorn*. 'What are you called?'

'The animal I am is called Man, and therefore the *hrossa* call me *Hmān*. But my own name is Ransom.'

'Man – Ren-soom,' said the *sorn*. He noticed that it spoke dif-ferently from the *hrossa*, without any suggestion of their persistent initial H.

It was sitting on its long, wedge-shaped buttocks with its feet drawn close up to it. A man in the same posture would have rest-ed his chin on his knees, but the *sorn*'s legs were too long for that. Its knees rose high above its shoulders on each side of its head – grotesquely suggestive of huge ears – and the head, down between them, rested its chin on the protruding breast. The creature seemed to have either a double chin or a beard; Ransom could not make out which in the firelight. It was mainly white or cream in colour and seemed to be clothed down to the ankles in some soft sub-stance that reflected the light. On the long fragile shanks, where the creature was closest to him, he saw that this was some natural kind of coat. It was not like fur but more like feathers. In fact it was almost exactly like feathers. The whole animal, seen at close quar-ters, was less terrifying than he had expected, and even a little

93

smaller. The face, it was true, took a good deal of getting used to – it was too long, too solemn and too colourless, and it was much more unpleasantly like a human face than any inhuman creature's face ought to be. Its eyes, like those of all very large creatures, seemed too small for it. But it was more grotesque than horrible. A new conception of the *sorns* began to arise in his mind: the ideas of 'giant' and 'ghost' receded behind those of 'goblin 'and 'gawk'.

'Perhaps you are hungry, Small One,' it said.

Ransom was. The *sorn* rose with strange spidery movements and began going to and fro about the cave, attended by its thin goblin shadow. It brought him the usual vegetable foods of Malacandra, and strong drink, with the very welcome addition of a smooth brown substance which revealed itself to nose, eye and palate, in defiance of all probability, as cheese. Ransom asked what it was.

The *sorn* began to explain painfully how the female of some animals secreted a fluid for the nourishment of its young, and would have gone on to describe the whole process of milking and cheesemaking, if Ransom had not interrupted it.

'Yes, yes,' he said. 'We do the same on Earth. What is the beast you use?'

'It is a yellow beast with a long neck. It feeds on the forests that grow in the *handramit*. The young ones of our people who are not yet fit for much else drive the beasts down there in the mornings and follow them while they feed; then before night they drive them back and put them in the caves.'

For a moment Ransom found something reassuring in the thought that the *sorns* were shepherds. Then he remembered that the Cyclops in Homer plied the same trade.

'I think I have seen one of your people at this very work,' he said. 'But the *hrossa* – they let you tear up their forests?'

'Why should they not?'

'Do you rule the *hrossa*?'

'Oyarsa rules them.'

'And who rules you?'

'Oyarsa.'

'But you know more than the *hrossa*?'

'The *hrossa* know nothing except about poems and fish and making things grow out of the ground.'

'And Oyarsa – is he a *sorn*?'

'No, no, Small One. I have told you he rules all *nau*' (so he pronounced *hnau*) 'and everything in Malacandra.'

'I do not understand this Oyarsa,' said Ransom. 'Tell me more.

'Oyarsa does not die,' said the *sorn*. 'And he does not breed. He is the one of his kind who was put into Malacandra to rule it when Malacandra was made. His body is not like ours, nor yours; it is hard to see and the light goes through it.'

'Like an *eldil*?'

'Yes, he is the greatest of *eldila* who ever come to a *handra*.'

'What are these *eldila*?'

'Do you tell me, Small One, that there are no *eldila* in your world?'

'Not that I know of. But what are *eldila*, and why can I not see them? Have they no bodies?'

'Of course they have bodies. There are a great many bodies you cannot see. Every animal's eyes see some things but not others. Do you not know of many kinds of body in Thulcandra?'

Ransom tried to give the *sorn* some idea of the terrestrial terminology of solids, liquids and gases. It listened with great attention.

'That is not the way to say it,' it replied. 'Body is movement. If it is at one speed, you smell something; if at another, you hear a sound; if at another, you see a sight; if at another, you neither see nor hear nor smell nor know the body in any way. But mark this, Small One, that the two ends meet.'

'How do you mean?'

'If movement is faster, then that which moves is more nearly in two places at once.'

'That is true.'

'But if the movement were faster still – it is difficult, for you do not know many words – you see that if you made it faster and faster, in the end the moving thing would be in all places at once, Small One.'

'I think I see that.'

'Well, then, that is the thing at the top of all bodies – so fast that it is at rest, so truly body that it has ceased being body at all. But we will not talk of that. Start from where we are, Small One. The swiftest thing that touches our senses is light. We do not truly see light, we only see slower things lit by it, so that for us light is on the edge – the last thing we know before things become too swift for us. But the body of an *eldil* is a movement swift as light; you may say its body is made of light, but not of that which is light for the *eldil*. His 'light' is a swifter movement which for us is nothing at all; and what we call light is for him a thing like water, a visible thing, a thing he can touch and bathe in – even a dark thing when not illumined by the swifter. And what we call firm things – flesh and earth – seems to him thinner, and harder to see, than our light, and more like clouds, and nearly nothing. To us the *eldil* is a thin, half-real body that can go through walls and rocks; to himself he goes through them because he is solid and firm and they are like cloud. And what is true light to him and fills the heaven, so that he will plunge into the rays of the sun to refresh himself from it, is to us the black nothing in the sky at night. These things are not strange, Small One, though they are beyond our senses. But it is strange that the *eldila* never visit Thulcandra.'

'Of that I am not certain,' said Ransom. It had dawned on him that the recurrent human tradition of bright, elusive people some-times appearing on the Earth – *alns*, *devas* and the like – might after all have another explanation than the anthropologists had yet given. True, it would turn the universe rather oddly inside out; but his experiences in the space-ship had prepared him for some such operation.

'Why does Oyarsa send for me?' he asked.

'Oyarsa has not told me,' said the *sorn*; 'But doubtless he would want to see any stranger from another *handra*.'

'We have no Oyarsa in my world,' said Ransom.

'That is another proof,' said the *sorn*, 'that you come from Thulcandra, the silent planet.'

'What has that to do with it?'

The *sorn* seemed surprised. 'It is not very likely if you had an Oyarsa that he would never speak to ours.'

'Speak to yours? But how could he – it is millions of miles away.'

'Oyarsa would not think of it like that.'

'Do you mean that he ordinarily receives messages from other planets?'

'Once again, he would not say it that way. Oyarsa would not say that he lives on Malacandra and that another Oyarsa lives on another earth. For him Malacandra is only a place in the heavens; it is in the heavens that he and the others live. Of course they talk together ...'

Ransom's mind shied away from the problem; he was getting sleepy and thought he must be misunderstanding the *sorn*.

'I think I must sleep, Augray,' he said. 'And I do not know what you are saying. Perhaps, too, I do not come from what you call Thulcandra.'

'We will both sleep presently,' said the *sorn*. 'But first I will show you Thulcandra.'

It rose and Ransom followed it into the back of the cave. Here he found a little recess and running up within it a winding stair. The steps, hewn for *sorns*, were too high for a man to climb with any comfort, but using hands and knees he managed to hobble up. The *sorn* preceded him. Ransom did not understand the light, which seemed to come from some small round object which the creature held in its hand. They went up a long way, almost as if they were climbing up the inside of a hollow mountain. At last, breathless, he found himself in a dark but warm chamber of rock, and heard the *sorn* saying:

'She is still well above the southern horizon.' It directed his attention to something like a small window. Whatever it was, it did not appear to work like an earthly telescope, Ransom thought;

though an attempt, made next day, to explain the principles of the telescope to the *sorn* threw grave doubts on his own ability to discern the difference. He leaned forward with his elbows on the sill of the aperture and looked. He saw perfect blackness and, floating in the centre of it, seemingly an arm's length away, a bright disk about the size of a half-crown. Most of its surface was featureless, shining silver; towards the bottom markings appeared, and below them a white cap, just as he had seen the polar caps in astronomical photographs of Mars. He wondered for a moment if it was Mars he was looking at; then, as his eyes took in the markings better, he recognised what they were – Northern Europe and a piece of North America. They were upside down with the North Pole at the bottom of the picture and this somehow shocked him. But it was Earth he was seeing – even, perhaps, England, though the picture shook a little and his eyes were quickly getting tired, and he could not be certain that he was not imagining it. It was all there in that little disk – London, Athens, Jerusalem, Shakespeare. There everyone had lived and everything had happened; and there, presumably, his pack was still lying in the porch of an empty house near Sterk.

'Yes,' he said dully to the *sorn*. 'That is my world.' It was the bleakest moment in all his travels.

16

Ransom awoke next morning with the vague feeling that a great weight had been taken off his mind. Then he remembered that he was the guest of a *sorn* and that the creature he had been avoiding ever since he landed had turned out to be as amicable as the *hrossa*, though he was far from feeling the same affection for it. Nothing then remained to be afraid of in Malacandra except Oyarsa ... 'The last fence', thought Ransom.

Augray gave him food and drink.

'And now,' said Ransom, 'how shall I find my way to Oyarsa?'

'I will carry you,' said the *sorn*. 'You are too small a one to make the journey yourself and I will gladly go to Meldilorn. The *hrossa* should not have sent you this way. They do not seem to know from looking at an animal what sort of lungs it has and what it can do. It is just like a *hross*. If you died on the *harandra* they would have made a poem about the gallant *hmān* and how the sky grew black and the cold stars shone and he journeyed on and journeyed on; and they would have put in a fine speech for you to say as you were dying ... and all this would seem to them just as good as if they had used a little forethought and saved your life by sending you the easier way round.'

'I like the *hrossa*,' said Ransom a little stiffly. 'And I think the way they talk about death is the right way.'

'They are right not to fear it, Ren-soom, but they do not seem to look at it reasonably as part of the very nature of our bodies – and therefore often avoidable at times when they would never see how to avoid it; For example, this has saved the life of many a *hross*, but a *hross* would not have thought of it.'

He showed Ransom a flask with a tube attached to it, and, at the end of the tube, a cup, obviously an apparatus for administering oxygen to oneself.

'Smell on it as you have need, Small One,' said the *sorn*. 'And close it up when you do not.'

Augray fastened the thing on his back and gave the tube over his shoulder into his hand; Ransom could not restrain a shudder at the touch of the *sorn*'s hands upon his body; they were fan-shaped, seven-fingered, mere skin over bone like a bird's leg, and quite cold. To divert his mind from such reactions he asked where the apparatus was made, for he had as yet seen nothing remotely like a factory or a laboratory;

'We thought it,' said the *sorn*, 'and the *pfifltriggi* made it.'

'Why do they make them?' said Ransom. He was trying once more, with his insufficient vocabulary, to find out the political and economic framework of Malacandrian life.

'They like making things,' said Augray. 'It is true they like best the making of things that are only good to look at and of no use. But sometimes when they are tired of that they will make things for us, things we have thought, provided they are difficult enough. They have not patience to make easy things however useful they would be. But let us begin our journey. You shall sit on my shoulder.'

The proposal was unexpected and alarming, but seeing that the *sorn* had already crouched down, Ransom felt obliged to climb on to the plume-like surface of its shoulder, to seat himself beside the long, pale face, casting his right arm as far as it would go round the huge neck, and to compose himself as well as he could for this precarious mode of travel. The giant rose cautiously to a standing position and he found himself looking down on the landscape from a height of about eighteen feet.

'Is all well, Small One?' it asked.

'Very well,' Ransom answered, and the journey began.

Its gait was perhaps the least human thing about it. It lifted its feet very high and set them down very gently. Ransom was reminded alternately of a cat stalking, a strutting barn-door fowl, and a high-stepping carriage horse; but the movement was not really like that of any terrestrial animal. For the passenger it was surprisingly comfortable. In a few minutes he had lost all sense of what was dizzying or unnatural in his position. Instead, ludicrous and even tender associations came crowding into his mind. It was like riding an elephant at the zoo in boyhood – like riding on his father's back at a still earlier age. It was fun. They seemed to be doing between six and seven miles an hour. The cold, though severe, was endurable; and thanks to the oxygen he had little difficulty with his breathing.

The landscape which he saw from his high, swaying post of observation was a solemn one. The *handramit* was nowhere to be seen. On each side of the shallow gully in which they were walking, a world of naked, faintly greenish rock, interrupted with wide patches of red, extended to the horizon. The heaven, darkest blue where the rock met it, was almost black at the zenith, and looking in any direction where sunlight did not blind him, he could see the stars. He learned from the *sorn* that he was right in thinking they were near the limits of the breathable. Already on the mountain fringe that borders the *harandra* and walls the *handramit*, or in the narrow depression along which their road led them, the air is of Himalayan rarity, ill breathing for a *hross*, and a few hundred feet higher, on the *harandra* proper, the true surface of the planet, it admits no life. Hence the brightness through which they walked was almost that of heaven – celestial light hardly at all tempered with an atmospheric veil.

The shadow of the *sorn*, with Ransom's shadow on its shoulder, moved over the uneven rock unnaturally distinct like the shadow of a tree before the headlights of a car; and the rock beyond the shadow hurt his eyes. The remote horizon seemed but an arm's length away. The fissures and moulding of distant slopes were clear as the background of a primitive picture made before men learned perspective. He was on the very frontier of that heaven he had known in the space-ship, and rays that the air-enveloped words cannot taste were once more at work upon his body. He felt the old lift of the heart, the soaring solemnity, the sense, at once sober and ecstatic, of life and power offered in unasked and unmeasured abundance. If there had been air enough in his lungs he would have laughed aloud; And now, even in the immediate landscape, beauty was drawing near. Over the edge of the valley, as if it had frothed down from the true *harandra*, came great curves of the rose-tinted, cumular stuff which he had seen so often from a distance. Now on a nearer view they appeared hard as stone in substance, but puffed above and stalked beneath like vegetation; His original simile of giant cauliflower turned out to be surprisingly correct – stone cauliflowers the size of cathedrals and the colour of pale rose. He asked the *sorn* what it was.

'It is the old forests of Malacandra,' said Augray. 'Once there was air on the *harandra* and it was warm. To this day, if you could get up there and live, you would see it all covered with the bones of ancient creatures; it was once full of life and noise; It was then these forests grew, and in and out among their stalks went a people that have vanished from the world these many thousand years. They were covered not with fur but with a coat like mine. They did not go in the water swimming or on the ground walking; they glided in the air on broad flat limbs which kept them up. It is said they were great singers, and in those days the red forests echoed with their music. Now the forests have become stone and only *eldila* can go among them.'

'We still have such creatures in our world,' said Ransom. 'We call them birds. Where was Oyarsa when all this happened to the *harandra*?'

'Where he is now.'

'And he could not prevent it?'

'I do not know. But a world is not made to last for ever, much less a race; that is not Maleldil's way.'

As they proceeded the petrified forests grew more numerous,

and often for half an hour at a time the whole horizon of the life-less, almost airless, waste blushed like an English garden in sum-mer. They passed many caves where, as Augray told him, *sorns* lived; sometimes a high cliff would be perforated with countless holes to the very top and unidentifiable noises came hollowly from within. 'Work' was in progress, said the *sorn*, but of what kind it could not make him understand. Its vocabulary was very different from that of the *hrossa*. Nowhere did he see anything like a village or city of *sorns*. who were apparently solitary not social creatures. Once or twice a long pallid face would show from a cavern mouth and exchange a horn-like greeting with the travellers, but for the most part the long valley, the rock-street of the silent people, was still and empty as the *harandra* itself.

Only towards afternoon, as they were about to descend into a dip of the road, they met three *sorns* together coming towards them down the opposite slope. They seemed to Ransom to be rather skating than walking. The lightness of their world and the perfect poise of their bodies allowed them to lean forward at right angles to the slope, and they came swiftly down like full-rigged ships before a fair wind. The grace of their movement, their lofty stature, and the softened glancing of the sunlight on their feathery sides, effected a final transformation in Ransom's feelings towards their race. 'Ogres' he had called them when they first met his eyes as he struggled in the grip of Weston and Devine; 'Titans' or 'Angels' he now thought would have been a better word. Even the faces, it seemed to him, he had not then seen aright. He had thought them spectral when they were only august, and his first human reaction to their lengthened severity of line and profound stillness of expression now appeared to him not so much coward-ly as vulgar. So might Parmenides or Confucius look to the eyes of a Cockney schoolboy! The great white creatures sailed towards Ransom and Augray and dipped like trees and passed.

In spite of the cold – which made him often dismount and take a spell on foot – he did not wish for the end of the journey; but Augray had his own plans and halted for the night long before sundown at the home of an older *sorn*. Ransom saw well enough that he was brought there to be shown to a great scientist. The cave, or, to speak more correctly, the system of excavations, was large and many-chambered, and contained a multitude of things that he did not understand. He was specially interested in a collection of rolls, seemingly of skin, covered with characters, which were clearly books; but he gathered that books were few in Malacandra.

'It is better to remember,' said the *sorns*.

When Ransom asked if valuable secrets might not thus be lost, they replied that Oyarsa always remembered them and would bring them to light if he thought fit.

'The *hrossa* used to have many books of poetry,' they added. 'But now they have fewer. They say that the writing of books destroys poetry.'

Their host in these caverns was attended by a number of other *sorns* who seemed to be in some way subordinate to him; Ransom thought at first that they were servants but decided later that they were pupils or assistants.

The evening's conversation was not such as would interest a terrestrial reader, for the *sorns* had determined that Ransom should not ask, but answer, questions. Their questioning was very different from the rambling, imaginative inquiries of the *hrossa*. They worked systematically from the geology of Earth to its present geography, and thence in turn to flora, fauna, human history, languages, politics and arts. When they found that Ransom could tell them no more on a given subject – and this happened pretty soon in most of their inquiries – they dropped it at once and went on to the next. Often they drew out of him indirectly much more knowledge than he consciously possessed, apparently working from a wide background of general science. A casual remark about trees when Ransom was trying to explain the manufacture of paper would fill up for them a gap in his sketchy answers to their botanical questions; his account of terrestrial navigation might illuminate mineralogy; and his description of the steam engine gave them a better knowledge of terrestrial air and water than Ransom had ever had. He had decided from the outset that he would be quite frank, for he now felt that it would be not *hnau*, and also that it would be unavailing, to do otherwise. They were astonished at what he had to tell them of human history – of war, slavery and prostitution.

'It is because they have no Oyarsa,' said one of the pupils.

'It is because every one of them wants to be a little Oyarsa himself,' said Augray.

'They cannot help it,' said the old *sorn*. 'There must be rule, yet how can creatures rule themselves? Beasts must be ruled by *hnau* and *hnau* by *eldila* and *eldila* by Maleldil. These creatures have no *eldila*. They are like one trying to lift himself by his own hair – or one trying to see over a whole country when he is on a level with it – like a female trying to beget young on herself.'

Two things about our world particularly stuck in their minds. One was the extraordinary degree to which problems of lifting and carrying things absorbed our energy. The other was the fact that we had only one kind of *hnau*: they thought this must have far-reaching effects in the narrowing of sympathies and even of thought.

'Your thought must be at the mercy of your blood,' said the old *sorn*. 'For you cannot compare it with thought that floats on a different blood.'

It was a tiring and very disagreeable conversation for Ransom. But when at last he lay down to sleep it was not of the human nakedness nor of his own ignorance that he was thinking. He thought only of the old forests of Malacandra and of what it might mean to grow up seeing always so few miles away a land of colour that could never be reached and had once been inhabited.

17

Early next day Ransom again took his seat on Augray's shoulder. For more than an hour they travelled through the same bright wilderness. Far to the north the sky was luminous with a cloud-like mass of dull red or ochre; it was very large and drove furiously westward about ten miles above the waste. Ransom, who had yet seen no cloud in the Malacandrian sky, asked what it was. The *sorn* told him it was sand caught up from the great northern deserts by the winds of that terrible country. It was often thus carried, sometimes at a height of seventeen miles, to fall again, perhaps in a *handramit*, as a choking and blinding dust storm. The sight of it moving with menace in the naked sky served to remind Ransom that they were indeed on the *outside* of Malacandra – no longer dwelling in a world but crawling over the surface of a strange planet. At last the cloud seemed to drop and burst far on the western horizon, where a glow, not unlike that of a conflagration, remained visible until a turn of the valley hid all that region from his view.

The same turn opened a new prospect to his eyes. What lay before him looked at first strangely like an earthly landscape – a landscape of grey downland ridges rising and falling like waves of the sea. Far beyond, cliffs and spires of the familiar green rock rose against the dark blue sky. A moment later he saw that what he had taken for downlands was but the ridged and furrowed surface of a blue-grey valley mist – a mist which would not appear a mist at all when they descended into the *handramit*. And already, as their road began descending, it was less visible and the many-coloured pattern of the low country showed vaguely through it. The descent grew quickly steeper; like the jagged teeth of a giant – a giant with very bad teeth – the topmost peaks of the mountain wall down which they must pass loomed up over the edge of their gulley. The look of the sky and the quality of the light were infinitesimally changed. A moment later they stood on the edge of such a slope as by earthly standards would rather be called a precipice; down and down this face, to where it vanished in a purple blush of vegetation, ran their road. Ransom refused absolutely to make the descent on Augray's shoulder. The *sorn*, though it did not fully understand his objection, stooped for him to dismount, and proceeded, with that same skating and forward sloping motion, to go down before him. Ransom followed, using gladly but stiffly his numb legs.

The beauty of this new *handramit* as it opened before him took his breath away. It was wider than that in which he had hitherto lived and right below him lay an almost circular lake – a sapphire twelve miles in diameter set in a border of purple forest. Amidst the lake there rose like a low and gently sloping pyramid, or like a woman's breast, an island of pale red, smooth to the summit, and on the summit, a grove of such trees as man had never seen. Their smooth columns had the gentle swell of the noblest beech trees: but these were taller than a cathedral spire on earth, and at their tops they broke rather into flower than foliage; into golden flower bright as tulip, still as rock, and huge as summer cloud. Flowers indeed they were, not trees, and far down among their roots he caught a pale hint of slab-like architecture. He knew before his guide told him that this was Meldilorn. He did not know what he had expected. The old dreams which he had brought from earth of some more than American complexity of offices or some engineers' paradise of vast machines had indeed been long laid aside. But he had not looked for anything quite so classic, so virginal, as this bright grove – lying so still, so secret, in its coloured valley, soaring with inimitable grace so many hundred feet into the wintry sunlight. At every step of his descent the comparative warmth of the valley came up to him more deliciously. He looked above – the sky was turning to a paler blue. He looked below – and sweet and faint the thin fragrance of the giant blooms came up to him. Distant crags were growing less sharp in outline, and surfaces less bright. Depth, dimness, softness and perspective were returning to the landscape. The lip or edge of rock from which they had started their descent was already far overhead; it seemed unlikely that they had really come from there. He was breathing freely. His toes, so long benumbed, could move delightfully inside his boots. He lifted the ear-flaps of his cap and found his ears instantly filled with the sound of falling water. And now he was treading on soft groundweed over level earth and the forest roof was above his head. They had conquered the *harandra* and were on the threshold of Meldilorn.

A short walk brought them into a kind of forest 'ride' – a broad avenue running straight as an arrow through the purple stems to where the rigid blue of the lake danced at the end of it. There they found a gong and hammer hung on a pillar of stone. These objects were all richly decorated, and the gong and hammer were of a greenish-blue metal which Ransom did not recognise. Augray struck the gong. An excitement was rising in Ransom's mind which almost prevented him from examining as coolly as he wished the ornamentation of the stone. It was partly pictorial, partly pure decoration. What chiefly struck him was a certain balance of packed and empty surfaces. Pure line drawings, as bare as the pre-historic pictures of reindeer on Earth, alternated with patches of design as close and intricate as Norse or Celtic jewellery; and then, as you looked at it, these empty and crowded areas turned out to be themselves arranged in larger designs. He was struck by the fact that the pictorial work was not confined to the emptier spaces; quite often large arabesques included as a subordinate detail intricate pictures. Elsewhere the opposite plan had been followed – and this alternation, too, had a rhythmical or patterned element in it. He was just beginning to find out that the pictures, though stylised, were obviously intended to tell a story, when Augray interrupted him. A ship had put out from the island shore of Meldilorn.

As it came towards them Ransom's heart warmed to see that it was paddled by a *hross*. The creature brought its boat up to the shore where they were waiting, stared at Ransom and then looked inquiringly at Augray.

'You may well wonder at this *nau*, Hrinha,' said the *sorn*, 'for you have never seen anything like it. It is called Ren-soom and has come through heaven from Thulcandra.'

'It is welcome, Augray,' said the *hross* politely. 'Is it coming to Oyarsa?'

'He has sent for it.'

'And for you also, Augray?'

'Oyarsa has not called me. If you will take Ren-soom over the water, I will go back to my tower.'

The *hross* indicated that Ransom should enter the boat. He attempted to express his thanks to the *sorn* and after a moment's consideration unstrapped his wrist-watch and offered it to him; it was the only thing he had which seemed a suitable present for a *sorn*. He had no difficulty in making Augray understand its purpose; but after examining it the giant gave it back to him, a little reluctantly, and said:

'This gift ought to be given to a *pfifltrigg*. It rejoices my heart, but they would make more of it. You are likely to meet some of the busy people in Meldilorn: give it to them. As for its use, do your people not know except by looking at this thing how much of the day has worn?'

'I believe there are beasts that have a sort of knowledge of that,' said Ransom, 'but our *hnau* have lost it.'

After this, his farewells to the *sorn* were made and he embarked. To be once more in a boat and with a *hross*, to feel the warmth of water on his face and to see a blue sky above him, was almost like coming home. He took off his cap and leaned back luxuriously in the bows, plying his escort with questions. He learned that the *hrossa* were not specially concerned with the service of Oyarsa, as he had surmised from finding a *hross* in charge of the ferry: all three species of *hnau* served him in their various capacities, and the ferry was naturally entrusted to those who understood boats. He learned that his own procedure on arriving in Meldilorn must be to go where he liked and do what he pleased until Oyarsa called for him. It might be an hour or several days before this happened. He would find huts near the landing place where he could sleep if necessary and where food would be given him. In return he related as much as he could make intelligible of his own world and his journey from it; and he warned the *hross* of the dangerous bent men who had brought him and who were still at large on Malacandra. As he did so, it occurred to him that he had not made this sufficiently clear to Augray; but he consoled himself with the reflection that Weston and Devine seemed to have already some liaison with the *sorns* and that they would not be likely to molest things so large and so comparatively man-like. At any rate, not yet. About Devine's ultimate designs he had no illusions; all he could do was to make a clean breast of them to Oyarsa. And now the ship touched land.

Ransom rose, while the *hross* was making fast, and looked about him. Close to the little harbour which they had entered, and to the left, were low buildings of stone – the first he had seen in Malacandra – and fires were burning. There, the *hross* told him, he could find food and shelter. For the rest the island seemed desolate, and its smooth slopes empty up to the grove that crowned them, where, again, he saw stonework. But this appeared to be neither temple nor house in the human sense, but a broad avenue of monoliths – a much larger Stonehenge, stately, empty and vanishing over the crest of the hill into the pale shadow of the flower-trunks. All was solitude; but as he gazed upon it he seemed to hear, against the background of morning silence, a faint, continual agitation of silvery sound – hardly a sound at all, if you attended to it, and yet impossible to ignore.

'The island is all full of *eldila*,' said the *hross* in a hushed voice.

He went ashore. As though half expecting some obstacle, he took a few hesitant paces forward and stopped, and then went on again in the same fashion.

Though the groundweed was unusually soft and rich and his feet made no noise upon it, he felt an impulse to walk on tiptoes. All his movements became gentle and sedate. The width of water about this island made the air warmer than any he had yet breathed in Malacandra; the climate was almost that of a warm earthly day in late September – a day that is warm but with a hint of frost to come. The sense of awe which was increasing upon him deterred him from approaching the crown of the hill, the grove and the avenue of standing stones.

He ceased ascending about half-way up the hill and began walking to his right, keeping a constant distance from the shore. He said to himself that he was having a look at the island, but his feeling was rather that the island was having a look at him. This was greatly increased by a discovery he made after he had been walking for about an hour, and which he ever afterwards found great difficulty in describing. In the most abstract terms it might be summed up by saying that the surface of the island was subject to tiny variations of light and shade which no change in the sky accounted for. If the air had not been calm and the groundweed too short and firm to move in the wind, he would have said that a faint breeze was playing with it, and working such slight alterations in the shading as it does in a cornfield on the Earth. Like the silvery noises in the air, these footsteps of light were shy of observation. Where he looked hardest they were least to be seen: on the edges of his field of vision they came crowding as though a complex arrangement of them were there in progress. To attend to any one of them was to make it invisible, and the minute brightness seemed often to have just left the spot where his eyes fell. He had no doubt that he was 'seeing' – as much as he ever would see – the *eldila*. The sensation it produced in him was curious. It was not exactly uncanny, not as if he were surrounded by ghosts. It was not even as if he were being spied upon; he had rather the sense of being looked at by things that had a right to look. His feeling was less than fear; it had in it something of embarrassment, something of shyness, something of submission, and it was profoundly uneasy.

He felt tired and thought that in this favoured land it would be warm enough to rest out of doors. He sat down. The softness of the weed, the warmth and the sweet smell which pervaded the whole island, reminded him of Earth and gardens in summer. He closed his eyes for a moment; then he opened them again and noticed buildings below him, and over the lake he saw a boat approaching. Recognition suddenly came to him. That was the ferry, and these buildings were the guesthouse beside the harbour; he had walked all round the island. A certain disappointment succeeded this discovery. He was beginning to feel hungry. Perhaps it would be a good plan to go down and ask for some food; at any rate it would pass the time.

But he did not do so. When he rose and looked more closely at the guesthouse he saw a considerable stir of creatures about it, and while he watched he saw that a full load of passengers was landing from the ferry-boat. In the lake he saw some moving objects which he did not at first identify but which turned out to be *sorns* up to their middles in the water and obviously wading to Meldilorn from the mainland. There were about ten of them. For some reason or other the island was receiving an influx of visitors. He no longer supposed that any harm would be done to him if he went down and mixed in the crowd, but he felt a reluctance to do so. The situation brought vividly back to his mind his experience as a new boy at school – new boys came a day early – hanging about and watching the arrival of the old hands. In the end he decided not to go down. He cut and ate some of the groundweed and dozed for a little.

In the afternoon, when it grew colder, he resumed his walking. Other *hnau* were roaming about the island by this time. He saw *sorns* chiefly, but this was because their height made them conspicuous. There was hardly any noise. His reluctance to meet these fellow-wanderers, who seemed to confine themselves to the coast of the island, drove him half consciously upwards and inwards. He found himself at last on the fringes of the grove and looking straight up the monolithic avenue. He had intended, for no very clearly defined reason, not to enter it, but he fell to studying the stone nearest to him, which was richly sculptured on all its four sides, and after that curiosity led him on from stone to stone.

The pictures were very puzzling. Side by side with representations of *sorns* and *hrossa* and what he supposed to be *pfifltriggi* there occurred again and again an upright wavy figure with only the suggestion of a face, and with wings. The wings were perfectly recognisable, and this puzzled him very much. Could it be that the traditions of Malacandrian art went back to that earlier geological and biological era when, as Augray had told him, there was life, including bird-life, on the *harandra*? The answer of the stones seemed to be Yes. He saw pictures of the old red forests with unmistakable birds flying among them, and many other creatures that he did not know. On another stone many of these were represented lying dead, and a fantastic *hnakra*-like figure, presumably symbolising the cold, was depicted in the sky above them shooting at them with darts. Creatures still alive were crowding round the winged, wavy figure, which he took to be Oyarsa, pictured as a winged flame. On the next stone Oyarsa appeared, followed by many creatures, and apparently making a furrow with some pointed instrument. Another picture showed the furrow being enlarged by *pfifltriggi* with digging tools. *Sorns* were piling the earth up in pinnacles on each side, and *hrossa* seemed to be making water channels. Ransom wondered whether this were a mythical account of the making of *handramits* or whether they were conceivably artificial in fact.

Many of the pictures he could make nothing of. One that particularly puzzled him showed at the bottom a segment of a circle, behind and above which rose three-quarters of a disk divided into concentric rings. He thought it was a picture of the sun rising behind a hill; certainly the segment at the bottom was full of Malacandrian scenes – Oyarsa in Meldilorn, *sorns* on the mountain edge of the *harandra*, and many other things both familiar to him and strange. He turned from it to examine the disk which rose behind it. It was not the sun. The sun was there, unmistakably, at the centre of the disk: round this the concentric circles revolved. In the first and smallest of these was pictured a little ball, on which rode a winged figure something like Oyarsa, but holding what appeared to be a trumpet. In the next, a similar ball carried another of the flaming figures. This one, instead of even the suggested face, had two bulges which after long inspection he decided were meant to be the udders or breasts of a female mammal. By this time he was quite sure that he was looking at a picture of the solar system. The first ball was Mercury, the second Venus – 'And what an extraordinary coincidence,' thought Ransom, 'that their mythology, like ours, associates some idea of the female with Venus.' The problem would have occupied him longer if a natural curiosity had not drawn his eyes on to the next ball which must represent the Earth. When he saw it, his whole mind stood still for a moment. The ball was there, but where the flame-like figure should have been, a deep depression of irregular shape had been cut as if to erase it. Once, then – but his speculations faltered and became silent before a series of unknowns. He looked at the next circle. Here there was no ball. Instead, the bottom of this circle touched the top of the big segment filled with Malacandrian scenes, so that Malacandra at this point touched the solar system and came out of it in perspective towards the spectator. Now that his mind had grasped the design, he was astonished at the vividness of it all. He stood back and drew a deep breath preparatory to tackling some of the mysteries in which he was engulfed. Malacandra, then, was Mars. The Earth – but at this point a sound of tapping or hammering, which had been going on for some time without gaining admission to his consciousness, became too insistent to be ignored. Some creature, and certainly not an *eldil*, was at work, close to him. A little startled – for he had been deep in thought – he turned round. There was nothing to be seen. He shouted out, idiotically, in English:

'Who's there?'

The tapping instantly stopped and a remarkable face appeared from behind a neighbouring monolith.

It was hairless like a man's or a *sorn*'s. It was long and pointed like a shrew's, yellow and shabby-looking, and so low in the forehead that but for the heavy development of the head at the back and behind the ears (like a bag-wig) it could not have been that of an intelligent creature. A moment later the whole of the thing came into view with a startling jump. Ransom guessed that it was a *pfifltrigg* – and was glad that he had not met one of this third race on his first arrival in Malacandra. It was much more insect-like or reptilian than anything he had yet seen. Its build was distinctly that of a frog, and at first Ransom thought it was resting, frog-like, on its 'hands'. Then he noticed that that part of its fore-limbs on which it was supported was really, in human terms, rather an elbow than a hand. It was broad and padded and clearly made to be walked on; but upwards from it, at an angle of about forty-five degrees, went the true fore-arms – thin, strong forearms, ending in enormous, sensitive, many-fingered hands. He realised that for all manual work from mining to cutting cameos this creature had the advantage of being able to work with its full strength from a supported elbow. The insect-like effect was due to the speed and jerkiness of its movements and to the fact that it could swivel its head almost all the way round like a mantis; and it was increased by a kind of dry, rasping, jingling quality in the noise of its moving. It was rather like a grasshopper, rather like one of Arthur Rackham's dwarfs, rather like a frog, and rather like a little old taxidermist whom Ransom knew in London.

'I come from another world,' began Ransom.

'I know, I know,' said the creature in a quick, twittering rather impatient voice. 'Come here, behind the stone. This way, this way. Oyarsa's orders. Very busy. Must begin at once. Stand there.'

Ransom found himself on the other side of the monolith, staring at a picture which was still in process of completion. The ground was liberally strewn with chips and the air was full of dust.

'There,' said the creature. 'Stand still. Don't look at me. Look over there.'

For a moment Ransom did not quite understand what was expected of him; then, as he saw the *pfifltrigg* glancing to and fro at him and at the stone with the unmistakable glance of artist from model to work which is the same in all worlds, he realised and almost laughed. He was standing for his portrait! From his position he could see that the creature was cutting the stone as if it were cheese and the swiftness of its movements almost baffled his eyes, but he could get no impression of the work done, though he could study the *pfifltrigg*. He saw that the jingling and metallic noise was due to the number of small instruments which it carried about its body. Sometimes, with an exclamation of annoyance, it would throw down the tool it was working with and select one of these; but the majority of those in immediate use it kept in its mouth. He realised also that this was an animal artificially clothed like himself, in some bright scaly substance which appeared richly decorated though coated in dust. It had folds of furry clothing about its throat like a comforter, and its eyes were protected by dark bulging goggles. Rings and chains of a bright metal – not gold, he thought – adorned its limbs and neck. All the time it was working it kept up a sort of hissing whisper to itself; and when it was excited – which it usually was – the end of its nose wrinkled like a rabbit's. At last it gave another startling leap, landed about ten yards away from its work, and said:

'Yes, yes. Not so good as I hoped. Do better another time. Leave it now. Come and see yourself.'

Ransom obeyed. He saw a picture of the planets, not now arranged to make a map of the solar system, but advancing in a single procession towards the spectator, and all, save one, bearing its fiery charioteer. Below lay Malacandra and there, to his surprise, was a very tolerable picture of the space-ship. Beside it stood three figures for all of which Ransom had apparently been the model. He recoiled from them in disgust. Even allowing for the strangeness of the subject from a Malacandrian point of view and for the stylisation of their art, still, he thought, the creature might have made a better attempt at the human form than these stock-like dummies, almost as thick as they were tall, and sprouting about the head and neck into something that looked like fungus.

He hedged. 'I expect it is like me as I look to your people,' he said. 'It is not how they would draw me in my own world.'

'No,' said the *pfifltrigg*. 'I do not mean it to be too like. Too like, and they will not believe it – those who are born after.' He added a good deal more which was difficult to understand; but while he was speaking it dawned upon Ransom that the odious figures were intended as an *idealisation* of humanity. Conversation languished for a little. To change the subject Ransom asked a question which had been in his mind for some time.

'I cannot understand,' he said, 'how you and the *sorns* and the *hrossa* all come to speak the same speech. For your tongues and teeth and throats must be very different.'

'You are right,' said the creature. 'Once we all had different speeches and we still have at home. But every one has learned the speech of the *hrossa*.'

'Why is that?' said Ransom, still thinking in terms of terrestrial history. 'Did the *hrossa* once rule the others?'

'I do not understand. They are our great speakers and singers. They have more words and better. No one learns the speech of my people, for what we have to say is said in stone and sun's blood and stars milk and all can see them. No one learns the *sorns*' speech, for you can change their knowledge into any words and it is still the same. You cannot do that with the songs of the *hrossa*. Their tongue goes all over Malacandra. I speak it to you because you are a stranger. I would speak it to a *sorn*. But we have our old tongues at home. You can see it in the names. The *sorns* have big-sounding names like Augray and Arkal and Belmo and Falmay. The *hrossa* have furry names like Hnoh and Hhihi and Hyoi and Hlithnahi.'

'The best poetry, then, comes in the roughest speech?'

'Perhaps,' said the *pfifltrigg*. 'As the best pictures are made in the hardest stone. But my people have names like Kalakaperi and Parakataru and Tafalakeruf. I am called Kanakaberaka.'

Ransom told it his name.

'In our country,' said Kanakaberaka, 'it is not like this. We are not pinched in a narrow *handramit*. There are the true forests, the green shadows, the deep mines. It is warm. It does not blaze with light like this, and it is not silent like this. I could put you in a place there in the forests where you could see a hundred fires at once and hear a hundred hammers. I wish you had come to our country. We do not live in holes like the *sorns* nor in bundles of weed like the *hrossa*. I could show you houses with a hundred pillars, one of sun's blood and the next of stars' milk, all the way ... and all the world painted on the walls.'

'How do you rule yourselves?' asked Ransom. 'Those who are digging in the mines – do they like it as much as those who paint the walls?'

'All keep the mines open; it is a work to be shared. But each digs for himself the thing he wants for his work. What else would he do?'

'It is not so with us.'

'Then you must make very bent work. How would a maker understand working in sun's blood unless he went into the home of sun's blood himself and knew one kind from another and lived with it for days out of the light of the sky till it was in his blood and his heart, as if he thought it and ate it and spat it?'

'With us it lies very deep and hard to get and those who dig it must spend their wholes lives on the skill.'

'And they love it?'

'I think not ... I do not know. They are kept at it because they are given no food if they stop.

Kanakaberaka wrinkled his nose. 'Then there is not food in plenty on your world?'

'I do not know,' said Ransom. 'I have often wished to know the answer to that question but no one can tell me. Does no one keep your people at their work, Kanakaberaka?'

'Our females,' said the *pfifltrigg* with a piping noise which was apparently his equivalent for a laugh.

'Are your females of more account among you than those of the other *hnau* among them?'

'Very greatly. The *sorns* make least account of females and we make most.'

18

That night Ransom slept in the guesthouse, which was a real house built by *pfifltriggi* and richly decorated. His pleasure at finding himself, in this respect, under more human conditions was qualified by the discomfort which, despite his reason, he could not help feeling in the presence, at close quarters, of so many Malacandrian creatures. All three species were represented. They seemed to have no uneasy feelings towards each other, though there were some differences of the kind that occur in a railway carriage on Earth – the *sorns* finding the house too hot and the *pfifltriggi* finding it too cold. He learned more of Malacandrian humour and of the noises that expressed it in this one night than he had learned during the whole of his life on the strange planet hitherto. Indeed, nearly all Malacandrian conversations in which he had yet taken part had been grave. Apparently the comic spirit arose chiefly from the meeting of the different kinds of *hnau*. The jokes of all three were equally incomprehensible to him. He thought he could see differences in kind – as that the *sorns* seldom got beyond irony, while the *hrossa* were extravagant and fantastic, and the *pfifltriggi* were sharp and excelled in abuse – but even when he understood all the words he could not see the points. He went early to bed.

It was at the time of early morning, when men on Earth go out to milk the cows, that Ransom was wakened. At first he did not know what had roused him. The chamber in which he lay was silent, empty and nearly dark. He was preparing himself to sleep again when a high pitched voice close beside him said, 'Oyarsa sends for you.' He sat up, staring about him. There was no one

119

there, and the voice repeated, 'Oyarsa sends for you.' The confusion of sleep was now clearing in his head, and he recognised that there was an *eldil* in the room. He felt no conscious fear, but while he rose obediently and put on such of his clothes as he had laid aside he found that his heart was beating rather fast. He was thinking less of the invisible creature in the room than of the interview that lay before him. His old terrors of meeting some monster or idol had quite left him: he felt nervous as he remembered feeling on the morning of an examination when he was an undergraduate. More than anything in the world he would have liked a cup of good tea.

The guest-house was empty. He went out. The bluish smoke was rising from the lake and the sky was bright behind the jagged eastern wall of the canyon; it was a few minutes before sunrise. The air was still very cold, the groundweed drenched with dew, and there was something puzzling about the whole scene which he presently identified with the silence. The *eldil* voices in the air had ceased and so had the shifting network of small lights and shades. Without being told, he knew that it was his business to go up to the crown of the island and the grove. As he approached them he saw with a certain sinking of heart that the monolithic avenue was full of Malacandrian creatures, and all silent. They were in two lines, one on each side, and all squatting or sitting in the various fashions suitable to their anatomies. He walked on slowly and doubtfully, not daring to stop, and ran the gauntlet of all those inhuman and unblinking eyes. When he had come to the very summit, at the middle of the avenue where the biggest of the stones rose, he stopped – he never could remember afterwards whether an *eldil* voice had told him to do so or whether it was an intuition of his own. He did not sit down, for the earth was too cold and wet and he was not sure if it would be decorous. He simply stood – motionless like a man on parade. All the creatures were looking at him and there was no noise anywhere.

He perceived, gradually, that the place was full of *eldila*. The lights, or suggestions of light, which yesterday had been scattered over the island, were now all congregated in this one spot, and were all stationary or very faintly moving. The sun had risen by now, and still no one spoke. As he looked up to see the first, pale sunlight upon the monoliths, he became conscious that the air above him was full of a far greater complexity of light than the sunrise could explain, and light of a different kind, *eldil*-light. The sky, no less than the earth, was full of them; the visible Malacandrians were but the smallest part of the silent consistory which surrounded him. He might, when the time came, be pleading his cause before thousands or before millions: rank behind rank about him, and rank above rank over his head, the creatures that had never yet seen man and whom man could not see, were waiting for his trial to begin. He licked his lips, which were quite dry, and wondered if he would be able to speak when speech was demanded of him. Then it occurred to him that perhaps this – this waiting and being looked at – *was* the trial; perhaps even now he was unconsciously telling them all they wished to know. But afterwards – a long time afterwards – there was a noise of movement. Every visible creature in the grove had risen to its feet and was standing, more hushed than ever, with its head bowed; and Ransom saw (if it could be called seeing) that Oyarsa was coming up between the long lines of sculptured stones. Partly he knew it from the faces of the Malacandrians as their lord passed them; partly he saw – he could not deny that he saw – Oyarsa himself. He never could say what it was like. The merest whisper of light – no, less than that, the smallest diminution of shadow – was travelling along the uneven surface of the groundweed; or rather some difference in the look of the ground, too slight to be named in the language of the five senses, moved slowly towards him. Like a silence spreading over a room full of people, like an infinitesimal coolness on a sultry day, like a passing memory of some long-forgotten sound or scent, like all that is stillest and smallest and most hard to seize in nature, Oyarsa passed between his subjects and drew near and came to rest, not ten yards away from Ransom, in the centre of Meldilorn. Ransom felt a tingling of his blood and a prickling on his fingers as if lightning were near him; and his heart and body seemed to him to be made of water.

Oyarsa spoke – a more unhuman voice than Ransom had yet heard, sweet and seemingly remote; an unshaken voice; a voice, as one of the *hrossa* afterwards said to Ransom, 'with no blood in it. Light is instead of blood for them.' The words were not alarming.

'What are you so afraid of, Ransom of Thulcandra?' it said.

'Of you, Oyarsa, because you are unlike me and I cannot see you.'

'Those are not great reasons,' said the voice. 'You are also unlike me, and, though I see you, I see you very faintly. But do not think we are utterly unlike. We are both copies of Maleldil. These are not the real reasons.'

Ransom said nothing.

'You began to be afraid of me before you set foot in my world. And you have spent all your time since then in flying from me. My servants saw your fear when you were in your ship in heaven. They saw that your own kind treated you ill, though they could not understand their speech. Then to deliver you out of the hands of those two I stirred up a *hnakra* to try if you would come to me of your own will. But you hid among the *hrossa* and though they told you to come to me, you would not. After that I sent my *eldil* to fetch you, but still you would not come. And in the end your own kind have chased you to me, and *hnau*'s blood has been shed.'

'I do not understand, Oyarsa. Do you mean that it was you who sent for me from Thulcandra?'

'Yes. Did not the other two tell you this? And why did you come with them unless you meant to obey my call? My servants could not understand their talk to you when your ship was in heaven.'

'Your servants … I cannot understand,' said Ransom.

'Ask freely,' said the voice.

'Have you servants out in the heavens?'

'Where else? There is nowhere else.'

'But you, Oyarsa, are here on Malacandra, as I am.'

'But Malacandra, like all worlds, floats in heaven. And I am not "here" altogether as you are, Ransom of Thulcandra. Creatures of your kind must drop out of heaven into a world; for us the worlds are places in heaven. But do not try to understand this now. It is enough to know that I and my servants are even now in heaven; they were around you in the sky-ship no less than they are around you here.'

'Then you knew of our journey before we left Thulcandra?'

'No. Thulcandra is the world we do not know. It alone is outside the heaven, and no message comes from it.'

Ransom was silent, but Oyarsa answered his unspoken questions.

'It was not always so. Once we knew the Oyarsa of your world – he was brighter and greater than I – and then we did not call it Thulcandra. It is the longest of all stories and the bitterest. He became bent. That was before any life came on your world. Those were the Bent Years of which we still speak in the heavens, when he was not yet bound to Thulcandra but free like us. It was in his mind to spoil other worlds besides his own. He smote your moon with his left hand and with his right he brought the cold death on my *harandra* before its time; if by my arm Maleldil had not opened the *handramits* and let out the hot springs, my world would have been unpeopled. We did not leave him so at large for long. There was great war, and we drove him back out of the heavens and bound him in the air of his own world as Maleldil taught us. There doubtless he lies to this hour, and we know no more of that planet: it is silent. We think that Maleldil would not give it up utterly to the Bent One, and there are stories among us that He has taken strange counsel and dared terrible things, wrestling with the Bent One in Thulcandra. But of this we know less than you; it is a thing we desire to look into.'

It was some time before Ransom spoke again and Oyarsa respected his silence. When he had collected himself he said:

'After this story, Oyarsa, I may tell you that our world is very bent. The two who brought me knew nothing of you, but only that the *sorns* had asked for me. They thought you were a false *eldil*, I think. There are false *eldila* in the wild parts of our world; men kill other men before them – they think the *eldil* drinks blood. They thought the *sorns* wanted me for this or for some other evil. They brought me by force. I was in terrible fear. The tellers of tales in our world make us think that if there is any life beyond our own air, it is evil.'

'I understand,' said the voice. 'And this explains things that I have wondered at. As soon as your journey had passed your own air and entered heaven, my servants told me that you seemed to be coming unwillingly and that the others had secrets from you. I did not think any creature could be so bent as to bring another of its own kind here by force.'

'They did not know what you wanted me for, Oyarsa. Nor do I know yet.'

'I will tell you. Two years ago – and that is about four of your years – this ship entered the heavens from your world. We followed its journey all the way hither and *eldila* were with it as it sailed over the *harandra*, and when at last it came to rest in the *handramit* more than half my servants were standing round it to see the strangers come out. All beasts we kept back from the place, and no *hnau* yet knew of it. When the strangers had walked to and fro on Malacandra and made themselves a hut and their fear of a new world ought to have worn off, I sent certain *sorns* to show themselves and to teach the strangers our language. I chose *sorns* because they are most like your people in form. The Thulcandrians feared the *sorns* and were very unteachable. The *sorns* went to them many times and taught them a little. They reported to me that the Thulcandrians were taking sun's blood wherever they could find it in the streams. When I could make nothing of them by report, I told the *sorns* to bring them to me, not by force but courteously. They would not come. I asked for one of them, but not even one of them would come. It would have been easy to take them; but though we saw they were stupid we did not know yet how bent they were, and I did not wish to stretch my authority beyond the creatures of my own world. I told the *sorns* to treat them like cubs, to tell them that they would be allowed to pick up no more of the sun's blood until one of their race came to me. When they were told this they stuffed as much as they could into the sky-ship and went back to their own world. We wondered at this, but now it is plain. They thought I wanted one of your race to eat and went to fetch one. If they had come a few miles to see me I would have received them honourably; now they have twice gone a voyage of millions of miles for nothing and will appear before me none the less. And you also, Ransom of Thulcandra, you have taken many vain troubles to avoid standing where you stand now.'

'That is true, Oyarsa. Bent creatures are full of fears. But I am here now and ready to know your will with me.'

'Two things I wanted to ask of your race. First I must know why you come here – so much is my duty to my world. And secondly I wish to hear of Thulcandra and of Maleldil's strange wars there with the Bent One; for that, as I have said, is a thing we desire to look into.'

'For the first question, Oyarsa, I have come here because I was brought. Of the others, one cares for nothing but the sun's blood, because in our world he can exchange it for many pleasures and powers. But the other means evil to you. I think he would destroy all your people to make room for our people; and then he would do the same with other worlds again. He wants our race to last for always, I think and he hopes they will leap from world to world … always going to a new sun when an old one dies … or something like that.'

'Is he wounded in his brain?'

'I do not know. Perhaps I do not describe his thoughts right. He is more learned than I.'

'Does he think he could go to the great worlds? Does he think Maleldil wants a race to live for ever?'

'He does not know there is any Maleldil. But what is certain, Oyarsa, is that he means evil to your world. Our kind must not be allowed to come here again. If you can prevent it only by killing all three of us, I am content.'

'If you were my own people I would kill them now, Ransom, and you soon; for they are bent beyond hope, and you, when you have grown a little braver, will be ready to go to Maleldil. But my authority is over my own world. It is a terrible thing to kill someone else's *hnau*. It will not be necessary.'

'They are strong, Oyarsa, and they can throw death many miles and can blow killing airs at their enemies.'

'The least of my servants could touch their ship before it reached Malacandra, while it was in the heaven, and make it a body of different movements – for you, no body at all. Be sure that no one of your race will come into my world again unless I call him. But enough of this. Now tell me of Thulcandra. Tell me all. We know nothing since the day when the Bent One sank out of heaven into the air of your world, wounded in the very light of his light. But why have you become afraid again?'

'I am afraid of the lengths of time, Oyarsa … or perhaps I do not understand. Did you not say this happened before there was life on Thulcandra?'

'Yes.'

'And you, Oyarsa? You have lived … and that picture on the stone where the cold is killing them on the *harandra*? Is that a picture of something that was before my world began?'

'I see you are *hnau* after all,' said the voice. 'Doubtless no stone that faced the air then would be a stone now. The picture has begun to crumble away and been copied again more times than there are *eldila* in the air above us. But it was copied right. In that way you are seeing a picture that was finished when your world was still half made. But do not think of these things. My people have a law never to speak much of sizes or numbers to you others, not even to *sorns*. You do not understand, and it makes you do reverence to nothings and pass by what is really great. Rather tell me what Maleldil has done in Thulcandra.'

'According to our traditions –' Ransom was beginning, when an unexpected disturbance broke in upon the solemn stillness of the assembly. A large party, almost a a procession, was approaching the grove, from the direction of the ferry. It consisted entirely, so far as he could see, of *hrossa*, and they appeared to be carrying something.

19

As the procession drew nearer Ransom saw that the foremost *hrossa* were supporting three long and narrow burdens. They carried them on their heads, four *hrossa* to each. After these came a number of others armed with harpoons and apparently guarding two creatures which he did not recognise. The light was behind them as they entered between the two farthest monoliths. They were much shorter than any animal he had yet seen on Malacandra, and he gathered that they were bipeds, though the lower limbs were so thick and sausage-like that he hesitated to call them legs. The bodies were a little narrower at the top than at the bottom so as to be very slightly pear-shaped, and the heads were neither round like those of *hrossa* nor long like those of *sorns*, but almost square. They stumped along on narrow, heavy-looking feet which they seemed to press into the ground with unnecessary violence. And now their faces were becoming visible as masses of lumped and puckered flesh of variegated colour fringed in some bristly, dark substance … Suddenly, with an indescribable change of feeling, he realised that he was looking at men. The two prisoners were Weston and Devine and he, for one privileged moment, had seen the human form with almost Malacandrian eyes.

The leaders of the procession had now advanced to within few yards of Oyarsa and laid down their burdens. These, he now saw, were three dead *hrossa* laid on biers of some unknown metal; they were on their backs and their eyes, not closed as we close the eyes of human dead, stared disconcertingly up at the far-off golden canopy of the grove. One of them he took to be Hyoi, and it was certainly Hyoi's brother, Hyahi, who now came forward, and after an obeisance to Oyarsa began to speak.

Ransom at first did not hear what he was saying, for his attention was concentrated on Weston and Devine. They were weaponless and vigilantly guarded by the armed *hrossa* about them. Both of them, like Ransom himself, had let their beards grow ever since they landed on Malacandra, and both were pale and travel stained. Weston was standing with folded arms, and his face wore a fixed, even an elaborate, expression of desperation. Devine, with his hands in his pockets, seemed to be in a state of furious sulks. Both clearly thought that they had good reason to fear, though neither was by any means lacking in courage. Surrounded by their guards as they were, and intent on the scene before them, they had not noticed Ransom.

He became aware of what Hyoi's brother was saying.

'For the death of these two, Oyarsa, I do not so much complain, for when we fell upon the *hmāna* by night they were in terror. You may say it was as a hunt and these two were killed as they might have been by a *hnakra*. But Hyoi they hit from afar with a coward's weapon when he had done nothing to frighten them. And now he lies there (and I do not say it because he was my brother, but all the *handramit* knows it) and he was a *hnakrapunt* and a great poet and the loss of him is heavy.'

The voice of Oyarsa spoke for the first time to the two men.

'Why have you killed my *hnau*?' it said.

Weston and Devine looked anxiously about them to identify the speaker.

'God!' exclaimed Devine in English. 'Don't tell me they've got a loudspeaker.'

'Ventriloquism,' replied Weston in a husky whisper. 'Quite common among savages. The witch-doctor or medicine-man pretends to go into a trance and he does it. The thing to do is to identify the medicine-man and address your remarks to *him* wherever the voice seems to come from; it shatters his nerve and shows you've seen through him. Do you see any of the brutes in a trance? By Jove – I've spotted him.'

Due credit must be given to Weston for his powers of observation: he had picked out the only creature in the assembly which was not standing in an attitude of reverence and attention. This was an elderly *hross* close beside him. It was squatting; and its eyes were shut. Taking a step towards it, he struck a defiant attitude and exclaimed in a loud voice (his knowledge of the language was elementary):

'Why you take our puff-bangs away? We very angry with you. We not afraid.'

On Weston's hypothesis his action ought to have been impressive. Unfortunately for him, no one else shared his theory of the elderly *hross*'s behaviour. The *hross* – who was well known to all of them, including Ransom – had not come with the funeral procession. It had been in its place since dawn. Doubtless it intended no disrespect to Oyarsa; but it must be confessed that it had yielded, at a much earlier stage in the proceedings, to an infirmity which attacks elderly *hnau* of all species, and was by this time enjoying a profound and refreshing slumber. One of its whiskers twitched a little as Weston shouted in its face, but its eyes remained shut.

The voice of Oyarsa spoke again. 'Why do you speak to him?' it said. 'It is I who ask you, why have you killed my *hnau*?'

'You let us go, then we talkee-talkee,' bellowed Weston at the sleeping *hross*. 'You think we no power, think you do all you like. You no can. Great big headman in sky he send us. You no do what I say, he come, blow you all up – Pouff! Bang!'

'I do not know what *bang* means,' said the voice. 'But why have you killed my *hnau*?'

'Say it was an accident,' muttered Devine to Weston in English.

'I've told you before,' replied Weston in the same language. 'You don't understand how to deal with natives. One sign of yielding and they'll be at our throats. The only thing is to intimidate them.'

'All right! Do your stuff, then,' growled Devine. He was obviously losing faith in his partner.

Weston cleared his throat and again rounded on the elderly *hross*.

'We kill him,' he shouted. 'Show what we can do. Everyone who no do all we say – pouff! bang! – kill him same as that one. You do all we say and we give you much pretty things. See! See!' To Ransom's intense discomfort, Weston at this point whipped out of his pocket a brightly coloured necklace of beads, the undoubted work of Mr Woolworth, and began dangling it in front of the faces of his guards, turning slowly round and round and repeating, 'Pretty, pretty! See! See!'

The result of this manoeuvre was more striking than Weston himself had anticipated. Such a roar of sounds as human ears had never heard before – baying of *hrossa*, piping of *pfifltriggi*, booming of *sorns* – burst out and rent the silence of that august place, waking echoes from the distant mountain walls. Even in the air above them there was a faint ringing of the *eldil* voices. It is greatly to Weston's credit that though he paled at this he did not lose his nerve.

'You no roar at me,' he thundered. 'No try make me afraid. Me no afraid of you.'

'You must forgive my people,' said the voice of Oyarsa – and even it was subtly changed – 'but they are not roaring at you. They are only laughing.'

But Weston did not know the Malacandrian word for laugh: indeed, it was not a word he understood very well in any language. Ransom, biting his lips with mortification, almost prayed that one experiment with the beads would satisfy the scientist; but that was because he did not know Weston. The latter saw that the clamour had subsided. He knew that he was following the most orthodox rules for frightening and then conciliating primitive races; and he was not the man to be deterred by one or two failures. The roar that went up from the throats of all spectators as he again began revolving like a slow motion picture of a humming-top, occasionally mopping his brow with his left hand and conscientiously jerking the necklace up and down with his right, completely drowned anything he might be attempting to say; but Ransom saw his lips moving and had little doubt that he was working away at 'Pretty, pretty!' Then suddenly the sound of laughter almost redoubled its volume. The stars in their courses were fighting against Weston. Some hazy memory of efforts made long since to entertain an infant niece had begun to penetrate his highly trained mind. He was bobbing up and down from the knees and holding his head on one side; he was almost dancing; and he was by now very hot indeed. For all Ransom knew he was saying 'Diddle, diddle, diddle.'

It was sheer exhaustion which ended the great physicist's performance – the most successful of its kind ever given on Malacandra – and with it the sonorous raptures of his audience. As silence returned Ransom heard Devine's voice in English:

'For God's sake stop making a buffoon of yourself, Weston,' it said. 'Can't you see it won't work?'

'It *doesn't* seem to be working,' admitted Weston, and I'm inclined to think they have even less intelligence than we supposed. Do you think, perhaps, if I tried it just once again – or would you like to try this time?'

'Oh, Hell!' said Devine, and, turning his back on his partner, sat down abruptly on the ground, produced his cigarette case and began to smoke.

'I'll give it to the witch-doctor,' said Weston during the moment of silence which Devine's action had produced among the mystified spectators; and before anyone could stop him he took a step forward and attempted to drop the string of beads round the elderly *hross's* neck. The *hross's* head was, however, too large for this operation and the necklace merely settled on its forehead like a crown, slightly over one eye. It shifted its head a little, like a dog worried with files, snorted gently, and resumed its sleep.

Oyarsa's voice now addressed Ransom. 'Are your fellow-creatures hurt in their brains, Ransom of Thulcandra?' it said. 'Or are they too much afraid to answer my questions?'

'I think, Oyarsa,' said Ransom, 'that they do not believe you are there. And they believe that all these *hnau* are – are like very young cubs. The thicker *hmān* is trying to frighten them and then to please them with gifts.'

At the sound of Ransom's voice the two prisoners turned sharply around. Weston was about to speak when Ransom interrupted him hastily in English:

'Listen, Weston. It is not a trick. There really is a creature there in the middle – there where you can see a kind of light, or a kind of something, if you look hard. And it is at least as intelligent as a man – they seem to live an enormous time. Stop treating it like a child and answer its questions. And if you take my advice, you'll speak the truth and not bluster.'

'The brutes seem to have intelligence enough to take you in, anyway,' growled Weston; but it was in a somewhat modified voice that he turned once more to the sleeping *hross* – the desire to wake up the supposed witch-doctor was becoming an obsession – and addressed it.

'We sorry we kill him,' he said, pointing to Hyoi. 'No go to kill him. *Sorns* tell us bring man, give him your big head. We got away back into sky. *He* come' (here he indicated Ransom) 'with us. He very bent man, run away, no do what *sorns* say like us. We run after him, get him back for *sorns*, want to do what we say and *sorns* tell us, see? He not let us. Run away, run, run. We run after. See a big black one, think he kill us, we kill him – pouff! bang! All for bent man. He no run away, he be good, we no run after, no kill big black one, see? You have bent man – bent man make all trouble – you plenty keep him, let us go. He afraid of you, we no afraid. Listen –'

At this moment Weston's continual bellowing in the face of the *hross* at last produced the effect he had striven for so long. The creature opened its eyes and stared mildly at him in some perplexity. Then, gradually realising the unpropriety of which it had been guilty, it rose slowly to its standing position, bowed respectfully to Oyarsa, and finally waddled out of the assembly still carrying the necklace draped over its right ear and eye. Weston, his mouth still open, followed the retreating figure with his gaze till it vanished among the stems of the grove.

It was Oyarsa who broke the silence. 'We have had mirth enough,' he said, 'and it is time to hear true answers to our questions. Something is wrong in your head, *hnau* from Thulcandra. There is too much blood in it. Is Firikitekila here?'

'Here Oyarsa,' said a *pfifltrigg*.

'Have you in your cisterns water that has been made cold?'

'Yes, Oyarsa.'

'Then let this thick *hnau* be taken to the guesthouse and let them bathe his head in cold water. Much water and many times. Then bring him again. Meanwhile I will provide for my killed *hrossa*.'

Weston did not clearly understand what the voice said – indeed, he was still too busy trying to find out where it came from – but terror smote him as he found himself wrapped in the strong arms of the surrounding *hrossa* and forced away from his place. Ransom would gladly have shouted out some reassurance, but Weston himself was shouting too loud to hear him. He was mixing English and Malacandrian now, and the last that was heard was a rising scream of 'Pay for this – pouff! bang! – Ransom, for God's sake – Ransom! Ransom!'

'And now,' said Oyarsa, when silence was restored, 'let us honour my dead *hnau*.'

At his words ten of the *hrossa* grouped themselves about the biers. Lifting their heads, and with no signal given as far as Ransom could see, they began to sing.

To every man, in his acquaintance with a new art, there comes a moment when that which before was meaningless first lifts, as it were, one corner of the curtain that hides its mystery, and reveals, in a burst of delight which later and fuller understanding can hardly ever equal, one glimpse of the indefinite possibilities within. For Ransom, this moment had now come in his understanding of Malacandrian song. Now first he saw that its rhythms were based on a different blood from ours, on a heart that beat more quickly, and a fiercer internal heat. Through his knowledge of the creatures and his love for them he began, ever so little, to hear it with their ears. A sense of great masses moving at visionary speeds, of giants dancing, of eternal sorrows eternally consoled, of he knew not what and yet what he had always known, awoke in him with the very first bars of the deep-mouthed dirge, and bowed down his spirit as if the gate of heaven had opened before him.

'Let it go hence,' they sang. 'Let it go hence, dissolve and be no body. Drop it, release it, drop it gently, as a stone is loosed from fingers drooping over a still pool. Let it go down, sink, fall away. Once below the surface there are no divisions, no layers in the water yielding all the way down; all one and all unwounded is that element. Send it voyaging; it will not come again. Let it go down; the *hnau* rises from it. This is the second life, the other beginning. Open, oh coloured world, without weight, without shore. You are second and better; this was first and feeble. Once the worlds were hot within and brought forth life, but only the pale plants, the dark plants. We see their children when they grow today, out of the sun's light in the sad places. After, the heaven made grow another kind of worlds; the high climbers, the bright-haired forests, cheeks of flowers. First were the darker, then the brighter. First was the worlds' brood, then the suns' brood.'

This was as much of it as he contrived later to remember and could translate. As the song ended Oyarsa said:

'Let us scatter the movements which were their bodies. So will Maleldil scatter all worlds when the first and feeble is worn.'

He made a sign to one of the *pfifltriggi*, who instantly arose and approached the corpses. The *hrossa*, now singing again but very softly, drew back at least ten paces. The *pfifltrigg* touched each of the three dead in turn with some small object that appeared to be made of glass or crystal – and then jumped away with one of his frog-like leaps. Ransom closed his eyes to protect them from a blinding light and felt something like a very strong wind blowing in his face, for a fraction of a second. Then all was calm again, and the three biers were empty.

'God! That would be a trick worth knowing on earth,' said Devine to Ransom. 'Solves the murderer's problem about the disposal of the body, eh?'

But Ransom, who was thinking of Hyoi, did not answer him; and before he spoke again everyone's attention was diverted by the return of the unhappy Weston among his guards.

·20·

The *hross* who headed this procession was a conscientious creature and began at once explaining itself in a rather troubled voice.

'I hope we have done right, Oyarsa,' it said. 'But we do not know. We dipped his head in the cold water seven times, but the seventh time something fell off it. We had thought it was the top of his head, but now we saw it was a covering made of the skin of some other creature. Then some said we had done your will with the seven dips, and others said not. In the end we dipped it seven times more. We hope that was right. The creature talked a lot between the dips, and most between the second seven, but we could not understand it.'

'You have done very well, Hnoo,' said Oyarsa. 'Stand away that I may see it, for now I will speak to it.'

The guards fell away on each side. Weston's usually pale face, under the bracing influence of the cold water, had assumed the colour of a ripe tomato, and his hair, which had naturally not been cut since he reached Malacandra, was plastered in straight, lank masses across his forehead. A good deal of water was still dripping over his nose and ears. His expression – unfortunately wasted on an audience ignorant of terrestrial physiognomy – was that of a brave man suffering in a great cause, and rather eager than reluctant to face the worst or even to provoke it. In explanation of his conduct it is only fair to remember that he had already that morning endured all the terrors of an expected martyrdom and all the anticlimax of fourteen compulsory cold douches. Devine, who knew his man, shouted out to Weston in English:

'Steady, Weston. These devils can split the atom or something pretty like it. Be careful what you say to them and don't let's have any of your bloody nonsense.'

'Huh!' said Weston. 'So you've gone native too?'

'Be silent,' said the voice of Oyarsa. 'You, thick one, have told me nothing of yourself, so I will tell it to you. In your own world you have attained great wisdom concerning bodies and by this you have been able to make a ship that can cross the heaven; but in all other things you have the mind of an animal. When first you came here, I sent for you, meaning you nothing but honour. The darkness in your mind filled you with fear. Because you thought I meant evil to you, you went as a beast goes against a beast of some other kind, and snared this Ransom. You would give him up to the evil you feared. Today, seeing him here, to save your own life, you would have given him to me a second time, still thinking I meant him hurt. These are your dealings with your own kind. And what you intend to my people, I know. Already you have killed some. And you have come here to kill them all. To you it is nothing whether a creature is *hnau* or not. At first I thought this was because you cared only whether a creature had a body like your own; but Ransom has that and you would kill him as lightly as any of my *hnau*. I did not know that the Bent One had done so much in your world and still I do not understand it. If you were mine, I would unbody you even now. Do not think follies; by my hand Maleldil does greater things than this, and I can unmake you even on the borders of your own world's air. But I do not yet resolve to do this. It is for you to speak. Let me see if there is anything in your mind besides fear and death and desire.'

Weston turned to Ransom. 'I see,' he said, 'that you have chosen the most momentous crisis in the history of the human race to betray it.' Then he turned in the direction of the voice.

'I know you kill us,' he said. 'Me not afraid. Others come, make it our world –'

But Devine had jumped to his feet, and interrupted him.

'No, no, Oyarsa,' he shouted. 'You no listen him. He very foolish man, he have dreams. We little people, only want pretty sun-bloods. You give us plenty sun-bloods, we go back into sky, you never see us no more. All done, see?'

'Silence,' said Oyarsa. There was an almost imperceptible change in the light, if it could be called light, out of which the voice came, and Devine crumpled up and fell back on the ground. When he resumed his sitting position he was white and panting.

'Speak on,' said Oyarsa to Weston.

'Me no … no …' began Weston in Malacandrian and then broke off. 'I can't say what I want in their accursed language,' he said in English.

'Speak to Ransom and he shall turn it into our speech,' said Oyarsa.

Weston accepted the arrangement at once. He believed that the hour of his death was come and he was determined to utter the thing – almost the only thing outside his own science – which he had to say. He cleared his throat, almost he struck a gesture, and began:

'To you I may seem a vulgar robber, but I bear on my shoulders the destiny of the human race. Your tribal life with its stone-age weapons and beehive huts, its primitive coracles and elementary social structure, has nothing to compare with our civilisation – with our science, medicine and law, our armies, our architecture, our commerce, and our transport system which is rapidly annihilating space and time. Our right to supersede you is the right of the higher over the lower. Life –'

'Half a moment,' said Ransom in English. 'That's about as much as I can manage at one go.' Then, turning to Oyarsa, he began translating as well as he could. The process was difficult and the result – which he felt to be rather unsatisfactory – was something like this:

'Among us, Oyarsa, there is a kind of *hnau* who will take other *hnaus*' food and – and things, when they are not looking. He says he is not an ordinary one of that kind. He says what he does now will make very different things happen to those of our people who are not yet born. He says that, among you, *hnau* of one kindred all live together and the *hrossa* have spears like those we used a very long time ago and your huts are small and round and your boats small and light and like our old ones, and you have one ruler. He says it is different with us. He says we know much. There is a thing happens in our world when the body of a living creature feels pains and becomes weak, and he says we sometimes know how to stop it. He says we have many bent people and we kill them or shut them in huts and that we have people for settling quarrels between the bent *hnau* about their huts and mates and things. He says we have many ways for the *hnau* of one land to kill those of another and some are trained to do it. He says we build very big and strong huts of stones and other things like the *pfifltriggi*. And he says we exchange many things among ourselves and can carry heavy weights very quickly a long way. Because of all this, he says it would not be the act of a bent *hnau* if our people killed all your people.'

As soon as Ransom had finished, Weston continued.

'Life is greater than any system of morality; her claims are absolute. It is not by tribal taboos and copy-book maxims that she has pursued her relentless march from the amoeba to man and from man to civilisation.'

'He says,' began Ransom, 'that living creatures are stronger than the question whether an act is bent or good – no, that cannot be right – he says it is better to be alive and bent than to be dead – no – he says, he says – I cannot say what he says, Oyarsa, in your language. But he goes on to say that the only good thing is that there should be very many creatures alive. He says there were many other animals before the first men and the later ones were better than the earlier ones; but he says the animals were not born because of what is said to the young about bent and good action by their elders. And he says these animals did not feel any pity.'

'She –' began Weston.

'I'm sorry,' interrupted Ransom, 'but I've forgotten who She is.'

'Life, of course,' snapped Weston. 'She has ruthlessly broken down all obstacles and liquidated all failures and today in her highest form – civilised man – and in me as his representative, she presses forward to that inter-planetary leap which will, perhaps, place her for ever beyond the reach of death.'

'He says,' resumed Ransom, 'that these animals learned to do many difficult things, except those who could not; and those ones died and the other animals did not pity them. And he says the best animal now is the kind of man who makes the big huts and carries the heavy weights and does all the other things I told you about; and he is one of these and he says that if the others all knew what he was doing they would be pleased. He says that if he could kill you all and bring our people to live in Malacandra, then they might be able to go on living here after something had gone wrong with our world. And then if something went wrong with Malacandra they might go and kill all the *hnau* in another world. And then another – and so they would never die out.'

'It is in her right,' said Weston, 'the right, or, if you will, the might of Life herself, that I am prepared without flinching to plant the flag of man on the soil of Malacandra: to march on, step by step, superseding, where necessary, the lower forms of life that we find, claiming planet after planet, system after system, till our posterity – whatever strange form and yet unguessed mentality they have assumed – dwell in the universe wherever the universe is habitable.'

'He says,' translated Ransom, 'that because of this it would *not* be a bent action – or else, he says, it *would* be a possible action – for him to kill you all and bring us here. He says he would feel no pity. He is saying again that perhaps they would be able to keep moving from one world to another and wherever they came they would kill everyone. I think he is now talking about worlds that go round other suns. He wants the creatures born from us to be in as many places as they can. He says he does not know what kind of creatures they will be.'

'I may fall,' said Weston. 'But while I live I will not, with such a key in my hand, consent to close the gates of the future on my race. What lies in that future, beyond our present ken, passes imagination to conceive: it is enough for me that there is a Beyond.'

'He is saying,' Ransom translated, 'that he will not stop trying to do all this unless you kill him. And he says that though he doesn't know what will happen to the creatures sprung from us, he wants it to happen very much.'

Weston, who had now finished his statement, looked round instinctively for a chair to sink into. On Earth he usually sank into a chair as the applause began. Finding none – he was not the kind of man to sit on the ground like Devine – he folded his arms and stared with a certain dignity about him.

'It is well that I have heard you,' said Oyarsa. 'For though your mind is feebler, your will is less bent than I thought. It is not for yourself that you would do all this.'

'No,' said Weston proudly in Malacandrian. 'Me die. Man live.'

'Yet you know that these creatures would have to be made quite unlike you before they lived on other worlds.'

'Yes, yes. All new. No one know yet. Strange! Big!'

'Then it is not the shape of body that you love?'

'No. Me no care how they shaped.'

'One would think, then, that it is for the mind you care. But that cannot be, or you would love *hnau* wherever you met it.'

'No care for *hnau*. Care for man.'

'But if it is neither man's mind, which is as the mind of all other *hnau* – is not Maleldil maker of them all? – nor his body, which will change – if you care for neither of these, what do you mean by man?'

This had to be translated to Weston. When he understood, he replied:

'Me care for man – care for our race – what man begets –' He had to ask Ransom the words for *race* and *beget*.

'Strange!' said Oyarsa. 'You do not love any one of your race – you would have let me kill Ransom. You do not love the mind of your race, nor the body. Any kind of creature will please you if only it is begotten by your kind as they now are. It seems to me,

Thick One, that what you really love is no completed creature but the very seed itself: for that is all that is left.'

'Tell him,' said Weston when he had been made to understand this, 'that I don't pretend to be a metaphysician. I have not come here to chop logic. If he cannot understand – as apparently you can't either – anything so fundamental as a man's loyalty to humanity, I can't make him understand it.'

But Ransom was unable to translate this and the voice of Oyarsa continued:

'I see now how the lord of the silent world has bent you. There are laws that all *hnau* know, of pity and straight dealing and shame and the like, and one of these is the love of kindred. He has taught you to break all of them except this one, which is not one of the greatest laws; this one he has bent till it becomes folly and has set it up, thus bent, to be a little blind Oyarsa in your brain. And now you can do nothing but obey it, though if we ask you why it is a law you can give no other reason for it than for all the other and greater laws which it drives you to disobey. Do you know why he has done this?'

'Me think no such person – me wise, new man – no believe all that old talk.'

'I will tell you. He has left you this one because a bent *hnau* can do more evil than a broken one. He has only bent you; but this Thin One who sits on the ground he has broken, for he has left him nothing but greed. He is now only a talking animal and in my world he could do no more evil than an animal. If he were mine I would unmake his body, for the *hnau* in it is already dead. But if you were mine I would try to cure you. Tell me, Thick One, why did you come here?'

'Me tell you. Make man live all the time.'

'But are your wise men so ignorant as not to know that Malacandra is older than your own world and nearer its death? Most of it is dead already. My people live only in the *handramits*; the heat and the water have been more and will be less. Soon now, very soon, I will end my world and give back my people to Maleldil.'

'Me know all that plenty. This only first try. Soon they go on another world.'

'But do you not know that all worlds will die?'

'Men go jump off each before it deads – on and on, see?'

'And when all are dead?'

Weston was silent. After a time Oyarsa spoke again.

'Do you not ask why my people, whose world is old, have not rather come to yours and taken it long ago.'

'Ho! Ho!' said Weston. 'You not know how.'

'You are wrong,' said Oyarsa. 'Many thousands of thousand years before this, when nothing yet lived on your world, the cold death was coming on my *harandra*. Then I was in deep trouble, not chiefly for the death of my *hnau* – Maleldil does not make them long-livers – but for the things which the lord of your world, who was not yet bound, put into their minds. He would have made them as your people are now – wise enough to see the death of their kind approaching but not wise enough to endure it. Bent counsels would soon have risen among them. They were well able to have made sky-ships. By me Maleldil stopped them. Some I cured, some I unbodied –'

'And see what come!' interrupted Weston. 'You now very few – shut up in *handramits* – soon all die.'

'Yes,' said Oyarsa, 'but one thing we left behind us on the *harandra*: fear. And with fear, murder and rebellion. The weakest of my people does not fear death. It is the Bent One, the lord of your world, who wastes your lives and befouls them with flying from what you know will overtake you in the end. If you were subjects of Maleldil you would have peace.'

Weston writhed in the exasperation born of his desire to speak and his ignorance of the language.

'Trash! Defeatist trash!' he shouted at Oyarsa in English; then, drawing himself up to his full height, he added in Malacandrian, 'You say your Maleldil let all go dead. Other one, Bent One, he fight, jump, live – not all talkee-talkee. Me no care Maleldil. Like Bent One better: me on his side.'

'But do you not see that he never will nor can,' began Oyarsa, and then broke off, as if recollecting himself. 'But I must learn more of your world from Ransom, and for that I need till night. I will not kill you, not even the thin one, for you are out of my world. Tomorrow you shall go hence again in your ship.'

Devine's face suddenly fell. He began talking rapidly in English.

'For God's sake, Weston, make him understand. We've been here for months – the Earth is not in opposition now. Tell him it can't be done. He might as well kill us at once.'

'How long will your journey be to Thulcandra?' asked Oyarsa.

Weston, using Ransom as his interpreter, explained that the journey, in the present position of the two planets, was almost impossible. The distance had increased by millions of miles. The angle of their course to the solar rays would be totally different from that which he had counted upon. Even if by a hundredth chance they could hit the Earth, it was almost certain that their supply of oxygen would be exhausted long before they arrived.

'Tell him to kill us now,' he added.

'All this I know,' said Oyarsa. 'And if you stay in my world I must kill you: no such creature will I suffer in Malacandra. I know there is small chance of your reaching your world; but small is not the same as none. Between now and the next noon choose which you will take. In the meantime, tell me this. If you reach it at all, what is the most time you will need?'

After a prolonged calculation, Weston, in a shaken voice, replied that if they had not made it in ninety days they would never make it, and they would, moreover, be dead of suffocation.

'Ninety days you shall have,' said Oyarsa. 'My *sorns* and *pfi-fltriggi* will give you air (we also have that art) and food for ninety days. But they will do something else to your ship. I am not minded that it should return into the heaven if once it reaches Thulcandra. You, Thick One, were not here when I unmade my dead *hrossa* whom you killed: the Thin One will tell you. This I can do, as Maleldil has taught me, over a gap of time or a gap of place. Before your sky-ship rises, my *sorns* will have so dealt with it that on the ninetieth day it will unbody, it will become what you call nothing. If that day finds it in heaven your death will be no bitterer because of this; but do not tarry in your ship if once you touch Thulcandra. Now lead these two away, and do you, my children, go where you will. But I must talk with Ransom.'

21

All that afternoon Ransom remained alone answering Oyarsa's questions. I am not allowed to record this conversation, beyond saying that the voice concluded it with the words:

'You have shown me more wonders than are known in the whole of heaven.'

After that they discussed Ransom's own future. He was given full liberty to remain in Malacandra or to attempt the desperate voyage to Earth. The problem was agonising to him. In the end he decided to throw in his lot with Weston and Devine.

'Love of our own kind,' he said, 'is not the greatest of laws, but you, Oyarsa, have said it is a law. If I cannot live in Thulcandra, it is better for me not to live at all.'

'You have chosen rightly,' said Oyarsa. 'And I will tell you two things. My people will take all the strange weapons out of the ship, but they will give one to you. And the *eldila* of deep heaven will be about your ship till it reaches the air of Thulcandra, and often in it. They will not let the other two kill you.'

It had not occurred to Ransom before that his own murder might be one of the first expedients for economising food and oxygen which would occur to Weston and Devine. He was now astonished at his obtuseness, and thanked Oyarsa for his protective measures. Then the great *eldil* dismissed him with these words:

'You are guilty of no evil, Ransom of Thulcandra, except a little fearfulness. For that, the journey you go on is your pain, and perhaps your cure: for you must be either mad or brave before it is ended. But I lay also a command on you; you must watch this Weston and this Devine in Thulcandra if ever you arrive there. They may yet do much evil in, and beyond, your world. From what you have told me, I begin to see that there are *eldila* who go down into your air, into the very stronghold of the Bent One; your world is not so fast shut as was thought in these parts of heaven. Watch those two bent ones. Be courageous. Fight them. And when you have need, some of our people will help. Maleldil will show them to you. It may even be that you and I shall meet again while you are still in the body; for it is not without the wisdom of Maleldil that we have met now and I have learned so much of your world. It seems to me that this is the beginning of more comings and goings between the heavens and the worlds and between one world and another – though not such as the Thick One hoped. I am allowed to tell you this. The year we are now in but – heavenly years are not as yours – has long been prophesied as a year of stirrings and high changes and the siege of Thulcandra may be near its end. Great things are on foot. If Maleldil does not forbid me, I will not hold aloof from them. And now, farewell.'

It was through vast crowds of all the Malacandrian species that the three human beings embarked next day on their terrible journey. Weston was pale and haggard from a night of calculations intricate enough to tax any mathematician even if his life did not hang on them. Devine was noisy, reckless and a little hysterical. His whole view of Malacandra had been altered overnight by the discovery that the 'natives' had an alcoholic drink, and he had even been trying to teach them to smoke. Only the *pfifltriggi* had made much of it. He was now consoling himself for an acute headache and the prospect of a lingering death by tormenting Weston. Neither partner was pleased to find that all weapons had been removed from the space-ship, but in other respects everything was as they wished it. At about an hour after noon Ransom took a last, long look at the blue waters, purple forest and remote green walls of the familiar *handramit*, and followed the other two through the manhole. Before it was closed Weston warned them that they must economise air by absolute stillness. No unnecessary movement must be made during their voyage; even talking must be prohibited.

'I shall speak only in an emergency,' he said.

'Thank God for that, anyway,' was Devine's last shot. Then they screwed themselves in.

Ransom went at once to the lower side of the sphere, into the chamber which was now most completely upside down, and stretched himself on what would later become its skylight. He was surprised to find that they were already thousands of feet up. The *handramit* was only a straight purple line across the rose-red surface of the *harandra*. They were above the junction of two *handramits*. One of them was doubtless that in which he had lived, the other that which contained Meldilorn. The gully by which he had cut off the corner between the two, on Augray's shoulders, was quite invisible.

Each minute more *handramits* came into view – long straight lines, some parallel, some intersecting, some building triangles. The landscape became increasingly geometrical. The waste between the purple lines appeared perfectly flat. The rosy colour of the petrified forests accounted for its tint immediately below him; but to the north and east the great sand deserts of which the *sorns* had told him were now appearing as illimitable stretches of yellow and ochre. To the west a huge discoloration began to show. It was an irregular patch of greenish blue that looked as if it were sunk below the level of the surrounding *harandra*. He concluded it was the forest low land of the *pfifltriggi* – or rather one of their forest lowlands, for now similar patches were appearing in all directions, some of them mere blobs at the intersection of *handramits*, some of vast extent. He became vividly conscious that his knowledge of Malacandra was minute, local, parochial. It was as if a *sorn* had journeyed forty million miles to the Earth and spent his stay there between Worthing and Brighton. He reflected that he would have very little to show for his amazing voyage if he survived it: a smattering of the language, a few landscapes, some half-understood physics – but where were the statistics, the history, the broad survey of extra-terrestrial conditions, which such a traveller ought to bring back? Those *handramits*, for example. Seen from the height which the space-ship had now attained, in all their unmistakable geometry, they put to shame his original impression that they were natural valleys. There were gigantic feats of engineering, about which he had learned nothing; feats accomplished, if all were true, before human history began ... before animal history began. Or was that only mythology? He knew it would seem like mythology when he got back to Earth (if he ever got back), but the presence of Oyarsa was still too fresh a memory to allow him any real doubts. It even occurred to him that the distinction between history and mythology might be itself meaningless outside the Earth.

The thought baffled him, and he turned again to the landscape below – the landscape which became every moment less of a landscape and more of a diagram. By this time, to the east, a much larger and darker patch of discoloration than he had yet seen was pushing its way into the reddish ochre of the Malacandrian world – a curiously shaped patch with long arms or horns extended on each side and a sort of bay between them, like the concave side of a crescent. It grew and grew. The wide dark arms seemed to be spread out to engulf the whole planet. Suddenly he saw a bright point of light in the middle of this dark patch and realised that it was not a patch on the surface of the planet at all, but the black sky showing behind her. The smooth curve was the edge of her disk. At this, for the first time since their embarkation, fear took hold of him. Slowly, yet not too slowly for him to see, the dark arms spread farther and even farther round the lighted surface till at last they met. The whole disk, framed in blackness, was before him. The faint percussions of the meteorites had long been audible; the window through which he was gazing was no longer definitely beneath him. His limbs, though already very light, were almost too stiff to move, and he was very hungry. He looked at his watch. He had been at his post, spellbound, for nearly eight hours.

He made his way with difficulty to the sunward side of the ship and reeled back almost blinded with the glory of the light.

Groping, he found his darkened glasses in his old cabin and got himself food and water: Weston had rationed them strictly in both. He opened the door of the control room and looked in. Both the partners, their faces drawn with anxiety, were seated before a kind of metal table; it was covered with delicate, gently vibrating instruments in which crystal and fine wire were the predominant materials. Both ignored his presence. For the rest of the silent journey he was free of the whole ship.

When he returned to the dark side, the world they were leaving hung in the star-strewn sky not much bigger than our earthly moon. Its colours were still visible – a reddish-yellow disk blotched with greenish blue and capped with white at the poles. He saw the two tiny Malacandrian moons – their movement quite perceptible – and reflected that they were among the thousand things he had not noticed during his sojourn there. He slept, and woke, and saw the disk still hanging in the sky. It was smaller than the Moon now. Its colours were gone except for a faint, uniform tinge of redness in its light; even the light was not now incomparably stronger than that of the countless stars which surrounded it. It had ceased to be Malacandra; it was only Mars.

He soon fell back into the old routine of sleeping and basking, punctuated with the making of some scribbled notes for his Malacandrian dictionary. He knew that there was very little chance of his being able to communicate his new knowledge to man, that unrecorded death in the depth of space would almost certainly be the end of their adventure. But already it had become impossible to think of it as 'space'. Some moments of cold fear he had; but each time they were shorter and more quickly swallowed up in a sense of awe which made his personal fate seem wholly insignificant. He could not feel that they were an island of life journeying through an abyss of death. He felt almost the opposite – that life was waiting outside the little iron eggshell in which they rode, ready at any moment to break in, and that, if it killed them, it would kill them by excess of its vitality. He hoped passionately that if they were to perish they would perish by the 'unbodying' of the space-ship and not by suffocation within it. To be let out, to be set free, to dissolve into the ocean of eternal noon, seemed to him at certain moments a consummation even more desirable than their return to Earth. And if he had felt some such lift of the heart when first he passed through heaven on their outward journey, he felt it now tenfold, for now he was convinced that the abyss was full of life in the most literal sense, full of living creatures.

His confidence in Oyarsa's words about the *eldila* increased rather than diminished as they went on. He saw none of them; the intensity of light in which the ship swam allowed none of the fugitive variations which would have betrayed their presence. But he heard, or thought he heard, all kinds of delicate sound, or vibrations akin to sound, mixed with the tinkling rain of meteorites, and often the sense of unseen presences even within the space-ship became irresistible. It was this, more than anything else, that made his own chances of life seem so unimportant. He and all his race showed small and ephemeral against a background of such immeasurable fullness. His brain reeled at the thought of the true population of the universe, the three-dimensional infinitude of their territory, and the unchronicled aeons of their past; but his heart became steadier than it had ever been.

It was well for him that he had reached this frame of mind before the real hardships of their journey began. Ever since their departure from Malacandra, the thermometer had steadily risen; now it was higher than it had stood at any time on their outward journey. And still it rose. The light also increased. Under his glasses he kept his eyes habitually tight shut, opening them only for the shortest time for necessary movements. He knew that if he reached Earth it would be with permanently damaged sight. But all this was nothing to the torment of heat. All three of them were awake for twenty-four hours out of the twenty-four, enduring with dilated eyeballs, blackened lips and froth-flecked cheeks the agony of thirst. It would be madness to increase their scanty rations of water: madness even to consume air in discussing the question.

He saw well enough what was happening. In his last bid for life Weston was venturing inside the Earth's orbit, leading them nearer the Sun than man, perhaps than life, had ever been. Presumably this was unavoidable; one could not follow a retreating Earth round the rim of its own wheeling course. They must be trying to meet it – to cut across … it was madness! But the question did not much occupy his mind; it was not possible for long to think of anything but thirst. One thought of water; then one thought of thirst; then one thought of thinking of thirst; then of water again. And still the thermometer rose. The walls of the ship were too hot to touch. It was obvious that a crisis was approaching. In the next few hours it must kill them or get less.

It got less. There came a time when they lay exhausted and shivering in what seemed the cold, though it was still hotter than any terrestrial climate. Weston had so far succeeded; he had risked the highest temperature at which human life could theoretically survive, and they had lived through it. But they were not the same men. Hitherto Weston had slept very little even in his watches off; always, after an hour or so of uneasy rest, he had returned to his charts and to his endless, almost despairing, calculations. You could see him fighting the despair – pinning his terrified brain down, and again down, to the figures. Now he never looked at them. He even seemed careless in the control room. Devine moved and looked like a somnambulist. Ransom lived increasingly on the dark side and for long hours he thought of nothing. Although the first great danger was past, none of them, at this time, had any serious hope of a successful issue to their journey. They had now been fifty days, without speech, in their steel shell, and the air was already very bad.

Weston was so unlike his old self that he even allowed Ransom to take his share in the navigation. Mainly by signs, but with the help of a few whispered words, he taught him all that was necessary at this stage of the journey. Apparently they were racing home – but with little chance of reaching it in time – before some sort of cosmic 'trade-wind'. A few rules of thumb enabled Ransom to keep the star which Weston pointed out to him in its position at the centre of the skylight, but always with his left hand on the bell to Weston's cabin.

This star was not the Earth. The days – the purely theoretical 'days' which bore such a desperately practical meaning for the travellers – mounted to fifty-eight before Weston changed course, and a different luminary was in the centre. Sixty days, and it was visibly a planet. Sixty-six, and it was like a planet seen through field-glasses. Seventy, and it was like nothing that Ransom had ever seen – a little dazzling disk too large for a planet and far too small for the Moon. Now that he was navigating, his celestial mood was shattered. Wild, animal thirst for life, mixed with homesick longing for the free airs and the sights and smells of earth – for grass and meat and beer and tea and the human voice – awoke in him. At first his chief difficulty on watch had been to resist drowsiness; now, though the air was worse, feverish excitement kept him vigilant. Often when he came off duty he found his right arm stiff and sore; for hours he had been pressing it unconsciously against the control board as if his puny thrust could spur the space-ship to yet greater speed.

Now they had twenty days to go. Nineteen – eighteen – and on the white terrestrial disk, now a little larger than a sixpence, he thought he could make out Australia and the south-east corner of Asia. Hour after hour, though the markings moved slowly across the disk with the Earth's diurnal revolution, the disk itself refused to grow larger. 'Get on! Get on!' Ransom muttered to the ship. Now ten days were left and it was like the Moon and so bright that they could not look steadily at it. The air in their little sphere was ominously bad, but Ransom and Devine risked a whisper as they changed watches.

'We'll do it,' they said. 'We'll do it yet.'

On the eighty-seventh day, when Ransom relieved Devine, he thought there was 'something wrong with the Earth. Before his watch was done, he was sure. It was no longer a true circle, but bulging a little on one side; it was almost pear-shaped. When Weston came on duty he gave one glance at the skylight, rang furiously on the bell for Devine, thrust Ransom aside, and took the navigating seat. His face was the colour of putty. He seemed to be about to do something to the controls, but as Devine entered the room he looked up and shrugged his shoulders with a gesture of despair. Then he buried his face in his hands and laid his head down on the control-board.

Ransom and Devine exchanged glances. They bundled Weston out of the seat – he was crying like a child – and Devine took his place. And now at last Ransom understood 'the mystery of the bulging Earth. What had appeared as a bulge on one side of her disk was becoming increasingly distinct as a second disk, a disk almost as large in appearance as her own. It was covering more than half of the Earth. It was the Moon – between them and the Earth, and two hundred and forty thousand miles nearer. Ransom did not know what fate this might mean for the space-ship. Devine obviously did, and never had he appeared so admirable. His face was as pale as Weston's, but his eyes were clear and preternaturally bright; he sat crouched over the controls like an animal about to spring and he was whistling very softly between his teeth.

Hours later Ransom understood what was happening. The Moon's disk was now larger than the Earth's, and very gradually it became apparent to him that both disks were diminishing in size. The space-ship was no longer approaching either the Earth or the Moon; it was farther away from them than it had been half an hour ago, and that was the meaning of Devine's feverish activity with the controls. It was not merely that the Moon was crossing their path and cutting them off from the Earth; apparently for some reason – probably gravitational – it was dangerous to get too close to the Moon, and Devine was standing off into space. In sight of harbour they were being forced to turn back to the open sea. He glanced up at the chronometer. It was the morning of the eighty-eighth day. Two days to make the Earth, and they were moving away from her.

'I suppose this finishes us?' he whispered.

'Expect so,' whispered Devine, without looking round. Weston presently recovered sufficiently to come back and stand beside

Devine. There was nothing for Ransom to do. He was sure, now, that they were soon to die. With this realisation, the agony of his suspense suddenly disappeared. Death, whether it came now or some thirty years later on earth, rose up and claimed his attention. There are preparations a man likes to make. He left the control room and returned into one of the sunward chambers, into the indifference of the moveless light, the warmth, the silence and the sharp-cut shadows. Nothing was farther from his mind than sleep. It must have been the exhausted atmosphere which made him drowsy. He slept.

He awoke in almost complete darkness in the midst of a loud continuous noise, which he could not at first identify. It reminded him of something – something he seemed to have heard in a previous existence. It was a prolonged drumming noise close above his head. Suddenly his heart gave a great leap.

'Oh God,' he sobbed. 'Oh God! It's *rain*.'

He was on Earth. The air was heavy and stale about him, but the choking sensations he had been suffering were gone. He realised that he was still in the spaceship. The others, in fear of its threatened 'unbodying', had characteristically abandoned it the moment it touched Earth and left him to his fate. It was difficult in the dark, and under the crushing weight of terrestrial gravity, to find his way out. But he managed it. He found the man-hole and slithered, drinking great draughts of air, down the outside of the sphere; slipped in mud, blessed the smell of it, and at last raised the unaccustomed weight of his body to its feet. He stood in pitch-black night under torrential rain. With every pore of his body he drank it in; with every desire of his heart he embraced the smell of the field about him – a patch of his native planet where grass grew, where cows moved, where presently he would come to hedges and a gate.

He had walked about half an hour when a vivid light behind him and a strong, momentary wind informed him that the spaceship was no more. He felt very little interest. He had seen dim lights, the lights of men, ahead. He contrived to get into a lane, then into a road, then into a village street. A lighted door was open. There were voices from within and they were speaking English. There was a familiar smell. He pushed his way in, regardless of the surprise he was creating, and walked to the bar.

'A pint of bitter, please,' said Ransom.

22

At this point, if I were guided by purely literary considerations, my story would end, but it is time to remove the mask and to acquaint the reader with the real and practical purpose for which this book has been written. At the same time he will learn how the writing of it became possible at all.

Dr Ransom – and at this stage it will become obvious that this is not his real name – soon abandoned the idea of his Malacandrian dictionary and indeed all idea of communicating his story to the world. He was ill for several months, and when he recovered he found himself in considerable doubt as to whether what he remembered had really occurred. It looked very like a delusion produced by his illness, and most of his apparent adventures could, he saw, be explained psychoanalytically. He did not lean very heavily on this fact himself, for he had long since observed that a good many 'real' things in the fauna and flora of our own world could be accounted for in the same way if you started with the assumption that they were illusions. But he felt that if he himself half doubted his own story, the rest of the world would disbelieve it completely. He decided to hold his tongue, and there the matter would have rested but for a very curious coincidence.

This is where I come into the story. I had known Dr Ransom slightly for several years and corresponded with him on literary and philological subjects, though we very seldom met. It was, therefore, quite in the usual order of things that I should write a letter some months ago, of which I will quote the relevant paragraph. It ran like this:

'I am now working at the Platonists of the twelfth century and incidentally discovering that they wrote damnably difficult Latin. In one of them, Bernardus Silvestris, there is a word I should particularly like your views on – the word *Oyarses*. It occurs in the description of a voyage through the heavens, and an *Oyarses* seems to be the 'intelligence' or tutelary spirit of a heavenly sphere, i.e. in our language, of a planet. I asked C. J. about it and he says it ought to be *Ousiarches*. That, of course, would make sense, but I do not feel quite satisfied. Have you by any chance ever come across a word like *Oyarses*, or can you hazard any guess as to what language it may be?'

The immediate result of this letter was an invitation to spend a weekend with Dr Ransom. He told me his whole story, and since then he and I have been almost continuously at work on the mystery. A good many facts, which I have no intention of publishing at present, have fallen into our hands; facts about planets in general and about Mars in particular, facts about medieval Platonists, and (not least in importance) facts about the Professor to whom I am giving the fictitious name of Weston. A systematic report of these facts might, of course, be given to the civilised world: but that would almost certainly result in universal incredulity and in a libel action from Weston. At the same time, we both feel that we cannot be silent. We are being daily confirmed in our belief that the *oyarses* of Mars was right when it said that the present 'celestial year' was to be a revolutionary one, that the long isolation of our own planets is nearing its end, and that great doings are on foot. We have found reason to believe that the medieval Platonists were living in the same celestial year as ourselves – in fact, that it began in the twelfth century of our era – and that the occurrence of the name Oyarsa (Latinized as *oyarses*) in Bernardus Silvestris is not an accident. And we have also evidence – increasing almost daily – that 'Weston', or the force or forces behind 'Weston', will play a very important part in the events of the next few centuries, and, unless we prevent them, a very disastrous one. We do not mean that they are likely to invade Mars – our cry is not merely 'Hands off Malacandra.' The dangers to be feared are not planetary but cosmic, or at least solar, and they are not temporal but eternal. More than this it would be unwise to say.

It was Dr Ransom who first saw that our only chance was to publish in the form of fiction what would certainly not be listened to as fact. He even thought – greatly overrating my literary powers – that this might have the incidental advantage of reaching a wider public, and that, certainly, it would reach a great many people sooner than 'Weston'. To my objection that if accepted as fiction, it would for that very reason be regarded as false, he replied that there would be indications enough in the narrative for the few readers – the very few – who *at present* were prepared to go farther into the matter.

'And they,' he said, 'will easily find out you, or me, and will easily identify Weston. Anyway,' he continued, 'what we need for the moment is not so much a body of belief as a body of people familiarised with certain ideas. If we could even effect in one per cent of our readers a change-over from the conception of Space to the conception of Heaven, we should have made a beginning.'

What neither of us foresaw was the rapid march of events which was to render the book out of date before it was published. These events have already made it rather a prologue to our story than the story itself. But we must let it go as it stands. For the later stages of the adventure – well, it was Aristotle, long before Kipling, who taught us the formula, 'That is another story.'

Postscript

*(Being extracts from a letter written by the original
of 'Dr Ransom' to the author)*

... I think you are right, and after the two or three corrections
(marked in red) the MS will have to stand. I won't deny that I am
disappointed, but then any attempt to tell such a story is bound to
disappoint the man who has really been there. I am not now referring to the ruthless way in which you have cut down all the philological part, though, as it now stands, we are giving our readers a
mere caricature of the Malacandrian language. I mean something
more difficult something which I couldn't possibly express. How
can one 'get across' the Malacandrian *smells*? Nothing comes back
to me more vividly in my dreams ... especially the early morning
smell in those purple woods, where the very mention of 'early
morning' and 'woods' is misleading because it must set you
thinking of earth and moss and cobwebs and the smell of our own
planet, but I'm thinking of something totally different. More 'aromatic' ... yes, but then it is not hot or luxurious or exotic as that
word suggests. Something aromatic, spicy, yet very cold, very
thin, tingling at the back of the nose – something that did to the
sense of smell what high, sharp violin notes do to the ear. And
mixed with that I always hear the sound of the singing – great
hollow hound-like music from enormous throats, deeper than
Chaliapin, a 'warm, dark noise'. I am homesick for my old
Malacandrian valley when I think of it; yet God knows when
I heard it there I was homesick enough for the Earth.

Of course you are right; if we are to treat it as a story you *must* telescope the time I spent in the village during which 'nothing happened'. But I grudge it. Those quiet weeks, the mere living among the *hrossa*, are to me the main thing that happened. I know them, Lewis; that's what you can't get into a mere story. For instance, because I always take a thermometer with me on a holiday (it has saved many a one from being spoiled) I know that the normal temperature of a *hross* is 103°. I know – though I can't remember learning it – that they live about 80 Martian years, or 160 earth years; that they marry at about 20 (= 40); that their droppings, like those of the horse, are not offensive to themselves, or to me, and are used for agriculture; that they don't shed tears, or blink; that they do get (as you would say) 'elevated' but not drunk on a gaudy night – of which they have many. But what can one do with these scraps of information? I merely analyse them out of a whole living memory that can never be put into words, and no one in this world will be able to build up from such scraps quite the right picture. For example, can I make even you understand how I know, beyond all question, why it is that the Malacandrians don't keep pets and, in general, don't feel about their 'lower animals' as we do about ours? Naturally it is the sort of thing they themselves could never have told me. One just sees why when one sees the three species together. Each of them is to the others *both* what a man is to us *and* what an animal is to us. They can talk to each other, they can co-operate, they have the same ethics; to that extent a *sorn* and a *hross* meet like two men. But then each finds the other different, funny, attractive as an animal is attractive. Some instinct starved in us, which we try to soothe by treating irrational creatures almost as if they were rational, is really satisfied in Malacandra. They don't need pets.

By the way, while we are on the subject of species, I am rather sorry that the exigencies of the story have been allowed to simplify the biology so much. Did I give you the impression that each of the three species was perfectly homogeneous? If so, I misled you. Take the *hrossa*; my friends were black *hrossa*, but there are also silver *hrossa*, and in some of the western *handramits* one finds the great crested *hross* – ten feet high, a dancer rather than a singer, and the noblest animal, after man, that I have ever seen. Only the males have the crest. I also saw a pure white *hross* at Meldilorn, but like a fool I never found out whether he represented a sub-species or was a mere freak like our terrestrial *albino*. There is also at least one other kind of *sorn* besides the kind I saw – the *soroborn* or red *sorn* of the desert, who lives in the sandy north. He's a corker by all accounts.

I agree, it is a pity I never saw the *pfifltriggi* at home. I know nearly enough about them to 'fake' a visit to them as an episode in the story, but I don't think we ought to introduce any mere fiction. 'True in substance' sounds all very well on earth, but I can't imagine myself explaining it to Oyarsa, and I have a shrewd suspicion (see my last' letter) that I have not heard the end of *him*. Anyway, why should our 'readers' (you seem to know the devil of a lot about them!), who are so determined to hear nothing about the language, be so anxious to know more of the *pfifltriggi*? But if you can work it in, there is, of course, no harm in explaining that they are oviparous and matriarchal, and short-lived compared with the other species. It is pretty plain that the great depressions which they inhabit are the old ocean-beds of Malacandra. *Hrossa*, who had visited them, described themselves as going down into deep forests over sand, 'the bone-stones [fossils] of ancient wave-borers above them'. No doubt these are the dark patches seen on the Martian disk from Earth. And that reminds me – the 'maps' of Mars which I have consulted since I got back are so inconsistent with one another that I have given up the attempt to identify my own *handramit*. If you want to try your hand, the desideratum is 'a roughly north-east and south-west "canal" cutting a north and south "canal" not more than twenty miles from the equator'. But astronomers differ very much as to what they can see.

Now as to your most annoying question: 'Did Augray, in describing the *eldila*, confuse the ideas of a subtler body and a superior being?' No. The confusion is entirely your, own. He said two things: that the *eldila* had bodies different from those of planetary animals, and that they were superior in intelligence. Neither he nor anyone else in Malacandra ever confused the one statement with the other or deduced the one from the other. In fact, I have reasons for thinking that there are also irrational animals with the *eldil* type of body (you remember Chaucer's 'airish beasts'?).

I wonder are you wise to say nothing about the problem of *eldil* speech? I agree that it would spoil the narrative to raise the question during the trial scene at Meldilorn, but surely many readers will have enough sense to ask how the *eldila*, who obviously don't breathe, can talk. It is true that we should have to admit we don't know, but oughtn't the readers to be told that? I suggested to J. – the only scientist here who is in my confidence – your theory that they might have instruments, or even organs, for manipulating the air around them and thus producing sounds indirectly, but he didn't seem to think much of it. He thought it probable that they directly manipulated the ears of those they were 'speaking' to. That sounds pretty difficult ... of course one must remember that we have really no knowledge of the shape or size of an *eldil*, or even of its relations to space (our space) in general. In fact, one wants to keep on insisting that we really know next to nothing about them. Like you, I can't help trying to fix their relation to the things that appear in terrestrial tradition – gods, angels, fairies. But we haven't the data. When I attempted to give Oyarsa some idea of our own Christian angelology, he certainly seemed to regard our 'angels' as different in some way from himself. But whether he meant that they were a different species, or only that they were some special military caste (since our poor old earth turns out to be a kind of Ypres Salient in the universe), I don't know.

Why must you leave out my account of how the shutter jammed just before our landing on Malacandra? Without this, your description of our sufferings from excessive light on the return journey raises the very obvious question, 'Why didn't they close their shutters?' I don't believe your theory that 'readers never notice that sort of thing'. I'm sure I should.

There are two scenes that I wish you could have worked into the book; no matter – they are worked into me. One or other of them is always before me when I close my eyes.

In one of them I see the Malacandrian sky at morning; pale blue, so pale that now, when I have grown once more accustomed to terrestrial skies, I think of it as almost white. Against it the nearer tops of the giant weeds – the 'trees' as you call them – show black, but far away, across miles of that blinding blue water, the remoter woods are water-colour purple. The shadows all around me on the pale forest floor are like shadows on snow. There are figures walking before me; slender yet gigantic forms, black and sleek as animated tall hats; their huge round heads, poised on their sinuous stalk-like bodies, give them the appearance of black tulips. They go down, singing, to the edge of the lake. The music fills the wood with its vibration, though it is so soft that I can hardly hear it: it is like dim organ music. Some of them embark, but most remain. It is done slowly; this is no ordinary embarkation, but some ceremony. It is, in fact, a *hross* funeral. Those three with the grey muzzles whom they have helped into the boat are going to Meldilorn to die. For in that world, except for some few whom the *hnakra* gets, no one dies before his time. All live out the full span allotted to their kind, and a death with them is as predictable as a birth with us. The whole village has known that those three will die this year, this month; it was an easy guess that they would die even this week. And now they are off; to receive the last counsel of Oyarsa, to die, and to be by him 'unbodied'. The corpses, as corpses, will exist only for a few minutes: there are no coffins in Malacandra, no sextons, churchyards, or undertakers. The valley is solemn at their departure, but I see no signs of passionate grief. They do not doubt their immortality, and friends of the same generation are not torn apart. You leave the world, as you entered it, with the 'men of your own year'. Death is not preceded by dread nor followed by corruption.

The other scene is a nocturne. I see myself bathing with Hyoi in the warm lake. He laughs at my clumsy swimming; accustomed to a heavier world, I can hardly get enough of me under water to make any headway. And then I see the night sky. The greater part of it is very like ours, though the depths are blacker and the stars brighter; but something that no terrestrial analogy will enable you fully to picture is happening in the west. Imagine the Milky Way magnified – the Milky Way seen through our largest telescope on the clearest night. And then imagine this, not painted across the zenith, but rising like a constellation behind the mountain tops – a dazzling necklace of lights brilliant as planets, slowly heaving itself up till it fills a fifth of the sky and now leaves a belt of blackness between itself and the horizon. It is too bright to look at for long, but it is only a preparation. Something else is coming. There is a glow like moonrise on the *harandra*. *Ahihra!* cries Hyoi, and other baying voices answer him from the darkness all about us. And now the true king of night is up, and now he is threading his way through that strange western galaxy and making its lights dim by comparison with his own. I turn my eyes away, for the little disk is far brighter than the Moon in her greatest splendour. The whole *handramit* is bathed in colourless light; I could count the stems of the forest on the far side of the lake; I see that my fingernails are broken and dirty. And now I guess what it is that I have seen – Jupiter rising beyond the Asteroids and forty million miles nearer than he has ever been to earthly eyes. But the Malacandrians would say 'within the Asteroids', for they have an odd habit, sometimes, of turning the solar system inside out. They call the Asteroids the 'dancers before the threshold of the Great Worlds'. The Great Worlds are the planets, as we should say, 'beyond' or 'outside' the Asteroids. Glundandra (Jupiter) is the greatest of these and has some importance in Malacandrian thought which I cannot fathom. He is 'the centre', 'great Meldilorn', 'throne' and 'feast'. They are, of course, well aware that he is uninhabitable, at least by animals of the planetary type; and they certainly have no pagan idea of giving a local habitation to Maleldil. But somebody or something of great importance is connected with Jupiter; as usual 'The *séroni* would know.' But they never told me. Perhaps the best comment is in the author whom I mentioned to you: 'For as it was well said of the great Africanus that he was never less alone than when alone, so, in our philosophy, no parts of this universal frame are less to be called solitarie than those which the vulgar esteem most solitarie, since the withdrawing of men and beasts signifieth but the greater frequency of more excellent creatures.'

More of this when you come. I am trying to read every old book on the subject that I can hear of. Now that 'Weston' has shut the door, the way to the planets lies through the past; if there is to be any more space-travelling, it will have to be time-travelling as well...!

Perelandra

TO SOME LADIES AT WANTAGE

Preface

This story can be read by itself but is also a sequel to *Out of the Silent Planet* in which some account was given of Ransom's adventures on Mars – or, as its inhabitants call it, *Malacandra*. All the human characters in this book are purely fictitious and none of them is allegorical, C.S.L.

1

As I left the railway station at Worchester and set out on the three-mile walk to Ransom's cottage, I reflected that no one on that platform could possibly guess the truth about the man I was going to visit. The flat heath which spread out before me (for the village lies all behind and to the north of the station) looked an ordinary heath. The gloomy five-o'clock sky was such as you might see on any autumn afternoon. The few houses and the clumps of red or yellowish trees were in no way remarkable. Who could imagine that a little farther on in that quiet landscape I should meet and shake by the hand a man who had lived and eaten and drunk in a world forty million miles distant from London, who had seen this Earth from where it looks like a mere point of green fire, and who had spoken face to face with a creature whose life began before our own planet was inhabitable?

For Ransom had met other things in Mars besides the Martians. He had met the creatures called *eldila*, and specially that great *eldil* who is the ruler of Mars or, in their speech, the *Oyarsa* of *Malacandra*. The *eldila* are very different from any planetary creatures. Their physical organism, if organism it can be called, is quite unlike either the human or the Martian. They do not eat, breed, breathe, or suffer natural death, and to that extent resemble thinking minerals more than they resemble anything we should recognise as an animal. Though they appear on planets and may even seem to our senses to be sometimes resident in them, the precise spatial location of an *eldil* at any moment presents great problems. They themselves regard space (or 'Deep Heaven') as their true habitat, and the planets are to them not closed worlds but merely moving points – perhaps even interruptions – in what we know as the Solar System and they as the Field of Arbol.

At present I was going to see Ransom in answer to a wire which had said 'Come down Thursday if possible. Business.' I guessed what sort of business he meant, and that was why I kept on telling myself that it would be perfectly delightful to spend a night with Ransom and also kept on feeling that I was not enjoying the prospect as much as I ought to. It was the *eldila* that were my trouble. I could just get used to the fact that Ransom had been to Mars … but to have met an *eldil*, to have spoken with something whose life appeared to be practically unending … Even the journey to Mars was bad enough. A man who has been in another world does not come back unchanged. One can't put the difference into words. When the man is a friend it may become painful: the old footing is not easy to recover. But much worse was my growing conviction that, since his return, the *eldila* were not leaving him alone. Little things in his conversation, little mannerisms, accidental allusions which he made and then drew back with an awkward apology, all suggested that he was keeping strange company; that there were – well, Visitors – at that cottage.

As I plodded along the empty, unfenced road which runs across the middle of Worchester Common I tried to dispel my growing sense of *malaise* by analysing it. What, after all, was I afraid of? The moment I had put this question I regretted it. I was shocked to find that I had mentally used the word 'afraid'. Up till then I had tried to pretend that I was feeling only distaste, or embarrassment, or even boredom. But the mere word *afraid* had let the cat out of the bag. I realised now that my emotion was neither more, nor less, nor other, than Fear. And I realised that I was afraid of two things – afraid that sooner or later I myself might meet an *eldil*, and afraid that I might get 'drawn in'. I suppose everyone knows this fear of getting 'drawn in' the moment at which a man realises that what had seemed mere speculations are on the point of landing him in the Communist Party or the Christian Church – the sense that a door has just slammed and left him on the inside. The thing was such sheer bad luck. Ransom himself had been taken to Mars (or Malacandra) against his will and almost by accident, and I had become connected with his affair by another accident. Yet here we were both getting more and more involved in what I could only describe as interplanetary politics. As to my intense wish never to come into contact with the *eldila* myself; I am not sure whether I can make you understand it. It was something more than a prudent desire to avoid creatures alien in kind, very powerful, and very intelligent. The truth was that all I heard about them served to connect two things which one's mind tends to keep separate, and that connecting gave one a sort of shock. We tend to think about non-human intelligences in two distinct categories which we label 'scientific' and 'supernatural' respectively. We think, in one mood, of Mr Wells' Martians (very unlike the real Malacandrians, by the bye), or his Selenites. In quite a different mood we let our minds loose on the possibility of angels, ghosts, fairies, and the like. But the very moment we are compelled to recognise a creature in either class as *real* the distinction begins to get blurred: and when it is a creature like an *eldil* the distinction vanishes altogether. These things were not animals – to that extent one had to classify them with the second group; but they had some kind of material vehicle whose presence could (in principle) be scientifically verified. To that extent they belonged to the first group. The distinction between natural and supernatural, in fact, broke down; and when it had done so, one realised how great a comfort it had been – how it had eased the burden of intolerable strangeness which this universe imposes on us by dividing it into two halves and encouraging the mind never to think of both in the same context. What price we may have paid for this comfort in the way of false security and accepted confusion of thought is another matter.

'This is a long, dreary road,' I thought to myself. 'Thank goodness I haven't anything to carry.' And then, with a start of realisation I remembered that I ought to be carrying a pack, containing my things for the night. I swore to myself. I must have left the thing in the train. Will you believe me when I say that my immediate impulse was to turn back to the station and 'do something about it'? Of course there was nothing to be done which could not equally well be done by ringing up from the cottage. That train, with my pack in it, must by this time be miles away.

I realise that now as clearly as you do. But at the moment it seemed perfectly obvious that I must retrace my steps, and I had indeed begun to do so before reason or conscience awoke and set me once more plodding forwards. In doing this I discovered more clearly than before how very little I wanted to do it. It was such hard work that I felt as if I were walking against a headwind; but in fact it was one of those still, dead evenings when no twig stirs, and beginning to be a little foggy.

The farther I went the more impossible I found it to think about anything except these *eldila*. What, after all, did Ransom really know about them? By his own account the sorts which he had met did not usually visit our own planet – or had only begun to do so since his return from Mars. We had *eldila* of our own, he said, Tellurian *eldila*, but they were of a different kind and mostly hostile to man. That, in fact, was why our world was cut off from communication with the other planets. He described us as being in a state of siege, as being, in fact, an enemy-occupied territory, held down by *eldila* who were at war both with us and with the *eldila* of 'Deep Heaven', or 'space'. Like the bacteria on the microscopic level, so these co-inhabiting pests on the macroscopic permeate our whole life invisibly and are the real explanation of that fatal bent which is the main lesson of history. If all this were true, then, of course, we should welcome the fact that *eldila* of a better kind had at last broken the frontier (it is, they say, at the Moon's orbit) and were beginning to visit us. Always assuming that Ransom's account was the correct one.

A nasty idea occurred to me. Why should not Ransom be a dupe? If something from outer space were trying to invade our planet, what better smoke-screen could it put up than this very story of Ransom's? Was there the slightest evidence, after all, for the existence of the supposed maleficent *eldila* on this earth? How if my friend were the unwitting bridge, the Trojan Horse, whereby some possible invader were effecting its landing on Tellus? And then once more, just as when I had discovered that I had no pack, the impulse to go no farther returned to me. 'Go back, go back,' it whispered to me, 'send him a wire, tell him you were ill, say you'll come some other time – anything.' The strength of the feeling astonished me. I stood still for a few moments telling myself not to be a fool, and when I finally resumed my walk I was wondering whether this might be the beginning of a nervous breakdown. No sooner had this idea occurred to me than it also became a new reason for not visiting Ransom. Obviously, I wasn't fit for any such jumpy 'business' as his telegram almost certainly referred to. I wasn't even fit to spend an ordinary weekend away from home. My only sensible course was to turn back at once and get safe home, before I lost my memory or became hysterical, and to put myself in the hands of a doctor. It was sheer madness to go on.

I was now coming to the end of the heath and going down a small hill, with a copse on my left and some apparently deserted industrial buildings on my right. At the bottom the evening mist was partly thick. 'They call it a Breakdown *at first*,' I thought. Wasn't there some mental disease in which quite ordinary objects looked to the patient unbelievably ominous? ... looked, in fact, just as that abandoned factory looks to me now? Great bulbous shapes of cement, strange brickwork bogeys, glowered at me over dry scrubby grass pock-marked with grey pools and intersected with the remains of a light railway. I was reminded of things which Ransom had seen in that other world: only there, they were people. Long spindle-like giants whom he calls *sorns*. What made it worse was that he regarded them as good people – very much nicer, in fact, than our own race. He was in league with them! How did I know he was even a dupe? He might be something worse ... and again I came to a standstill.

The reader, not knowing Ransom, will not understand how contrary to all reason this idea was. The rational part of my mind, even at that moment, knew perfectly well that even if the whole universe were crazy and hostile, Ransom was sane and wholesome and honest. And this part of my mind in the end sent me forward – but with a reluctance and a difficulty I can hardly put into words. What enabled me to go on was the knowledge (deep down inside me) that I was getting nearer at every stride to the one friend: but I *felt* that I was getting nearer to the one enemy – the traitor, the sorcerer, the man in league with 'them' … walking into the trap with my eyes open, like a fool. 'They call it a breakdown at first,' said my mind, 'and send you to a nursing home; later on they move you to an asylum.'

I was past the dead factory now, down in the fog, where it was very cold. Then came a moment – the first one – of absolute terror and I had to bite my lip to keep myself from screaming. It was only a cat that had run across the road, but I found myself completely unnerved. 'Soon you will really be screaming,' said my inner tormentor, 'running round and round, screaming, and you won't be able to stop it.'

There was a little empty house by the side of the road, with most of the windows boarded up and one staring like the eye of a dead fish. Please understand that at ordinary times the idea of a 'haunted house' means no more to me than it does to you. No more; but also, no less. At that moment it was nothing so definite as the thought of a ghost that came to me. It was just the word 'haunted'. 'Haunted' … 'haunting' … what a quality there is in that first syllable! Would not a child who had never heard the word before and did not know its meaning shudder at the mere sound if, as the day was closing in, it heard one of its elders say to another 'This house is haunted'?

At last I came to the crossroads by the little Wesleyan chapel where I had to turn to the left under the beech trees. I ought to be seeing the lights from Ransom's windows by now – or was it past blackout time? My watch had stopped, and I didn't know. It was dark enough but that might be due to the fog and the trees. It wasn't the dark I was afraid of, you understand. We have all known times when inanimate objects seemed to have almost a facial expression, and it was the expression of this bit of road which I did not like. 'It's not true,' said my mind, 'that people who are really going mad never think they're going mad.' Suppose that real insanity had chosen this place in which to begin? In that case, of course, the black enmity of those dripping trees – their horrible expectancy – would be a hallucination. But that did not make it any better. To think that the spectre you see is an illusion does not rob him of his terrors: it simply adds the further terror of madness itself – and then on top of that the horrible surmise that those whom the rest call mad have, all along, been the only people who see the world as it really is.

This was upon me now. I staggered on into the cold and the darkness, already half convinced that I must be entering what is called Madness. But each moment my opinion about sanity changed. Had it ever been more than a convention – a comfortable set of blinkers, an agreed mode of wishful thinking, which excluded from our view the full strangeness and malevolence of the universe we are compelled to inhabit? The things I had begun to know during the last few months of my acquaintance with Ransom already amounted to more than 'sanity' would admit; but I had come much too far to dismiss them as unreal. I doubted his interpretation, or his good faith. I did not doubt the existence of the things he had met in Mars – the *pfifltriggi*, the *hrossa*, and the *sorns* – nor of these interplanetary *eldila*. I did not even doubt the reality of that mysterious being whom the *eldila* call Maleldil and to whom they appear to give a total obedience such as no Tellurian dictator can command. I knew what Ransom supposed Maleldil to be.

Surely that was the cottage. It was very well blacked-out. A childish, whining thought arose on my mind: why was he not out at the gate to welcome me? An even more childish thought followed. Perhaps he *was* in the garden waiting for me, hiding. Perhaps he would jump on me from behind. Perhaps I should see a figure that looked like Ransom standing with its back to me and when I spoke to it, it would turn round and show a face that was not human at all ...

I have naturally no wish to enlarge on this phase of my story. The state of mind I was in was one which I look back on with humiliation. I would have passed it over if I did not think that some account of it was necessary for a full understanding of what follows – and, perhaps, of some other things as well. At all events, I *can't* really describe how I reached the front door of the cottage. Somehow or other, despite the loathing and dismay that pulled me back and a sort of invisible wall of resistance that met me in the face, fighting for each step, and almost shrieking as a harmless spray of the hedge touched my face, I managed to get through the gate and up the little path. And there I was, drumming on the door and wringing the handle and shouting to him to let me in as if my life depended on it.

There was no reply – not a sound except the echo of the sounds I had been making myself. There was only something white fluttering on the knocker. I guessed, of course, that it was a note. In striking a match to read it by, I discovered how very shaky my hands had become; and when the match went out I realised how dark the evening had grown. After several attempts I read the thing. 'Sorry. Had to go up to Cambridge. Shan't be back till the late train. Eatables in larder and bed made up in your usual room. Don't wait supper for me unless you feel like it – E. R.' And immediately the impulse to retreat, which had already assailed me several times, leaped upon me with a sort of demoniac violence. Here was my retreat left open, positively inviting me. Now was my chance. If anyone expected me to go into that house and sit there alone for several hours, they were mistaken! But then, as the thought of the return journey began to take shape in my mind, I faltered. The idea of setting out to traverse the avenue of beech trees again (it was really dark now) with this house behind me (one had the absurd feeling that it could follow one) was not attractive. And then, I hope, something better came into my mind – some rag of sanity and some reluctance to let Ransom down. At least I could try the door to see if it were really unlocked. I did. And it was. Next moment, I hardly know how, I found myself inside and let it slam behind me.

It was quite dark, and warm. I groped a few paces forward, hit my shin violently against something, and fell. I sat still for a few seconds nursing my leg. I thought I knew the layout of Ransom's hall-sitting-room pretty well and couldn't imagine what I had blundered into. Presently I groped in my pocket, got out my matches, and tried to strike a light. The head of the match flew off. I stamped on it and sniffed to make sure it was not smouldering on the carpet. As soon as I sniffed I became aware of a strange smell in the room. I could not for the life of me make out what it was. It had an unlikeness to ordinary domestic smells as great as that of some chemicals, but it was not a chemical kind of smell at all. Then I struck another match. It flickered and went out almost at once – not unnaturally, since I was sitting on the door-mat and there are few front doors even in better built houses than Ransom's country cottage which do not admit a draught. I had seen nothing by it except the palm of my own hand hollowed in an attempt to guard the flame. Obviously I must get away from the door. I rose gingerly and felt my way forward. I came at once to an obstacle – something smooth and very cold that rose a little higher than my knees. As I touched it I realised that it was the source of the smell. I groped my way along this to the left and finally came to the end of it. It seemed to present several surfaces and I couldn't picture the shape. It was not a table, for it had no top. One's hand groped along the rim of a kind of low wall – the thumb on the outside and the fingers down inside the enclosed space. If it had felt like wood I should have supposed it to be a large packing-case. But it was not wood. I thought for a moment that it was wet, but soon decided that I was mistaking coldness for moisture. When I reached the end of it I struck my third match.

I saw something white and semi-transparent rather like ice. A great big thing, very long: a kind of box, an open box: and of a disquieting shape which I did not immediately recognise. It was big enough to put a man into. Then I took a step back, lifting the lighted match higher to get a more comprehensive view, and instantly tripped over something behind me. I found myself sprawling in darkness, not on the carpet, but on more of the cold substance with the odd smell. How many of the infernal things were there?

I was just preparing to rise again and hunt systematically round the room for a candle when I heard Ransom's name pronounced; and almost, but not quite, simultaneously I saw the thing I had feared so long to see. I heard Ransom's name pronounced: but I should not like to say I heard a voice pronounce it. The sound was quite astonishingly unlike a voice. It was perfectly articulate: it was even, I suppose, rather beautiful. But it was, if you understand me, inorganic. We feel the difference between animal voices (including those of the human animal) and all other noises pretty clearly, I fancy, though it is hard to define. Blood and lungs and the warm, moist cavity of the mouth are somehow indicated in every Voice. Here they were not. The two syllables sounded more as if they were played on an instrument than as if they were spoken: and yet they did not sound mechanical either. A machine is something we make out of natural materials; this was more as if rock or crystal or light had spoken of itself. And it went through me from chest to groin like the thrill that goes through you when you think you have lost your hold while climbing a cliff.

That was what I heard. What I saw was simply a very faint rod or pillar of light. I don't think it made a circle of light either on the floor or the ceiling, but I am not sure of this. It certainly had very little power of illuminating its surroundings. So far, all is plain sailing. But it had two other characteristics which are less easy to grasp. One was its colour. Since I saw the thing I must obviously have seen it either white or coloured; but no efforts of my memory can conjure up the faintest image of what that colour was. I try blue, and gold, and violet, and red, but none of them will fit. How it is possible to have a visual experience which immediately and ever after becomes impossible to remember, I do not attempt to explain. The other was its angle. It was not at right angles to the floor. But as soon as I have said this, I hasten to add that this way of putting it is a later reconstruction. What one actually felt at the moment was that the column of light was vertical but the floor was not horizontal – the whole room seemed to have heeled over as if it were on board ship. The impression, however produced, was that this creature had reference to some horizontal, to some whole system of directions, based outside the Earth, and that its mere presence imposed that alien system on me and abolished the terrestrial horizontal.

I had no doubt at all that I was seeing an *eldil*, and little doubt that I was seeing the archon of Mars, the Oyarsa of Malacandra. And now that the thing had happened I was no longer in a condition of abject panic. My sensations were, it is true, in some ways very unpleasant. The fact that it was quite obviously not organic – the knowledge that intelligence was somehow located in this homogeneous cylinder of light but not related to it as our consciousness is related to our brains and nerves – was profoundly disturbing.[1] It

[1] In the text I naturally keep to what I thought and felt at the time, since this alone is first-hand evidence: but there is obviously room for more further speculation about the form in which *eldila* appear to our senses. The only serious considerations of the problem so far are to be sought in the early seventeenth century. As a starting point for future investigation I recommend the following from Natvilcius (*De Aethereo et aerio Corpore*, Basel. 1627, II. xii.); *liquet simplicem flammem sensibus nostris subjectam non esse corpus proprie dictum angeli vel daemonis, sed potius aut illius corporis sensorium aut superficiem corporis in coelesti dispositione locorum supra cogitationes humanas existentis* ('It appears that the homogeneous flame perceived by our senses is not the body, properly so called, of an angel or daemon, but rather either the sensorium of that body or the surface of a body which exists after a manner beyond our conception in the celestial flame of spatial references'). By the 'celestial frame of references' I take him to mean what we should now call 'multi-dimensional space'. Not, of course, that Natvilcius knew anything about multi-dimensional geometry, but that he had reached empirically what mathematics has since reached on theoretical grounds.

would not fit into our categories. The response which we ordinarily make to a living creature and that which we make to an inanimate object were here both equally inappropriate. On the other hand, all those doubts which I had felt before I entered the cottage as to whether these creatures were friend or foe, and whether Ransom were a pioneer or a dupe, had for the moment vanished. My fear was now of another kind. I felt sure that the creature was what we call 'good', but I wasn't sure whether I liked 'goodness' so much as I had supposed. This is a very terrible experience. As long as what you are afraid of is something evil, you may still hope that the good may come to your rescue. But suppose you struggle through to the good and find that it also dreadful? How if food itself turns out to be the very thing you can't eat, and home the very place you can't live, and your very comforter the person who makes you uncomfortable? Then, indeed, there is no rescue possible: the last card has been played. For a second or two I was nearly in that condition. Here at last was a bit of that world from beyond the world, which I had always supposed that I loved and desired, breaking through and appearing to my senses: and I didn't like it, I wanted it to go away. I wanted every possible distance, gulf, curtain, blanket and barrier to be placed between it and me. But I did not fall quite into the gulf. Oddly enough my very sense of helplessness saved me and steadied me. For now I was quite obviously 'drawn in'. The struggle was over. The next decision did not lie with me.

Then, like a noise from a different world, came the opening of the door and the sound of boots on the doormat, and I saw, silhouetted against the greyness of the night in the open doorway, a figure which I recognised as Ransom. The speaking which was not a voice came again out of the rod of light: and Ransom, instead of moving, stood still and answered it. Both speeches were in a strange polysyllabic language which I had not heard before. I make no attempt to excuse the feelings which awoke in me when I heard the unhuman sound addressing my friend and my friend answering it in the unhuman language They are, in fact, inexcusable; but if you think they are improbable at such a juncture, I must tell you plainly that you have read neither history nor your own heart to much effect. They were feelings of resentment, horror and jealousy. It was in my mind to shout out, 'Leave your familiar alone, you damned magician, and attend to Me.'

What I actually said was, 'Oh, Ransom. Thank God you've come.'

2

The door was slammed (for the second time that night) and after a moment's groping Ransom had found and lit a candle. I glanced quickly round and could see no one but ourselves. The most noticeable thing in the room was the big white object. I recognised the shape well enough this time. It was a large coffin-shaped casket, open. On the floor beside it lay its lid, and it was doubtless this that I had tripped over. Both were made of the same white material, like ice, but more cloudy and less shining.

'By Jove, I'm glad to see you,' said Ransom, advancing and shaking hands with me. 'I'd hoped to be able to meet you at the station, but everything has had to be arranged in such a hurry and I found at the last moment that I'd got to go up to Cambridge. I never intended to leave you to make *that* journey alone.' Then, seeing, I suppose, that I was still staring at him rather stupidly, he added, 'I say – you're *all right*, aren't you? You got through the barrage without any damage?'

'The barrage? – I don't understand.'

'I was thinking you would have met some difficulties in getting here.'

'Oh, *that*!' said I. 'You mean it wasn't just my nerves? There really was something in the way?'

'Yes. They didn't want you to get here. I was afraid some thing of the sort might happen but there was no time to do anything about it. I was pretty sure you'd get through somehow.'

'By *they* you mean the others – our own *eldila*?'

'Of course. They've got wind of what's on hand …'

I interrupted him. 'To tell you the truth, Ransom,' I said, 'I'm getting more worried every day about the whole business. It came into my head as I was on my way here –'

'Oh, they'll put all sorts of things into your head if you let them,' said Ransom lightly. 'The best plan is to take no notice, and keep straight on. Don't try to answer them. They like drawing you into an interminable argument.'

'But, look here,' said I. 'This isn't child's play. Are you quite certain that this Dark Lord, this depraved Oyarsa of Tellus, really exists? Do you know for certain either that there are two sides, or which side is ours?'

He fixed me suddenly with one of his mild, but strangely formidable, glances.

'You are in *real* doubt about either, are you?' he asked.

'No,' said I, after a pause, and felt rather ashamed.

'That's all right, then,' said Ransom cheerfully. 'Now let's get some supper and I'll explain as we go along.'

'What's that coffin affair?' I asked as we moved into the kitchen.

'That is what I'm to travel in.'

'Ransom!' I exclaimed. 'He – it – the *eldil* – is not going to take you back to Malacandra?'

'Don't!' said he. 'Oh, Lewis, you don't understand. Take me back to Malacandra? If only he would! I'd give anything I possess ... just to look down one of those gorges again and see the blue, blue water winding in and out among the woods. Or to be up on top – to see a *sorn* go gliding along the slopes. Or to be back there of an evening when Jupiter was rising, too bright to look at, and all the asteroids like a Milky Way, with each star in it as bright as Venus looks from Earth! And the smells! It is hardly ever out of my mind. You'd expect it to be worse at night when Malacandra is up and I can actually see it. But it isn't then that I get the real twinge. It's on hot summer days – looking up at the deep blue and thinking that *in there,* millions of miles deep where I can never, never get back to it, there's a place I know, and flowers at that very moment growing over Meldilorn, and friends of mine, going about their business, who would welcome me back. No. No such luck. It's not Malacandra I'm being sent to. It's Perelandra.'

'That's what we call Venus, isn't it?'

'Yes.'

'And you say you're being sent.'

'Yes. If you remember, before I left Malacandra the Oyarsa hinted to me that my going there at all might be the beginning of a whole new phase in the life of the Solar System – the Field of Arbol. It might mean, he said, that the isolation of our world, the siege, was beginning to draw to an end.'

'Yes. I remember.'

'Well, it really does look as if something of the sort were afoot. For one thing, the two sides, as you call them, have begun to appear much more clearly, much less mixed, here on Earth, in our own human affairs – to show in something a little more like their true colours.'

'I see that all right.'

'The other thing is this. The black archon – our own bent Oyarsa – is meditating some sort of attack on Perelandra.'

'But is he at large like that in the Solar System? Can he get there?'

'That's just the point. He can't get there in his own person, in his own photosome or whatever we should call it. As you know, he was driven back within these bounds centuries before any human life existed on our planet. If he ventured to show himself outside the Moon's orbit he'd be driven back again by main force. That would be a different kind of war. You or I could contribute no more to it than a flea could contribute to the defence of Moscow. No. He must be attempting Perelandra in some different way.'

'And where do you come in?'

'Well – simply I've been ordered there.'

'By the – by Oyarsa, you mean?'

'No. The order comes from much higher up. They all do, you know, in the long run.'

'And what have you got to do when you get there?'

'I haven't been told.'

'You are just part of the Oyarsa's *entourage*?'

'Oh no. He isn't going to be there. He is to transport me to Venus – to deliver me there. After that, as far as I know, I shall be alone.'

'But, look here, Ransom – I mean ...' my voice trailed away.

'I know!' said he with one of his singularly disarming smiles. 'You are feeling the absurdity of it. Dr Elwin Ransom setting out single-handed to combat powers and principalities. You may even be wondering if I've got megalomania.'

'I didn't mean that quite,' said I.

'Oh, but I think you did. At any rate that is what I have been feeling myself ever since the thing was sprung on me. But when you come to think of it, is it odder than what all of us have to do every day? When the Bible used that very expression about fighting with principalities and powers and depraved hypersomatic beings at great heights (our translation is very misleading at that point, by the way) it meant that quite ordinary people were to do the fighting.'

'Oh, I dare say,' said I. 'But that's rather different. That refers to a moral conflict.'

Ransom threw back his head and laughed. 'Oh, Lewis, Lewis,' he said, 'you are inimitable, simply inimitable!'

'Say what you like, Ransom, there *is* a difference.'

'Yes. There is. But not a difference that makes it megalomania to think that any of us might have to fight either way. I'll tell you how I look at it. Haven't you noticed how in our own little war here on earth, there are different phases, and while any one phase is going on people get into the habit of thinking and behaving as if it was going to be permanent? But really the thing is changing under your hands all the time, and neither your assets nor your dangers this year are the same as the year before. Now your idea that ordinary people will never have to meet the Dark *Eldila* in any form except a psychological or moral form – as temptations or the like – is simply an idea that held good for a certain phase of the cosmic war: the phase of the great siege, the phase which gave to our planet its name of Thulcandra, the *silent* planet. But supposing that phase is passing? In the next phase it may be anyone's job to meet them … well, in some quite different mode.'

'I see.'

'Don't imagine I've been selected to go to Perelandra because I'm anyone in particular. One never can see, or not till long afterwards, why *any* one was selected for *any* job. And when one does, it is usually some reason that leaves no room for vanity. Certainly, it is never for what the man himself would have regarded as his chief qualifications. I rather fancy I am being sent because those two blackguards who kidnapped me and took me to Malacandra, did something which they never intended: namely, gave a human being a chance to learn that language.'

'What language do you mean?'

'*Hressa-Hlab*, of course. The language I learned in Malacandra.'

'But surely you don't imagine they will speak the same language on Venus?'

'Didn't I tell you about that?' said Ransom, leaning forward. We were now at table and had nearly finished our cold meat and beer and tea. 'I'm surprised I didn't, for I found out two or three months ago, and scientifically it is one of the most interesting things about the whole affair. It appears we were quite mistaken in thinking *Hressa-Hlab* the peculiar speech of Mars. It is really what may be called Old Solar, *Hlab-Eribol-ef-Cordi*.'

'What on earth do you mean?'

'I mean that there was originally a common speech for all rational creatures inhabiting the planets of our system: those that were ever inhabited, I mean – what the *eldila* call the Low Worlds. Most of them, of course, have never been inhabited and never will be. At least not what we'd call inhabited. That original speech was lost on Thulcandra, our own world, when our whole tragedy took place. No human language now known in the world is descended from it.

'But what about the other two languages on Mars?'

'I admit I don't understand about them. One thing I do know, and I believe I could prove it on purely philological grounds. They are incomparably less ancient than *Hressa-Hlab*, specially *Surnibur*, the speech of the *sorns*. I believe it could be shown that *Surnibur* is, by Malacandrian standards, quite a modern development. I doubt if its birth can be put farther back than a date which would fall within our Cambrian Period.'

'And you think you will find *Hressa-Hlab*, or Old Solar, spoken on Venus?'

'Yes. I shall arrive knowing the language. It saves a lot of trouble – though, as a philologist, I find it rather disappointing.'

'But you've no idea what you are to do, or what conditions you will find?'

'No idea at all what I'm to do. There are jobs, you know where it is essential that one should *not* know too much beforehand ... things one might have to say which one couldn't say effectively if one had prepared them. As to conditions, well, I don't know much. It will be warm: I'm to go naked. Our astronomers don't know anything about the surface of Perelandra at all. The outer layer of her atmosphere is too thick. The main problem, apparently, is whether she revolves on her own axis or not, and at what speed. There are two schools of thought. There's a man called Schiaparelli who thinks she revolves once on herself in the same time it takes her to go once round Arbol – I mean, the Sun. The other people think she revolves on her own axis once in every twenty-three hours. That's one of the things I shall find out.'

'If Schiaparelli is right there'd be perpetual day on one side of her and perpetual night on the other?'

He nodded, musing. 'It'd be a funny frontier,' he said presently. 'Just think of it. You'd come to a country of eternal twilight, getting colder and darker every mile you went. And then presently you wouldn't be able to go farther because there'd be no more air. I wonder can you stand in the day, just on the right side of the frontier, and look *into* the night which you can never reach? And perhaps see a star or two – the only place you *could* see them, for of course in the Day-Lands they would never be visible ... Of course if they have a scientific civilisation they may have diving-suits or things like submarines on wheels for going into the Night.'

His eyes sparkled, and even I, who had been mainly thinking of how I should miss him and wondering what chances there were of my ever seeing him again, felt a vicarious thrill of wonder and of longing to know. Presently he spoke again.

'You haven't yet asked me where *you* come in,' he said.

'Do you mean I'm to go too?' said I, with a thrill of exactly the opposite kind.

'Not at all. I mean you are to pack me up, and to stand by to unpack me when I return – if all goes well.'

'Pack you? Oh, I'd forgotten about that coffin affair. Ransom, how on earth are you going to travel in that thing? What's the motive power? What about air – and food – and water? There's only just room for you to lie in it.'

'The Oyarsa of Malacandra himself will be the motive power. He will simply move it to Venus. Don't ask me how. I have no idea what organs or instruments they use. But a creature who has kept a planet in its orbit for several billions of years will be able to manage a packing-case!'

'But what will you eat? How will you breathe?'

'He tells me I shall need to do neither. I shall be in some state of suspended animation, as far as I can make out. I can't understand him when he tries to describe it. But that's his affair.'

'Do you feel quite happy about it?' said I, for a sort of horror was beginning once more to creep over me.

'If you mean, Does my reason accept the view that he will (accidents apart) deliver me safe on the surface of Perelandra? – the answer is Yes,' said Ransom. 'If you mean, Do my nerves and my imagination respond to this view? – I'm afraid the answer is No. One can believe in anaesthetics and yet feel in a panic when they actually put the mask over your face. I think I feel as a man who believes in the future life feels when he is taken out to face a firing party. Perhaps it's good practice.'

'And I'm to pack you into that accursed thing?' said I.

'Yes,' said Ransom. 'That's the first step. We must get out into the garden as soon as the sun is up and point it so that there are no trees or buildings in the way. Across the cabbage bed will do. Then I get in – with a bandage across my eyes, for those walls won't keep out all the sunlight once I'm beyond the air – and you screw me down. After that, I think you'll just see it glide off.'

'And then?'

'Well, then comes the difficult part. You must hold yourself in readiness to come down here again the moment you are summoned, to take off the lid and let me out when I return.'

'When do you expect to return?'

'Nobody can say. Six months – a year – twenty years. That's the trouble. I'm afraid I'm laying a pretty heavy burden on you.'

'I might be dead.'

'I know. I'm afraid part of your burden is to select a successor: at once, too. There are four or five people whom we can trust'

'What will the summons be?'

'Oyarsa will give it. It won't be mistakable for anything else. You needn't bother about that side of it. One other point. I've no particular reason to suppose I shall come back wounded. But just in case – if you can find a doctor whom we can let into the secret, it might be just as well to bring him with you when you come down to let me out.'

'Would Humphrey do?'

'The very man. And now for some more personal matters. I've had to leave you out of my will, and I'd like you to know why.'

'My dear chap, I never thought about your will till this moment.'

'Of course not. But I'd like to have left you something. The reason I haven't, is this. I'm going to disappear. It is possible I may not come back. It's just conceivable there might be a murder trial, and if so one can't be too careful. I mean, for your sake. And now for one or two other private arrangements.'

We laid our heads together and for a long time we talked about those matters which one usually discusses with relatives and not with friends. I got to know a lot more about Ransom than I had known before, and from the number of odd people whom he recommended to my care, 'If ever I happened to be able to do anything', I came to realise the extent and intimacy of his charities. With every sentence the shadow of approaching separation and a kind of graveyard gloom began to settle more emphatically upon us. I found myself noticing and loving all sorts of little mannerisms and expressions in him such as we notice always in a woman we love, but notice in a man only as the last hours of his leave run out or the date of the probably fatal operation draws near. I felt our nature's incurable incredulity; and could hardly believe that what was now so close, so tangible and (in a sense) so much at my command, would in a few hours be wholly inaccessible, an image – soon, even an elusive image – in my memory. And finally a sort of shyness fell between us because each knew what the other was feeling. It had got very cold.

'We must be going soon,' said Ransom.

'Not till he – the Oyarsa – comes back,' said I – though, indeed, now that the thing was so near I wished it to be over.

'He has never left us,' said Ransom, 'he has been in the cottage all the time.'

'You mean he has been waiting in the next room all these hours?'

'Not waiting. They never have that experience. You and I are conscious of waiting, because we have a body that grows tired or restless, and therefore a sense of cumulative duration. Also we can distinguish duties and spare time and therefore have a conception of leisure. It is not like that with him. He has been here all this time, but you can no more call it waiting than you can call the whole of his existence waiting. You might as well say that a tree in a wood was waiting, or the sunlight waiting on the side of a hill.' Ransom yawned. 'I'm tired,' he said, 'and so are you. I shall sleep well in that coffin of mine. Come. Let us lug it out.'

We went into the next room and I was made to stand before the featureless flame which did not wait but just was, and there, with

Ransom as our interpreter, I was in some fashion presented and with my own tongue sworn in to this great business. Then we took down the blackout and let in the grey, comfortless morning. Between us we carried out the casket and the lid, so cold they seemed to burn our fingers. There was a heavy dew on the grass and my feet were soaked through at once. The *eldil* was with us, outside there, on the little lawn; hardly visible to my eyes at all in the daylight. Ransom showed me the clasps of the lid and how it was to be fastened on, and then there was some miserable hanging about, and then the final moment when he went back into the house and reappeared, naked; a tall, white, shivering, weary scarecrow of a man at that pale, raw hour. When he had got into the hideous box he made me tie a thick black bandage round his eyes and head. Then he lay down. I had no thoughts of the planet Venus now and no real belief that I should see him again. If I had dared I would have gone back on the whole scheme: but the other thing – the creature that did not wait – was there, and the fear of it was upon me. With feelings that have since often returned to me in nightmare I fastened the cold lid down on top of the living man and stood back. Next moment I was alone. I didn't see how it went. I went back indoors and was sick. A few hours later I shut up the cottage and returned to Oxford.

Then the months went past and grew to a year and a little more than a year, and we had raids and bad news and hopes deferred and all the earth became full of darkness and cruel habitations, till the night when Oyarsa came to me again. After that there was a journey in haste for Humphrey and me, standings in crowded corridors and waitings at small hours on windy platforms, and finally the moment when we stood in clear early sunlight in the little wilderness of deep weeds which Ransom's garden had now become and saw a black speck against the sunrise and then, almost silently, the casket had glided down between us. We flung ourselves upon it and had the lid off in about a minute and a half.

'Good God! All smashed to bits,' I cried at my first glance of the interior.

'Wait a moment,' said Humphrey. And as he spoke the figure in the coffin began to stir and then sat up, shaking off as it did so a mass of red things which had covered its head and shoulders and which I had momentarily mistaken for ruin and blood. As they streamed off him and were caught in the wind I perceived them to be flowers. He blinked for a second or so, then called us by our names, gave each of us a hand, and stepped out on the grass.

'How are you both?' he said. 'You're looking rather knocked up.'

I was silent for a moment, astonished at the form which had risen from that narrow house – almost a new Ransom, glowing with health and rounded with muscle and seemingly ten years younger. In the old days he had been beginning to show a few grey hairs; but now the beard which swept his chest was pure gold.

'Hullo, you've cut your foot;' said Humphrey: and I saw now that Ransom was bleeding from the heel.

'Ugh, it's cold down here,' said Ransom. 'I hope you've got the boiler going and some hot water – and some clothes.'

'Yes,' said I, as we followed him into the house. 'Humphrey thought of all that. I'm afraid I shouldn't have.'

Ransom was now in the bathroom, with the door open, veiled in clouds of steam, and Humphrey and I were talking to him from the landing. Our questions were more numerous than he could answer.

'That idea of Schiaparelli's is all wrong,' he shouted. 'They have an ordinary day and night there,' and 'No, my heel doesn't hurt – or, at least, it's only just begun to,' and 'Thanks, any old clothes. Leave them on the chair,' and 'No, thanks. I don't somehow feel like bacon or eggs or anything of that kind. No fruit, you say? Oh well, no matter. Bread or porridge or something,' and 'I'll be down in five minutes now.'

He kept on asking if we were really all right and seemed to think we looked ill. I went down to get the breakfast, and Humphrey said he would stay and examine and dress the cut on Ransom's heel. When he rejoined me I was looking at one of the red petals which had come in the casket.

'That's rather a beautiful flower,' said I, handing it to him. 'Yes,' said Humphrey, studying it with the hands and eyes of a scientist. 'What extraordinary delicacy! It makes an English violet seem like a coarse weed.'

'Let's put some of them in water.'

'Not much good. Look – it's withered already.'

'How do you think he is?'

'Tip-top in general. But I don't quite like that heel. He says the haemorrhage has been going on for a long time.'

Ransom joined us, fully dressed, and I poured out the tea. And all that day and far into the night he told us the story that follows.

3

What it is like to travel in a celestial coffin was a thing that Ransom never described. He said he couldn't. But odd hints about that journey have come out at one time or another when he was talking of quite different matters.

According to his own account he was not what we call conscious, and yet at the same time the experience was a very positive one with a quality of its own. On one occasion, someone had been talking about 'seeing life' in the popular sense of knocking about the world and getting to know people, and B., who was present (and who is an Anthroposophist), said something I can't quite remember about 'seeing life 'in a very different sense. I think he was referring to some system of meditation which claimed to make 'the form of Life itself' visible to the inner eye. At any rate Ransom let himself in for a long cross-examination by failing to conceal the fact that he attached some very definite idea to this. He even went so far – under extreme pressure – as to say that life appeared to him, in that condition, as a 'coloured shape'. Asked 'what colour?', he gave a curious look and could only say 'what colours! yes, what colours!' But then he spoiled it all by adding, 'of course it wasn't colour at all really. I mean, not what we'd call colour,' and shutting up completely for the rest of the evening. Another hint came out when a sceptical friend of ours called McPhee was arguing against the Christian doctrine of the resurrection of the human body. I was his victim at the moment, and he was pressing on me in his Scots way with such questions as 'So you think you're going to have guts and palate for ever in a world where there'll be no eating, and genital organs in a world without copulation? Man, ye'll have a grand time of it!' when Ransom suddenly burst out with great excitement, 'Oh, don't you see, you ass, that there's a difference between a trans-sensuous life and a non-sensuous life?' That, of course, directed McPhee's fire to him. What emerged was that in Ransom's opinion the present functions and appetites of the body would disappear, not because they were atrophied but because they were, as he said 'engulfed'. He used the word 'trans-sexual', I remember, and began to hunt about for some similar words to apply to eating (after rejecting 'trans-gastronomic'), and since he was not the only philologist present, that diverted the conversation into different channels. But I am pretty sure he was thinking of something he had experienced on his voyage to Venus. But perhaps the most mysterious thing he ever said about it was this. I was questioning him on the subject – which he doesn't often allow – and had incautiously said, 'Of course I realise it's all rather too vague for you to put into words,' when he took me up rather sharply, for such a patient man, by saying, 'On the contrary, it is words that are vague. The reason why the thing can't be expressed is that it's too *definite* for language.' And that is about all I can tell you of his journey. One thing is certain, that he came back from Venus even more changed than he had come back from Mars. But of course that may have been because of what happened to him after his landing.

To that landing, as Ransom narrated it to me, I will now proceed. He seems to have been awakened (if that is the right word) from his indescribable celestial state by the sensation of falling – in other words, when he was near enough to Venus to feel Venus as something in the downward direction. The next thing he noticed was that he was very warm on one side and very cold on the other, though neither sensation was so extreme as to be really painful. Anyway, both were soon swallowed up in the prodigious white light from below which began to penetrate through the semi-opaque walls of the casket. This steadily increased and became distressing in spite of the fact that his eyes were protected. There is no doubt this was the *albedo*, the outer veil of very dense atmosphere with which Venus is surrounded and which reflects the sun's rays with intense power. For some obscure reason he was not conscious, as he had been on his approach to Mars, of his own rapidly increasing weight. When the white light was just about to become unbearable, it disappeared altogether, and very soon after the cold on his left side and the heat on his right began to decrease and to be replaced by an equable warmth. I take it he was now in the outer layer of the Perelandrian atmosphere – at first in a pale, and later in a tinted, twilight. The prevailing colour, as far as he could see through the sides of the casket, was golden or coppery. By this time he must have been very near the surface of the planet, with the length of the casket at right angles to that surface – falling feet downwards like a man in a lift. The sensation of falling – helpless as he was and unable to move his arms – became frightening. Then suddenly there came a great green darkness, an unidentifiable noise – the first message from the new world – and a marked drop in temperature. He seemed now to have assumed a horizontal position and also, to his great surprise, to be moving not downwards but upwards; though, at the moment, he judged this to be an illusion. All this time he must have been making faint, unconscious efforts to move his limbs, for now he suddenly found that the sides of his prison-house yielded to pressure. He *was* moving his limbs, encumbered with some viscous substance. Where was the casket? His sensations were very confused. Sometimes he seemed to be falling, sometimes to be soaring upwards, and then again to be moving in the horizontal plane. The viscous substance was white. There seemed to be less of it every moment … white, cloudy stuff just like the casket, only not solid. With a horrible shock he realised that it *was* the casket, the casket melting, dissolving away, giving place to an indescribable confusion of colour – a rich, varied world in which nothing, for the moment, seemed palpable. There was no casket now. He was turned out – deposited – solitary. He was in Perelandra.

His first impression was of nothing more definite than of something slanted – as though he were looking at a photograph which had been taken when the camera was not held level. And even this lasted only for an instant. The slant was replaced by a different slant; then two slants rushed together and made a peak, and the peak flattened suddenly into a horizontal line, and the horizontal line tilted and became the edge of a vast gleaming slope which rushed furiously towards him. At the same moment he felt that he was being lifted. Up and up he soared till it seemed as if he must reach the burning dome of gold that hung above him instead of a sky. Then he was at a summit; but almost before his glance had taken in a huge valley that yawned beneath him – shining green like glass and marbled with streaks of scummy white – he was rushing down into that valley at perhaps thirty miles an hour. And now he realised that there was a delicious coolness over every part of him except his head, that his feet rested on nothing, and that he had for some time been performing unconsciously the actions of a swimmer. He was riding the foamless swell of an ocean, fresh and cool after the fierce temperatures of Heaven, but warm by earthly standards – as warm as a shallow bay with sandy bottom in a sub-tropical climate. As he rushed smoothly up the great convex hill-side of the next wave he got a mouthful of the water. It was hard-ly at all flavoured with salt; it was drinkable – like fresh water and only, by an infinitesimal degree, less insipid. Though he had not been aware of thirst till now, his drink gave him a quite astonishing pleasure. It was almost like meeting Pleasure itself for the first time. He buried his flushed face in the green translucence, and when he withdrew it, found himself once more on the top of a wave.

There was no land in sight. The sky was pure, flat gold like the background of a medieval picture. It looked very distant – as far off as a cirrhus cloud looks from earth. The ocean was gold too, in the offing, flecked with innumerable shadows. The nearer waves, though golden where their summits caught the light, were green on their slopes: first emerald, and lower down a lustrous bottle green, deepening to blue where they passed beneath the shadow of other waves.

All this he saw in a flash; then he was speeding down once more into the trough. He had somehow turned on his back. He saw the golden roof of that world quivering with a rapid variation of paler lights as a ceiling quivers at the reflected sunlight from the bath-water when you step into your bath on a summer morning. He guessed that this was the reflection of the waves wherein he swam. It is a phenomenon observable three days out of five in the planet of love. The queen of those seas views herself continually in a celestial mirror.

Up again to the crest, and still no sight of land. Something that looked like clouds – or could it be ships? – far away on his left. Then, down, down, down – he thought he would never reach the end of it ... this time he noticed how dim the light was. Such tepid revelry in water – such glorious bathing, as one would have called it on earth, suggested as its natural accompaniment a blazing sun. But here there was no such thing. The water gleamed, the sky burned with gold, but all was rich and dim, and his eyes fed upon it undazzled and unaching. The very names of green and gold, which he used perforce in describing the scene, are too harsh for the tenderness, the muted iridescence, of that warm, maternal, del-icately gorgeous world. It was mild to look upon as evening, warm like summer noon, gentle and winning like early dawn. It was alto-gether pleasurable. He sighed.

There was a wave ahead of him now so high that it was dread-ful. We speak idly in our own world of seas mountain high when they are not much more than mast high. But this was the real thing. If the huge shape had been a hill of land and not of water he might have spent a whole forenoon or longer walking the slope before he reached the summit. It gathered him into itself and hurled him up to that elevation in a matter of seconds. But before he reached the top, he almost cried out in terror. For this wave had not a smooth top like the others. A horrible crest appeared; jagged and billowy and fantastic shapes, unnatural, even unliquid, in appearance, sprouted from the ridge. Rocks? Foam? Beasts? The question hardly had time to flash through his mind before the thing was upon him. Involuntarily he shut his eyes. Then he found himself once more rushing downhill. Whatever it was, it had gone past him. But it had been something. He had been struck in the face. Dabbing with his hands he found no blood. He had been struck by something soft which did him no harm but merely stung like a lash because of the speed at which he met it. He turned round on his back again – already, as he did so, soaring thousands of feet aloft to the high water of the next ridge. Far below him in a vast, momentary valley he saw the thing that had missed him. It was an irregularly shaped object with many curves and re-entrants. It was variegated in colour like a patch-work quilt – flame-colour, ultra-marine, crimson, orange, gamboge and violet. He could not say more about it for the whole glimpse lasted so short a time. Whatever the thing was, it was floating, for it rushed up the slope of the opposite wave and over the summit and out of sight. It sat to the water like a skin, curving as the water curved. It took the wave's shape at the top, so that for a moment half of it was already out of sight beyond the ridge and the other half still lying on the higher slope. It behaved rather like a mat of weeds on a river – a mat of weeds that takes on every contour of the little ripples you make by rowing past it – but on a very different scale. This thing might have been thirty acres or more in area.

Words are slow. You must not lose sight of the fact that his whole life on Venus up till now had lasted less than five minutes. He was not in the least tired, and not yet seriously alarmed as to his power of surviving in such a world. He had confidence in those who had sent him there, and for the meantime the coolness of the water and the freedom of his limbs were still a novelty and a delight; but more than all these was something else at which I have already hinted and which can hardly be put into words – the strange sense of excessive pleasure which seemed somehow to be communicated to him through all his senses at once. I use the word 'excessive' because Ransom himself could only describe it by say-ing that for his first few days on Perelandra he was haunted, not by a feeling of guilt, but by surprise that he had no such feeling. There was an exuberance or prodigality of sweetness about the mere act of living which our race finds it difficult not to associate with forbidden and extravagant actions. Yet it is a violent world too. Hardly had he lost sight of the floating object when his eyes were stabbed by an unendurable light. A grading, blue-to-violet illumination made the golden sky seem dark by comparison and in a moment of time revealed more of the new planet than he had yet seen. He saw the waste of waves spread illimitably before him, and far, far away, at the end of the world, against the sky, a single smooth column of ghastly green standing up, the one thing fixed and vertical in this universe of shining slopes. Then the rich twilight rushed back (now seeming almost darkness) and he heard thunder. But it has a different *timbre* from terrestrial thunder, more resonance, and even, when distant, a kind of tinkling. It is the laugh, rather than the roar, of heaven. Another flash followed, and another, and then the storm was all about him. Enormous purple clouds came driving between him and the golden sky, and with no preliminary drops a rain such as he had never experienced began to fall. There were no lines in it; the water above him seemed only less continuous than the sea, and he found it difficult to breathe. The flashes were incessant. In between them, when he looked in any direction except that of the clouds, he saw a completely changed world. It was like being at the centre of a rainbow, or in a cloud of multi-coloured steam. The water which now filled the air was turning sea and sky into a bedlam of flaming and writhing transparencies. He was dazzled and now for the first time a little frightened. In the flashes he saw, as before, only the endless sea and the still green column at the end of the world. No land anywhere – not the suggestion of a shore from one horizon to the other.

The thunder was ear-splitting and it was difficult to get enough air. All sorts of things seemed to be coming down in the rain – living things apparently. They looked like preternaturally airy and graceful frogs – sublimated frogs – and had the colour of dragonflies, but he was in no plight to make careful observations. He was beginning to feel the first symptoms of exhaustion and was completely confused by the riot of colours in the atmosphere. How long this state of affairs lasted he could not say, but the next thing that he remembers noticing with any accuracy was that the swell was decreasing. He got the impression of being near the end of a range of water-mountains and looking down into lower country. For a long time he never reached this lower country; what had seemed, by comparison with the seas which he had met on his first arrival, to be calm water, always turned out to be only slightly smaller waves when he rushed down into them. There seemed to be a good many of the big floating objects about. And these, again, from some distance looked like an archipelago, but always, as he drew nearer and found the roughness of the water they were riding, they became more like a fleet. But in the end there was no doubt that the swell was subsiding. The rain stopped. The waves were merely of Atlantic height. The rainbow colours grew fainter and more transparent and the golden sky first showed timidly through them and then established itself again from horizon to horizon. The waves grew smaller still. He began to breathe freely. But he was now really tired, and beginning to find leisure to be afraid.

One of the great patches of floating stuff was sidling down a wave not more than a few hundred yards away. He eyed it eagerly, wondering whether he could climb on to one of these things for rest. He strongly suspected that they would prove mere mats of weed, or the topmost branches of submarine forests, incapable of supporting him. But while he thought this, the particular one on which his eyes were fixed crept up a wave and came between him and the sky. It was not flat. From its tawny surface a whole series of feathery and billowy shapes arose, very unequal in height; they looked darkish against the dim glow of the golden roof. Then they all tilted one way as the thing which carried them curled over the crown of the water and dipped out of sight. But here was another, not thirty yards away and bearing down on him. He struck out towards it, noticing as he did so how sore and feeble his arms were and feeling his first thrill of true fear. As he approached it he saw that it ended in a fringe of undoubtedly vegetable matter; it trailed, in fact, a dark red skirt of tubes and strings and bladders. He grabbed at them and found he was not yet near enough. He began swimming desperately, for the thing was gliding past him at some ten miles an hour. He grabbed again and got a handful of whip-like red strings, but they pulled out of his hand and almost cut him. Then he thrust himself right in among them, snatching wildly straight before him. For one second he was in a kind of vegetable broth of gurgling tubes and exploding bladders; next moment his hands caught something firmer ahead, something almost like very soft wood. Then, with the breath nearly knocked out of him and a bruised knee, he found himself lying face downward on a resistant surface. He pulled himself an inch or so farther. Yes – there was no doubt now; one did not go through; it was something one could lie on.

It seems that he must have remained lying on his face, doing nothing and thinking nothing for a very long time. When he next began to take any notice of his surroundings he was, at all events, well rested. His first discovery was that he lay on a dry surface, which on examination turned out to consist of something very like heather, except for the colour which was coppery. Burrowing idly with his fingers he found something friable like dry soil, but very little of it, for almost at once he came upon a base of tough inter-locked fibres. Then he rolled on his back, and in doing so discovered the extreme resilience of the surface on which he lay. It was something much more than the pliancy of the heather-like vegetation, and felt more as if the whole floating island beneath that vegetation were a kind of mattress. He turned and looked 'inland' – if that is the right word – and for one instant what he saw looked very like a country. He was looking up a long lonely valley with a copper-coloured floor bordered on each side by gentle slopes clothed in a kind of many-coloured forest. But even as he took this in, it became a long copper-coloured ridge with the forest sloping *down* on each side of it. Of course he ought to have been prepared for this, but he says that it gave him an almost sickening shock. The thing had looked, in that first glance, so like a real country that he had forgotten it was floating – an island if you like, with hills and valleys, but hills and valleys which changed places every minute so that only a cinematograph could make a contour map of it. And that is the nature of the floating islands of Perelandra. A photograph, omitting the colours and the perpetual variation of shape, would make them look deceptively like landscapes in our own world, but the reality is very different; for they are dry and fruitful like land but their only shape is the inconstant shape of the water beneath them. Yet the land-like appearance proved hard to resist. Although he had now grasped with his brain what was happening, Ransom had not yet grasped it with his muscles and nerves. He rose to take a few paces inland – and downhill, as it was at the moment of his rising – and immediately found himself flung down on his face, unhurt because of the softness of the weed. He scrambled to his feet – saw that he now had a steep slope to ascend – and fell a second time. A blessed relaxation of the strain in which he had been living since his arrival dissolved him into weak laughter. He rolled to and fro on the soft fragrant surface in a real schoolboy fit of the giggles.

This passed. And then for the next hour or two he was teaching himself to walk. It was much harder than getting your sealegs on a ship, for whatever the sea is doing, the deck of the ship remains a plane. But this was like learning to walk on water itself. It took him several hours to get a hundred yards away from the edge, or coast, of the floating island; and he was proud when he could go five paces without a fall, arms outstretched, knees bent in readiness for sudden change of balance, his whole body swaying and tense like that of one who is learning to walk the tight-rope. Perhaps he would have learned more quickly if his falls had not been so soft, if it had not been so pleasant, having fallen, to lie still and gaze at the golden roof and hear the endless soothing noise of the water and breathe in the curiously delightful smell of the herbage. And then, too, it was so strange, after rolling head over heels down into some little dell, to open his eyes and find himself seated on the central mountain peak of the whole island looking down like Robinson Crusoe on field and forest to the shores in every direction, that a man could hardly help sitting there a few minutes longer – and then being detained again because, even as he made to rise, mountain and valley alike had been obliterated and the whole island had become a level plain.

At long last he reached the wooded part. There was an undergrowth of feathery vegetation, about the height of gooseberry bushes, coloured like sea anemones. Above this were the taller growths – strange trees with tube-like trunks of grey and purple spreading rich canopies above his head, in which orange, silver and blue were the predominant colours. Here, with the aid of the tree trunks, he could keep his feet more easily. The smells in the forest were beyond all that he had ever conceived. To say that they made him feel hungry and thirsty would be misleading; almost, they created a new kind of hunger and thirst, a longing that seemed to flow over from the body into the soul and which was a heaven to feel. Again and again he stood still, clinging to some branch to steady himself, and breathed it all in, as if breathing had become a kind of ritual. And at the same time the forest landscape furnished what would have been a dozen landscapes on Earth – now level wood with trees as vertical as towers, now a deep bottom where it was surprising not to find a stream, now a wood growing on a hillside, and now again, a hilltop whence one looked down through slanted boles at the distant sea. Save for the inorganic sound of waves there was utter silence about him. The sense of his solitude became intense without becoming at all painful – only adding, as it were, a last touch of wildness to the unearthly pleasures that surrounded him. If he had any fear now, it was a faint apprehension that his reason might be in danger. There was something in Perelandra that might overload a human brain.

Now he had come to a part of the wood where great globes of yellow fruit hung from the trees – clustered as toy-balloons are clustered on the back of the balloon-man and about the same size. He picked one of them and turned it over and over. The rind was smooth and firm and seemed impossible to tear open. Then by accident one of his fingers punctured it and went through into coldness. After a moment's hesitation he put the little aperture to his lips. He had meant to extract the smallest, experimental sip, but the first taste put his caution all to flight. It was, of course, a taste, just as his thirst and hunger had been thirst and hunger. But then it was so different from every other taste that it seemed mere pedantry to call it a taste at all. It was like the discovery of a totally new genus of pleasures, something unheard of among men, out of all reckoning, beyond all covenant. For one draught of this on Earth wars would be fought and nations betrayed. It could not be classified. He could never tell us, when he came back to the world of men, whether it was sharp or sweet, savoury or voluptuous, creamy or piercing. 'Not like that' was all he could ever say to such inquiries. As he let the empty gourd fall from his hand and was about to pluck a second one, it came into his head that he was now neither hungry nor thirsty. And yet to repeat a pleasure so intense and almost so spiritual seemed an obvious thing to do. His reason, or what we commonly take to be reason in our own world, was all in favour of tasting this miracle again; the child-like innocence of fruit, the labours he had undergone, the uncertainty of the future, all seemed to commend the action. Yet something seemed opposed to this 'reason'. It is difficult to suppose that this opposition came from desire, for what desire would turn from so much deliciousness? But for whatever cause, it appeared to him better not to taste again. Perhaps the experience had been so complete that repetition would be a vulgarity – like asking to hear the same symphony twice in a day.

As he stood pondering over this and wondering how often in his life on Earth he had reiterated pleasures not through desire, but in the teeth of desire and in obedience to a spurious rationalism, he noticed that the light was changing. It was darker behind him than it had been; ahead, the sky and sea shone through the wood with a changed intensity. To step out of the forest would have been a minute's work on Earth; on this undulating island it took him longer, and when he finally emerged into the open an extraordinary spectacle met his eyes. All day there had been no variation at any point in the golden roof to mark the sun's position, but now the whole of one half-heaven revealed it. The orb itself remained invisible, but on the rim of the sea rested an arc of green so luminous that he could not look at it, and beyond that, spreading almost to the zenith, a great fan of colour like a peacock's tail. Looking over his shoulder he saw the whole island ablaze with blue, and across it and beyond it, even to the ends of the world, his own enormous shadow. The sea, far calmer now than he had yet seen it, smoked towards heaven in huge dolomites and elephants of blue and purple vapour, and a light wind, full of sweetness, lifted the hair on his forehead. The day was burning to death. Each moment the waters grew more level; something not far removed from silence began to be felt. He sat down cross-legged on the edge of the island, the desolate lord, it seemed, of this solemnity. For the first time it crossed his mind that he might have been sent to an uninhabited world, and the terror added, as it were, a razor-edge to all that profusion of pleasure.

Once more, a phenomenon which reason might have anticipated took him by surprise. To be naked yet warm, to wander among summer fruits and lie in sweet heather – all this had led him to count on a twilit night, a mild midsummer greyness. But before the great apocalyptic colours had died out in the west, the eastern heaven was black. A few moments, and the blackness had reached the western horizon. A little reddish light lingered at the zenith for a time, during which he crawled back to the woods. It was already, in common parlance, 'too dark to see your way'. But before he had lain down among the trees the real night had come – seamless darkness, not like night but like being in a coal-cellar, darkness in which his own hand held before his face was totally invisible. Absolute blackness, the undimensioned, the impenetrable, pressed on his eye balls. There is no moon in that land, no star pierces the golden roof. But the darkness was warm. Sweet new scents came stealing out of it. The world had no size now. Its boundaries were the length and breadth of his own body and the little patch of soft fragrance which made his hammock, swaying ever more and more gently. Night covered him like a blanket and kept all loneliness from him. The blackness might have been his own room. Sleep came like a fruit which falls into the hand almost before you have touched the stem.

4

At Ransom's waking something happened to him which perhaps never happens to a man until he is out of his own world: he saw reality, and thought it was a dream. He opened his eyes and saw a strange heraldically coloured tree loaded with yellow fruits and silver leaves. Round the base of the indigo stem was coiled a small dragon covered with scales of red gold. He recognised the garden of the Hesperides at once. 'This is the most vivid dream I have ever had,' he thought. By some means or other he then realised that he was awake; but extreme comfort and some trance-like quality, both in the sleep which had just left him and in the experience to which he had awaked, kept him lying motionless. He remembered how in the very different world called Malacandra – that cold, archaic world, as it now seemed to him – he had met the original of the Cyclops, a giant in a cave and a shepherd. Were all the things which appeared as mythology on Earth scattered through other worlds as realities? Then the realisation came to him: 'You are in an unknown planet, naked and alone, and that may be a dangerous animal.' But he was not badly frightened. He knew that the ferocity of terrestrial animals was, by cosmic standards, an exception, and had found kindness in stranger creatures than this. But he lay quiet a little longer and looked at it. It was a creature of the lizard type, about the size of a St Bernard dog, with a serrated back. Its eyes were open.

Presently he ventured to rise on one elbow. The creature went on looking at him. He noticed that the island was perfectly level. He sat up and saw, between the stems of the trees, that they were in calm water. The sea looked like gilded glass. He resumed his study of the dragon. Could this be a rational animal – a *hnau* as they said in Malacandra – and the very thing he had been sent there to meet? It did not look like one, but it was worth trying. Speaking in the Old Solar tongue he formed his first sentence – and his own voice sounded to him unfamiliar.

'Stranger,' he said, 'I have been sent to your world through the Heaven by the servants of Maleldil. Do you give me welcome?'

The thing looked at him very hard and perhaps very wisely. Then, for the first time, it shut its eyes. This seemed an unpromising start. Ransom decided to rise to his feet. The dragon reopened its eyes. He stood looking at it while you could count twenty, very uncertain how to proceed. Then he saw that it was beginning to uncoil itself. By a great effort of will he stood his ground; whether the thing were rational or irrational, flight could hardly help him for long. It detached itself from the tree, gave itself a shake, and opened two shining reptilian wings – bluish gold and bat-like. When it had shaken these and closed them again, it gave Ransom another long stare, and at last, half waddling and half crawling, made its way to the edge of the island and buried its long metallic-looking snout in the water. When it had drunk it raised its head and gave a kind of croaking bleat which was not entirely unmusical. Then it turned, looked yet again at Ransom and finally approached him. 'It's madness to wait for it,' said the false reason, but Ransom set his teeth and stood. It came right up and began nudging him with its cold snout about his knees. He was in great perplexity. Was it rational and was this how it talked? Was it irrational but friendly – and if so, how should he respond? You could hardly stroke a creature with scales! Or was it merely scratching itself against him? At that moment, with a suddenness which convinced him it was only a beast, it seemed to forget all about him, turned away, and began tearing up the herbage with great avidity. Feeling that honour was now satisfied, he also turned away back to the woods.

There were trees near him loaded with the fruit which he had already tasted, but his attention was diverted by a strange appearance a little farther off. Amid the darker foliage of a greenish-grey thicket something seemed to be sparkling. The impression, caught out of the corner of his eye, had been that of a greenhouse roof with the sun on it. Now that he looked at it squarely it still suggested glass, but glass in perpetual motion. Light seemed to be coming and going in a spasmodic fashion. Just as he was moving to investigate this phenomenon he was startled by a touch on his left leg. The beast had followed him. It was once more nosing and nudging. Ransom quickened his pace. So did the dragon. He stopped; so did it. When he went on again it accompanied him so closely that its side pressed against his thighs and sometimes its cold, hard, heavy foot descended on his. The arrangement was so little to his satisfaction that he was beginning to wonder seriously how he could put an end to it when suddenly his whole attention was attracted by something else. Over his head there hung from a hairy tube-like branch a great spherical object, almost transparent, and shining. It held an area of reflected light in it and at one place a suggestion of rainbow colouring. So this was the explanation of the glass-like appearance in the wood. And looking round he perceived innumerable shimmering globes of the same kind in every direction. He began to examine the nearest one attentively. At first he thought it was moving, then he thought it was not. Moved by a natural impulse he put out his hand to touch it. Immediately his head, face and shoulders were drenched with what seemed (in that warm world) an ice-cold shower bath, and his nostrils filled with a sharp, shrill, exquisite scent that somehow brought to his mind the verse in Pope, 'die of a rose in aromatic pain'. Such was the refreshment that he seemed to himself to have been, till now, but half awake. When he opened his eyes – which had closed involuntarily at the shock of moisture – all the colours about him seemed richer and the dimness of that world seemed clarified. A re-enchantment fell upon him. The golden beast at his side seemed no longer either a danger or a nuisance. If a naked man and a wise dragon were indeed the sole inhabitants of this floating paradise, then this also was fitting, for at that moment he had a sensation not of following an adventure but of enacting a myth. To be the figure that he was in this unearthly pattern appeared sufficient.

He turned again to the tree. The thing that had drenched him was quite vanished. The tube or branch, deprived of its pendent globe, now ended in a little quivering orifice from which there hung a bead of crystal moisture. He looked round in some bewilderment. The grove was still full of its iridescent fruit but now he perceived that there was a slow continual movement. A second later he had mastered the phenomenon. Each of the bright spheres was very gradually increasing in size, and each, on reaching a certain dimension, vanished with a faint noise, and in its place there was a momentary dampness on the soil and a soon-fading, delicious fragrance and coldness in the air. In fact, the things were not fruit at all but bubbles. The trees (he christened them at that moment) were bubble trees. Their life, apparently, consisted in drawing up water from the ocean and then expelling it in this form) but enriched by its short sojourn in their sappy inwards. He sat down to feed his eyes upon the spectacle. Now that he knew the secret he could explain to himself why this wood looked and felt so different from every other part of the island. Each bubble, looked at individually, could be seen to emerge from its parent-branch as a mere bead, the size of a pea, and swell and burst; but looking at the wood as a whole, one was conscious only of a continual faint disturbance of light, an elusive interference with the prevailing Perelandrian silence, an unusual coolness in the air, and a fresher quality in the perfume. To a man born in our world it felt a more outdoor place than the open parts of the island, or even the sea. Looking at a fine cluster of the bubbles which hung above his head he thought how easy it would be to get up and plunge oneself through the whole lot of them and to feel, all at once, that magical refreshment multiplied tenfold. But he was restrained by the same sort of feeling which had restrained him over-night from tasting a second gourd. He had always disliked the people who encored a favourite air in an opera – 'That just spoils it' had been his comment. But this now appeared to him as a principle of far wider application and deeper moment. This itch to have things over again, as if life were a film that could be unrolled twice or even made to work backwards ... was it possibly the root of all evil? No: of course the love of money was called that. But money itself – perhaps one valued it chiefly as a defence against chance, a security for being able to have things over again, a means of arresting the unrolling of the film.

He was startled from his meditation by the physical discomfort of some weight on his knees. The dragon had lain down and deposited its long, heavy head across them. 'Do you know,' he said to it in English, 'that you are a considerable nuisance?' It never moved. He decided that he had better try and make friends with it. He stroked the hard dry head, but the creature took no notice. Then his hand passed lower down and found softer surface, or even a chink in the mail. Ah ... that was where it liked being tickled. It grunted and shot out a long cylindrical slate-coloured tongue to lick him. It rolled round on its back revealing an almost white belly, which Ransom kneaded with his toes. His acquaintance with the dragon prospered exceedingly. In the end it went to sleep.

He rose and got a second shower from a bubble tree. This made him feel so fresh and alert that he began to think of food. He had forgotten whereabouts on the island the yellow gourds were to be found, and as he set out to look for them he discovered that it was difficult to walk. For a moment he wondered whether the liquid in the bubbles had some intoxicating quality, but a glance around assured him of the real reason. The plain of copper-coloured heather before him, even as he watched, swelled into a low hill and the low hill moved in his direction. Spellbound anew at the sight of land rolling towards him, like water, in a wave, he forgot to adjust himself to the movement and lost his feet. Picking himself up, he proceeded more carefully. This time there was no doubt about it. The sea was rising. Where two neighbouring woods made a vista to the edge of this living raft he could see troubled water, and the warm wind was now strong enough to ruffle his hair. He made his way gingerly towards the coast, but before he reached it he passed some bushes which carried a rich crop of oval green berries, about three times the size of almonds. He picked one and broke it in two. The flesh was dryish and bread-like, something of the same kind as a banana. It turned out to be good to eat. It did not give the orgiastic and almost alarming pleasure of the gourds, but rather the specific pleasure of plain food – the delight of munching and being nourished, a 'Sober certainty of waking bliss'. A man, or at least a man like Ransom, felt he ought to say grace over it; and so he presently did. The gourds would have required rather an oratorio or a mystical meditation. But the meal had its unexpected highlights. Every now and then one struck a berry which had a bright red centre: and these were so savoury, so memorable among a thousand tastes, that he would have begun to look for them and to feed on them only, but that he was once more forbidden by that same inner adviser which had already spoken to him twice since he came to Perelandra. 'Now on earth,' thought Ransom, 'they'd soon discover how to breed these redhearts, and they'd cost a great deal more than the others.' Money, in fact, would provide the means of saying *encore* in a voice that could not be disobeyed.

When he had finished his meal he went down to the water's edge to drink, but before he arrived there it was already 'up' to the water's edge. The island at that moment was a little valley of bright land nestling between hills of green water, and as he lay on his belly to drink he had the extraordinary experience of dipping his mouth in a sea that was higher than the shore. Then he sat upright for a bit with his legs dangling over the edge among the red weeds that fringed this little country. His solitude became a more persistent element in his consciousness. What had he been brought here to do? A wild fancy came into his head that this empty world had been waiting for him as for its first inhabitant, that he was singled out to be the founder, the beginner. It was strange that the utter loneliness through all these hours had not troubled him so much as one night of it on Malacandra. He thought the difference lay in this, that mere chance, or what he took for chance, had turned him adrift in Mars, but here he knew that he was part of a plan. He was no longer unattached, no longer on the outside.

As his country climbed the smooth mountains of dimly lustrous water he had frequent opportunity to see that many other islands were close at hand. They varied from his own island and from one another in their colouring more than he would have thought possible. It was a wonder to see these big mats or carpets of land tossing all around him like yachts in harbour on a rough day – their trees each moment at a different angle just as the masts of the yachts would be. It was a wonder to see some edge of vivid green or velvety crimson come creeping over the top of a wave far above him and then wait till the whole country unrolled itself down the wave's side for him to study. Sometimes his own land and a neighbouring land would be on opposite slopes of a trough, with only a narrow strait of water between them; and then, for the moment, you were cheated with the semblance of a terrestrial landscape. It looked exactly as though you were in a well-wooded valley with a river at the bottom of it. But while you watched, that seeming river did the impossible. It thrust itself up so that the land on either side sloped downwards from it; and then up farther still and shouldered half the landscape out of sight beyond its ridge; and became a huge greeny-gold hog's back of water hanging in the sky and threatening to engulf your own land, which now was concave and reeled backwards to the next roller, and rushing upwards, became convex again.

A clanging, whirring noise startled him. For a moment he fancied he was in Europe and that a plane was flying low over his head. Then he recognised his friend the dragon. Its tail was streaked out straight behind it so that it looked like a flying worm, and it was heading for an island about half a mile away. Following its course with his eyes, he saw two long lines of winged objects, dark against the gold firmament, approaching the same island from the left and right. But they were not batwinged reptiles. Peering hard into the distance, he decided that they were birds, and a musical chattering noise, presently wafted to him by a change of the wind, confirmed this belief. They must have been a little larger than swans. Their steady approach to the same island for which the dragon was heading fixed his attention and filled him with a vague feeling of expectation. What followed next raised this to positive excitement. He became aware of some creamily foamed disturbance in the water, much nearer, and making for the same island. A whole fleet of objects was moving in formation. He rose to his feet. Then the lift of a wave cut them off from his sight. Next moment they were visible again, hundreds of feet below him. Silver-coloured objects, all alive with circling and frisking movements ... he lost them again, and swore. In such a very uneventful world they had become important. Ah ...! here they were again. Fish certainly. Very large, obese, dolphin-like fish, two long lines together, some of them spouting columns of rainbow-coloured water from their noses, and one leader. There was something queer about the leader, some sort of projection or malformation on the back. If only the things would remain visible for more than fifty seconds at a time. They had almost reached that other island now, and the birds were all descending to meet them at its edge. There was the leader again, with his hump or pillar on his back. A moment of wild incredulity followed, and then Ransom was balanced, with legs wide apart, on the utmost fringe of his own island and shouting for all he was worth. For at the very moment when the leading fish had reached that neighbouring land, the land had risen up on a wave between him and the sky; and he had seen, in perfect and unmistakable silhouette, the thing on the fish's back reveal itself as a human form – a human form which stepped ashore, turned with a slight inclination of its body towards the fish and then vanished from sight as the whole island slid over the shoulder of the billow. With beating heart Ransom waited till it was in view again. This time it was not between him and the sky. For a second or so the human figure was undiscoverable. A stab of something like despair pierced him. Then he picked it out again – a tiny darkish shape moving slowly between him and a patch of blue vegetation. He waved and gesticulated and shouted till his throat was hoarse, but it took no notice of him. Every now and then he lost sight of it. Even when he found it again, he sometimes doubted whether it were not an optical illusion – some chance figuration of foliage which his intense desire had assimilated to the shape of a man. But always, just before he had despaired, it would become unmistakable again. Then his eyes began to grow tired and he knew that the longer he looked the less he would see. But he went on looking none the less.

At last, from mere exhaustion, he sat down. The solitude, which up till now had been scarcely painful, had become a horror. Any return to it was a possibility he dared not face. The drugging and entrancing beauty had vanished from his surroundings; take that one human form away and all the rest of this world was now pure nightmare, a horrible cell or trap in which he was imprisoned. The suspicion that he was beginning to suffer from hallucinations crossed his mind. He had a picture of living for ever and ever on this hideous island, always really alone but always haunted by the phantoms of human beings, who would come up to him with smiles and outstretched hands, and then fade away as he approached them. Bowing his head on his knees, he set his teeth and endeavoured to restore some order in his mind. At first he found he was merely listening to his own breathing and counting the beats of his heart; but he tried again and presently succeeded. And then, like revelation, came the very simple idea that if he wished to attract the attention of this man-like creature he must wait till he was on the crest of a wave and then stand up so that it would see him outlined against the sky.

Three times he waited till the shore whereon he stood became a ridge, and rose, swaying to the movement of his strange country, gesticulating. The fourth time he succeeded. The neighbouring island was, of course, lying for the moment beneath him like a valley. Quite unmistakably the small dark figure waved back. It detached itself from a confusing background of greenish vegetation and began running towards him – that is, towards the nearer coast of its own island – across an orange-coloured field. It ran easily:

the heaving surface of the field did not seem to trouble it. Then his own land reeled downwards and backwards and a great wall of water pushed its way up between the two countries and cut each off from sight of the other. A moment later, and Ransom, from the valley in which he now stood, saw the orange-coloured land pouring itself like a moving hillside down the slightly convex slope of a wave far above him. The creature was still running. The width of water between the two islands was about thirty feet, and the creature was less than a hundred yards away from him. He knew now that it was not merely man-like, but a man – a green man on an orange field, green like the beautifully coloured green beetle in an English garden, running downhill towards him with easy strides and very swiftly. Then the seas lifted his own land and the green man became a foreshortened figure far below him, like an actor seen from the gallery at Covent Garden. Ransom stood on the very brink of his island, straining his body forward and shouting. The green man looked up. He was apparently shouting too, with his hands arched about his mouth; but the roar of the seas smothered the noise and the next moment Ransom's island dropped into the trough of the wave and the high green ridge of sea cut off his view. It was maddening. He was tortured with the fear that the distance between the islands might be increasing. Thank God: here came the orange land over the crest following him down into the pit. And there was the stranger, now on the very shore, face to face with him. For one second the alien eyes looked at his full of love and welcome. Then the whole face changed: a shock as of disappointment and astonishment passed over it. Ransom realised, not without a disappointment of his own, that he had been mistaken for someone else. The running, the waving, the shouts, had not been intended for him. And the green man was not a man at all, but a woman.

It is difficult to say why this surprised him so. Granted the human form, he was presumably as likely to meet a female as a male. But it did surprise him, so that only when the two islands once more began to fall apart into separate wave-valleys did he realise that he had said nothing to her, but stood staring like a fool. And now that she was out of sight he found his brain on fire with doubts. Was this what he had been sent to meet? He had been expecting wonders, had been prepared for wonders, but not prepared for a goddess carved apparently out of green stone, yet alive. And then it flashed across his mind – he had not noticed it while the scene was before him – that she had been strangely accompanied. She had stood up amidst a throng of beasts and birds as a tall sapling stands among bushes – big pigeon-coloured birds and flame-coloured birds, and dragons, and beaver-like creatures about the size of rats, and heraldic-looking fish in the sea at her feet. Or had he imagined that? Was this the beginning of the hallucinations he had feared? Or another myth coming out into the world of fact – perhaps a more terrible myth, of Circe or Alcina? And the expression on her … what had she expected to find that made the finding of him such a disappointment?

The other island became visible again. He had been right about the animals. They surrounded her ten or twenty deep, all facing her, most of them motionless, but some of them finding their places, as at a ceremony, with delicate noiseless movements. The birds were in long lines and more of them seemed to be alighting on the island every moment and joining these lines. From a wood of bubble trees behind her half a dozen creatures like very short-legged and elongated pigs – the dachshunds of the pig world – were waddling up to join the assembly. Tiny frog-like beasts, like those he had seen falling in the rain, kept leaping about her, sometimes higher than her head, sometimes alighting on her shoulders; their colours were so vivid that at first he mistook them for kingfishers. Amidst all this she stood looking at him; her feet together, her arms hanging at her sides, her stare level and unafraid, communicating nothing. Ransom determined to speak, using the Old Solar tongue. 'I am from another world,' he began and then stopped. The Green Lady had done something for which he was quite unprepared. She raised her arm and pointed at him: not as in menace, but as though inviting the other creatures to behold him. At the same moment her face changed again, and for a second he thought she was going to cry. Instead she burst into laughter – peal upon peal of laughter till her whole body shook with it, till she bent almost double, with her hands resting on her knees, still laughing and repeatedly pointing at him. The animals, like our own dogs in similar circumstances, dimly understood that there was merriment afoot; all manner of gambolling, wing-clapping, snorting, and standing upon hind legs began to be displayed. And still the Green Lady laughed till yet again the wave divided them and she was out of sight.

Ransom was thunderstruck. Had the *eldila* sent him to meet an idiot? Or an evil spirit that mocked him? Or was it after all a hallucination? – for this was just how a hallucination might be expected to behave. Then an idea occurred to him which would have taken much longer, perhaps, to occur to me or you. It might not be she who was mad but he who was ridiculous. He glanced down at himself. Certainly his legs presented an odd spectacle, for one was brownish-red (like the flanks of a Titian satyr) and the other was white – by comparison, almost a leprous white. As far as self-inspection could go, he had the same parti-coloured appearance all over – no unnatural result of his one-sided exposure to the sun during the voyage. Had this been the joke? He felt a momentary impatience with the creature who could mar the meeting of two worlds with laughter at such a triviality. Then he smiled in spite of himself at the very undistinguished career he was having on Perelandra. For dangers he had been prepared; but to be first a disappointment and then an absurdity ... Hullo! Here were the Lady and her island in sight again.

She had recovered from her laughter and sat with her legs trailing in the sea, half unconsciously caressing a gazelle-like creature which had thrust its soft nose under her arm. It was difficult to believe that she had ever laughed, ever done anything but sit on the shore of her floating isle. Never had Ransom seen a face so calm, and so unearthly, despite the full humanity of every feature. He decided afterwards that the unearthly quality was due to the complete absence of that element of resignation which mixes, in however slight a degree, with all profound stillness in terrestrial faces. This was a calm which no storm had ever preceded. It might be idiocy, it might be immortality, it might be some condition of mind to which terrestrial experience offered no due at all. A curious and rather horrifying sensation crept over him. On the ancient planet Malacandra he had met creatures who were not even remotely human in form but who had turned out, on further acquaintance, to be rational and friendly. Under an alien exterior he had discovered a heart like his own. Was he now to have the reverse experience? For now he realised that the word 'human' refers to something more than the bodily form or even to the rational mind. It refers also to that community of blood and experience which unites all men and women on the Earth. But this creature was not of his race; no windings, however intricate, of any genealogical tree could ever establish a connection between himself and her. In that sense, not one drop in her veins was 'human'. The universe had produced her species and his quite independently.

All this passed through his mind very quickly, and was speedily interrupted by his consciousness that the light was changing. At first he thought that the green Creature had, of herself, begun to turn bluish and to shine with a strange electric radiance. Then he noticed that the whole landscape was a blaze of blue and purple – and almost at the same time that the two islands were not so close together as they had been. He glanced at the sky. The many-coloured furnace of the shortlived evening was kindled all about him. In a few minutes it would be pitch black ... and the islands were drifting apart. Speaking slowly in that ancient language, he cried out to her, 'I am a stranger. I come in peace. Is it your will that I swim over to your land?'

The Green Lady looked quickly at him with an expression of curiosity.

'What is "peace"?' she asked.

Ransom could have danced with impatience. Already it was visibly darker and there was no doubt now that the distance between the islands was increasing. Just as he was about to speak again a wave rose between them and once more she was out of sight; and as that wave hung above him, shining purple in the light of the sunset, he noticed how dark the sky beyond it had become. It was already through a kind of twilight that he looked down from the next ridge upon the other island far below him. He flung himself into the water. For some seconds he found a difficulty in getting clear of the shore. Then he seemed to succeed and struck out. Almost at once he found himself back again among the red weeds and bladders. A moment or two of violent struggling followed and then he was free – and swimming steadily – and then, almost without warning, swimming in total darkness. He swam on, but despair of finding the other land, or even of saving his life, now gripped him. The perpetual change of the great swell abolished all sense of direction. It could only be by chance that he would land anywhere. Indeed, he judged from the time he had already been in the water that he must have been swimming *along* the space between the islands instead of across it. He tried to alter his course; then doubted the wisdom of this, tried to return to his original course, and became so confused that he could not be sure he had done either. He kept on telling himself that he must keep his head. He was beginning to be tired. He gave up all attempts to guide himself. Suddenly, a long time after, he felt vegetation sliding past him. He gripped and pulled. Delicious smells of fruit and flowers came to him out of the darkness. He pulled harder still on his aching arms. Finally he found himself, safe and panting, on the dry, sweet-scented, undulating surface of an island.

5

Ransom must have fallen asleep almost as soon as he landed, for he remembered nothing more till what seemed the song of a bird broke in upon his dreams. Opening his eyes, he saw that it was a bird indeed, a long-legged bird like a very small stork, singing rather like a canary. Full daylight – or what passes for such in Perelandra – was all about him, and in his heart such a premonition of good adventure as made him sit up forthwith and brought him, a moment later, to his feet. He stretched his arms and looked around. He was not on the orange-coloured island, but on the same island which had been his home ever since he came to this planet. He was floating in a dead calm and therefore had no difficulty in making his way to the shore. And there he stopped in astonishment. The Lady's island was floating beside his, divided only by five feet or so of water. The whole look of the world had changed. There was no expanse of sea now visible – only a flat wooded landscape as far as the eye could reach in every direction. Some ten or twelve of the islands, in fact, were here lying together and making a short-lived continent. And there walking before him, as if on the other side of a brook, was the Lady herself – walking with her head a little bowed and her hands occupied in plaiting together some blue flowers. She was singing to herself in a low voice but stopped and turned as he hailed her and looked him full in the face.

'I was young yesterday,' she began, but he did not hear the rest of her speech. The meeting, now that it had actually come about, proved overwhelming. You must not misunderstand the story at this point. What overwhelmed him was not in the least the fact that she, like himself, was totally naked. Embarrassment and desire were both a thousand miles away from his experience: and if he was a little ashamed of his own body, that was a shame which had nothing to do with difference of sex and turned only on the fact that he knew his body to be a little ugly and a little ridiculous. Still less was her colour a source of horror to him. In her own world that green was beautiful and fitting; it was his pasty white and angry sunburn which were the monstrosity. It was neither of these; but he found himself unnerved. He had to ask her presently to repeat what she had been saying.

'I was young yesterday,' she said. 'When I laughed at you. Now I know that the people in your world do not like to be laughed at.'

'You say you were young?'

'Yes.'

'Are you not young today also?'

She appeared to be thinking for a few moments, so intently that the flowers dropped, unregarded, from her hand.

'I see it now,' she said presently. 'It is very strange to say one is young at the moment one is speaking. But tomorrow I shall be older. And then I shall say I was young today. You are quite right. This is great wisdom you are bringing, O Piebald Man.'

'What do you mean?'

'This looking backward and forward along the line and seeing how a day has one appearance as it comes to you, and another when you are in it, and a third when it has gone past. Like the waves.'

'But you are very little older than yesterday.'

'How do you know that?'

'I mean,' said Ransom, 'a night is not a very long time.'

She thought again, and then spoke suddenly, her face lightening. 'I see it now,' she said. 'You think times have lengths. A night is always a night whatever you do in it, as from this tree to that is always so many paces whether you take them quickly or slowly. I suppose that is true in a way. But the waves do not always come at equal distances. I see that you come from a wise world ... if this is wise. I have never done it before – stepping out of life into the Alongside and looking at oneself living as if one were not alive. Do they all do that in your world, Piebald?'

'What do you know about other worlds?' said Ransom.

'I know this. Beyond the roof it is all deep heaven, the high place. And the low is not really spread out as it seems to be' (here she indicated the whole landscape) 'but is rolled up into little balls: little lumps of the low swimming in the high. And the oldest and greatest of them have on them that which we have never seen nor heard and cannot at all understand. But on the younger Maleldil has made to grow the things like us, that breathe and breed.'

'How have you found all this out? Your roof is so dense that your people cannot see through into Deep Heaven and look at the other worlds.'

Up till now her face had been grave. At this point she clapped her hands and a smile such as Ransom had never seen changed her. One does not see that smile here except in children, but there was nothing of the child about it there.

'Oh, I see it,' she said. 'I am older now. Your world has no roof. You look right out into the high place and see the great dance with your own eyes. You live always in that terror and that delight, and what we must only believe you can behold. Is not this a wonderful invention of Maleldil's? When I was young I could imagine no beauty but this of our own world. But He can think of all, and all different.'

'That is one of the things that is bewildering me,' said Ransom. 'That you are not different. You are shaped like the women of my own kind. I had not expected that. I have been in one other world beside my own. But the creatures there are not at all like you and me.'

'What is bewildering about it?'

'I do not see why different worlds should bring forth like creatures. Do different trees bring forth like fruit?'

'But that other world was older than yours,' she said.

'How do you know that?' asked Ransom in amazement.

'Maleldil is telling me,' answered the woman. And as she spoke the landscape had become different, though with a difference none of the senses would identify. The light was dim, the air gentle, and all Ransom's body was bathed in bliss, but the garden world where he stood seemed to be packed quite full, and as if an unendurable pressure had been laid upon his shoulders, his legs failed him and he half sank, half fell, into a sitting position.

'It all comes into my mind now,' she continued. 'I see the big furry creatures, and the white giants – what is it you called them? – the *sorns*, and the blue rivers. Oh, what a strong pleasure it would be to see, them with my outward eyes, to touch them, and the stronger because there are no more of that kind to come. It is only in the ancient worlds they linger yet.'

'Why?' said Ransom in a whisper, looking up at her.

'You must know that better than I,' she said. 'For was it not in your own world that all this happened?'

'All what?'

'I thought it would be you who would tell me of it,' said the woman, now in her turn bewildered.

'What are you talking about?' said Ransom.

'I mean,' said she, 'that in your world Maleldil first took Himself this form, the form of your race and mine.'

'You know that?' said Ransom sharply. Those who have had a dream which is very beautiful but from which, nevertheless, they have ardently desired to awake, will understand his sensations.

'Yes, I know that. Maleldil has made me older to that amount since we began speaking.' The expression on her face was such as he had never seen, and could not steadily look at. The whole of this adventure seemed to be slipping out of his hands. There was a long silence. He stooped down to the water and drank before he spoke again.

'Oh, my Lady,' he said, 'why do you say that such creatures linger only in the ancient worlds?'

'Are you so young?' she answered. 'How could they come again? Since our Beloved became a man, how should Reason in any world take on another form? Do you not understand? That is all over. Among times there is a time that turns a corner and everything this side of it is new. Times do not go backward.'

'And can one little world like mine be the corner?'

'I do not understand. Corner with us is not the name of a size.'

'And do you,' said Ransom with some hesitation – 'and do you know *why* He came thus to my world?'

All through this part of the conversation he found it difficult to look higher than her feet, so that her answer was merely a voice in the air above him. 'Yes,' said the voice. 'I know the reason. But it is not the reason you know. There was more than one reason, and there is one I know and cannot tell to you, and another that you know and cannot tell to me.'

'And after this,' said Ransom, 'it will all be men.'

'You say it as if you were sorry.'

'I think,' said Ransom, 'I have no more understanding than a beast. I do not well know what I am saying. But I loved the furry people whom I met in Malacandra, that old world. Are they to be swept away? Are they only rubbish in the Deep Heaven?'

'I do not know what *rubbish* means,' she answered, 'nor what you are saying. You do not mean they are worse because they come early in the history and do not come again? They are their own part of the history and not another. We are on this side of the wave and they on the far side. All is new.'

One of Ransom's difficulties was an inability to be quite sure who was speaking at any moment in this conversation. It may (or may not) have been due to the fact that he could not look long at her face. And now he wanted the conversation to end. He had 'had enough' – not in the half-comic sense whereby we use those words to mean that a man has had too much, but in the plain sense. He had had his fill, like a man who has slept or eaten enough. Even an hour ago, he would have found it difficult to express this quite bluntly; but now it came naturally to him to say:

'I do not wish to talk any more. But I would like to come over to your island so that we may meet again when we wish.'

'Which do you call my island?' said the Lady.

'The one you are on,' said Ransom. 'What else?'

'Come,' she said, with a gesture that made that whole world a house and her a hostess. He slid into the water and scrambled out beside her. Then he bowed, a little clumsily as all modern men do, and walked away from her into a neighbouring wood. He found his legs unsteady and they ached a little; in fact a curious physical exhaustion possessed him. He sat down to rest for a few minutes and fell immediately into dreamless sleep.

He awoke completely refreshed but with a sense of insecurity. This had nothing to do with the fact that he found himself, on waking, strangely attended. At his feet, and with its snout partially resting upon them, lay the dragon; it had one eye shut and one open. As he rose on his elbow and looked about him he found that he had another custodian at his head: a furred animal something like a wallaby but yellow. It was the yellowest thing he had ever seen. As soon as he moved both beasts began nudging him. They would not leave him alone till he rose, and when he had risen they would not let him walk in any direction but one. The dragon was much too heavy for him to shove it out of the way, and the yellow beast danced round him in a fashion that headed him off from every direction but the one it wanted him to go. He yielded to their pressure and allowed himself to be shepherded, first through a wood of higher and browner trees than he had yet seen and then across a small open space and into a kind of alley of bubble trees and beyond that into large fields of silver flowers that grew waist-high. And then he saw that they had been bringing him to be shown to their mistress. She was standing a few yards away, motionless but not apparently disengaged – doing something with her mind, perhaps even with her muscles, that he did not understand. It was the first time he had looked steadily at her, himself unobserved, and she seemed more strange to him than before. There was no category in the terrestrial mind which would fit her. Opposites met in her and were fused in a fashion for which we have no images. One way of putting it would be to say that neither our sacred nor our profane art could make her portrait. Beautiful, naked, shameless, young – she was obviously a goddess: but then the face, the face so calm that it escaped insipidity by the very concentration of its mildness, the face that was like the sudden coldness and stillness of a church when we enter it from a hot street – that made her a Madonna. The alert, inner silence which looked out from those eyes overawed him; yet at any moment she might laugh like a child, or run like Artemis or dance like a Maenad. All this against the golden sky which looked as if it were only an arm's length above her head. The beasts raced forward to greet her, and as they rushed through the feathery vegetation they startled from it masses of the frogs, so that it looked as if huge drops of vividly coloured dew were being tossed in the air. She turned as they approached her and welcomed them, and once again the picture was half like many earthly scenes but in its total effect unlike them all. It was not really like a woman making much of a horse, nor yet a child playing with a puppy. There was in her face an authority, in her caresses a condescension, which by taking seriously the inferiority of her adorers made them somehow less inferior – raised them from the status of pets to that of slaves. As Ransom reached her she stooped and whispered something in the ear of the yellow creature, and then, addressing the dragon, bleated to it almost in its own voice. Both of them, having received their *congé*, darted back into the woods.

'The beasts in your world seem almost rational,' said Ransom.

'We make them older every day,' she answered. 'Is not that what it means to be a beast?'

But Ransom clung to her use of the word *we*.

'That is what I have come to speak to you about,' he said. 'Maleldil has sent me to your world for some purpose. Do you know what it is?'

She stood for a moment almost like one listening and then answered 'No.'

'Then you must take me to your home and show me to your people.'

'People? I do not know what you are saying.'

'Your kindred – the others of your kind.'

'Do you mean the King?'

'Yes. If you have a King, I had better be brought before him.'

'I cannot do that,' she answered. 'I do not know where to find him.'

'To your own home then.'

'What is *home*?'

'The place where people live together and have their possessions and bring up their children.'

She spread out her hands to indicate all that was in sight. 'This is my home,' she said.

'Do you live here alone?' asked Ransom.

'What is *alone*?'

Ransom tried a fresh start. 'Bring me where I shall meet others of our kind.'

'If you mean the King, I have already told you I do not know where he is. When we were young – many days ago – we were leaping from island to island, and when he was on one and I was on another the waves rose and we were driven apart.'

'But can you take me to some other of your kind? The King cannot be the only one.'

'He is the only one. Did you not know?'

'But there must be others of your kind – your brothers and sisters, your kindred, your friends.'

'I do not know what these words mean.'

'Who is this King?' said Ransom in desperation.

'He is himself, he is the King,' said she. 'How can one answer such a question?'

'Look here,' said Ransom. 'You must have had a mother. Is she alive? Where is she? When did you see her last?'

'I have a mother?' said the Green Lady, looking full at him with eyes of untroubled wonder. 'What do you mean? I am the Mother.' And once again there fell upon Ransom the feeling that it was not she, or not she only, who had spoken. No other sound came to his ears, for the sea and the air were still, but a phantom sense of vast choral music was all about him. The awe which her apparently witless replies had been dissipating for the last few minutes returned upon him.

'I do not understand,' he said.

'Nor I,' answered the Lady. 'Only my spirit praises Maleldil who comes down from Deep Heaven into this lowness and will make me to be blessed by all the times that are rolling towards us. It is He who is strong and makes me strong and fills empty worlds with good creatures.'

'If you are a mother, where are your children?'

'Not yet,' she answered.

'Who will be their father?'

'The King – who else?'

'But the King – had he no father?'

'He *is* the Father.'

'You mean,' said Ransom slowly, 'that you and he are the only two of your kind in the whole world?'

'Of course.' Then presently her face changed. 'Oh, how young I have been,' she said. 'I see it now. I had known that there were many creatures in that ancient world of the *hrossa* and the *sorns*. But I had forgotten that yours also was an older world than ours. I see – there are many of you by now. I had been thinking that of you also there were only two. I thought you were the King and Father of your world. But there are children of children of children by now, and you perhaps are one of these.'

'Yes,' said Ransom.

'Greet your Lady and Mother well from me when you return to your own world,' said the Green Woman. And now for the first time there was a note of deliberate courtesy, even of ceremony, in her speech. Ransom understood. She knew now at last that she was not addressing an equal. She was a queen sending a message to a queen through a commoner, and her manner to him was henceforward more gracious. He found it difficult to make his next answer.

'Our Mother and Lady is dead,' he said.

'What is *dead*?'

'With us they go away after a time. Maleldil takes the soul out of them and puts it somewhere else – in Deep Heaven, we hope. They call it death.'

'Do not wonder, O Piebald Man, that your world should have been chosen for time's corner. You live looking out always on heaven itself, and as if this were not enough Maleldil takes you all thither in the end. You are favoured beyond all worlds.'

Ransom shook his head. 'No. It is not like that,' he said.

'I wonder,' said the woman, 'if you were sent here to teach us *death*.'

'You don't understand,' he said. 'It is not like that. It is horrible. It has a foul smell. Maleldil Himself wept when He saw it.' Both his voice and his facial expression were apparently something new to her. He saw the shock, not of horror, but of utter bewilderment, on her face for one instant and then, without effort, the ocean of her peace swallowed it up as if it had never been, and she asked him what he meant.

'You could never understand, Lady,' he replied. 'But in our world not all events are pleasing or welcome. There may be such a thing that you could cut off both your arms and your legs to prevent it happening – and yet it happens: with us.'

'But how can one wish any of those waves not to reach us which Maleldil is rolling towards us?'

Against his better judgment Ransom found himself goaded into argument.

'But even you,' he said, 'when you first saw me, I know now you were expecting and hoping that I was the King. When you found I was not, your face changed. Was that event not unwelcome? Did you not wish it to be otherwise?'

'Oh,' said the Lady. She turned aside with her head bowed and her hands clasped in an intensity of thought. She looked up and said, 'You make me grow older more quickly than I can bear,' and walked a little farther off. Ransom wondered what he had done. It was suddenly borne in upon him that her purity and peace were not, as they had seemed, things settled and inevitable like the purity and peace of an animal – that they were alive and therefore breakable, a balance maintained by a mind and therefore, at least in theory, able to be lost. There is no reason why a man on a smooth road should lose his balance on a bicycle; but he could. There was no reason why she should step out of her happiness into the psychology of our own race; but neither was there any wall between to prevent her doing so. The sense of precariousness terrified him: but when she looked at him again he changed that word to Adventure, and then all words died out of his mind. Once more he could not look steadily at her. He knew now what the old painters were trying to represent when they invented the halo. Gaiety and gravity together, a splendour as of martyrdom yet with no pain in it at all, seemed to pour from her countenance. Yet when she spoke her words were a disappointment.

'I have been so young till this moment that all my life now seems to have been a kind of sleep. I have thought that I was being carried, and behold, I was walking.'

Ransom asked what she meant.

'What you have made me see,' answered the Lady, 'is as plain as the sky, but I never saw it before. Yet it has happened every day. One goes into the forest to pick food and already the thought of one fruit rather than another has grown up in one's mind. Then, it may be, one finds a different fruit and not the fruit one thought of. One joy was expected and another is given. But this I had never noticed before that at the very moment of the finding there is in the mind a kind of thrusting back, or a setting aside. The picture of the fruit you have not found is still, for a moment, before you. And if you wished – if it were possible to wish – you could keep it there. You could send your soul after the good you had expected, instead of turning it to the good you had got. You could refuse the real good; you could make the real fruit taste insipid by thinking of the other.'

Ransom interrupted. 'That is hardly the same thing as finding a stranger when you wanted your husband.'

'Oh, that is how I came to understand the whole thing. You and the King differ more than two kinds of fruit. The joy of finding him again and the joy of all the new knowledge I have had from you are more unlike than two tastes; and when the difference is as great as that, and each of the two things so great, then the first picture does stay in the mind quite a long time – many beats of the heart – after the other good has come. And this, O Piebald, is the glory and wonder you have made me see; that it is I, I myself, who turn from the good expected to the given good. Out of my own heart I do it. One can conceive a heart which did not: which clung to the good it had first thought of and turned the good which was given it into no good.'

'I don't see the wonder and the glory of it,' said Ransom.

Her eyes flashed upon him such a triumphant flight above his thoughts as would have been scorn in earthly eyes; but in that world it was not scorn.

'I thought,' she said, 'that I was carried in the will of Him I love, but now I see that I walk with it. I thought that the good things He sent me drew me into them as the waves lift the islands; but now I see that it is I who plunge into them with my own legs and arms, as when we go swimming. I feel as if I were living in that roofless world of yours when men walk undefended beneath naked heaven. It is delight with terror in it! One's own self to be walking from one good to another, walking beside Him as Himself may walk, not even holding hands. How has He made me so separate from Himself? How did it enter His mind to conceive such a thing? The world is so much larger than I thought. I thought we went along paths – but it seems there are no paths. The going itself is the path.'

'And have you no fear,' said Ransom, 'that it will ever be hard to turn your heart from the thing you wanted to the thing Maleldil sends?'

'I see,' said the Lady presently. 'The wave you plunge into may be very swift and great. You may need all your force to swim into it. You mean, He might send me a good like that?'

'Yes – or like a wave so swift and great that all your force was too little.'

'It often happens that way in swimming,' said the Lady. 'Is not that part of the delight?'

'But are you happy without the King? Do you not want the King?'

'Want him?' she said. 'How could there be anything I did not want?'

There was something in her replies that began to repel Ransom. 'You can't want him very much if you are happy without him,' he said: and was immediately surprised at the sulkiness of his own voice.

'Why?' said the Lady. 'And why, O Piebald, are you making little hills and valleys in your forehead and why do you give a little lift of your shoulders? Are these the signs of something in your world?'

'They mean nothing,' said Ransom hastily. It was a small lie; but there it would not do. It tore him as he uttered it, like a vomit. It became of infinite importance. The silver meadow and the golden sky seemed to fling it back at him. As if stunned by some measureless anger in the very air he stammered an emendation: 'They mean nothing I could explain to you.' The Lady was looking at him with a new and more judicial expression. Perhaps in the presence of the first mother's son she had ever seen, she was already dimly forecasting the problems that might arise when she had children of her own.

'We have talked enough now,' she said at last. At first he thought she was going to turn away and leave him. Then, when she did not move, he bowed and drew back a step or two. She still said nothing and seemed to have forgotten about him. He turned and retraced his way through the deep vegetation until they were out of sight of each other. The audience was at an end.

6

As soon as the Lady was out of sight Ransom's first impulse was to run his hands through his hair, to expel the breath from his lungs in a long whistle, to light a cigarette, to put his hands in his pockets, and in general, to go through all that ritual of relaxation which a man performs on finding himself alone after a rather trying interview. But he had no cigarettes and no pockets: nor indeed did he feel himself alone. That sense of being in Someone's Presence which had descended on him with such unbearable pressure during the very first moments of his conversation with the Lady did not disappear when he had left her. It was, if anything, increased. Her society had been, in some degree, a protection against it, and her absence left him not to solitude but to a more formidable kind of privacy. At first it was almost intolerable; as he put it to us, in telling the story, 'There seemed no room.' But later on, he discovered that it was intolerable only at certain moments – at just those moments in fact (symbolised by his impulse to smoke and to put his hands in his pockets) when a man asserts his independence and feels that now at last he's on his own. When you felt like that, then the very air seemed too crowded to breathe; a complete fulness seemed to be excluding you from a place which, nevertheless, you were unable to leave. But when you gave in to the thing, gave yourself up to it, there was no burden to be borne. It became not a load but a medium, a sort of splendour as of eatable, drinkable, breathable gold, which fed and carried you and not only poured into you but out from you as well. Taken the wrong way, it suffocated; taken the right way, it made terrestrial life seem, by comparison, a vacuum. At first, of course, the wrong moments occurred pretty often. But like a man who has a wound that hurts him in certain positions and who gradually learns to avoid those positions, Ransom learned not to make that inner gesture. His day became better and better as the hours passed.

During the course of the day he explored the island pretty thoroughly. The sea was still calm and it would have been possible in many directions to have reached neighbouring islands by a mere jump. He was placed, however, at the edge of this temporary archipelago, and from one shore he found himself looking out on the open sea. They were lying, or else very slowly drifting, in the neighbourhood of the huge green column which he had seen a few moments after his arrival in Perelandra. He had an excellent view of this object at about a mile's distance. It was clearly a mountainous island. The column turned out to be really a cluster of columns – that is, of crags much higher than they were broad, rather like exaggerated dolomites, but smoother: so much smoother in fact that it might be truer to describe them as pillars from the Giant's Causeway magnified to the height of mountains. This huge upright mass did not, however, rise directly from the sea. The island had a base of rough country, but with smoother land at the coast, and a hint of valleys with vegetation in them between the ridges, and even of steeper and narrower valleys which ran some way up between the central crags. It was certainly land, real fixed land with its roots in the solid surface of the planet. He could dimly make out the texture of true rock from where he sat. Some of it was inhabitable land. He felt a great desire to explore it. It looked as if a landing would present no difficulties, and even the great mountain itself might turn out to be climbable.

He did not see the Lady again that day. Early next morning, after he had amused himself by swimming for a little and eaten his first meal, he was again seated on the shore looking out towards the Fixed Land. Suddenly he heard her voice behind him and looked round. She had come forth from the woods with some beasts, as usual, following her. Her words had been words of greeting, but she showed no disposition to talk. She came and stood on the edge of the floating island beside him and looked with him towards the Fixed Land.

'I will go there,' she said at last.

'May I go with you?' asked Ransom.

'If you will,' said the Lady. 'But you see it is the Fixed Land.'

'That is why I wish to tread on it,' said Ransom. 'In my world all the lands are fixed, and it would give me pleasure to walk in such a land again.'

She gave a sudden exclamation of surprise and stared at him.

'Where, then, do you live in your world?' she asked.

'On the lands.'

'But you said they are all fixed.'

'Yes. We live on the fixed lands.'

For the first time since they had met, something not quite unlike an expression of horror or disgust passed over her face.

'But what do you do during the nights?'

'During the nights?' said Ransom in bewilderment. 'Why, we sleep, of course.'

'But where?'

'Where we live. On the land.'

She remained in deep thought so long that Ransom feared she was never going to speak again. When she did, her voice was hushed and once more tranquil, though the note of joy had not yet returned to it.

'He has never bidden you not to,' she said, less as a question than as a statement.

'No,' said Ransom.

'There can, then, be different laws in different worlds.'

'Is there a law in your world not to sleep in a Fixed Land?'

'Yes,' said the Lady. 'He does not wish us to dwell there. We may land on them and walk on them, for the world is ours. But to stay there to sleep and awake there ...' she ended with a shudder.

'You couldn't have that law in our world,' said Ransom. 'There *are* no floating lands with us.'

'How many of you are there?' asked the Lady suddenly.

Ransom found that he didn't know the population of the Earth, but contrived to give her some idea of many millions. He had expected her to be astonished, but it appeared that numbers did not interest her. 'How do you all find room on your Fixed Land?' she asked.

'There is not one fixed land, but many,' he answered. 'And they are big: almost as big as the sea.'

'How do you endure it?' she burst out. 'Almost half your world empty and dead. Loads and loads of land, all tied down. Does not the very thought of it crush you?'

'Not at all,' said Ransom. 'The very thought of a world which was all sea like yours would make my people unhappy and afraid.'

'Where will this end?' said the Lady, speaking more to herself than to him. 'I have grown so old in these last few hours that all my life before seems only like the stem of a tree, and now I am like the branches shooting out in every direction. They are getting so wide apart that I can hardly bear it. First to have learned that I walk from good to good with my own feet ... that was a stretch enough. But now it seems that good is not the same in all worlds; that Maleldil has forbidden in one what He allows in another.'

'Perhaps my world is wrong about this,' said Ransom rather feebly, for he was dismayed at what he had done.

'It is not so,' said she. 'Maleldil Himself has told me now. And it could not be so, if your world has no floating lands. But He is not telling me why He has forbidden it to us.'

'There's probably some good reason,' began Ransom, when he was interrupted by her sudden laughter.

'Oh, Piebald, Piebald,' she said, still laughing. 'How often the people of your race speak!'

'I'm sorry,' said Ransom, a little put out.

'What are you sorry for?'

'I am sorry if you think I talk too much.'

'Too much? How can I tell what would be too much for you to talk?'

'In our world when they say a man talks much they mean they wish him to be silent.'

'If that is what they mean, why do they not say it?'

'What made you laugh?' asked Ransom, finding her question too hard.

'I laughed, Piebald, because you were wondering, as I was, about this law which Maleldil has made for one world and not for another. And you had nothing to say about it and yet made the nothing up into words.'

'I *had* something to say, though,' said Ransom almost under his breath. 'At least,' he added in a louder voice, 'this forbidding is no hardship in such a world as yours.'

'That also is a strange thing to say,' replied the Lady. 'Who thought of its being hard? The beasts would not think it hard if I told them to walk on their heads. It would become their delight to walk on their heads. I am His beast, and all His biddings are joys. It is not that which makes me thoughtful. But it was coming into my mind to wonder whether there are two kinds of bidding.'

'Some of our wise men have said ...' began Ransom, when she interrupted him.

'Let us wait and ask the King,' she said. 'For I think, Piebald, you do not know much more about this than I do.'

'Yes, the King, by all means,' said Ransom. 'If only we can find him.' Then, quite involuntarily, he added in English, 'By Jove! What was that?' She also had exclaimed. Some thing like a shooting star seemed to have streaked across the sky, far away on their left, and some seconds later an indeterminate noise reached their ears.

'What was that?' he asked again, this time in Old Solar.

'Something has fallen out of Deep Heaven,' said the Lady. Her face showed wonder and curiosity: but on Earth we so rarely see these emotions without some admixture of defensive fear that her expression seemed strange to him.

'I think you're right,' said he. 'Hullo! What's this?' The calm sea had swelled and all the weeds at the edge of their island were in movement. A single wave passed under their island and all was still again.

'Something has certainly fallen into the sea,' said the Lady. Then she resumed the conversation as if nothing had happened.

'It was to look for the King that I had resolved to go over today to the Fixed Land. He is on none of these islands here, for I have searched them all. But if we climbed high up on the Fixed Land and looked about, then we should see a long way. We could see if there are any other islands near us.'

'Let us do this,' said Ransom. 'If we can swim so far.'

'We shall ride,' said the Lady. Then she knelt down on the shore – and such grace was in all her movements that it was a wonder to see her kneel – and gave three low calls all on the same note. At first no result was visible. But soon Ransom saw broken water coming rapidly towards them. A moment later and the sea beside the island was a mass of the large silver fishes: spouting, curling their bodies, pressing upon one another to get nearer, and the nearest ones nosing the land. They had not only the colour but the smoothness of silver. The biggest were about nine feet long and all were thick-set and powerful-looking. They were very unlike any terrestrial species, for the base of the head was noticeably wider than the foremost part of the trunk. But then the trunk itself grew thicker again towards the tail. Without this tailward bulge they would have looked like giant tadpoles. As it was, they suggested rather pot-bellied and narrow-chested old men with very big heads. The Lady seemed to take a long time in selecting two of them. But the moment she had done so the others all fell back for a few yards and the two successful candidates wheeled round and lay still with their tails to the shore, gently moving their fins. 'Now, Piebald, like this,' she said, and seated herself astride the narrow part of the right-hand fish. Ransom followed her example. The great head in front of him served instead of shoulders so that there was no danger of sliding off. He watched his hostess. She gave her fish a slight kick with her heels. He did the same to his. A moment later they were gliding out to sea at about six miles an hour. The air over the water was cooler and the breeze lifted his hair. In a world where he had as yet only swum and walked, the fish's progress gave the impression of quite an exhilarating speed. He glanced back and saw the feathery and billowy mass of the islands receding and the sky growing larger and more emphatically golden. Ahead, the fantastically shaped and coloured mountain dominated his whole field of vision. He noticed with interest that the whole school of rejected fish were still with them – some following, but the majority gambolling in wide extended wings to left and right.

'Do they always follow like this?' he asked.

'Do the beasts not follow in your world?' she replied. 'We cannot ride more than two. It would be hard if those we did not choose were not even allowed to follow.'

'Was that why you took so long to choose the two fish, Lady?' he asked.

'Of course,' said the Lady. 'I try not to choose the same fish too often.'

The land came towards them apace and what had seemed level coastline began to open into bays and thrust itself forward into promontories. And now they were near enough to see that in this apparently calm ocean there was an invisible swell, a very faint rise and fall of water on the beach. A moment later the fishes lacked depth to swim any further, and following the Green Lady's example, Ransom slipped both his legs to one side of his fish and groped down with his toes. Oh, ecstasy! – they touched solid pebbles. He had not realised till now that he was pining for 'fixed land'. He looked up. Down to the bay in which they were landing ran a steep narrow valley with low cliffs and outcroppings of a reddish rock and, lower down, banks of some kind of moss and a few trees. The trees might almost have been terrestrial: planted in any southern country of our own world they would not have seemed remarkable to anyone except a trained botanist. Best of all, down the middle of the valley – and welcome to Ransom's eyes and ears as a glimpse of home or of heaven – ran a little stream, a dark translucent stream where a man might hope for trout.

'You love this land, Piebald?' said the Lady, glancing at him.

'Yes,' said he, 'it is like my own world.'

They began to walk up the valley to its head. When they were under the trees the resemblance of an early country was diminished, for there is so much less light in that world that the glade which should have cast only a little shadow cast a forest gloom. It was about a quarter of a mile to the top of the valley, where it narrowed into a mere cleft between low rocks. With one or two grips and a leap the Lady was up these, and Ransom followed. He was amazed at her strength. They emerged into a steep upland covered with a kind of turf which would have been very like grass but that there was more blue in it. It seemed to be closely cropped and dotted with white fluffy objects as far as the eye could reach.

'Flowers?' asked Ransom. The Lady laughed.

'No. These are the Piebalds. I named you after them.' He was puzzled for a moment but presently the objects began to move, and soon to move quickly, towards the human pair whom they had apparently winded – for they were already so high that there was a strong breeze. In a moment they were bounding all about the Lady and welcoming her. They were white beasts with black spots about the size of sheep but with ears so much larger, noses so much more mobile, and tails so much longer, that the general impression was rather of enormous mice. Their claw-like or almost hand-like paws were clearly built for climbing, and the bluish turf was their food. After a proper interchange of courtesies with these creatures, Ransom and the Lady continued their journey. The circle of golden sea below them was now spread out in an enormous expanse and the green rock pillars above seemed almost to overhang. But it was a long and stiff climb to their base. The temperature here was much lower, though it was still warm. The silence was also noticeable. Down below, on the islands, though one had not remarked it at the time, there must have been a continual background of water noises, bubble noises, and the movement of beasts.

They were now entering into a kind of bay or re-entrant of turf between two of the green pillars. Seen from below these had appeared to touch one another; but now, though they had gone in so deep between two of them that most of the view was cut off on either hand, there was still room for a battalion to march in line. The slope grew steeper every moment; and as it grew steeper the space between the pillars also grew narrower. Soon they were scrambling on hands and knees in a place where the green walls hemmed them in so that they must go in single file, and Ransom, looking up, could hardly see the sky overhead. Finally they were faced with a little bit of real rock work—a neck of stone about eight feet high which joined, like a gum of rock, the roots of the two monstrous teeth of the mountain. 'I'd give a good deal to have a pair of trousers on,' thought Ransom to himself as he looked at it. The Lady, who was ahead, stood on tiptoe and raised her arms to catch a projection on the lip of the ridge. Then he saw her pull, apparently intending to lift her whole weight on her arms and swing herself to the top in a single movement. 'Look here, you can't do it that way,' he began, speaking inadvertently in English, but before he had time to correct himself she was standing on the edge above him. He did not see exactly how it was done, but there was no sign that she had taken any unusual exertion. His own climb was a less dignified affair, and it was a panting and perspiring man with a smudge of blood on his knee who finally stood beside her. She was inquisitive about the blood, and when he had explained the phenomenon to her as well as he could, wanted to scrape a little skin off her own knee to see if the same would happen. This led him to try to explain to her what was meant by pain, which only made her more anxious to try the experiment. But at the last moment Maleldil apparently told her not to.

Ransom now turned to survey their surroundings. High overhead, and seeming by perspective to lean inwards towards each other at the top and almost to shut out the sky, rose the immense piers of rock – not two or three of them, but nine. Some of them, like those two between which they had entered the circle, were close together. Others were many yards apart. They surrounded a roughly oval plateau of perhaps seven acres, covered with a finer turf than any known on our planet and dotted with tiny crimson flowers. A high, singing wind carried, as it were, a cooled and refined quintessence of all the scents from the richer world below, and kept these in continual agitation. Glimpses of the far-spread sea, visible between pillars, made one continually conscious of great height; and Ransom's eyes, long accustomed to the medley of curves and colours in the floating islands, rested on the pure lines and stable masses of this place with great refreshment. He took a few paces forward into the cathedral spaciousness of the plateau, and when he spoke his voice woke echoes.

'Oh, this is good,' he said. 'But perhaps you – you to whom it is forbidden – do not feel it so.' But a glance at the Lady's face told him he was wrong. He did not know what was in her mind; but her face, as once or twice before, seemed to shine with something before which he dropped his eyes. 'Let us examine the sea,' she said presently.

They made the circle of the plateau methodically. Behind them lay the group of islands from which they had set out that morning. Seen from this altitude it was larger even than Ransom had supposed. The richness of its colours – its orange, its silver, its purple and (to his surprise) its glossy blacks – made it seem almost heraldic. It was from this direction that the wind came; the smell of those islands though faint, was like the sound of running water to a thirsty man. But on every other side they saw nothing but the ocean. At least, they saw no islands. But when they had made almost the whole circuit, Ransom shouted and the Lady pointed almost at the same moment. About two miles off, dark against the coppery-green of the water, there was some small round object. If he had been looking down on an earthly sea Ransom would have taken it, at first sight, for a buoy.

'I do not know what it is,' said the Lady. 'Unless it is the thing that fell out of Deep Heaven this morning.'

'I wish I had a pair of field-glasses,' thought Ransom, for the Lady's words had awakened in him a sudden suspicion. And the longer he stared at the dark blob the more his suspicion was confirmed. It appeared to be perfectly spherical; and he thought he had seen something like it before.

You have already heard that Ransom had been in that world which men call Mars but whose true name is Malacandra. But he had not been taken thither by the *eldila*. He had been taken by men, and taken in a space-ship, a hollow sphere of glass and steel. He had, in fact, been kidnapped by men who thought that the ruling powers of Malacandra demanded a human sacrifice. The whole thing had been a misunderstanding. The great Oyarsa who has governed Mars from the beginning (and whom my own eyes beheld, in a sense, in the hall of Ransom's cottage) had done him no harm and meant him none. But his chief captor, Professor Weston, had meant plenty of harm. He was a man obsessed with the idea which is at this moment circulating all over our planet in obscure works of 'scientification', in little Interplanetary Societies and Rocketry Clubs, and between the covers of monstrous magazines, ignored or mocked by the intellectuals, but ready, if ever the power is put into its hands, to open a new chapter of misery for the universe. It is the idea that humanity, having now sufficiently corrupted the planet where it arose, must at all costs contrive to seed itself over a larger area: that the vast astronomical distances which are God's quarantine regulations, must somehow be overcome. This for a start. But beyond this lies the sweet poison of the false infinite – the wild dream that planet after planet, system after system, in the end galaxy after galaxy, can be forced to sustain, everywhere and for ever, the sort of life which is contained in the loins of our own species – a dream begotten by the hatred of death upon the fear of true immortality, fondled in secret by thousands of ignorant men and hundreds who are not ignorant. The destruction or enslavement of other species in the universe, if such there are, is to these minds a welcome corollary. In Professor Weston the power had at last met the dream. The great physicist had discovered a motive power for his spaceship. And that little black object, now floating beneath him on the sinless waters of Perelandra, looked to Ransom more like the space-ship every moment. 'So that,' he thought, 'that is why I have been sent here. He failed on Malacandra and now he is coming here. And it's up to me to do something about it.' A terrible sense of inadequacy swept over him. Last time – in Mars – Weston had had only one accomplice. But he had had firearms. And how many accomplices might he have this time? And in Mars he had been foiled not by Ransom but by the *eldila*, and specially the great *eldil*, the Oyarsa, of that world. He turned quickly to the Lady.

'I have seen no *eldila* in your world,' he said.

'*Eldila*?' she repeated as if it were a new name to her. 'Yes. *Eldila*,' said Ransom, 'the great and ancient servants of Maleldil. The creatures that neither breed nor breathe. Whose bodies are made of light. Whom we can hardly see. Who ought to be obeyed.'

She mused for a moment and then spoken 'Sweetly and gently this time Maleldil makes me older. He shows me all the natures of these blessed creatures. But there is no obeying them *now*, not in this world. That is all the old order, Piebald, the far side of the wave that has rolled past us and will not come again. That very ancient world to which you journeyed was put under the *eldila*. In your own world also they ruled once: but not since our Beloved became a Man. In your world they linger still. But in our world, which is the first of worlds to wake after the great change, they have no power. There is nothing now between us and Him. They have grown less and we have increased. And now Maleldil puts it into my mind that this is their glory and their joy. They received us – us things of the low worlds, who breed and breathe – as weak and small beasts whom their lightest touch could destroy; and their glory was to cherish us and make us older till we were older than they – till they could fall at our feet. It is a joy we shall not have. However I teach the beasts they will never be better than I. But it is a joy beyond all. Not that it is better joy than ours. Every joy is beyond all others. The fruit we are eating is always the best fruit of all.'

'There have been *eldila* who did not think it a joy,' said Ransom.

'How?'

'You spoke yesterday, Lady, of clinging to the old good instead of taking the good that came.'

'Yes – for a few heart-beats.'

'There was an *eldil* who clung longer – who has been clinging since before the worlds were made.'

'But the old good would cease to be a good at all if he did that.'

'Yes. It has ceased. And still he clings.'

She stared at him in wonder and was about to speak, but he interrupted her.

'There is not time to explain,' he said.

'No time? What has happened to the time?' she asked.

'Listen,' he said. 'That thing down there has come through Deep Heaven from my world. There is a man in it: perhaps many men –'

'Look,' she said, 'it is turning into two – one big and one small.'

Ransom saw that a small black object had detached itself from the space-ship and was beginning to move uncertainly away from it. It puzzled him for a moment. Then it dawned on him that Weston – if it was Weston – probably knew the watery surface he had to expect on Venus and had brought some kind of collapsible boat. But could it be that he had not reckoned with tides or storms and did not foresee that it might be impossible for him ever to recover the space-ship? It was not like Weston to cut off his own retreat. And Ransom certainly did not wish Weston's retreat to be cut off. A Weston who could not, even if he chose, return to Earth, was an insoluble problem. Anyway, what could he, Ransom, possibly do without support from the *eldila*? He began to smart under a sense of injustice. What was the good of sending him – a mere scholar – to cope with a situation of this sort? Any ordinary pugilist, or, better still, any man who could make good use of a tommy-gun, would have been more to the purpose. If only they could find this King whom the Green Woman kept on talking about ...

But while these thoughts were passing through his mind he became aware of a dim murmuring or growling sound which had gradually been encroaching on the silence for some time. 'Look,' said the Lady suddenly, and pointed to the mass of islands. Their surface was no longer level. At the same moment he realised that the noise was that of waves: small waves as yet, but definitely beginning to foam on the rocky headlands of the Fixed Island. 'The sea is rising,' said the Lady. 'We must go down and leave this land at once. Soon the waves will be too great – and I must not be here by night.'

'Not that way,' shouted Ransom. 'Not where you will meet the man from my world.'

'Why?' said the Lady. 'I am Lady and Mother of this world. If the King is not here, who else should greet a stranger?'

'I will meet him.'

'It is not your world, Piebald,' she replied.

'You do not understand,' said Ransom. 'This man – he is a friend of that *eldil* of whom I told you – one of those who cling to the wrong good.'

'Then I must explain it to him,' said the Lady. 'Let us go and make him older,' and with that she slung herself down the rocky edge of the plateau and began descending the mountain slope. Ransom took longer to manage the rocks; but once his feet were again on the turf he began running as fast as he could. The Lady cried out in surprise as he flashed past her, but he took no notice. He could now see clearly which bay the little boat was making for and his attention was fully occupied in directing his course and making sure of his feet. There was only one man in the boat. Down and down the long slope he raced. Now he was in a fold: now in a winding valley which momentarily cut off the sight of the sea. Now at last he was in the cove itself. He glanced back and saw to his dismay that the Lady had also been running and was only a few yards behind. He glanced forward again. There were waves, though not yet very large ones, breaking on the pebbly beach. A man in shirt and shorts and a pith helmet was ankle-deep in the water, wading ashore and pulling after him a little canvas punt. It was certainly Weston, though his face had something about it which seemed subtly unfamiliar. It seemed to Ransom of vital importance to prevent a meeting between Weston and the Lady. He had seen Weston murder an inhabitant of Malacandra. He turned back, stretching out both arms to bar her way and shouting 'Go back!' She was too near. For a second she was almost in his arms. Then she stood back from him, panting from the race, surprised, her mouth opened to speak. But at that moment he heard Weston's voice, from behind him, saying in English, 'May I ask you, Dr Ransom, what is the meaning of this?'

7

In all the circumstances it would have been reasonable to expect that Weston would be much more taken aback at Ransom's presence than Ransom could be at his. But if he were, he showed no sign of it, and Ransom could hardly help admiring the massive egoism which enabled this man in the very moment of his arrival on an unknown world to stand there unmoved in all his authoritative vulgarity, his arms akimbo, his face scowling, and his feet planted as solidly on that unearthly soil as if he had been standing with his back to the fire in his own study. Then, with a shock, he noticed that Weston was speaking to the Lady in the Old Solar language with perfect fluency. On Malacandra, partly from incapacity, and much more from his contempt for the inhabitants, he had never acquired more than a smattering of it. Here was an inexplicable and disquieting novelty. Ransom felt that his only advantage had been taken from him. He felt that he was now in the presence of the incalculable. If the scales had been suddenly weighted in this one respect, what might come next?

He awoke from his abstraction to find that Weston and the Lady had been conversing fluently, but without mutual understanding. 'It is no use,' she was saying. 'You and I are not old enough to speak together, it seems. The sea is rising; let us go back to the islands. Will he come with us, Piebald?'

'Where are the two fishes?' said Ransom.

'They will be waiting in the next bay,' said the Lady.

'Quick, then,' said Ransom to her; and then, in answer to her look: 'No, he will not come.' She did not, presumably, understand his urgency, but her eye was on the sea and she understood her own reason for haste. She had already begun to ascend the side of the valley, with Ransom following her, when Weston shouted, 'No, you don't.' Ransom turned and found himself covered by a revolver. The sudden heat which swept over his body was the only sign by which he knew that he was frightened. His head remained clear.

'Are you going to begin in this world also by murdering one of its inhabitants?' he asked.

'What are you saying?' asked the Lady, pausing and looking back at the two men with a puzzled, tranquil face.

'Stay where you are, Ransom,' said the Professor. 'That native can go where she likes; the sooner the better.'

Ransom was about to implore her to make good her escape when he realised that no imploring was needed. He had irrationally supposed that she would understand the situation; but apparently she saw nothing more than two strangers talking about something which she did not at the moment understand – that, and her own necessity of leaving the Fixed Land at once.

'You and he do not come with me, Piebald?' she asked.

'No,' said Ransom, without turning round. 'It may be that you and I shall not meet soon again. Greet the King for me if you find him and speak of me always to Maleldil. I stay here.'

'We shall meet when Maleldil pleases,' she answered, 'or if not, some greater good will happen to us instead.' Then he heard her footsteps behind him for a few seconds, and then he heard them no more and knew he was alone with Weston.

'You allowed yourself to use the word Murder just now, Dr Ransom,' said the Professor, 'in reference to an accident that occurred when we were in Malacandra. In any case, the creature killed was not a human being. Allow me to tell you that I consider the seduction of a native girl as an almost equally unfortunate way of introducing civilisation to a new planet.

'Seduction?' said Ransom. 'Oh, I see. You thought I was making love to her.'

'When I find a naked civilised man embracing a naked savage woman in a solitary place, that is the name I give to it.'

'I wasn't embracing her,' said Ransom dully, for the whole business of defending himself on this score seemed at that moment a mere weariness of the spirit. 'And no one wears clothes here. But what does it matter? Get on with the job that brings you to Perelandra.'

'You ask me to believe that you have been living here with that woman under these conditions in a state of sexless innocence?'

'Oh, sexless!' said Ransom disgustedly. 'All right, if you like. It's about as good a description of living in Perelandra as it would be to say that a man had forgotten water because Niagara Falls didn't immediately give him the idea of making it into cups of tea. But you're right enough if you mean that I have had no more thought of desiring her than – than ...' Comparisons failed him and his voice died. Then he began again: 'But don't say I'm asking you to believe it, or to believe anything. I am asking you nothing but to begin and end as soon as possible whatever butcheries and robberies you have come to do.'

Weston eyed him for a moment with a curious expression: then, unexpectedly, he returned his revolver to its holster.

'Ransom,' he said, 'you do me a great injustice.'

For several seconds there was silence between them. Long breakers with white woolpacks of foam on them were now rolling into the cove exactly as on Earth.

'Yes,' said Weston at last, 'and I will begin with a frank admission. You may make what capital of it you please. I shall not be deterred. I deliberately say that I was, in some respects, mistaken – seriously mistaken – in my conception of the whole interplanetary problem when I went to Malacandra.'

Partly from the relaxation which followed the disappearance of the pistol, and partly from the elaborate air of magnanimity with which the great scientist spoke, Ransom felt very much inclined to laugh. But it occurred to him that this was possibly the first occasion in his whole life in which Weston had ever acknowledged himself in the wrong, and that even the false dawn of humility, which is still ninety-nine per cent of arrogance, ought not to be rebuffed – or not by him.

'Well, that's very handsome,' he said. 'How do you mean?'

'I'll tell you presently,' said Weston. 'In the meantime I must get my things ashore.' Between them they beached the punt, and began carrying Weston's primus-stove and tins and tent and other packages to a spot about two hundred yards inland. Ransom, who knew all the paraphernalia to be needless, made no objection, and in about a quarter of an hour something like an encampment had been established in a mossy place under some blue-trunked silver-leaved trees beside a rivulet. Both men sat down and Ransom listened at first with interest, then with amazement, and finally with incredulity. Weston cleared his throat, threw out his chest, and assumed his lecturing manner. Throughout the conversation that followed, Ransom was filled with a sense of crazy irrelevance. Here were two human beings, thrown together in an alien world under conditions of inconceivable strangeness; the one separated from his spaceship, the other newly released from the threat of instant death. Was it sane – was it imaginable – that they should find themselves at once engaged in a philosophical argument which might just as well have occurred in a Cambridge combination room? Yet that, apparently, was what Weston insisted upon. He showed no interest in the fate of his space-ship; he even seemed to feel no curiosity about Ransom's presence on Venus. Could it be that he had travelled more than thirty million miles of space in search of – conversation? But as he went on talking, Ransom felt himself more and more in the presence of a monomaniac. Like an actor who cannot think of anything but his celebrity, or a lover who can think of nothing but his mistress, tense, tedious, and unescapable, the scientist pursued his fixed idea.

'The tragedy of my life,' he said, 'and indeed of the modern intellectual world in general, is the rigid specialisation of knowledge entailed by the growing complexity of what is known. It is my own share in that tragedy that an early devotion to physics has prevented me from paying any proper attention to Biology until I reached the fifties. To do myself justice, I should make it clear that the false humanist ideal of knowledge as an end in itself never appealed to me. I always wanted to know in order to achieve utility. At first, that utility naturally appeared to me in a personal form – I wanted scholarships, an income, and that generally recognised position in the world without which a man has no leverage. When those were attained, I began to look farther: to the utility of the human race!'

He paused as he rounded his period and Ransom nodded to him to proceed.

'The utility of the human race,' continued Weston, 'in the long run depends rigidly on the possibility of interplanetary, and even inter-sidereal, travel. That problem I solved. The key of human destiny was placed in my hands. It would be unnecessary – and painful to us both – to remind you how it was wrenched from me in Malacandra by a member of a hostile intelligent species whose existence, I admit, I had not anticipated.'

'Not hostile exactly,' said Ransom, 'but go on.'

'The rigours of our return journey from Malacandra led to a serious breakdown in my health –'

'Mine too,' said Ransom.

Weston looked somewhat taken aback at the interruption and went on. 'During my convalescence I had that leisure for reflection which I had denied myself for many years. In particular I reflected on the objections you had felt to that liquidation of the non-human inhabitants of Malacandra which was, of course, the necessary preliminary to its occupation by our own species. The traditional and, if I may say so, the humanitarian form in which you advanced those objections had till then concealed from me their true strength. That strength I now began to perceive. I began to see that my own exclusive devotion to human utility was really based on an unconscious dualism.'

'What do you mean?'

'I mean that all my life I had been making a wholly unscientific dichotomy or antithesis between Man and Nature – had conceived myself fighting *for* Man against his non-human environment. During my illness I plunged into Biology, and particularly into what may be called biological philosophy. Hitherto, as a physicist, I had been content to regard Life as a subject outside my scope. The conflicting views of those who drew a sharp line between the organic and the inorganic and those who held that what we call Life was inherent in matter from the very beginning had not interested me. Now it did. I saw almost at once that I could admit no break, no discontinuity, in the unfolding of the cosmic process. I became a convinced believer in emergent evolution. All is one. The stuff of mind, the unconsciously purposive dynamism, is present from the very beginning.

Here he paused. Ransom had heard this sort of thing pretty often before and wondered when his companion was coming to the point. When Weston resumed it was with an even deeper solemnity of tone.

'The majestic spectacle of this blind, inarticulate purposiveness thrusting its way upward and ever upward in an endless unity of differentiated achievements towards an ever-increasing complexity of organisation, towards spontaneity and spirituality, swept away all my old conception of a duty to Man as such. Man in himself is nothing. The forward movements of Life – the growing spirituality – is everything. I say to you quite freely, Ransom, that I should have been wrong in liquidating the Malacandrians. It was a mere prejudice that made me prefer our own race to theirs. To spread spirituality, not to spread the human race, is henceforth my mission. This sets the coping-stone on my career. I worked first for myself; then for science; then for humanity; but now at last for Spirit itself I might say, borrowing language which will be more familiar to you, the Holy Spirit.'

'Now what exactly do you mean by that?' asked Ransom. 'I mean,' said Weston, 'that nothing now divides you and me except a few outworn theological technicalities with which organised religion has unhappily allowed itself to get incrusted. But I have penetrated that crust. The Meaning beneath it is as true and living as ever. If you will excuse me for putting it that way, the essential truth of the religious view of life finds a remarkable witness in the fact that it enabled you, on Malacandra, to grasp, in your own mythical and imaginative fashion, a truth which was hidden from me.'

'I don't know much about what people call the religious view of life,' said Ransom, wrinkling his brow. 'You see, I'm a Christian. And what we mean by the Holy Ghost is *not* a blind, inarticulate purposiveness.'

'My dear Ransom,' said Weston, 'I understand you perfectly. I have no doubt that my phraseology will seem strange to you, and perhaps even shocking. Early and revered associations may have put it out of your power to recognise in this new form the very same truths which religion has so long preserved and which science is now at last re-discovering. But whether you can see it or not, believe me, we are talking about exactly the same thing.'

'I'm not at all sure that we are.'

'That, if you will permit me to say so, is one of the real weaknesses of organised religion – that adherence to formulae, that failure to recognise one's own friends. God is a spirit, Ransom. Get hold of that. You're familiar with that already. Stick to it. God is a spirit.'

'Well, of course. But what then?'

'What then? Why, spirit – mind – freedom – spontaneity – that's what I'm talking about. That is the goal towards which the whole cosmic process is moving. The final disengagement of that freedom, that spirituality, is the work to which I dedicate my own life and the life of humanity. The goal, Ransom, the goal: think of it! *Pure* spirit: the final vortex of self-thinking, self-originating activity.'

'Final?' said Ransom. 'You mean it doesn't yet exist?'

'Ah,' said Weston, 'I see what's bothering you. Of course I know. Religion pictures it as being there from the beginning. But surely that is not a real difference? To make it one, would be to take time too seriously. When it has once been attained, you might then say it had been at the beginning just as well as at the end. Time is one of the things it will transcend.'

'By the way,' said Ransom, 'is it in any sense at all personal – is it alive?'

An indescribable expression passed over Weston's face. He moved a little nearer to Ransom and began speaking in a lower voice.

'That's what none of them understand,' he said. It was such a gangster's or a schoolboy's whisper and so unlike his usual orotund lecturing style that Ransom for a moment felt a sensation almost of disgust.

'Yes,' said Weston, 'I couldn't have believed, myself, till recently. Not a person, of course. Anthropomorphism is one of the childish diseases of popular religion' (here he had resumed his public manner), 'but the opposite extreme of excessive abstraction has perhaps in the aggregate proved more disastrous. Call it a Force. A great, inscrutable Force, pouring up into us from the dark bases of being. A Force that can choose its instruments. It is only lately, Ransom, that I've learned from actual experience something which you have believed all your life as part of your religion.' Here he suddenly subsided again into a whisper – a croaking whisper unlike his usual voice. 'Guided,' he said. 'Chosen. Guided. I've become conscious that I'm a man set apart. Why did I do physics? Why did I discover the Weston rays? Why did I go to Malacandra? It – the Force – has pushed me on all the time. I'm being guided. I know now that I am the greatest scientist the world has yet produced. I've been made so for a purpose. It is through me that Spirit itself is at this moment pushing on to its goal.'

'Look here,' said Ransom, 'one wants to be careful about this sort of thing. There are spirits and spirits, you know.'

'Eh?' said Weston. 'What are you talking about?'

'I mean a thing might be a spirit and not good for you.'

'But I thought you agreed that Spirit was the good – the end of the whole process? I thought you religious people were all out for spirituality? What is the point of asceticism – fasts and celibacy and all that? Didn't we agree that God is a spirit? Don't you worship Him because He is pure spirit?'

'Good heavens, no! We worship Him because He is wise and good. There's nothing specially fine about simply being a spirit. The Devil is a spirit.'

'Now your mentioning the Devil is very interesting,' said Weston, who had by this time quite recovered his normal manner. 'It is a most interesting thing in popular religion, this tendency to fissiparate, to breed pairs of opposites: heaven and hell, God and Devil. I need hardly say that in my view no real dualism in the universe is admissible; and on that ground I should have been disposed, even a few weeks ago, to reject these pairs of doublets as pure mythology. It would have been a profound error. The cause of this universal religious tendency is to be sought much deeper. The doublets are really portraits of Spirit, of cosmic energy – self-portraits, indeed, for it is the Life-Force itself which has deposited them in our brains.'

'What on earth do you mean?' said Ransom. As he spoke he rose to his feet and began pacing to and fro. A quite appalling weariness and malaise had descended upon him.

'*Your* Devil and *your* God,' said Weston, 'are both pictures of the same Force. Your heaven is a picture of the perfect spirituality ahead; your hell a picture of the urge or *nisus* which is driving us on to it from behind. Hence the static peace of the one and the fire and darkness of the other. The next stage of emergent evolution, beckoning us forward, is God; the transcended stage behind, ejecting us, is the Devil. Your own religion, after all, says that the devils are fallen angels.'

'And you are saying precisely the opposite, as far as I can make out – that angels are devils who've risen in the world.'

'It comes to the same thing,' said Weston.

There was another long pause. 'Look here,' said Ransom, 'it's easy to misunderstand one another on a point like this. What you are saying sounds to me like the most horrible mistake a man could fall into. But that may be because in the effort to accommodate it to my supposed 'religious views', you're saying a good deal more than you mean. It's only a metaphor, isn't it, all this about spirits and forces? I expect all you really mean is that you feel it your duty to work for the spread of civilisation and knowledge and that kind of thing.' He had tried to keep out of his voice the involuntary anxiety which he had begun to feel. Next moment he recoiled in horror at the cackling laughter, almost an infantile or senile laughter, with which Weston replied.

'There you go, there you go,' he said. 'Like all you religious people. You talk and talk about these things all your life, and the moment you meet the reality you get frightened.'

'What proof,' said Ransom (who indeed did feel frightened), 'what proof have you that you are being guided or supported by anything except your own individual mind and other people's books?'

'You didn't notice, dear Ransom,' said Weston, 'that I'd improved a bit since we last met in my knowledge of extra terrestrial language. You are a philologist, they tell me.'

Ransom started. 'How did you do it?' he blurted out.

'Guidance, you know, guidance,' croaked Weston. He was squatting at the roots of his tree with his knees drawn up, and his face, now the colour of putty, wore a fixed and even slightly twisted grin. 'Guidance. Guidance,' he went on. 'Things coming into my head. I'm being prepared all the time. Being made a fit receptacle for it.'

'That ought to be fairly easy,' said Ransom impatiently. 'If this Life-Force is something so ambiguous that God and the Devil are equally good portraits of it, I suppose any receptacle is equally fit, and anything you can do is equally an expression of it.'

'There's such a thing as the main current,' said Weston. 'It's a question of surrendering yourself to that – making yourself the conductor of the live, fiery, central purpose – becoming the very finger with which it reaches forward.'

'But I thought that was the Devil aspect of it, a moment ago.'

'That is the fundamental paradox. The thing we are reaching

forward to is what you would call God. The reaching forward, the dynamism, is what people like you always call the Devil. The people like me, who do the reaching forward, are always martyrs. You revile us, and by us come to your goal.'

'Does that mean in plainer language that the things the Force wants you to do are what ordinary people call diabolical?'

'My dear Ransom, I wish you would not keep relapsing on to the popular level. The two things are only moments in the single, unique reality. The world leaps forward through great men and greatness always transcends mere moralism. When the leap has been made our 'diabolism' as you would call it becomes the morality of the next stage; but while we are making it, we are called criminals, heretics, blasphemers ...'

'How far does it go? Would you still obey the Life-Force if you found it prompting you to murder me?'

'Yes.'

'Or to sell England to the Germans?'

'Yes.'

'Or to print lies as serious research in a scientific periodical?'

'Yes.'

'God help you!' said Ransom.

'You are still wedded to your conventionalities,' said Weston. 'Still dealing in abstractions. Can you not even conceive a total commitment – a commitment to something which utterly overrides all our petty ethical pigeon-holes?'

Ransom grasped at the straw. 'Wait, Weston,' he said abruptly. 'That may be a point of contact. You say it's a total commitment. That is, you're giving up yourself. You're not out for your own advantage. No, wait half a second. This is the point of contact between your morality and mine. We both acknowledge –'

'Idiot,' said Weston. His voice was almost a howl and he had risen to his feet. 'Idiot,' he repeated. 'Can you understand nothing? Will you always try to press everything back into the miserable framework of your old jargon about self and self-sacrifice? That is the old accursed dualism in another form. There is no possible distinction in concrete thought between me and the universe. In so far as I am the conductor of the central forward pressure of the universe, I am it. Do you see, you timid, scruple-mongering fool? I *am* the Universe. I, Weston, am your God and your Devil. I call that Force into me completely ...'

Then horrible things began happening. A spasm like that preceding a deadly vomit twisted Weston's face out of recognition. As it passed, for one second something like the old Weston reappeared the old Weston, staring with eyes of horror and howling, 'Ransom, Ransom! For Christ's sake don't let them –' and instantly his whole body spun round as if he had been hit by a revolver bullet and he fell to the earth, and was there rolling at Ransom's feet, slavering and chattering and tearing up the moss by handfuls. Gradually the convulsions decreased. He lay still, breathing heavily, his eyes open but without expression. Ransom was kneeling beside him now. It was obvious that the body was alive, and Ransom wondered whether this were a stroke or an epileptic fit, for he had never seen either. He rummaged among the packages and found a bottle of brandy which he uncorked and applied to the patient's mouth. To his consternation the teeth opened, closed on the neck of the bottle and bit it through. No glass was spat out. 'O God, I've killed him,' said Ransom. But beyond a spurt of blood at the lips there was no change in his appearance. The face suggested that either he was in no pain or in a pain beyond all human comprehension. Ransom rose at last, but before doing so he plucked the revolver from Weston's belt, then, walking down to the beach, he threw it as far as he could into the sea.

He stood for some moments gazing out upon the bay and undecided what to do. Presently he turned and climbed up the turfy ridge that bordered the little valley on his left hand. He found himself on a fairly level upland with a good view of the sea, now running high and teased out of its level gold into a continually changing pattern of lights and shadows. For a second or two he could catch no sight of the islands. Then suddenly their tree-tops appeared, hanging high up against the sky, and widely separated.

The weather, apparently, was already driving them apart – and even as he thought this they vanished once more into some unseen valley of the waves. What was his chance, he wondered, of ever finding them again? A sense of loneliness smote him, and then a feeling of angry frustration. If Weston were dying, or even if Weston were to live, imprisoned here with him on an island they could not leave, what had been the danger he was sent to avert from Perelandra? And so, having begun to think of himself, he realised that he was hungry. He had seen neither fruit nor gourd on the Fixed Land. Perhaps it was a death trap. He smiled bitterly at the folly which had made him so glad, that morning, to exchange those floating paradises, where every grove dropped sweetness, for this barren rock. But perhaps it was not barren after all. Determined, despite the weariness which was every moment descending upon him, to make a search for food, he was just turning inland when the swift changes of colour that announce the evening of that world overtook him. Uselessly he quickened his pace. Before he had got down into the valley, the grove where he had left Weston was a mere cloud of darkness. Before he had reached it he was in seamless, undimensioned night. An effort or two to grope his way to the place where Weston's stores had been deposited only served to abolish his sense of direction altogether. He sat down perforce. He called Weston's name aloud once or twice but, as he expected, received no answer. 'I'm glad I removed his gun, all the same,' thought Ransom; and then, 'Well, *qui dort dine* and I suppose I must make the best of it till the morning.' When he lay down he discovered that the solid earth and moss of the Fixed Land was very much less comfortable than the surfaces to which he had lately been accustomed. That, and the thought of the other human being lying, no doubt, close at hand with open eyes and teeth clenched on splintered glass, and the sullen recurring pound of breakers on the beach, all made the night comfortless. 'If I lived on Perelandra,' he muttered, 'Maleldil wouldn't need to *forbid* this island. I wish I'd never set eyes on it.'

8

He woke, after a disturbed and dreamful sleep, in full daylight. He had a dry mouth, a crick in his neck, and a soreness in his limbs. It was so unlike all previous wakings in the world of Venus, that for a moment he supposed himself back on Earth: and the dream (for so it seemed to him) of having lived and walked on the oceans of the Morning Star rushed through his memory with a sense of lost sweetness that was well-nigh unbearable. Then he sat up and the facts came back to him. 'It's jolly nearly the same as having waked from a dream, though,' he thought. Hunger and thirst became at once his dominant sensations, but he conceived it a duty to look first at the sick man – though with very little hope that he could help him. He gazed round. There was the grove of silvery trees all right, but he could not see Weston. Then he glanced at the bay; there was no punt either. Assuming that in the darkness he had blundered into the wrong valley, he rose and approached the stream for a drink. As he lifted his face from the water with a long sigh of satisfaction, his eyes suddenly fell on a little wooden box – and then beyond it on a couple of tins. His brain was working rather slowly and it took him a few seconds to realise that he was in the right valley after all, and a few more to draw conclusions from the fact that the box was open and empty, and that some of the stores had been removed and others left behind. But was it possible that a man in Weston's physical condition could have recovered sufficiently during the night to strike camp and to go away laden with some kind of pack? Was it possible that any man could have faced a sea like that in a collapsible punt? It was true, as he now noticed for the first time, that the

269

storm (which had been a mere squall by Perelandrian standards) appeared to have blown itself out during the night; but there was still a quite formidable swell and it seemed out of the question that the Professor could have left the island. Much more probably he had left the valley on foot and carried the punt with him. Ransom decided that he must find Weston at once: he must keep in touch with his enemy. For if Weston had recovered, there was no doubt he meant mischief of some kind. Ransom was not at all certain that he had understood all his wild talk on the previous day; but what he did understand he disliked very much, and suspected that this vague mysticism about 'spirituality' would turn out to be something even nastier than his old and comparatively simple programme of planetary imperialism. It would be unfair to take seriously the things the man had said immediately before his seizure, no doubt; but there was enough without that.

The next few hours Ransom passed in searching the island for food and for Weston. As far as food was concerned, he was rewarded. Some fruit like bilberries could be gathered in handfuls on the upper slopes, and the wooded valleys abounded in a kind of oval nut. The kernel had a toughly soft consistency, rather like cork or kidneys, and the flavour, though somewhat austere and prosaic after the fruit of the floating islands, was not unsatisfactory. The giant mice were as tame as other Perelandrian beasts but seemed stupider. Ransom ascended to the central plateau. The sea was dotted with islands in every direction, rising and falling with the swell, and all separated from one another by wide stretches of water. His eye at once picked out an orange-coloured island, but he did not know whether it was that on which he had been living, for he saw at least two others in which the same colour predominated. At one time he counted twenty-three floating islands in all. That, he thought, was more than the temporary archipelago had contained, and allowed him to hope that any one of those he saw might hide the King – or that the King might even at this moment be re-united to the Lady. Without thinking it out very clearly, he had come to rest almost all his hopes on the King.

Of Weston he could find no trace. It really did seem, in spite of all improbabilities, that he had somehow contrived to leave the Fixed Island; and Ransom's anxiety was very great. What Weston, in his new vein, might do, he had no idea. The best to hope for was that he would simply ignore the master and mistress of Perelandra as mere savages or 'natives'.

Late in the day, being tired, he sat down on the shore. There was very little swell now and the waves, just before they broke, were less than knee-deep. His feet, made soft by the mattress-like surface which one walks on in those floating islands, were hot and sore. Presently he decided to refresh them by a little wading. The delicious quality of the water drew him out till he was waist-deep. As he stood there, deep in thought, he suddenly perceived that what he had taken to be an effect of light on the water was really the back of one of the great silvery fish. 'I wonder would it let me ride it?' he thought; and then, watching how the beast nosed towards him and kept itself as near the shallows as it dared, it was borne in upon him that it was trying to attract his attention. Could it have been *sent*? The thought had no sooner darted through his mind than he decided to make the experiment. He laid his hand across the creature's back, and it did not flinch from his touch. Then with some difficulty he scrambled into a sitting position across the narrow part behind its head, and while he was doing this it remained as nearly stationary as it could; but as soon as he was firmly in the saddle it whisked itself about and headed for the sea.

If he had wished to withdraw, it was very soon impossible to do so. Already the green pinnacles of the mountain, as he looked back, had withdrawn their summits from the sky and the coastline of the island had begun to conceal its bays and nesses. The breakers were no longer audible – only the prolonged sibilant or chattering noises of the water about him. Many floating islands were visible, though seen from this level they were mere feather silhouettes. But the fish seemed to be heading for none of these. Straight on, as if it well knew its way, the beat of the great fins carried him for more than an hour. Then green and purple splashed the whole world, and after that darkness.

Somehow he felt hardly any uneasiness when he found himself swiftly climbing and descending the low hills of water through the black night. And here it was not all black. The heavens had vanished, and the surface of the sea; but far, far below him in the heart of the vacancy through which he appeared to be travelling, strange bursting star shells and writhing streaks of a bluish-green luminosity appeared. At first they were very remote, but soon, as far as he could judge, they were nearer. A whole world of phosphorescent creatures seemed to be at play not far from the surface – coiling eels and darting things in complete armour, and then heraldically fantastic shapes to which the sea-horse of our own waters would be commonplace. They were all round him – twenty or thirty of them often in sight at once. And mixed with all this riot of sea-centaurs and sea-dragons he saw yet stranger forms: fishes, if fishes they were, whose forward part was so nearly human in shape that when he first caught sight of them he thought he had fallen into a dream and shook himself to awake. But it was no dream. There – and there again – it was unmistakable: now a shoulder, now a profile, and then for one second a full face: veritable mermen or mermaids. The resemblance to humanity was indeed greater, not less, than he had first supposed. What had for a moment concealed it from him was the total absence of human expression. Yet the faces were not idiotic; they were not even brutal parodies of humanity like those of our terrestrial apes. They were more like human faces asleep, or faces in which humanity slept while some other life, neither bestial nor diabolic, but merely elvish, out of our orbit, was irrelevantly awake. He remembered his old suspicion that what was myth in one world might always be fact in some other. He wondered also whether the King and Queen of Perelandra, though doubtless the first human pair of this planet, might on the physical side have a marine ancestry. And if so, what then of the man-like things before men in our own world? Must they in truth have been the wistful brutalities whose pictures we see in popular books on evolution?

Or were the old myths truer than the modern myths? Had there in truth been a time when satyrs danced in the Italian woods? But he said 'Hush' to his mind at this stage, for the mere pleasure of breathing in the fragrance which now began to steal towards him from the blackness ahead. Warm and sweet, and every moment sweeter and purer, and every moment stronger and more filled with all delights, it came to him. He knew well what it was. He would know it henceforward out of the whole universe – the night breath of a floating island in the star Venus. It was strange to be filled with homesickness for places where his sojourn had been so brief and which were, by any objective standard, so alien to all our race. Or were they? The cord of longing which drew him to the invisible isle seemed to him at that moment to have been fastened long, long before his coming to Perelandra, long before the earliest times that memory could recover in his childhood, before his birth, before the birth of man himself, before the origins of time. It was sharp, sweet, wild and holy, all in one, and in any world where men's nerves have ceased to obey their central desires would doubtless have been aphrodisiac too, but not in Perelandra. The fish was no longer moving. Ransom put out his hand. He found he was touching weed. He crawled forward over the head of the monstrous fish, and levered himself on to the gently moving surface of the island. Short as his absence from such places had been, his earth-trained habits of walking had reasserted themselves, and he fell more than once as he groped his way on the heaving lawn. But it did not harm falling here; good luck to it! There were trees all about him in the dark and when a smooth, cool, rounded object came away in his hand he put it, unfearing, to his lips. It was none of the fruits he had tasted before. It was better than any of them. Well might the Lady say of her world that the fruit you ate at any moment was, at that moment, the best. Wearied with his day's walking and climbing, and, still more, borne down by absolute satisfaction, he sank into dreamless sleep.

He felt that it was several hours later when he awoke and found himself still in darkness. He knew, too, that he had been suddenly waked: and a moment later he was listening to the sound that had waked him. It was the sound of voices – a man's voice and a woman's in earnest conversation. He judged that they were very close to him – for in a Perelandrian night an object is no more visible six inches than six miles away. He perceived at once who the speakers were: but the voices sounded strange, and the emotions of the speakers were obscure to him, with no facial expression to eke them out.

'I am wondering,' said the woman's voice, 'whether all the people of your world have the habit of talking about the same thing more than once. I have said already that we are forbidden to dwell on the Fixed Land. Why do you not either talk of something else or stop talking?'

'Because this forbidding is such a strange one,' said the man's voice. 'And so unlike the ways of Maleldil in my world. And He has not forbidden you to think about dwelling on the Fixed Land.'

'That would be a strange thing – to think about what will never happen.'

'Nay, in our world we do it all the time. We put words together to mean things that have never happened and places that never were: beautiful words, well put together. And then tell them to one another. We call it stories or poetry. In that old world you spoke of, Malacandra, they did the same. It is for mirth and wonder and wisdom.'

'What is the wisdom in it?'

'Because the world is made up not only of what is but of what might be. Maleldil knows both and wants us to know both.'

'This is more than I ever thought of. The other – the Piebald one – has already told me things which made me feel like a tree whose branches were growing wider and wider apart. But this goes beyond all. Stepping out of what is into what might be and talking and making things out there ... alongside the world. I will ask the King what he thinks of it.'

'You see, that is what we always come back to. If only you had not been parted from the King.'

'Oh, I see. That also is one of the things that might be. The world might be so made that the King and I were never parted.'

'The world would not have to be different – only the way you live. In a world where people live on the Fixed Lands they do not become suddenly separated.'

'But you remember we are not to live on the Fixed Land.'

'No, but He has never forbidden you to think about it. Might not that be one of the reasons why you are forbidden to do it – so that you may have a Might Be to think about, to make Story about as we call it?'

'I will think more of this. I will get the King to make me older about it.'

'How greatly I desire to meet this King of yours! But in the matter of Stories he may be no older than you himself.'

'That saying of yours is like a tree with no fruit. The King is always older than I, and about all things.'

'But Piebald and I have already made you older about certain matters which the King never mentioned to you. That is the new good which you never expected. You thought you would always learn all things from the King; but now Maleldil has sent you other men whom it had never entered your mind to think of and they have told you things the King himself could not know.'

'I begin to see now why the King and I were parted at this time. This is a strange and great good He intended for me.'

'And if you refused to learn things from me and keep on saying you would wait and ask the King, would that not be like turning away from the fruit you had found to the fruit you had expected?'

'These are deep questions, Stranger. Maleldil is not putting much into my mind about them.'

'Do you not see why?'

'No.'

'Since Piebald and I have come to your world we have put many things into your mind which Maleldil has not. Do you not see that He is letting go of your hand a little?'

'How could He? He is wherever we go.'

'Yes, but in another way. He is making you older – making you to learn things not straight from Him but by your own meetings with other people and your own questions and thoughts.'

'He is certainly doing that.'

'Yes. He is making you a full woman, for up till now you were only half made – like the beasts who do nothing of themselves. This time, when you meet the King again, it is you who will have things to tell him. It is you who will be older than he and who will make him older.'

'Maleldil would not make a thing like that happen. It would be like a fruit with no taste.'

'But it would have a taste for *him*. Do you not think the King must sometimes be tired of being the older? Would he not love you more if you were wiser than he?'

'Is this what you call a Poetry or do you mean that it really is?'

'I mean a thing that really is.'

'But how could anyone love anything more? It is like saying a thing could be bigger than itself.'

'I only meant you could become more like the women of my world.'

'What are they like?'

'They are of a great spirit. They always reach out their hands for the new and unexpected good, and see that it is good long before the men understand it. Their minds run ahead of what Maleldil has told them. They do not need to wait for Him to tell them what is good, but know it for themselves as He does. They are, as it were, little Maleldils. And because of their wisdom, their beauty is as much greater than yours as the sweetness of these gourds surpasses the taste of water. And because of their beauty the love which the men have for them is as much greater than the King's love for you as the naked burning of Deep Heaven seen from my world is more wonderful than the golden roof of yours.'

'I wish I could see them.'

'I wish you could.'

'How beautiful is Maleldil and how wonderful are all His works: perhaps He will bring out of me daughters as much greater than I as I am greater than the beasts. It will be better than I thought. I had thought I was to be always Queen and Lady. But I see now that I may be as the *eldila*. I may be appointed to cherish when they are small and weak children who will grow up and overtop me and at whose feet I shall fall. I see it is not only questions and thoughts that grow out wider and wider like branches. Joy also widens out and comes where we had never thought.'

'I will sleep now,' said the other voice. As it said this it became, for the first time, unmistakably the voice of Weston and of Weston disgruntled and snappish. Up till now Ransom, though constantly resolving to join the conversation, had been kept silent in a kind of suspense between two conflicting states of mind. On the one hand he was certain, both from the voice and from many of the things it said, that the male speaker was Weston. On the other hand, the voice, divided from the man's appearance, sounded curiously unlike itself. Still more, the patient persistent manner in which it was used was very unlike the Professor's usual alternation between pompous lecturing and abrupt bullying. And how could a man fresh from such a physical crisis as he had seen Weston undergo have recovered such mastery of himself in a few hours? And how could he have reached the floating island? Ransom had found himself throughout their dialogue confronted with an intolerable contradiction. Something which was and was not Weston was talking: and the sense of this monstrosity, only a few feet away in the darkness, had sent thrills of exquisite horror tingling along his spine, and raised questions in his mind which he tried to dismiss as fantastic. Now that the conversation was over he realised, too, with what intense anxiety he had followed it. At the same moment he was conscious of a sense of triumph. But it was not he who was triumphant. The whole darkness about him rang with victory. He started and half raised himself. Had there been any actual sound? Listening hard he could hear nothing but the low murmurous noise of warm wind and gentle swell. The suggestion of music must have been from within. But as soon as he lay down again he felt assured that it was not. From without, most certainly from without, but not by the sense of hearing, festal revelry and dance and splendour poured into him – no sound, yet in such fashion that it could not be remembered or thought of except as music. It was like having a new sense. It was like being present when the morning stars sang together. It was as if Perelandra had that moment been created – and perhaps in some sense it had. The feeling of a great disaster averted was forced upon his mind, and with it came the hope that there would be no second attempt; and then, sweeter than all, the suggestion that he had been brought there not to do anything but only as a spectator or a witness. A few minutes later he was asleep.

9

The weather had changed during the night. Ransom sat looking out from the edge of the forest in which he had slept, on a flat sea where there were no other islands in view. He had waked a few minutes before and found himself lying alone in a close thicket of stems that were rather reed-like in character but stout as those of birch trees and which carried an almost flat roof of thick foliage. From this there hung fruits as smooth and bright and round as holly-berries, some of which he ate. Then he found his way to open country near the skirts of the island and looked about him. Neither Weston nor the Lady was in sight, and he began walking in a leisurely fashion beside the sea. His bare feet sank a little into a carpet of saffron-coloured vegetation, which covered them with an aromatic dust. As he was looking down at this he suddenly noticed something else. At first he thought it was a creature of more fantastic shape than he had yet seen on Perelandra. Its shape was not only fantastic but hideous. Then he dropped on one knee to examine it. Finally he touched it, with reluctance. A moment later he drew back his hands like a man who had touched a snake.

It was a damaged animal. It was, or had been, one of the brightly coloured frogs. But some accident had happened to it. The whole back had been ripped open in a sort of V-shaped gash, the point of the V being a little behind the head. Some thing had torn a widening wound backward – as we do in opening an envelope – along the trunk and pulled it out so far behind the animal that the hoppers or hind legs had been almost torn off with it. They were so damaged that the frog could not leap. On earth it would have been merely a nasty sight, but up to this moment Ransom had as yet seen nothing dead or spoiled in Perelandra, and it was like a blow in the face. It was like the first spasm of well-remembered pain warning a man who had thought he was cured that his family have deceived him and he is dying after all. It was like the first lie from the mouth of a friend on whose truth one was willing to stake a thousand pounds. It was irrevocable. The milk-warm wind blowing over the golden sea, the blues and silvers and greens of the floating garden, the sky itself – all these had become, in one instant, merely the illuminated margin of a book whose text was the struggling little horror at his feet, and he himself, in that same instant, had passed into a state of emotion which he could neither control nor understand. He told himself that a creature of that kind probably had very little sensation. But it did not much mend matters. It was not merely pity for pain that had suddenly changed the rhythm of his heart-beats. The thing was an intolerable obscenity which afflicted him with shame. It would have been better, or so he thought at that moment, for the whole universe never to have existed than for this one thing to have happened. Then he decided, in spite of his theoretical belief that it was an organism too low for much pain, that it had better be killed. He had neither boots nor stone nor stick. The frog proved remarkably hard to kill. When it was far too late to desist he saw clearly that he had been a fool to make the attempt. Whatever its sufferings might be he had certainly increased and not diminished them. But he had to go through with it. The job seemed to take nearly an hour. And when at last the mangled result was quite still and he went down to the water's edge to wash, he was sick and shaken. It seems odd to say this of a man who had been on the Somme; but the architects tell us that nothing is great or small save by position.

At last he got up and resumed his walk. Next moment he started and looked at the ground again. He quickened his pace, and then once more stopped and looked. He stood stock-still and covered his face. He called aloud upon heaven to break the nightmare or to let him understand what was happening. A trail of mutilated frogs lay along the edge of the island. Picking his footsteps with care, he followed it. He counted ten, fifteen, twenty: and the twenty-first brought him to a place where the wood came down to the water's edge. He went into the wood and came out on the other side. There he stopped dead and stared. Weston, still clothed but without his pith helmet, was standing about thirty feet away: and as Ransom watched he was tearing a frog – quietly and almost surgically inserting his forefinger, with its long sharp nail, under the skin behind the creature's head and ripping it open. Ransom had not noticed before that Weston had such remarkable nails. Then he finished the operation, threw the bleeding ruin away, and looked up. Their eyes met.

If Ransom said nothing, it was because he could not speak. He saw a man who was certainly not ill, to judge from his easy stance and the powerful use he had just been making of his fingers. He saw a man who was certainly Weston, to judge from his height and build and colouring and features. In that sense he was quite recognisable. But the terror was that he was also unrecognisable. He did not look like a sick man: but he looked very like a dead one. The face which he raised from torturing the frog had that terrible power which the face of a corpse sometimes has of simply rebuffing every conceivable human attitude one can adopt towards it. The expressionless mouth, the unwinking stare of the eyes, something heavy and inorganic in the very folds of the cheek, said clearly: 'I have features as you have, but there is nothing in common between you and me.' It was this that kept Ransom speechless. What could you say – what appeal or threat could have any meaning – to *that*? And now, forcing its way up into consciousness, thrusting aside every mental habit and every longing not to believe, came the conviction that this, in fact, was not a man: that Weston's body was kept, walking and undecaying, in Perelandra by some wholly different kind of life, and that Weston himself was gone.

It looked at Ransom in silence and at last began to smile. We have all often spoken – Ransom himself had often spoken – of a devilish smile. Now he realised that he had never taken the words seriously. The smile was not bitter, nor raging, nor, in an ordinary sense, sinister; it was not even mocking. It seemed to summon Ransom, with a horrible naïveté of welcome, into the world of its own pleasures, as if all men were at one in those pleasures, as if they were the most natural thing in the world and no dispute could ever have occurred about them. It was not furtive, nor ashamed, it had nothing of the conspirator in it. It did not defy goodness, it ignored it to the point of annihilation. Ransom perceived that he had never before seen anything but half-hearted and uneasy attempts at evil. This creature was whole-hearted. The extremity of its evil had passed beyond all struggle into some state which bore a horrible similarity to innocence. It was beyond vice as the Lady was beyond virtue.

The stillness and the smiling lasted for perhaps two whole minutes: certainly not less. Then Ransom made to take a step towards the thing, with no very clear notion of what he would do when he reached it. He stumbled and fell. He had a curious difficulty in getting to his feet again, and when he got to them he overbalanced and fell for the second time. Then there was a moment of darkness filled with a noise of roaring express trains. After that the golden sky and coloured waves returned and he knew he was alone and recovering from a faint. As he lay there, still unable and perhaps unwilling to rise, it came into his mind that in certain old philosophers and poets he had read that the mere sight of the devils was one of the greatest among the torments of Hell. It had seemed to him till now merely a quaint fancy. And yet (as he now saw) even the children know better: no child would have any difficulty in understanding that there might be a face the mere beholding of which was final calamity. The children, the poets, and the philosophers were right. As there is one Face above all worlds merely to see which is irrevocable joy, so at the bottom of all worlds that face is waiting whose sight alone is the misery from which none who beholds it can recover. And though there seemed to be, and indeed were, a thousand roads by which a man could walk through the world, there was not a single one which did not lead sooner or later either to the Beatific or the Miserific Vision. He himself had, of course, seen only a mask or faint adumbration of it; even so, he was not quite sure that he would live.

When he was able, he got up and set out to search for the thing. He must either try to prevent it from meeting the Lady or at least be present when they met. What he could do, he did not know; but it was clear beyond all evasion that this was what he had been sent for. Weston's body, travelling in a space-ship, had been the bridge by which something else had invaded Perelandra – whether that supreme and original evil whom in Mars they call The Bent One, or one of his lesser followers, made no difference. Ransom was all goose flesh, and his knees kept getting in each other's way. It surprised him that he could experience so extreme a terror and yet be walking and thinking – as men in war or sickness are surprised to find how much can be borne. 'It will drive us mad,' 'It will kill us outright,' we say; and then it happens and we find ourselves neither mad nor dead, still held to the task.

The weather changed. The plain on which he was walking swelled to a wave of land. The sky grew paler: it was soon rather primrose than gold. The sea grew darker, almost the colour of bronze. Soon the island was climbing considerable hills of water. Once or twice he had to sit down and rest. After several hours (for his progress was very slow) he suddenly saw two human figures on what was for the moment a skyline. Next moment they were out of sight as the country heaved up between them and him. It took about half an hour to reach them. Weston's body was standing swaying and balancing itself to meet each change of the ground in a manner of which the real Weston would have been incapable. It was talking to the Lady. And what surprised Ransom most was that she continued to listen to it without turning to welcome him or even to comment on his arrival when he came and sat down beside her on the soft turf.

'It *is* a great branching out,' it was saying. 'This making of story or poetry about things that might be but are not. If you shrink back from it, are you not drawing back from the fruit that is offered you?'

'It is not from the making a story that I shrink back, O Stranger,' she answered, 'but from this one story that you have put into my head. I can make myself stories about my children or the King. I can make it that the fish fly and the land beasts swim. But if I try to make the story about living on Fixed Land I do not know how to make it about Maleldil. For if I make it that He has changed His command, that will not go. And if I make it that we are living there against His command, that is like making the sky all black and the water so that we cannot drink it and the air so that we cannot breathe it. But also, I do not see what is the pleasure of trying to make these things.'

'To make you wiser, older,' said Weston's body.

'Do you know for certain that it will do that?' she asked.

'Yes, for certain,' it replied. 'That is how the women of my world have become so great and so beautiful.'

'Do not listen to him,' broke in Ransom; 'send him away. Do not hear what he says, do not think of it.'

She turned to Ransom for the first time. There had been some very slight change in her face since he had last seen her. It was not sad, nor deeply bewildered, but the hint of something precarious had increased. On the other hand she was clearly pleased to see him, though surprised at his interruption; and her first words revealed that her failure to greet him at his arrival had resulted from her never having envisaged the possibility of a conversation between more than two speakers. And throughout the rest of their talk, her ignorance of the technique of general conversation gave a curious and disquieting quality to the whole scene. She had no notion of how to glance rapidly from one face to another or to disentangle two remarks at once. Sometimes she listened wholly to Ransom, sometimes wholly to the other, but never to both.

'Why do you start speaking before this man has finished, Piebald?' she inquired. 'How do they do in your world where you are many and more than two must often be together? Do they not talk in turns; or have you an art to understand even when all speak together? I am not old enough for that.'

'I do not want you to hear him at all,' said Ransom. 'He is –' and then he hesitated. 'Bad', 'liar', 'enemy', none of these words would, as yet, have any meaning for her. Racking his brains he thought of their previous conversation about the great *eldil* who had held on to the old good and refused the new one. Yes; that would be her only approach to the idea of badness. He was just about to speak but it was too late. Weston's voice anticipated him.

'This Piebald,' it said, 'does not want you to hear me, because he wants to keep you young. He does not want you to go on to the new fruits that you have never tasted before.'

'But how could he want to keep me younger?'

'Have you not seen already,' said Weston's body, 'that Piebald is one who always shrinks back from the wave that is coming towards us and would like, if he could, to bring back the wave that is past? In the very first hour of his talking with you, did he not betray this? He did not know that all was new since Maleldil became a man and that now all creatures with reason will be men. You had to teach him this. And when he had learned it he did not welcome it. He was sorry that there would be no more of the old furry people. He would bring back that old world if he could. And when you asked him to teach you Death, he would not. He wanted you to remain young, not to learn Death. Was it not he who first put into your mind the very thought that it was possible not to desire the wave that Maleldil was rolling towards us; to shrink so much that you would cut off your arms and legs to prevent it coming?'

'You mean he is so young?'

'He is what in my world we call Bad,' said Weston's body. 'One who rejects the fruit he is given for the sake of the fruit he expected or the fruit he found last time.'

'We must make him older, then,' said the Lady, and though she did not look at Ransom, all the Queen and Mother in her were revealed to him and he knew that she wished him, and all things, infinitely well. And he – he could do nothing. His weapon had been knocked out of his hand.

'And will you teach us Death?' said the Lady to Weston's shape, where it stood above her.

'Yes,' it said, 'it is for this that I came here, that you may have Death in abundance. But you must be very courageous.'

'*Courageous*. What is that?'

'It is what makes you to swim on a day when the waves are so great and swift that something inside you bids you to stay on land.'

'I know. And those are the best days of all for swimming.'

'Yes. But to find Death, and with Death the real oldness and the strong beauty and the uttermost branching out, you must plunge into things greater than waves.'

'Go on. Your words are like no other words that I have ever heard. They are like the bubble breaking on the tree. They make me think of – of – I do not know what they make me think of.'

'I will speak greater words than these; but I must wait till you are older.'

'Make me older.'

'Lady, Lady,' broke in Ransom, 'will not Maleldil make you older in His own time and His own way, and will not that be far better?'

Weston's face did not turn in his direction either at this point or at any other time during the conversation, but his voice, addressed wholly to the Lady, answered Ransom's interruption.

'You see?' it said. 'He himself, though he did not mean nor wish to do so, made you see a few days ago that Maleldil is beginning to teach you to walk by yourself, without holding you by the hand. That was the first branching out. When you came to know that, you were becoming really old. And since then Maleldil has let you learn much – not from His own voice, but from mine. You are becoming your own. That is what Maleldil wants you to do. That is why He has let you be separated from the King and even, in a way, from Himself. His way of making you older is to make you make yourself older. And yet this Piebald would have you sit still and wait for Maleldil to do it all.'

'What must we do to Piebald to make him older?' said the Lady.

'I do not think you can help him till you are older yourself,' said the voice of Weston. 'You cannot help anyone yet. You are as a tree without fruit.'

'It is very true,' said the Lady. 'Go on.'

'Then listen,' said Weston's body. 'Have you understood that to wait for Maleldil's voice when Maleldil wishes you to walk on your own is a kind of disobedience?'

'I think I have.'

'The wrong kind of obeying itself can be a disobeying.'

The Lady thought for a few moments and then clapped her hands. 'I see,' she said, 'I see! Oh, how old you make me. Before now I have chased a beast for mirth. And it has understood and run away from me. If it had stood still and let me catch it, that would have been a sort of obeying – but not the best sort.'

'You understand very well. When you are fully grown you will be even wiser and more beautiful than the women of my own world. And you see that it might be so with Maleldil's biddings.'

'I think I do not see quite clearly.'

'Are you certain that He really wishes to be always obeyed?'

'How can we not obey what we love?'

'The beast that ran away loved you.'

'I wonder,' said the Lady, 'if that is the same. The beast knows very well when I meant to run away and when I want it to come to me. But Maleldil has never said to us that any word or work of His was a jest. How could our Beloved need to jest or frolic as we do? He is all a burning joy and a strength. It is like thinking that He needed sleep or food.'

'No, it would not be a jest. That is only a thing like it, not the thing itself. But could the taking away of your hand from His – the full growing up – the walking in your own way – could that ever be perfect unless you had, if only once, *seemed* to disobey Him?'

'How could one *seem* to disobey?'

'By doing what He only *seemed* to forbid. There might be a commanding which He wished you to break.'

'But if He told us we were to break it, then it would be no command. And if He did not, how should we know?'

'How wise you are growing, beautiful one,' said Weston's mouth. 'No. If He told you to break what He commanded, it would be no true command, as you have seen. For you are right, He makes no jests. A real disobeying, a real branching out, this is what He secretly longs for: secretly, because to tell you would spoil all.'

'I begin to wonder,' said the Lady after a pause, 'whether you are so much older than I. Surely what you are saying is like fruit with no taste! How can I step out of His will save into something that cannot be wished? Shall I start trying not to love Him – or the King – or the beasts? It would be like trying to walk on water or swim through islands. Shall I try not to sleep or to drink or to laugh? I thought your words had a meaning. But now it seems they have none. To walk out of His will is to walk into nowhere.'

'That is true of all His commands except one.'

'But can that one be different?'

'Nay, you see of yourself that it is different. These other commands of His – to love, to sleep, to fill this world with your children – you see for yourself that they are good. And they are the same in all worlds. But the command against living on the Fixed Island is not so. You have already learned that He gave no such command to my world. And you cannot see where the goodness of it is. No wonder. If it were really good, must He not have commanded it to all worlds alike? For how could Maleldil not command what was good? There is *no* good in it. Maleldil Himself is showing you that, this moment, through your own reason. It is mere command. It is forbidding for the mere sake of forbidding.'

'But why ...?'

'In order that you may break it. What other reason can there be? It is not good. It is not the same for other worlds. It stands between you and all settled life, all command of your own days. Is not Maleldil showing you as plainly as He can that it was set up as a test – as a great wave you have to go over, that you may become really old, really separate from Him.'

'But if this concerns me so deeply, why does He put none of this into my mind? It is all coming from you, Stranger. There is no whisper, even, of the Voice saying Yes to your words.'

'But do you not see that there cannot be? He longs – oh, how greatly He longs – to see His creature become fully itself, to stand up in its own reason and its own courage even against Him. But how can He tell it to do this? That would spoil all. Whatever it did after that would only be one more step taken with Him. This is the one thing of all the things He desires in which He must have no finger. Do you think He is not weary of seeing nothing but Himself in all that He has made? If that contented Him, why should He create at all? To find the Other – the thing whose will is no longer His – that is Maleldil's desire.'

'If I could but know this –'

'He must not tell you. He cannot tell you. The nearest He can come to telling you is to let some other creature tell it for Him. And behold, He has done so. Is it for nothing, or without His will, that I have journeyed through Deep Heaven to teach you what He would have you know but must not teach you Himself?'

'Lady,' said Ransom, 'if I speak, will you hear me?'

'Gladly, Piebald.'

'This man has said that the law against living on the Fixed Island is different from the other Laws, because it is not the same for all worlds and because we cannot see the goodness in it. And so far he says well. But then he says that it is thus different in order that you may disobey it. But there might be another reason.'

'Say it, Piebald.'

'I think He made one law of that kind in order that there might be obedience. In all these other matters what you call obeying Him is but doing what seems good in your own eyes also. Is love content with that? You do them, indeed, because they are His will, but not only because they are His will. Where can you taste the joy of obeying unless He bids you do something for which His bidding is the *only* reason? When we spoke last you said that if you told the beasts to walk on their heads, they would delight to do so. So I know that you understand well what I am saying.'

'Oh, brave Piebald,' said the Green Lady, 'this is the best you have said yet. This makes me older fare: yet it does not feel like the oldness this other is giving me. Oh, how well I see it! We cannot walk out of Maleldil's will: but He has given us a way to walk out of *our* will. And there could be no such way except a command like this. Out of our own will. It is like passing out through the world's roof into Deep Heaven. All beyond is Love Himself. I knew there was joy in looking upon the Fixed Island and laying down all thought of ever living there, but I did not till now understand.' Her face was radiant as she spoke, but then a shade of bewilderment crossed it. 'Piebald,' she said, 'if you are so young, as this other says, how do you know these things?'

'He says I am young, but I say not.'

The voice of Weston's face spoke suddenly, and it was louder and deeper than before and less like Weston's voice.

'I am older than he,' it said, 'and he dare not deny it. Before the mothers of the mothers of his mother were conceived, I was already older than he could reckon. I have been with Maleldil in Deep Heaven where he never came and heard the eternal councils. And in the order of creation I am greater than he, and before me he is of no account. Is it not so?' The corpse-like face did not even now turn towards him, but the speaker and the Lady both seemed to wait for Ransom to reply. The falsehood which sprang to his mind died on his lips. In that air, even when truth seemed fatal, only truth would serve. Licking his lips and choking down a feeling of nausea, he answered:

'In our world to be older is not always to be wiser.'

'Look on him,' said Weston's body to the Lady; 'consider how white his cheeks have turned and how his forehead is wet. You have not seen such things before: you will see them more often hereafter. It is what happens – it is the beginning of what happens – to little creatures when they set themselves against great ones.

An exquisite thrill of fear travelled along Ransom's spine. What saved him was the face of the Lady. Untouched by the evil so close to her, removed as it were ten years' journey deep within the region of her own innocence, and by that innocence at once so protected and so endangered, she looked up at the standing Death above her, puzzled indeed, but not beyond the bounds of cheerful curiosity, and said:

'But he was right, Stranger, about this forbidding. It is you who need to be made older. Can you not see?'

'I have always seen the whole whereof he sees but the half. It is most true that Maleldil has given you a way of walking out of your own will – but out of your deepest will.'

'And what is that?'

'Your deepest will, at present, is to obey Him – to be always as you are now, only His beast or His very young child. The way out of that is hard. It was made hard that only the very great, the very wise, the very courageous should dare to walk in it, to go on – on out of this smallness in which you now live – through the dark wave of His forbidding, into the real life, Deep Life, with all its joy and splendour and hardness.'

'Listen, Lady,' said Ransom. 'There is something he is not telling you. All this that we are now talking has been talked before. The thing he wants you to try has been tried before. Long ago, when our world began, there was only one man and one woman in it, as you and the King are in this. And there once before he stood, as he stands now, talking to the woman. He had found her alone as he has found you alone. And she listened, and did the thing Maleldil had forbidden her to do. But no joy and splendour came of it. What came of it I cannot tell you because you have no image of it in your mind. But all love was troubled and made cold, and Maleldil's voice became hard to hear so that wisdom grew little among them; and the woman was against the man and the mother against the child; and when they looked to eat there was no fruit on their trees, and hunting for food took all their time, so that their life became narrower, not wider.'

'He has hidden the half of what happened,' said Weston's corpse-like mouth. 'Hardness came out of it but also splendour. They made with their own hands mountains higher than your Fixed Island. They made for themselves Floating Islands greater than yours which they could move at will through the ocean faster than any bird can fly. Because there was not always food enough, a woman could give the only fruit to her child or her husband and eat death instead – could give them all, as you in your little narrow life of playing and kissing and riding fishes have never done, nor shall do till you break the commandment. Because knowledge was harder to find, those few who found it became beautiful and excelled their fellows as you excel the beasts; and thousands were striving for their love ...'

'I think I will go to sleep now,' said the Lady quite suddenly. Up to this point she had been listening to Weston's body with open mouth and wide eyes, but as he spoke of the women with the thousands of lovers she yawned, with the unconcealed and unpremeditated yawn of a young cat.

'Not yet,' said the other. 'There is more. He has not told you that it was this breaking of the commandment which brought Maleldil to our world and because of which He was made man. He dare not deny it.'

'Do you say this, Piebald?' asked the Lady.

Ransom was sitting with his fingers locked so tightly that his knuckles were white. The unfairness of it all was wounding him like barbed wire. Unfair ... unfair. How could Maleldil expect him to fight against this, to fight with every weapon taken from him, forbidden to lie and yet brought to places where truth seemed fatal? It was unfair! A sudden impulse of hot rebellion arose in him. A second later, doubt, like a huge wave, came breaking over him. How if the enemy were right after all? *Felix peccatum Adae.* Even the Church would tell him that good came of disobedience in the end. Yes, and it was true too that he, Ransom, was a timid creature, a man who shrank back from new and hard things. On which side, after all, did the temptation lie? Progress passed before his eyes in a great momentary vision: cities, armies, tall ships and libraries and fame, and the grandeur of poetry spurting like a fountain out of the labours and ambitions of men. Who could be certain that Creative Evolution was not the deepest truth? From all sorts of secret crannies in his own mind whose very existence he had never before suspected, something wild and heady and delicious began to rise, to pour itself towards the shape of Weston. 'It is a spirit, it is a spirit,' said this inner voice, 'and you are only a man. It goes on from century to century. You are only a man ...'

'Do you say this, Piebald?' asked the Lady a second time.

The spell was broken.

'I will tell you what I say,' answered Ransom, jumping to his feet. 'Of course good came of it. Is Maleldil a beast that we can stop His path, or a leaf that we can twist His shape? Whatever you do, He will make good of it. But not the good He had prepared for you if you had obeyed Him. That is lost for ever. The first King and first Mother of our world did the forbidden thing; and He brought good of it in the end. But what they did was not good; and what they lost we have not seen. And there were some to whom no good came nor ever will come.' He turned to the body of Weston. 'You,' he said, 'tell her all. What good came to you? Do *you* rejoice that Maleldil became a man? Tell her of *your* joys, and of what profit you had when you made Maleldil and death acquainted.'

In the moment that followed this speech two things happened that were utterly unlike terrestrial experience. The body that had been Weston's threw up its head and opened its mouth and gave a long melancholy howl like a dog; and the Lady lay down, wholly unconcerned, and closed her eyes and was instantly asleep. And while these two things were happening the piece of ground on which the two men stood and the woman lay was rushing down a great hillside of water.

Ransom kept his eyes fixed upon the enemy, but it took no notice of him. Its eyes moved like the eyes of a living man but it was hard to be sure what it was looking at, or whether it really used the eyes as organs of vision at all. One got the impression of a force that cleverly kept the pupils of those eyes fixed in a suitable direction while the mouth talked but which, for its own purpose, used wholly different modes of perception. The thing sat down close to the Lady's head on the far side of her from Ransom. If you could call it sitting down. The body did not reach its squatting position by the normal movements of a man: it was more as if some external force manoeuvred it into the right position and then let it drop. It was impossible to point to any particular motion which was definitely non-human. Ransom had the sense of watching an imitation of living motions which had been very well studied and was technically correct: but somehow it lacked the master touch. And he was chilled with an inarticulate, night-nursery horror of the thing he had to deal with – the managed corpse, the bogey, the Un-man.

There was nothing to do but to watch: to sit there, for ever if need be, guarding the Lady from the Un-man while their island climbed interminably over the Alps and Andes of burnished water. All three were very still. Beasts and birds came often and looked upon them. Hours later the Un-man began to speak. It did not even look in Ransom's direction; slowly and cumbrously, as if by some machinery that needed oiling, it made its mouth and lips pronounce his name.

'Ransom,' it said.

'Well?' said Ransom.

'Nothing,' said the Un-man. He shot an inquisitive glance at it. Was the creature mad? But it looked, as before, dead rather than mad, sitting there with the head bowed and the mouth a little open, and some yellow dust from the moss settled in the creases of its cheeks, and the legs crossed tailor-wise, and the hands, with their long metallic-looking nails, pressed flat together on the ground before it. He dismissed the problem from his mind and returned to his own uncomfortable thoughts.

'Ransom,' it said again.

'What is it?' said Ransom sharply.

'Nothing,' it answered.

Again there was silence; and again, about a minute later, the horrible mouth said:

'Ransom!' This time he made no reply. Another minute and it uttered his name again; and then, like a minute gun, 'Ransom ... Ransom ... Ransom,' perhaps a hundred times.

'What the Hell do you want?' he roared at last. 'Nothing,' said the voice. Next time he determined not to answer; but when it had called on him about a thousand times he found himself answering whether he would or no, and 'Nothing,' came the reply. He taught himself to keep silent in the end: not that the torture of resisting his impulse to speak was less than the torture of response but because something with him rose up to combat the tormentor's assurance that he must yield in the end. If the attack had been of some more violent kind it might have been easier to resist. What chilled and almost cowed him was the union of malice with something nearly childish. For temptation, for blasphemy, for a whole battery of horrors, he was in some sort prepared: but hardly for this petty, indefatigable nagging as of a nasty little boy at a preparatory school. Indeed no imagined horror could have surpassed the sense which grew within him as the slow hours passed, that this creature was, by all human standards, inside out – its heart on the surface and its shallowness at the heart. On the surface, great designs and an antagonism to Heaven which involved the fate of worlds: but deep within, when every veil had been pierced, was there, after all, nothing but a black puerility, an aimless empty spitefulness content to sate itself with the tiniest cruelties, as love does not disdain the smallest kindness? What kept him steady, long after all possibility of thinking about something else had disappeared, was the decision that if he must hear either the word Ransom or the word Nothing a million times, he would prefer the word Ransom.

And all the time the little jewel-coloured land went soaring up into the yellow firmament and hung there a moment and tilted its woods and went racing down into the warm lustrous depths between the waves: and the Lady lay sleeping with one arm bent beneath her head and her lips a little parted. Sleeping assuredly –

for her eyes were shut and her breathing regular – yet not looking quite like those who sleep in our world, for her face was full of expression and intelligence, and the limbs looked as if they were ready at any moment to leap up, and altogether she gave the impression that sleep was not a thing that happened to her but an action which she performed.

Then all at once it was night. 'Ransom ... Ransom ... Ransom ... Ransom,' went on the voice. And suddenly it crossed his mind that though he would some time require sleep, the Un-man might not.

10

Sleep proved to be indeed the problem. For what seemed a great time, cramped and wearied, and soon hungry and thirsty as well, he sat still in the darkness trying not to attend to the unflagging repetition of 'Ransom – Ransom – Ransom.' But presently he found himself listening to a conversation of which he knew he had not heard the beginning and realised that he had slept. The Lady seemed to be saying very little. Weston's Voice was speaking gently and continuously. It was not talking about the Fixed Land nor even about Maleldil. It appeared to be telling, with extreme beauty and pathos, a number of stories, and at first Ransom could not perceive any connecting link between them. They were all about women, but women who had apparently lived at different periods of the world's history and in quite different circumstances. From the Lady's replies it appeared that the stories contained much that she did not understand; but oddly enough the Un-man did not mind. If the questions aroused by any one story proved at all difficult to answer, the speaker simply dropped that story and instantly began another. The heroines of the stories seemed all to have suffered a great deal – they had been oppressed by fathers, cast off by husbands, deserted by lovers. Their children had risen up against them and society had driven them out. But the stories all ended, in a sense, happily: sometimes with honours and praises to a heroine still living, more often with tardy acknowledgment and unavailing tears after her death. As the endless speech proceeded, the Lady's questions grew always fewer; some meaning for the words Death and Sorrow – though what kind of meaning

Ransom could not even guess – was apparently being created in her mind by mere repetition. At last it dawned upon him what all these stories were about. Each one of these women had stood forth alone and braved a terrible risk for her child, her lover, or her people. Each had been misunderstood, reviled and persecuted: but each also magnificently vindicated by the event. The precise details were often not very easy to follow. Ransom had more than a suspicion that many of these noble pioneers had been what in ordinary terrestrial speech we call witches or perverts. But that was all in the background. What emerged from the stories was rather an image than an idea – the picture of the tall, slender form, unbowed though the world's weight rested upon its shoulders, stepping forth fearless and friendless into the dark to do for others what those others forbade it to do yet needed to have done. And all the time, as a sort of background to these goddess shapes, the speaker was building up a picture of the other sex. No word was directly spoken on the subject: but one felt them there as a huge, dim multitude of creatures pitifully childish and complacently arrogant; timid, meticulous, unoriginating; sluggish and ox-like, rooted to the earth almost in their indolence, prepared to try nothing, to risk nothing, to make no exertion, and capable of being raised into full life only by the unthanked and rebellious virtue of their females. It was very well done. Ransom, who had little of the pride of sex, found himself for a few moments all but believing it.

In the midst of this the darkness was suddenly torn by a flash of lightning; a few seconds later came a revel of Perelandrian thunder, like the playing of a heavenly tambourine, and after that warm rain. Ransom did not much regard it. The flash had shown him the Un-man sitting bolt upright, the Lady raised on one elbow, the dragon lying awake at her head, a grove of trees beyond, and great waves against the horizon. He was thinking of what he had seen. He was wondering how the Lady could see that face – those jaws monotonously moving as if they were rather munching than talking – and not know the creature to be evil. He saw, of course, that this was unreasonable of him. He himself was doubtless an uncouth figure in her eyes; she could have no knowledge either about evil or about the normal appearance of terrestrial man to guide her. The expression on her face, revealed in the sudden light, was one that he had not seen there before. Her eyes were not fixed on the narrator: as far as that went, her thoughts might have been a thousand miles away. Her lips were shut and a little pursed. Her eyebrows were slightly raised. He had not yet seen her look so like a woman of our own race; and yet her expression was one he had not very often met on earth – except, as he realised with a shock, on the stage. 'Like a tragedy queen' was the disgusting comparison that arose in his mind. Of course it was a gross exaggeration. It was an insult for which he could not forgive himself. And yet ... and yet ... the tableau revealed by the lightning had photographed itself on his brain. Do what he would, he found it impossible not to think of that new look in her face. A very good tragedy queen, no doubt. The heroine of a very great tragedy, very nobly played by an actress who was a good woman in real life. By earthly standards, an expression to be praised, even to be revered: but remembering all that he had read in her countenance before, the unselfconscious radiance, the frolic sanctity, the depth of stillness that reminded him sometimes of infancy and sometimes of extreme old age while the hard youth and valiancy of face and body denied both, he found this new expression horrifying. The fatal touch of invited grandeur, of enjoyed pathos – the assumption, however slight, of a rôle – seemed a hateful vulgarity. Perhaps she was doing no more— he had good hope that she was doing no more – than responding in a purely imaginative fashion to this new art of Story or Poetry. But by God she'd better not! And for the first time the thought 'This can't go on' formulated itself in his mind.

'I will go where the leaves cover us from the rain,' said her voice in the darkness. Ransom had hardly noticed that he was getting wet – in a world without clothes it is less important. But he rose when he heard her move and followed her as well as he could by ear. The Un-man seemed to be doing the same. They progressed in total darkness on a surface as variable as that of water. Every now and then there was another flash. One saw the Lady walking erect, the Un-man slouching by her side with Weston's shirt and shorts now sodden and clinging to it, and the dragon puffing and waddling behind. At last they came to a place where the carpet under their feet was dry and there was a drumming noise of rain on firm leaves above their heads. They lay down again. 'And another time,' began the Un-man at once, 'there was a queen in our world who ruled over a little land—'

'Hush!' said the Lady, 'let us listen to the rain.' Then, after a moment, she added, 'What was that? It was some beast I never heard before' – and indeed, there had been something very like a low growl close beside them.

'I do not know,' said the voice of Weston.

'I think I do,' said Ransom.

'Hush!' said the Lady again, and no more was said that night.

This was the beginning of a series of days and nights which Ransom remembered with loathing for the rest of his life. He had been only too correct in supposing that his enemy required no sleep. Fortunately the Lady did, but she needed a good deal less than Ransom and possibly, as the days passed, came to take less than she needed. It seemed to Ransom that whenever he dozed he awoke to find the Un-man already in conversation with her. He was dead tired. He could hardly have endured it all but for the fact that their hostess quite frequently dismissed them both from her presence. On such occasions Ransom kept close to the Un-man. It was a rest from the main battle, but was a very imperfect rest. He did not dare to let the enemy out of his sight for a moment, and every day its society became more unendurable. He had full opportunity to learn the falsity of the maxim that the Prince of Darkness is a gentleman. Again and again he felt that a suave and subtle Mephistopheles with red cloak and rapier and a feather in his cap, or even a sombre tragic Satan out of *Paradise Lost*, would have been a welcome release from the thing he was actually doomed to watch. It was not like dealing with a wicked politician at all: it was much more like being set to guard an imbecile or a monkey or a very nasty child. What had staggered and disgusted him when it first began saying, 'Ransom ... Ransom ...' continued to disgust him every day and every hour. It showed plenty of subtlety and intelligence when talking to the Lady; but Ransom soon perceived that it regarded intelligence simply and solely as a weapon, which it had no more wish to employ in its off-duty hours than a soldier has to do bayonet practice when he is on leave. Thought was for it a device necessary to certain ends, but thought in itself did not interest it. It assumed reason as externally and inorganically as it had assumed Weston's body. The moment the Lady was out of sight it seemed to relapse. A great deal of his time was spent in protecting the animals from it. Whenever it got out of sight, or even a few yards ahead, it would make a grab at any beast or bird within its reach and pull out some fur or feathers. Ransom tried whenever possible to get between it and its victim. On such occasions there were nasty moments when the two stood facing each other. It never came to a fight, for the Un-man merely grinned and perhaps spat and fell back a little, but before that happened Ransom usually had opportunity to discover how terribly he feared it. For side by side with his disgust, the more childlike terror of living with a ghost or a mechanised corpse never left him for many minutes together. The fact of being *alone* with it sometimes rushed upon his mind with such dismay that it took all his reason to resist his longing for society – his impulse to rush madly over the island until he found the Lady and to beg her protection. When the Un-man could not get animals it was content with plants. It was fond of cutting their outer rinds through with its nails, or grubbing up roots, or pulling off leaves, or even tearing up handfuls of turf. With Ransom himself it had innumerable games to play. It had a whole repertory of obscenities to perform with its own – or rather with Weston's – body: and the mere silliness of them was almost worse than the dirtiness. It would sit making grimaces at him for hours together; and then, for hours more, it would go back to its old repetition of 'Ransom ... Ransom.' Often its grimaces achieved a horrible resemblance to people whom

Ransom had known and loved in our own world. But worst of all were those moments when it allowed Weston to come back into its countenance. Then its voice, which was always Weston's voice, would begin a pitiful, hesitant mumbling, 'You be very careful, Ransom. I'm down in the bottom of a big black hole. No, I'm not, though. I'm on Perelandra. I can't think very well now, but that doesn't matter, he does all my thinking for me. It'll get quite easy presently. That boy keeps on shutting the windows. That's all right, they've taken off my head and put someone else's on me. I'll soon be all right now. They won't let me see my press cuttings. So then I went and told him that if they didn't want me in the First Fifteen they could jolly well do without me, see. We'll tell that young whelp it's an insult to the examiners to show up this kind of work. What I want to know is why I should pay for a first-class ticket and then be crowded out like this. It's not fair. Not fair. I never meant any harm. Could you take some of this weight off my chest, I don't want all those clothes. Let me alone. Let me alone. It's not fair. It's not fair. What enormous bluebottles. They say you get used to them' – and then it would end in the canine howl. Ransom never could make up his mind whether it was a trick or whether a decaying psychic energy that had once been Weston were indeed fitfully and miserably alive within the body that sat there beside him. He discovered that any hatred he had once felt for the Professor was dead. He found it natural to pray fervently for his soul. Yet what he felt for Weston was not exactly pity. Up till that moment, whenever he had thought of Hell, he had pictured the lost souls as being still human; now, as the frightful abyss which parts ghosthood from manhood yawned before him, pity was almost swallowed up in horror – in the unconquerable revulsion of the life within him from positive and self-consuming Death. If the remains of Weston were, at such moments, speaking through the lips of the Un-man, then Weston was not now a man at all. The forces which had begun, perhaps years ago, to eat away his humanity had now completed their work. The intoxicated will which had been slowly poisoning the intelligence and the affections had now at last poisoned itself and the whole psychic organism had fallen to pieces. Only a ghost was left – an everlasting unrest, a crumbling, a ruin, an odour of decay. 'And this,' thought Ransom, 'might be my destination; or hers.'

But of course the hours spent alone with the Un-man were like hours in a back area. The real business of life was the interminable conversation between the Tempter and the Green Lady. Taken hour by hour the progress was hard to estimate; but as the days passed Ransom could not resist the conviction that the general development was in the enemy's favour. There were, of course, ups and downs. Often the Un-man was unexpectedly repulsed by some simplicity which it seemed not to have anticipated. Often, too, Ransom's own contributions to the terrible debate were for the moment successful. There were times when he thought, 'Thank God! We've won at last.' But the enemy was never tired, and Ransom grew more weary all the time; and presently he thought he could see signs that the Lady was becoming tired too. In the end he taxed her with it and begged her to send them both away. But she rebuked him, and her rebuke revealed how dangerous the situation had already become. 'Shall I go and rest and play,' she asked, 'while all this lies on our hands? Not till I am certain that there is no great deed to be done by me for the King and for the children of our children.'

It was on those lines that the enemy now worked almost exclusively. Though the Lady had no word for Duty he had made it appear to her in the light of a Duty that she should continue to fondle the idea of disobedience, and convinced her that it would be a cowardice if she repulsed him. The idea of the Great Deed, of the Great Risk, of a kind of martyrdom, were presented to her every day, varied in a thousand forms. The notion of waiting to ask the King before a decision was made had been unobtrusively shuffled aside. Any such 'cowardice' was not not to be thought of. The whole point of her action – the whole grandeur – would lie in taking it without the King's knowledge, in leaving him utterly free to repudiate it, so that all the benefits should be his, and all the risks hers; and with the risk, of course, all the magnanimity, the pathos, the tragedy, and the originality. And also, the Tempter hinted, it would be no use asking the King, for he would certainly *not* approve the action: men were like that. The King must be forced to be free. Now, while she was on her own – now or never – the noble thing must be achieved; and with that 'Now or never' he began to play on a fear which the Lady apparently shared with the women of earth – the fear that life might be wasted, some great opportunity let slip. 'How if I were as a tree that could have borne gourds and yet bore none,' she said. Ransom tried to convince her that children were fruit enough. But the Un-man asked whether this elaborate division of the human race into two sexes could possibly be meant for no other purpose than offspring? – a matter which might have been more simply provided for, as it was in many of the plants. A moment later it was explaining that men like Ransom in his own world – men of that intensely male and backward-looking type who always shrank away from the new good – had continuously laboured to keep woman down to mere child-bearing and to ignore the high destiny for which Maleldil had actually created her. It told her that such men had already done incalculable harm. Let her look to it that nothing of the sort happened on Perelandra. It was at this stage that it began to teach her many new words: words like Creative and Intuition and Spiritual. But that was one of its false steps. When she had at last been made to understand what 'creative' meant she forgot all about the Great Risk and the tragic loneliness and laughed for a whole minute on end. Finally she told the Un-man that it was younger even than Piebald, and sent them both away.

Ransom gained ground over that; but on the following day he lost it all by losing his temper. The enemy had been pressing on her with more than usual ardour the nobility of self-sacrifice and self-dedication, and the enchantment seemed to be deepening in her mind every moment, when Ransom, goaded beyond all patience, had leaped to his feet and really turned upon her, talking far too quickly and almost shouting, and even forgetting his Old Solar and intermixing English words. He tried to tell her that he'd seen this kind of 'unselfishness' in action: to tell her of women making themselves sick with hunger rather than begin the meal before the man of the house returned, though they knew perfectly well that there was nothing he disliked more; of mothers wearing themselves to a ravelling to marry some daughter to a man whom she detested; of Agrippina and of Lady Macbeth. 'Can you not see,' he shouted, 'that he is making you say words that mean nothing? What is the good of saying you would do this for the King's sake when you know it is what the King would hate most? Are you Maleldil that you should determine what is good for the King?' But she understood only a very small part of what he said and was bewildered by his manner. The Un-man made capital out of this speech.

But through all these ups and downs, all changes of the front line, all counter-attacks and stands and withdrawals, Ransom came to see more and more clearly the strategy of the whole affair. The Lady's response to the suggestion of becoming a risk-bearer, a tragic pioneer, was still a response made chiefly out of her love for the King and for her unborn children, and even, in a sense, of Maleldil Himself. The idea that He might not really wish to be obeyed to the letter was the sluice through which the whole flood of suggestion had been admitted to her mind. But mixed with this response, from the moment when the Un-man began its tragic stories, there was the faintest touch of theatricality, the first hint of a self-admiring inclination to seize a grand rôle in the drama of her world. It was clear that the Un-man's whole effort was to increase this element. As long as this was but one drop, so to speak, in the sea of her mind, he would not really succeed. Perhaps, while it remained so, she was protected from actual disobedience: perhaps no rational creature, until such a motive became dominant, could really throw away happiness for anything quite so vague as the Tempter's chatter about Deeper Life and the Upward Path. The veiled egoism in the conception of noble revolt must be increased. And Ransom thought, despite many rallies on her part and many set-backs suffered by the enemy, that it was, very slowly and yet perceptibly, increasing. The matter was, of course, cruelly complicated. What the Un-man said was always very nearly true. Certainly it must be part of the Divine plan that this happy creature should mature, should become more and more a creature of free choice, should become, in a sense, more distinct from God and from her husband in order thereby to be at one with them in a richer fashion. In fact, he had seen this very process going on from the moment at which he met her, and had, unconsciously, assisted it. This present temptation, if conquered, would itself be the next, and greatest, step in the same direction: an obedience freer, more reasoned, more conscious than any she had known before, was being put in her power. But for that very reason the fatal false step which, once taken, would thrust her down into the terrible slavery of appetite and hate and economics and government which our race knows so well, could be made to sound so like the true one. What made him feel sure that the dangerous element in her interest was growing was her progressive disregard of the plain intellectual bones of the problem. It became harder to recall her mind to the *data* – a command from Maleldil, a complete uncertainty about the results of breaking it, and a present happiness so great that hardly any change could be for the better. The turgid swell of indistinctly splendid images which the Un-man aroused, and the transcendent importance of the central image, carried all this away. She was still in her innocence. No evil intention had been formed in her mind. But if her will was uncorrupted, half her imagination was already filled with bright, poisonous shapes. 'This can't go on,' thought Ransom for the second time. But all his arguments proved in the long run unavailing, and it did go on.

There came a night when he was so tired that towards morning he fell into a leaden sleep and slept far into the following day. He woke to find himself alone. A great horror came over him. 'What could I have done? What could I have done?' he cried out, for he thought that all was lost. With sick heart and sore head he staggered to the edge of the island: his idea was to find a fish and to pursue the truants to the Fixed Land where he felt little doubt that they had gone. In the bitterness and confusion of his mind he forgot that he had no notion in which direction that land now lay nor how far it was distant. Hurrying through the woods, he emerged into an open place and suddenly found that he was not alone. Two human figures, robed to their feet, stood before him, silent under the yellow sky. Their clothes were of purple and blue, their heads wore chaplets of silver leaves, and their feet were bare. They seemed to him to be, the one the ugliest, and the other the most beautiful, of the children of man. Then one of them spoke and he realised that they were none other than the Green Lady herself and the haunted body of Weston. The robes were of feathers, and he knew well the Perelandrian birds from which they had been derived; the art of the weaving, if weaving it could be called, was beyond his comprehension.

'Welcome, Piebald,' said the Lady. 'You have slept long. What do you think of us in our leaves?'

'The birds,' said Ransom. 'The poor birds! What has he done to them?'

'He has found the feathers somewhere,' said the Lady carelessly. 'They drop them.'

'Why have you done this, Lady?'

'He has been making me older again. Why did you never tell me, Piebald?'

'Tell you what?'

'We never knew. This one showed me that the trees have leaves and the beasts have fur, and said that in your world the men and women also hung beautiful things about them. Why do you not tell us how we look? Oh, Piebald, Piebald, I hope this is not going to be another of the new goods from which you draw back your hand. It cannot be new to you if they all do it in your world.'

'Ah,' said Ransom, 'but it is different there. It is cold.'

'So the Stranger said,' she answered. 'But not in all parts of your world. He says they do it even where it is warm.'

'Has he said why they do it?'

'To be beautiful. Why else?' said the Lady, with some wonder in her face.

'Thank Heaven,' thought Ransom, 'he is only teaching her vanity'; for he had feared something worse. Yet could it be possible, in the long run, to wear clothes without learning modesty, and through modesty lasciviousness?

'Do you think we are more beautiful?' said the Lady, interrupting his thoughts.

'No,' said Ransom; and then, correcting himself, 'I don't know.' It was, indeed, not easy to reply. The Un-man, now that Weston's prosaic shirt and shorts were concealed, looked a more exotic and therefore a more imaginatively, less squalidly, hideous figure. As for the Lady – that she looked in some way worse was not doubtful. Yet there is a plainness in nudity – as we speak of 'plain' bread. A sort of richness, a flamboyancy, a concession, as it were, to lower conceptions of the beautiful, had come with the purple robe. For the first (and last) time she appeared to him at that moment as a woman whom an earthborn man might conceivably love. And this was intolerable. The ghastly inappropriateness of the idea had, all in one moment, stolen something from the colours of the landscape and the scent of the flowers.

'Do you think we are more beautiful?' repeated the Lady.

'What does it matter?' said Ransom dully.

'Everyone should wish to be as beautiful as they can,' she answered. 'And we cannot see ourselves.'

'We can,' said Weston's body.

'How can this be?' said the Lady, turning to it. 'Even if you could roll your eyes right round to look inside they would see only blackness.'

'Not that way,' it answered. 'I will show you.' It walked a few paces away to where Weston's pack lay in the yellow turf. With that curious distinctness which often falls upon us when we are anxious and preoccupied Ransom noticed the exact make and pattern of the pack. It must have been from the same shop in London where he had bought his own: and that little fact, suddenly reminding him that Weston had once been a man, that he too had once had pleasures and pains and a human mind, almost brought the tears into his eyes. The horrible fingers which Weston would never use again worked at the buckles and brought out a small bright object – an English pocket mirror that might have cost three-and-six. He handed it to the Green Lady. She turned it over in her hands.

'What is it? What am I to do with it?' she said.

'Look in it,' said the Un-man.

'How?'

'Look!' he said. Then taking it from her he held it up to her face. She stared for quite an appreciable time without apparently making anything of it. Then she started back with a cry and covered her face. Ransom started too. It was the first time he had seen her the mere passive recipient of any emotion. The world about him was big with change.

'Oh – oh,' she cried. 'What is it? I saw a face.'

'Only your own face, beautiful one,' said the Un-man.

'I know,' said the Lady, still averting her eyes from the mirror. 'My face – out there – looking at me. Am I growing older or is it something else? I feel … I feel … my heart is beating too hard. I am not warm. What is it?' She glanced from one of them to the other. The mysteries had all vanished from her face. It was as easy to read as that of a man in a shelter when a bomb is coming.

'What is it?' she repeated.

'It is called Fear,' said Weston's mouth. Then the creature turned its face full on Ransom and grinned.

'Fear,' she said. 'This is Fear,' pondering the discovery; then, with abrupt finality, 'I do not like it.'

'It will go away,' said the Un-man, when Ransom interrupted.

'It will never go away if you do what he wishes. It is into more and more fear that he is leading you.'

'It is,' said the Un-man, 'into the great waves and through them and beyond. Now that you know Fear, you see that it must be you who shall taste it on behalf of your race. You know the King will not. You do not wish him to. But there is no cause for fear in this little thing: rather for joy. What is fearful in it?'

'Things being two when they are one,' replied the Lady decisively. 'That thing' (she pointed at the mirror) 'is me and not me.'

'But if you do not look you will never know how beautiful you are.'

'It comes into my mind, Stranger,' she answered, 'that a fruit does not eat itself, and a man cannot be together with himself.'

'A fruit cannot do that because it is only a fruit,' said the Un-man. 'But we can do it. We call this thing a mirror. A man can love himself, and be together with himself. That is what it means to be a man or a woman – to walk alongside oneself as if one were a second person and to delight in one's own beauty. Mirrors were made to teach this art.'

'Is it a good?' said the Lady.

'No,' said Ransom.

'How can you find out without trying?' said the Un-man. 'If you try it and it is not good,' said Ransom, 'how do you know whether you will be able to stop doing it?'

'I am walking alongside myself already,' said the Lady. 'But I do not yet know what I look like. If I have become two I had better know what the other is. As for you, Piebald, one look will show me this woman's face and why should I look more than once?'

She took the mirror, timidly but firmly, from the Un-man and looked into it in silence for the better part of a minute. Then she let it sink and stood holding it at her side.

'It is very strange,' she said at last.

'It is very beautiful,' said the Un-man. 'Do you not think so?'

'Yes.'

'But you have not yet found what you set out to find.'

'What was that? I have forgotten.'

'Whether the robe of feathers made you more beautiful or less.'

'I saw only a face.'

'Hold it further away and you will see the whole of the alongside woman – the other who is yourself. Or no – I will hold it.'

The commonplace suggestions of the scene became grotesque at this stage. She looked at herself first with the robe, then without it, then with it again; finally she decided against it and threw it away. The Un-man picked it up.

'Will you not keep it?' he said; 'you might wish to carry it on some days even if you do not wish for it on all days.'

'*Keep* it?' she asked, not clearly understanding.

'I had forgotten,' said the Un-man. 'I had forgotten that you would not live on the Fixed Land nor build a house nor in any way become mistress of your own days. *Keeping* means putting a thing where you know you can always find it again, and where rain, and beasts, and other people cannot reach it. I would give you this mirror to keep. It would be the Queen's mirror, a gift brought into the world from Deep Heaven: the other women would not have it. But you have reminded me. There can be no gifts, no keeping, no foresight while you live as you do – from day to day, like the beasts.'

But the Lady did not appear to be listening to him. She stood like one almost dazed with the richness of a day-dream. She did not look in the least like a woman who is thinking about a new dress. The expression of her face was noble. It was a great deal too noble. Greatness, tragedy, high sentiment – these were obviously what occupied her thoughts. Ransom perceived that the affair of the robes and the mirror had been only superficially concerned with what is commonly called female vanity. The image of her beautiful body had been offered to her only as a means to awake the far more perilous image of her great soul. The external and, as it were, dramatic conception of the self was the enemy's true aim. He was making her mind a theatre in which that phantom self should hold the stage. He had already written the play.

11

Because he had slept so late that morning Ransom found it easy to keep awake the following night. The sea had become calm and there was no rain. He sat upright in the darkness with his back against a tree. The others were close beside him – the Lady, to judge by her breathing, asleep and the Un-man doubtless waiting to arouse her and resume its solicitations the moment Ransom should doze. For the third time, more strongly than ever before, it came into his head, 'This can't go on.'

The Enemy was using Third Degree methods. It seemed to Ransom that, but for a miracle, the Lady's resistance was bound to be worn away in the end. Why did no miracle come? Or rather, why no miracle on the right side? For the presence of the Enemy was in itself a kind of Miracle. Had Hell a prerogative to work wonders? Why did Heaven work none? Not for the first time he found himself questioning Divine Justice. He could not understand why Maleldil should remain absent when the Enemy was there in person.

But while he was thinking this, as suddenly and sharply as if the solid darkness about him had spoken with articulate voice, he knew that Maleldil was not absent. That sense – so very welcome yet never welcomed without the overcoming of a certain resistance – that sense of the Presence which he had once or twice before experienced on Perelandra, returned to him. The darkness was packed quite full. It seemed to press upon his trunk so that he could hardly use his lungs: it seemed to close in on his skull like a crown of intolerable weight so that for a space he could hardly think. Moreover, he became aware in some indefinable fashion that it had never been absent, that only some unconscious activity of his own had succeeded in ignoring it for the past few days.

Inner silence is for our race a difficult achievement. There is a chattering part of the mind which continues, until it is corrected, to chatter on even in the holiest places. Thus, while one part of Ransom remained, as it were, prostrated in a hush of fear and love that resembled a kind of death, something else inside him, wholly unaffected by reverence, continued to pour queries and objections into his brain. 'It's all very well,' said this voluble critic, 'a presence of *that* sort! But the Enemy is really here, really saying and doing things. Where is Maleldil's representative?'

The answer which came back to him, quick as a fencer's or a tennis player's *riposte*, out of the silence and the darkness, almost took his breath away. It seemed blasphemous. 'Anyway, what can I do?' babbled the voluble self. 'I've done all I can. I've talked till I'm sick of it. It's no good, I tell you.' He tried to persuade himself that he, Ransom, could not possibly be Maleldil's representative as the Unman was the representative of Hell. The suggestion was, he argued, itself diabolical – a temptation to fatuous pride, to megalomania. He was horrified when the darkness simply flung back this argument in his face, almost impatiently. And then – he wondered how it had escaped him till now – he was forced to perceive that his own coming to Perelandra was at least as much of a marvel as the Enemy's. That miracle on the right side, which he had demanded, had in fact occurred. He himself was the miracle.

'Oh, but this is nonsense,' said the voluble self. He, Ransom, with his ridiculous piebald body and his ten times defeated arguments – what sort of a miracle was that? His mind darted hopefully down a side-alley that seemed to promise escape. Very well then. He *had* been brought here miraculously. He was in God's hands. As long as he did his best – and he *had* done his best – God would see to the final issue. He had not succeeded. But he had done his best. No one could do more. ''Tis not in mortals to command success.' He must not be worried about the final result. Maleldil would see

313

to that. And Maleldil would bring him safe back to Earth after his very real, though unsuccessful, efforts. Probably Maleldil's real intention was that he should publish to the human race the truths he had learned on the planet Venus. As for the fate of Venus, that could not really rest upon his shoulders. It was in God's hands. One must be content to leave it there. One must have Faith ...

It snapped like a violin string. Not one rag of all this evasion was left. Relentlessly, unmistakably, the Darkness pressed down upon him the knowledge that this picture of the situation was utterly false. His journey to Perelandra was not a moral exercise, nor a sham fight. If the issue lay in Maleldil's hands, Ransom and the Lady were those hands. The fate of a world really depended on how they behaved in the next few hours. The thing was irreducibly, nakedly real. They could, if they chose, decline to save the innocence of this new race, and if they declined its innocence would not be saved. It rested with no other creature in all time or all space. This he saw clearly, though as yet he had no inkling of what he could do.

The voluble self protested, wildly, swiftly, like the propeller of a ship racing when it is out of the water. The imprudence, the unfairness, the absurdity of it! Did Maleldil *want* to lose worlds? What was the sense of so arranging things that anything really important should finally and absolutely depend on such a man of straw as himself? And at that moment, far away on Earth, as he now could not help remembering, men were at war, and whitefaced subalterns and freckled corporals who had but lately begun to shave, stood in horrible gaps or crawled forward in deadly darkness, awaking, like him, to the preposterous truth that all really depended on their actions; and far away in time Horatius stood on the bridge, and Constantine settled in his mind whether he would or would not embrace the new religion, and Eve herself stood looking upon the forbidden fruit and the Heaven of Heavens waited for her decision. He writhed and ground his teeth, but could not help seeing. Thus, and not otherwise, the world was made. Either something or nothing must depend on individual choices. And if something, who could set bounds to it? A stone may determine the course of a river. He was that stone at this horrible moment which had become the centre of the whole universe. The *eldila* of all worlds, the sinless organisms of everlasting light, were silent in Deep Heaven to see what Elwin Ransom of Cambridge would do.

Then came blessed relief. He suddenly realised that he did not know what he *could* do. He almost laughed with joy. All this horror had been premature. No definite task was before him. All that was being demanded of him was a general and preliminary resolution to oppose the Enemy in any mode which circumstances might show to be desirable: in fact – and he flew back to the comforting words as a child flies back to its mother's arms – 'to do his best' – or rather, to go on doing his best, for he had really been doing it all along. 'What bugbears we make of things unnecessarily!' he murmured, settling himself in a slightly more comfortable position. A mild flood of what appeared to him to be cheerful and rational piety rose and engulfed him.

Hullo! What was this? He sat straight upright again, his heart beating wildly against his side. His thoughts had stumbled on an idea from which they started back as a man starts back when he has touched a hot poker. But this time the idea was really too childish to entertain. This time it *must* be a deception, risen from his own mind. It stood to reason that a struggle with the Devil meant a *spiritual* struggle ... the notion of a physical combat was only fit for a savage. If only it were as simple as that ... but here the voluble self had made a fatal mistake. The habit of imaginative honesty was too deeply engrained in Ransom to let him toy for more than a second with the pretence that he feared bodily strife with the Un-man less than he feared anything else. Vivid pictures crowded upon him ... the deadly cold of those hands (he had touched the creature accidentally some hours before) ... the long metallic nails ... ripping off narrow strips of flesh, pulling out tendons. One would die slowly. Up to the very end that cruel idiocy would smile into one's face. One would give way long before one died – beg for mercy, promise it help, worship, anything.

It was fortunate that something so horrible should be so obviously out of the question. Almost, but not quite, Ransom decreed that whatever the Silence and the Darkness seemed to be saying about this, no such crude, materialistic struggle could possibly be what Maleldil really intended. Any suggestion to the contrary must be only his own morbid fancy. It would degrade the spiritual warfare to the condition of mere mythology. But here he got another check. Long since on Mars, and more strongly since he came to Perelandra, Ransom had been perceiving that the triple distinction of truth from myth and of both from fact was purely terrestrial – was part and parcel of that unhappy division between soul and body which resulted from the Fall. Even on Earth the sacraments existed as a permanent reminder that the division was neither wholesome nor final. The Incarnation had been the beginning of its disappearance. In Perelandra it would have no meaning at all. Whatever happened here would be of such a nature that earth-men would call it mythological. All this he had thought before. Now he knew it. The Presence in the darkness, never before so formidable, was putting these truths into his hands, like terrible jewels.

The voluble self was almost thrown out of its argumentative stride – became for some seconds as the voice of a mere whimpering child begging to be let off, to be allowed to go home. Then it rallied. It explained precisely where the absurdity of a physical battle with the Un-man lay. It would be quite irrelevant to the spiritual issue. If the Lady were to be kept in obedience only by the forcible removal of the Tempter, what was the use of that? What would it prove? And if the temptation were not a proving or testing, why was it allowed to happen at all? Did Maleldil suggest that our own world might have been saved if the elephant had accidentally trodden on the serpent a moment before Eve was about to yield? Was it as easy and as un-moral as that? The thing was patently absurd!

The terrible silence went on. It became more and more like a face, a face not without sadness, that looks upon you while you are telling lies, and never interrupts, but gradually you know that it knows, and falter, and contradict yourself, and lapse into silence. The voluble self petered out in the end. Almost the Darkness said to Ransom, 'You know you are only wasting time.' Every minute it became clearer to him that the parallel he had tried to draw between Eden and Perelandra was crude and imperfect. What had happened on Earth, when Maleldil was born a man at Bethlehem, had altered the universe for ever. The new world of Perelandra was not a mere repetition of the old world Tellus. Maleldil never repeated Himself. As the Lady had said, the same wave never came twice. When Eve fell, God was not Man. He had not yet made men members of His body: since then He had, and through them henceforward He would save and suffer. One of the purposes for which He had done all this was to save Perelandra not through Himself but through Himself in Ransom. If Ransom refused, the plan, so far, miscarried. For that point in the story, a story far more complicated than he had conceived, it was he who had been selected. With a strange sense of 'fallings from him, vanishings', he perceived that you might just as well call Perelandra, not Tellus, the centre. You might look upon the Perelandrian story as merely an indirect consequence of the Incarnation on earth: or you might look on the Earth story as mere preparation for the new worlds of which Perelandra was the first. The one was neither more nor less true than the other. Nothing was more or less important than anything else, nothing was a copy or model of anything else.

At the same time he also perceived that his voluble self had begged the question. Up to this point the Lady had repelled her assailant. She was shaken and weary, and there were some stains perhaps in her imagination, but she had stood. In that respect the story already differed from anything that he certainly knew about the mother of our own race. He did not know whether Eve had resisted at all, or if so, for how long. Still less did he know how the story would have ended if she had. If the 'serpent' had been foiled, and returned the next day, and the next … what then? Would the trial have lasted for ever? How would Maleldil have stopped it?

Here on Perelandra his own intuition had been not that no temptation must occur but that 'This can't go on.' This stopping of a third-degree solicitation, already more than once refused, was a problem to which the terrestrial Fall offered no clue – a new task, and for that new task a new character in the drama, who appeared (most unfortunately) to be himself. In vain did his mind hark back, time after time, to the Book of Genesis, asking 'What would have happened?' But to this the Darkness gave him no answer. Patiently and inexorably it brought him back to the here and the now, and to the growing certainty of what was here and now demanded. Almost he felt that the words 'would have happened' were meaningless – mere invitations to wander in what the Lady would have called an 'alongside world' which had no reality. Only the actual was real: and every actual situation was new. Here in Perelandra the temptation would be stopped by Ransom, or it would not be stopped at all. The Voice – for it was almost with a Voice that he was now contending – seemed to create around this alternative an infinite vacancy. This chapter, this page, this very sentence, in the cosmic story was utterly and eternally itself; no other passage that had occurred or ever would occur could be substituted for it.

He fell back on a different line of defence. How *could* he fight the immortal enemy? Even if he were a fighting man – instead of a sedentary scholar with weak eyes and a baddish wound from the last war – what use was there in fighting it? It couldn't be killed, could it? But the answer was almost immediately plain. Weston's body could be destroyed; and presumably that body was the Enemy's only foothold in Perelandra. By that body, when that body still obeyed a human will, it had entered the new world: expelled from it, it would doubtless have no other habitation. It had entered that body at Weston's own invitation, and without such invitation could enter no other. Ransom remembered that the unclean spirits, in the Bible, had a horror of being cast out into the 'deep'. And thinking of these things he perceived at last, with a sinking of heart, that if physical action were indeed demanded of him, it was an action, by ordinary standards, neither impossible nor hopeless. On the physical plane it was one middle-aged, seden-tary body against another, and both unarmed save for fists and teeth and nails. At the thought of these details, terror and disgust overcame him. To kill the thing with such weapons (he remem-bered his killing of the frog) would be a nightmare; to be killed – who knew how slowly? – was more than he could face. That he would be killed he felt certain. 'When,' he asked, 'did I even win a fight in all my life?'

He was no longer making efforts to resist the conviction of what he must do. He had exhausted all his efforts. The answer was plain beyond all subterfuge. The Voice out of the night spoke it to him in such unanswerable fashion that, though there was no noise, he almost felt it must wake the woman who slept close by. He was faced with the impossible. This he must do: this he could not do. In vain he reminded himself of the things that unbelieving boys might at this moment be doing on Earth for a lesser cause. His will was in that valley where the appeal to shame becomes useless – nay, makes the valley darker and deeper. He believed he could face the Un-man with firearms: even that he could stand up unarmed and face certain death if the creature had retained Weston's revolver. But to come to grips with it, to go voluntarily into those dead yet living arms, to grapple with it, naked chest to naked chest … Terrible follies came into his mind. He would fail to obey the Voice, but it would be all right because he would repent later on, when he was back on Earth. He would lose his nerve as St Peter had done, and be, like St Peter, forgiven. Intellectually, of course, he knew the answer to these temptations perfectly well; but he was at one of those moments when all the utterances of intellect sound like twice-told tales. Then some cross wind of the mind changed his mood. Perhaps he would fight and win, perhaps not even be badly mauled. But no faintest hint of a guarantee in that direction came to him from the darkness. The future was black as the night itself.

'It is not for nothing that you are named Ransom,' said the Voice.

And he knew that this was no fancy of his own. He knew it for a very curious reason – because he had known for many years that his surname was derived not from *ransom* but from *Ranolf's son*. It would never have occurred to him thus to associate the two words. To connect the name Ransom with the act of ransoming would have been for him a mere pun. But even his voluble self did not now dare to suggest that the Voice was making a play upon words. All in a moment of time he perceived that what was, to human philologists, a mere accidental resemblance of two sounds, was in truth no accident. The whole distinction between things accidental and things designed, like the distinction between fact and myth, was purely terrestrial. The pattern is so large that within the little frame of earthly experience there appear pieces of it between which we can see no connection, and other pieces between which we can. Hence we rightly, for our use, distinguish the accidental from the essential. But step outside that frame and the distinction drops down into the void, fluttering useless wings. He had been forced out of the frame, caught up into the larger pattern. He knew now why the old philosophers had said that there is no such thing as chance or fortune beyond the Moon. Before his Mother had borne him, before his ancestors had been called Ransoms, before *ransom* had been the name for a payment that delivers, before the world was made, all these things had so stood together in eternity that the very significance of the pattern at this point lay in their coming together in just this fashion. And he bowed his head and groaned and repined against his fate – to be still a man and yet to be forced up into the metaphysical world, to enact what philosophy only thinks.

'My name also is Ransom,' said the Voice.

It was some time before the purport of this saying dawned upon him. He whom the other worlds call Maleldil, was the world's ransom, his own ransom, well he knew. But to what purpose was it said now? Before the answer came to him he felt its insufferable approach and held out his arms before him as if he could keep it from forcing open the door of his mind. But it came. So *that* was the real issue. If he now failed, this world also would hereafter be redeemed. If he were not the ransom, Another would be. Yet nothing was ever repeated. Not a second crucifixion: perhaps – who knows – not even a second Incarnation … some act of even more appalling love, some glory of yet deeper humility. For he had seen already how the pattern grows and how from each world it sprouts into the next through some other dimension. The small external evil which Satan had done in Malacandra was only as a line: the deeper evil he had done in Earth was as a square: if Venus fell, her evil would be a cube – her Redemption beyond conceiving. Yet redeemed she would be. He had long known that great issues hung on his choice; but as he now realised the true width of the frightful freedom that was being put into his hands – a width to which all merely spatial infinity seemed narrow – he felt like a man brought out under naked heaven, on the edge of a precipice, into the teeth of a wind that came howling from the Pole. He had pictured himself, till now, standing before the Lord, like Peter. But it was worse. He sat before Him like Pilate. It lay with him to save or to spill. His hands had been reddened, as all men's hands have been, in the slaying before the foundation of the world; now, if he chose, he would dip them again in the same blood. 'Mercy,' he groaned; and then, 'Lord, why not me?' But there was no answer.

The thing still seemed impossible. But gradually something happened to him which had happened to him only twice before in his life. It had happened once while he was trying to make up his mind to do a very dangerous job in the last war. It had happened again while he was screwing his resolution to go and see a certain man in London and make to him an excessively embarrassing confession which justice demanded. In both cases the thing had seemed a sheer impossibility: he had not thought but known that, being what he was, he was psychologically incapable of doing it; and then, without any apparent movement of the will, as objective and unemotional as the reading on a dial, there had arisen before him, with perfect certitude, the knowledge 'about this time tomorrow you will have done the impossible'. The same thing happened now. His fear, his shame, his love, all his arguments, were not altered in the least. The thing was neither more nor less dreadful than it had been before. The only difference was that he knew – almost as a historical proposition – that it was going to be done. He might beg, weep, or rebel – might curse or adore – sing like a martyr or blaspheme like a devil. It made not the slightest difference. The thing was going to be done. There was going to arrive, in the course of time, a moment at which he would have done it. The future act stood there, fixed and unalterable as if he had already performed it. It was a mere irrelevant detail that it happened to occupy the position we call future instead of that which we call past. The whole struggle was over, and yet there seemed to have been no moment of victory. You might say, if you liked, that the power of choice had been simply set aside and an inflexible destiny substituted for it. On the other hand, you might say that he had been delivered from the rhetoric of his passions and had emerged into unassailable freedom. Ransom could not, for the life of him, see any difference between these two statements. Predestination and freedom were apparently identical. He could no longer see any meaning in the many arguments he had heard on this subject.

No sooner had he discovered that he would certainly try to kill the Un-man tomorrow than the doing of it appeared to him a smaller matter than he had supposed. He could hardly remember why he had accused himself of megalomania when the idea first occurred to him. It was true that if he left it undone, Maleldil Himself would do some greater thing instead. In that sense, he stood for Maleldil: but no more than Eve would have stood for Him by simply not eating the apple, or than any man stands for Him in doing any good action. As there was no comparison in person, so there was none in suffering – or only such comparison as may be between a man who burns his finger putting out a spark and a fireman who loses his life in fighting a conflagration because that spark was not put out. He asked no longer 'Why me?' It might as well be he as another. It might as well be any other choice as this. The fierce light which he had seen resting on this moment of decision rested in reality on all.

'I have cast your Enemy into sleep,' said the Voice. 'He will not wake till morning. Get up. Walk twenty paces back into the wood; there sleep. Your sister sleeps also.'

12

When some dreaded morning comes we usually wake fully to it at once. Ransom passed with no intermediate stages from dreamless sleep to a full consciousness of his task. He found himself alone – the island gently rocking on a sea that was neither calm nor stormy. The golden light, glinting through indigo trunks of trees, told him in which direction the water lay. He went to it and bathed. Then, having landed again, he lay down and drank. He stood for a few minutes running his hands through his wet hair and stroking his limbs. Looking down at his own body he noticed how greatly the sunburn on one side and the pallor on the other had decreased. He would hardly be christened Piebald if the Lady were now to meet him for the first time. His colour had become more like ivory: and his toes, after so many days of nakedness, had begun to lose the cramped, squalid shape imposed by boots. Altogether he thought better of himself as a human animal than he had done before. He felt pretty certain that he would never again wield an un-maimed body until a greater morning came for the whole universe, and he was glad that the instrument had been thus tuned up to concert pitch before he had to surrender it. 'When I wake up after Thy image, I shall be satisfied,' he said to himself.

Presently he walked into the woods. Accidentally – for he was at the moment intent on food – he blundered through a whole cloud of the arboreal bubbles. The pleasure was as sharp as when he had first experienced it, and his very stride was different as he emerged from them. Although this was to be his last meal, he did not even now feel it proper to look for any favourite fruit. But what met him was gourds. 'A good breakfast on the morning you're hanged,' he thought whimsically as he let the empty shell drop from his hand – filled for the moment with such pleasure as seemed to make the whole world a dance. 'All said and done,' he thought, 'it's been worth it. I have had a time. I have lived in Paradise.'

He went a little farther in the wood, which grew thickly here about, and almost tripped over the sleeping form of the Lady. It was unusual for her to be sleeping at this time of the day, and he assumed it was Maleldil's doing. 'I shall never see her again,' he thought; and then, 'I shall never again look on a female body in quite the same way as I look on this.' As he stood looking down on her, what was most with him was an intense and orphaned longing that he might, if only for once, have seen the great Mother of his own race thus, in her innocence and splendour. 'Other things, other blessings, other glories,' he murmured. 'But never that. Never in all worlds, that. God can make good use of all that happens. But the loss is real.' He looked at her once again and then walked abruptly past the place where she lay. 'I was right,' he thought, 'it couldn't have gone on. It was time to stop it.'

It took him a long time, wandering like this, in and out of the dark yet coloured thickets, before he found his Enemy. He came on his old friend the dragon, just as he had first seen it, coiled about the trunk of a tree, but it also was asleep; and now he noticed that ever since he awoke he had perceived no chattering of birds, no rustling of sleek bodies or peering of brown eyes through the leafage, nor heard any noise but that of water. It seemed that the Lord God had cast that whole island or perhaps that whole world into deep sleep. For a moment this gave him a sense of desolation, but almost at once he rejoiced that no memory of blood and rage should be left imprinted in these happy minds.

After about an hour, suddenly rounding a little clump of bubble trees he found himself face to face with the Un-man. 'Is it wounded already?' he thought as the first vision of a blood-stained chest broke on him. Then he saw that of course it was not its own blood.

A bird, already half plucked and with beak wide open in the soundless yell of strangulation, was feebly struggling in its long clever hands. Ransom found himself acting before he knew what he had done. Some memory of boxing at his preparatory school must have awaked, for he found he had delivered a straight left with all his might on the Un-man's jaw. But he had forgotten that he was not fighting with gloves; what recalled him to himself was the pain as his fist crashed against the jaw-bone – it seemed almost to have broken his knuckles – and the sickening jar all up his arm. He stood still for a second under the shock of it and this gave the Un-man time to fall back about six paces. It too had not liked the first taste of the encounter. It had apparently bitten its tongue, for blood came bubbling out of the mouth when it tried to speak. It was still holding the bird.

'So you mean to try strength,' it said in English, speaking thick.

'Put down that bird,' said Ransom.

'But this is very foolish,' said the Un-man. 'Do you not know who I am?'

'I know *what* you are,' said Ransom. 'Which of them doesn't matter.'

'And you think, little one,' it answered, 'that you can fight with me? You think He will help you, perhaps? Many thought that. I've known Him longer than you, little one. They all think He's going to help them – till they come to their senses screaming recantations too late in the middle of the fire, mouldering in concentration camps, writhing under saws, jibbering in mad-houses, or nailed on to crosses. Could He help Himself?' – and the creature suddenly threw back its head and cried in a voice so loud that it seemed the golden sky-roof must break, '*Eloi, Eloi, lama sabachthani.*'

And the moment it had done so, Ransom felt certain that the sounds it had made were perfect Aramaic of the First Century. The Un-man was not quoting; it was remembering. These were the very words spoken from the Cross, treasured through all those years in the burning memory of the outcast creature which had heard them, and now brought forward in hideous parody; the horror made him momentarily sick. Before he had recovered the Un-man was upon him, howling like a gale, with eyes so wide opened that they seemed to have no lids, and with all its hair rising on its scalp. It had him caught tightly to its chest, with its arms about him, and its nails were ripping great strips off his back. His own arms were inside its embrace and, pummelling wildly, he could get no blow at it. He turned his head and bit deeply into the muscle of its right arm, at first without success, then deeper. It gave a howl, tried to hold on, and then suddenly he was free. Its defence was for an instant unready and he found himself raining punches about the region of its heart, faster and harder than he had supposed possible. He could hear through its open mouth the great gusts of breath that he was knocking out of it. Then its hands came up again, fingers arched like claws. It was not trying to box. It wanted to grapple. He knocked its right arm aside with a horrible shock of bone against bone and caught it a jab on the fleshy part of the chin: at the same moment its nails tore his right. He grabbed at its arms. More by luck than by skill he got it held by both wrists.

What followed for the next minute or so would hardly have looked like a fight at all to any spectator. The Un-man was trying with every ounce of power it could find in Weston's body to wrench its arms free from Ransom's hands, and he, with every ounce of his power, was trying to retain his manacle hold round its wrists. But this effort, which sent streams of sweat down the backs of both combatants, resulted in a slow and seemingly leisurely, and even aimless, movement of both pairs of arms. Neither could for the moment hurt the other. The Un-man bent forward its head and tried to bite, but Ransom straightened his arms and kept it at arm's length. There seemed no reason why this should ever end.

Then suddenly it shot out its leg and crooked it behind his knee. He was nearly taken off his feet. Movements became quick and flurried on both sides. Ransom in his turn tried to trip, and failed. He started bending the enemy's left arm back by main force with some idea of breaking or at least spraining it. But in the effort to do so he must have weakened his hold on the other wrist. It got its right free. He had just time to close his eyes before the nails tore fiercely down his cheek and the pain put an end to the blows his left was already raining on its ribs. A second later – he did not know quite how it happened – they were standing apart, their chests heaving in great gasps, each staring at the other.

Both were doubtless sorry spectacles. Ransom could not see his own wounds but he seemed to be covered with blood. The enemy's eyes were nearly closed and the body, wherever the remains of Weston's shirt did not conceal it, was a mass of what would soon be bruises. This, and its laboured breathing, and the very taste of its strength in their grapples, had altered Ransom's state of mind completely. He had been astonished to find it no stronger. He had all along, despite what reason told him, expected that the strength of its body would be superhuman, diabolical. He had reckoned on arms that could no more be caught and stopped than the blades of an aeroplane's propeller. But now he knew, by actual experience, that its bodily strength was merely that of Weston. On the physical plane it was one middle-aged scholar against another. Weston had been the more powerfully built of the two men, but he was fat; his body would not take punishment well. Ransom was nimbler and better breathed. His former certainty of death now seemed to him ridiculous. It was a very fair match. There was no reason why he should not win – and live.

This time it was Ransom who attacked and the second bout was much the same as the first. What it came to was that whenever he could box Ransom was superior; whenever he came under tooth and claw he was beaten. His mind, even in the thick of it, was now quite clear. He saw that the issue of the day hung on a very simple question – whether loss of blood would undo him before heavy blows on heart and kidneys undid the other.

All that rich world was asleep about them. There were no rules, no umpire, no spectators; but mere exhaustion, constantly compelling them to fall apart, divided the grotesque duel into rounds as accurately as could be wished. Ransom could never remember how many of these rounds were fought. The thing became like the frantic repetitions of delirium, and thirst a greater pain than any the adversary could inflict. Sometimes they were both on the ground together. Once he was actually astride the enemy's chest, squeezing its throat with both hands and – he found to his surprise – shouting a line out of *The Battle of Maldon*: but it tore his arms so with its nails and so pounded his back with its knees that he was thrown off.

Then he remembers – as one remembers an island of consciousness preceded and followed by long anaesthesia – going forward to meet the Un-man for what seemed the thousandth time and knowing clearly that he could not fight much more. He remembers seeing the Enemy for a moment looking not like Weston but like a mandrill, and realising almost at once that this was delirium. He wavered. Then an experience that perhaps no good man can ever have in our world came over him – a torrent of perfectly unmixed and lawful hatred. The energy of hating, never before felt without some guilt, without some dim knowledge that he was failing fully to distinguish the sinner from the sin, rose into his arms and legs till he felt that they were pillars of burning blood. What was before him appeared no longer a creature of corrupted will. It was corruption itself to which will was attached only as an instrument. Ages ago it had been a Person: but the ruins of personality now survived in it only as weapons at the disposal of a furious self-exiled negation. It is perhaps difficult to understand why this filled Ransom not with horror but with a kind of joy. The joy came from finding at last what hatred was made for. As a boy with an axe rejoices on finding a tree, or a boy with a box of coloured chalks rejoices on finding a pile of perfectly white paper, so he rejoiced in the perfect congruity between his emotion and its object. Bleeding and trembling with weariness as he was, he felt that nothing was beyond his power, and when he flung himself upon the living Death, the eternal Surd in the universal mathematic, he was astonished, and yet (on a deeper level) not astonished at all, at his own strength. His arms seemed to move quicker than his thought. His hands taught him terrible things. He felt its rib break, he heard its jaw-bone crack. The whole creature seemed to be crackling and splitting under his blows. His own pains, where it tore him, somehow failed to matter. He felt that he could so fight, so hate with a perfect hatred, for a whole year.

All at once he found he was beating the air. He was in such a state that at first he could not understand what was happening – could not believe that the Un-man had fled. His momentary stupidity gave it a start; and when he came to his senses he was just in time to see it vanishing into the wood, with a limping uneven stride, with one arm hanging useless, and with its doglike howl. He dashed after it. For a second or so it was concealed from him by the tree trunks. Then it was once more in sight. He began running with all his power, but it kept its lead.

It was a fantastic chase, in and out of the lights and shadows and up and down the slowly moving ridges and valleys. They passed the dragon where it slept. They passed the Lady, sleeping with a smile on her face. The Un-man stooped low as it passed her with the fingers of its left hand crooked for scratching. It would have torn her if it dared, but Ransom was close behind and it could not risk the delay. They passed through a flock of large orange-coloured birds all fast asleep, each on one leg, each with its head beneath its wing, so that they looked like a grove of formal and flowery shrubs. They picked their steps where pairs and families of the yellow wallabies lay on their backs with eyes fast shut and their small forepaws folded on their breasts as if they were crusaders carved on tombs. They stooped beneath branches which were bowed down because on them lay the tree-pigs, making a comfortable noise like a child's snore. They crashed through thickets of bubble trees and forgot, for the moment, their weariness. It was a large island. They came out of the woods and rushed across wide fields of saffron or of silver, sometimes deep to their ankles and sometimes to their waists in the cool or poignant scents. They rushed down into yet other woods which lay, as they approached them, at the bottom of secret valleys, but rose before they reached them to crown the summits of lonely hills. Ransom could not gain on his quarry. It was a wonder that any creature so maimed as its uneven strides showed it to be, could maintain that pace. If the ankle were really sprained, as he suspected, it must suffer indescribably at every step. Then the horrible thought came into his mind that perhaps it could somehow hand over the pain to be borne by whatever remnants of Weston's consciousness yet survived in its body. The idea that something which had once been of his own kind and fed at a human breast might even now be imprisoned in the thing he was pursuing redoubled his hatred, which was unlike nearly all other hatreds he had ever known, for it increased his strength.

As they emerged from about the fourth wood he saw the sea before them not thirty yards away. The Un-man rushed on as if it made no distinction between land and water and plunged in with a great splash. He could see its head, dark against the coppery sea, as it swam. Ransom rejoiced, for swimming was the only sport in which he had ever approached excellence. As he took the water he lost sight of the Un-man for a moment; then, looking up and shaking the wet hair from his face as he struck out in pursuit (his hair was very long by now), he saw its whole body upright and above the surface as though it were sitting on the sea. A second glance and he realised that it had mounted a fish. Apparently the charm'd slumber extended only to the island, for the Un-man on his mount was making good speed. It was stooping down doing something to its fish, Ransom could not see what. Doubtless it would have many ways of urging the animal to quicken its pace.

For a moment he was in despair: but he had forgotten the man-loving nature of these sea-horses. He found almost at once that he was in a complete shoal of the creatures, leaping and frisking to attract his attention. In spite of their good will it was no easy matter to get himself on to the slippery surface of the fine specimen which his grabbing hands first reached: while he was struggling to mount, the distance widened between him and the fugitive. But at last it was done. Settling himself behind the great goggle-eyed head he nudged the animal with his knees, kicked it with his heels, whispered words of praise and encouragement, and in general did all he could to awake its metal. It began threshing its way forward. But looking ahead Ransom could no longer see any sign of the Un-man, but only the long empty ridge of the next wave coming towards him. Doubtless the quarry was beyond the ridge. Then he noticed that he had no cause to be bothered about the direction. The slope of water was dotted all over with the great fish, each marked by a heap of yellow foam and some of them spouting as well. The Un-man possibly had not reckoned on the instinct which made them follow as leader any of their company on whom a human being sat. They were all forging straight ahead, no more uncertain of their course than homing rooks or bloodhounds on a scent. As Ransom and his fish rose to the top of the wave, he found himself looking down on a wide shallow trough shaped much like a valley in the home counties. Far away and now approaching the opposite slope was the little, dark puppet-like silhouette of the Un-man: and between it and him the whole school of fish was spread out in three or four lines. Clearly there was no danger of losing touch. Ransom was hunting him with the fish and they would not cease to follow. He laughed aloud. 'My hounds are bred out of the Spartan kind, so flew'd so sanded,' he roared.

Now for the first time the blessed fact that he was no longer fighting nor even standing thrust itself upon his attention. He made to assume a more relaxed position and was pulled up sharp by a grinding pain across his back. He foolishly put back his hand to explore his shoulders, and almost screamed at the pain of his own touch. His back seemed to be in shreds and the shreds seemed to be all stuck together. At the same time he noticed that he had lost a tooth and that nearly all the skin was gone from his knuckles; and underneath the smarting surface pains, deeper and more ominous aches racked him from head to foot. He had not known he was so knocked up.

Then he remembered that he was thirsty. Now that he had begun to cool and stiffen he found the task of getting a drink from the water that raced by him extremely difficult. His first idea had been to stoop low till his head was almost upside down and bury his face in the water: but a single attempt cured him of that. He was reduced to putting down his cupped hands, and even this, as his stiffness grew upon him, had to be done with infinite caution and with many groans and gasps. It took many minutes to get a tiny sip which merely mocked his thirst. The quenching of that thirst kept him employed for what seemed to be half an hour – a half hour of sharp pains and insane pleasures. Nothing had ever tasted so good. Even when he had done drinking he went on taking up water and splashing it over himself. This would have been among the happiest moments of his life – if only the smarting of his back did not seem to be getting worse and if only he were not afraid that there was poison in the cuts. His legs kept on getting stuck to the fish and having to be unstuck with pain and care. Every now and then blackness threatened to come over him. He could easily have fainted, but he thought 'This will never do' and fixed his eyes on objects close at hand and thought plain thoughts and so retained his consciousness.

All this time the Un-man rode on before him, up-wave and down-wave, and the fishes followed and Ransom followed the fishes. There seemed to be more of them now, as if the chase had met other shoals and gathered them up into itself in snowball fashion: and soon there were creatures other than fish. Birds with long necks like swans – he could not tell their colour for they looked black against the sky – came, wheeling at first, overhead, but afterwards they settled in long straight files – all following the Un-man. The crying of these birds was often audible, and it was the wildest sound that Ransom had ever heard, the loneliest, and the one that had least to do with Man. No land was in sight, nor had been for many hours. He was on the high seas, the waste places of Perelandra, as he had not been since his first arrival. The sea noises continuously filled his ear: the sea smell, unmistakable and stirring as that of our Tellurian oceans, but quite different in its warmth and golden sweetness, entered into his brain. It also was wild and strange. It was not hostile: if it had been, its wildness and strangeness would have been the less, for hostility is a relation and an enemy is not a total stranger. It came into his head that he knew nothing at all about this world. Some day, no doubt, it would be peopled by the descendants of the King and Queen. But all its millions of years in the unpeopled past, all its uncounted miles of laughing water in the lonely present ... did they exist solely for that? It was strange that he to whom a wood or a morning sky on earth had sometimes been a kind of meal, should have had to come to another planet in order to realise Nature as a thing in her own right The diffused meaning, the inscrutable character, which had been both in Tellus and Perelandra since they split off from the Sun, and which would be, in one sense, displaced by the advent of imperial man, yet, in some other sense, not displaced at all, enfolded him on every side and caught him into itself.

13

Darkness fell upon the waves as suddenly as if it had been poured out of a bottle. As soon as the colours and the distances were thus taken away, sound and pain became more emphatic. The world was reduced to a dull ache, and sudden stabs, and the beating of the fish's fins, and the monotonous yet infinitely varied noises of the water. Then he found himself almost falling off the fish, recovered his seat with difficulty, and realised that he had been asleep, perhaps for hours. He foresaw that this danger would continually recur. After some consideration he levered himself painfully out of the narrow saddle behind its head and stretched his body at full length along the fish's back. He parted his legs and wound them about the creature as far as he could and did the same with his arms, hoping that thus he could retain his mount even while sleeping. It was the best he could do. A strange thrilling sensation crept over him, communicated doubtless from the movement of its muscles. It gave him the illusion of sharing in its strong bestial life, as if he were himself becoming a fish.

Long after this he found himself staring into something like a human face. It ought to have terrified him but, as sometimes happens to us in a dream, it did not. It was a bluish-greenish face shining apparently by its own light. The eyes were much larger than those of a man and gave it a goblin appearance. A fringe of corrugated membranes at the sides suggested whiskers. With a shock he realised that he was not dreaming, but awake. The thing was real. He was still lying, sore and wearied, on the body of the fish and this face belonged to something that was swimming alongside him.

He remembered the swimming submen or mermen whom he had seen before. He was not at all frightened, and he guessed that the creature's reaction to him was the very same as his to it – an uneasy, though not hostile, bewilderment. Each was wholly irrelevant to the other. They met as the branches of different trees meet when the wind brings them together.

Ransom now raised himself once more to a sitting position. He found that the darkness was not complete. His own fish swam in a bath of phosphorescence and so did the stranger at his side. All about him were other blobs and daggers of blue light and he could dimly make out from the shapes which were fish and which were the water-people. Their movements faintly indicated the contours of the waves and introduced some hint of perspective into the night. He noticed presently that several of the water-people in his immediate neighbourhood seemed to be feeding. They were picking dark masses of something off the water with their webbed frog-like hands and devouring it. As they munched, it hung out of their mouths in bushy and shredded bundles and looked like moustaches. It is significant that it never occurred to him to try to establish any contact with these beings, as he had done with every other animal on Perelandra, nor did they try to establish any with him. They did not seem to be the natural subjects of man as the other creatures were. He got the impression that they simply shared a planet with him as sheep and horses share a field, each species ignoring the other. Later, this came to be a trouble in his mind: but for the moment he was occupied with a more practical problem. The sight of their eating had reminded him that he was hungry and he was wondering whether the stuff they ate were eatable by him. It took him a long time, scooping the water with his fingers, to catch any of it. When at last he did it turned out to be of the same general structure as one of our smaller seaweeds, and to have little bladders that popped when one pressed them. It was tough and slippery, but not salt like the weeds of a Tellurian sea. What it tasted like, he could never properly describe. It is to be noted all through this story that while Ransom was on Perelandra his sense of taste had become something more than it was on Earth: it gave knowledge as well as pleasure, though not a knowledge that can be reduced to words. As soon as he had eaten a few mouthfuls of the seaweed he felt his mind oddly changed. He felt the surface of the sea to be the top of the world. He thought of the floating islands as we think of clouds; he saw them in imagination as they would appear from below – mats of fibre with long streamers handing down from them, and became startlingly conscious of his own experience in walking on the topside of them as a miracle or a myth. He felt his memory of the Green Lady and all her promised descendants and all the issues which had occupied him ever since he came to Perelandra rapidly fading from his mind, as a dream fades when we wake, or as if it were shouldered aside by a whole world of interests and emotions to which he could give no name. It terrified him. In spite of his hunger he threw the rest of the weed away.

He must have slept again, for the next scene that he remembers was in daylight. The Un-man was still visible ahead, and the shoal of fishes was still spread out between it and him. The birds had abandoned the chase. And now at last a full and prosaic sense of his position descended upon him. It is a curious flaw in the reason, to judge from Ransom's experience, that when a man comes to a strange planet he at first quite forgets its size. That whole world is so small in comparison with his journey through space that he forgets the distances within it: any two places in Mars, or in Venus, appear to him like places in the same town. But now, as Ransom looked round once more and saw nothing in every direction but golden sky and tumbling waves, the full absurdity of this delusion was borne in upon him. Even if there were continents in Perelandra, he might well be divided from the nearest of them by the breadth of the Pacific or more. But he had no reason to suppose that there were any. He had no reason to suppose that even the floating islands were very numerous, or that they were equally distributed over the surface of the planet. Even if their loose archipelago spread over a thousand square miles, what would that be but a negligible freckling in a landless ocean that rolled for ever round a globe not much smaller than the World of Men? Soon his fish would be tired. Already, he fancied, it was not swimming at its original speed. The Un-man would doubtless torture its mount to swim till it died. But he could not do that. As he was thinking of these things and staring ahead, he saw something that turned his heart cold. One of the other fish deliberately turned out of line, spurted a little column of foam, dived, and reappeared some yards away, apparently drifting. In a few minutes it was out of sight. It had had enough.

And now the experiences of the past day and night began to make a direct assault upon his faith. The solitude of the seas and, still more, the experiences which had followed his taste of the sea-weed, had insinuated a doubt as to whether this world in any real sense belonged to those who called themselves its King and Queen. How could it be made for them when most of it, in fact, was unin-habitable by them? Was not the very idea naive and anthropomorphic in the highest degree? As for the great prohibition, on which so much had seemed to hang – was it really so important? What did these roarers with the yellow foam, and these strange people who lived in them, care whether two little creatures, now far away, lived or did not live on one particular rock? The parallelism between the scenes he had lately witnessed and those recorded in the Book of Genesis, and which had hitherto given him the feeling of knowing by experience what other men only believe, now began to shrink in importance. Need it prove anything more than that similar irrational *taboos* had accompanied the dawn of reason in two different worlds? It was all very well to talk of Maleldil: but where was Maleldil now? If this illimitable ocean said anything, it said something very different. Like all solitudes it was, indeed, haunted: but not by an anthropomorphic Deity, rather by the wholly inscrutable to which man and his life remained eternally irrelevant. And beyond this ocean was space itself. In vain did Ransom try to remember that he had been in 'space' and found it Heaven, tingling with a fulness of life for which infinity itself was not one cubic inch too large. All that seemed like a dream. That opposite mode of thought which he had often mocked and called in mockery The Empirical Bogey, came surging into his mind – the great myth of our century with its gases and galaxies, its light years and evolutions, its nightmare perspectives of simple arithmetic in which everything that can possibly hold significance for the mind becomes the mere by-product of essential disorder. Always till now he had belittled it, had treated with a certain disdain its flat superlatives, its clownish amazement that different things should be of different sizes, its glib munificence of ciphers. Even now, his reason was not quite subdued, though his heart would not listen to his reason. Part of him still knew that the size of a thing is the least important characteristic, that the material universe derived from the comparing and mythopoeic power within him that very majesty before which he was now asked to abase himself, and that mere numbers could not overawe us unless we lent them, from our own resources, that awfulness which they themselves could no more supply than a banker's ledger. But this knowledge remained an abstraction. Mere bigness and loneliness overbore him.

These thoughts must have taken several hours and absorbed all his attention. He was aroused by what he least expected – the sound of a human voice. Emerging from his reverie he saw that all the fishes had deserted him. His own was swimming feebly: and there a few yards away, no longer fleeing him but moving slowly towards him, was the Un-man. It sat hugging itself, its eyes almost shut up with bruises, its flesh the colour of liver, its leg apparently broken, its mouth twisted with pain.

'Ransom,' it said feebly.

Ransom held his tongue. He was not going to encourage it to start that game again.

'Ransom,' it said again in a broken voice, 'for God's sake speak to me.'

He glanced at it in surprise. Tears were on its cheeks. 'Ransom, don't cold-shoulder me,' it said. 'Tell me what has happened. What have they done to us? You – you're all bleeding. My leg's broken …' its voice died away in a whimper.

'Who are you?' he asked sharply.

'Oh, don't pretend you don't know me,' mumbled Weston's voice. I'm Weston. You're Ransom – Elwin Ransom of Leicester, Cambridge, the philologist. We've had our quarrels, I know. I'm sorry. I dare say I've been in the wrong. Ransom, you'll not leave me to die in this horrible place, will you?'

'Where did you learn Aramaic?' asked Ransom, keeping his eyes on the other.

'Aramaic?' said Weston's voice. 'I don't know what you're talking about. It's not much of a game to make fun of a dying man.'

'But are you really Weston?' said Ransom, for he began to think that Weston had actually come back.

'Who else should I be?' came the answer, with a burst of weak temper, on the verge of tears.

'Where have you been?' asked Ransom.

Weston – if it was Weston – shuddered. 'Where are we now?' he asked presently.

'In Perelandra – Venus, you know,' answered Ransom.

'Have you found the space-ship?' asked Weston. 'I never saw it except at a distance,' said Ransom. 'And I've no idea where it is now – a couple of hundred miles away for all I know.'

'You mean we're trapped?' said Weston, almost in a scream. Ransom said nothing and the other bowed his head and cried like a baby.

'Come,' said Ransom at last, 'there's no good taking it like that. Hang it all, you'd not be much better off if you were on Earth. You remember they're having a war there. The Germans may be bombing London to bits at this moment!' Then seeing the creature still crying, he added, 'Buck up, Weston. It's only death, all said and done. We should have to die some day, you know. We shan't lack water, and hunger – without thirst – isn't too bad. As for drowning – well, a bayonet wound, or cancer, would be worse.'

'You mean to say you're going to leave me,' said Weston. 'I can't, even if I wanted to,' said Ransom. 'Don't you see I'm in the same position as yourself?'

'You'll promise not to go off and leave me in the lurch?' said Weston.

'All right, I'll promise if you like. Where could I go to?'

Weston looked very slowly all round and then urged his fish little nearer to Ransom's.

'Where is … it?' he asked in a whisper. 'You know,' and he made meaningless gestures.

'I might ask you the same question,' said Ransom.

'Me?' said Weston. His face was, in one way and another, so disfigured that it was hard to be sure of its expression.

'Have you any idea of what's been happening to you for the last few days?' said Ransom.

Weston once more looked all round him uneasily.

'It's all true, you know,' he said at last.

'What's all true?' said Ransom.

Suddenly Weston turned on him with a snarl of rage. 'It's all very well for you,' he said. 'Drowning doesn't hurt and death is bound to come anyway, and all that nonsense. What do you know about death? It's all true, I tell you.'

'What are you talking about?'

'I've been stuffing myself up with a lot of nonsense all my life,' said Weston. 'Trying to persuade myself that it matters what happens to the human race … trying to believe that anything you can do will make the universe bearable. It's all rot, do you see?'

'And something else is truer!'

'Yes,' said Weston, and then was silent for a long time.

'We'd better turn our fishes head on to this,' said Ransom presently, his eyes on the sea, 'or we'll be driven apart.' Weston obeyed without seeming to notice what he did, and for a time the two men were riding very slowly side by side.

'I'll tell you what's true,' said Weston presently.

'What?'

'A little child that creeps upstairs when nobody's looking and very slowly turns the handle to take one peep into the room where its grandmother's dead body is laid out – and then runs away and has bad dreams. An enormous grandmother, you understand.'

'What do you mean by saying that's truer?'

'I mean that child knows something about the universe which all science and all religion is trying to hide.'

Ransom said nothing.

'Lots of things,' said Weston presently. 'Children are afraid to go through a churchyard at night, and the grown-ups tell them not to be silly: but the children know better than the grown-ups. People in Central Africa doing beastly things with masks on in the middle of the night – and missionaries and civil servants say it's all superstition. Well, the blacks know more about the universe than the white people. Dirty priests in back streets in Dublin frightening half-witted children to death with stories about it. You'd say they are unenlightened. They're not: except that they think there is a way of escape. There isn't. That is the real universe, always has been, always will be. That's what it all *means*.'

'I'm not quite clear –' began Ransom, when Weston interrupted him.

'That's why it's so important to live as long as you can. All the good things are now – a thin little rind of what we call life, put on for show, and then – the *real* universe for ever and ever. To thicken the rind by one centimetre – to live one week, one day, one half hour longer – that's the only thing that matters. Of course you don't know it: but every man who is waiting to be hanged knows it. You say 'What difference does a short reprieve make?' What difference!!'

'But nobody need go there,' said Ransom.

'I know that's what you believe,' said Weston. 'But you're wrong. It's only a small parcel of civilised people who think that. Humanity as a whole knows better. It knows – Homer knew – that *all* the dead have sunk down into the inner darkness: under the rind. All witless, all twittering, gibbering, decaying. Bogeymen. Every savage knows that *all* ghosts hate the living who are still enjoying the rind: just as old women hate girls who still have their good looks. It's quite right to be afraid of the ghosts. You're going to be one all the same.'

'You don't believe in God,' said Ransom.

'Well, now, that's another point,' said Weston. 'I've been to church as well as you when I was a boy. There's more sense in parts of the Bible than you religious people know. Doesn't it say He's the God of the living, not of the dead? That's just it. Perhaps your God does exist – but it makes no difference whether He does or not. No, of course you wouldn't see it; but one day you will. I don't think you've got the idea of the rind – the thin outer skin which we call life – really clear. Picture the universe as an infinite glove with this very thin crust on the outside. But remember its thickness is a thickness of *time*. It's about seventy years thick in the best places. We are born on the surface of it and all our lives we are sinking through it. When we've got all the way through then we are what's called Dead: we've got into the dark part inside, the real globe. If your God exists, He's not in the globe – He's outside, like a moon. As we pass into the interior we pass out of His ken. He doesn't follow us in. You would express it by saying He's not in time – which you think comforting! In other words He stays put: out in the light and air, outside. But we are in time. We 'move with the times'. That is, from His point of view, we move *away*, into what He regards as nonentity, where He never follows. That is all there is to us, all there ever was. He may be there in what you call 'Life', or He may not. What difference does it make? *We're* not going to be there for long!'

'That could hardly be the whole story,' said Ransom. 'If the whole universe were like that, then we, being parts of it, would feel at home in such a universe. The very fact that it strikes us as monstrous –'

'Yes,' interrupted Weston, 'that would be all very well if it wasn't that reasoning itself is only valid as long as you stay in the rind. It has nothing to do with the real universe. Even the ordinary scientists – like what I used to be myself – are beginning to find that out. Haven't you seen the real meaning of all this modern stuff about the dangers of extrapolation and bent space and the indeterminacy of the atom? They don't say it in so many words, of course, but what they're getting to, even before they die nowadays, is what all men get to when they're dead – the knowledge that reality is neither rational nor consistent nor anything else. In a sense you might say it isn't there. 'Real' and 'Unreal', 'true' and 'false' – they're all only on the surface. They give way the moment you press them.'

'If all this were true,' said Ransom, 'what would be the point of saying it?'

'Or of anything else?' replied Weston. 'The only point in anything is that there isn't any point. Why do ghosts want to frighten? Because they *are* ghosts. What else is there to do?'

'I get the idea;' said Ransom. 'That the account a man gives of the universe, or of any other building, depends very much on where he is standing.'

'But specially,' said Weston, 'on whether he's inside or out. All the things you like to dwell upon are outsides. A planet like our own, or like Perelandra, for instance. Or a beautiful human body. All the colours and pleasant shapes are merely where it ends, where it ceases to be. Inside, what do you get? Darkness, worms, heat, pressure, salt, suffocation, stink.'

They ploughed forward for a few minutes in silence over waves which were now growing larger. The fish seemed to be making little headway.

'Of course you don't care,' said Weston. 'What do you people in the rind care about us? You haven't been pulled down yet. It's like a dream I once had, though I didn't know then how true it was. I dreamed I was lying dead – you know, nicely laid out in the ward in a nursing home with my face settled by the undertaker and big lilies in the room. And then a sort of a person who was all falling to bits – like a tramp, you know, only it was himself not his clothes that was coming to pieces – came and stood at the foot of the bed, just hating me. "All right," he said, "all right. You think you're mighty fine with your clean sheet and your shiny coffin being got ready. I began like that. We all did. Just wait and see what you come down to in the end." '

'Really,' said Ransom, 'I think you might just as well shut up.

'Then there's Spiritualism,' said Weston, ignoring this suggestion. 'I used to think it all nonsense. But it isn't. It's all true. You've noticed that all *pleasant* accounts of the dead are traditional or philosophical? What actual experiment discovers is quite different. Ectoplasm – slimy films coming out of a medium's belly and making great, chaotic, tumbledown faces. Automatic writing producing reams of rubbish.'

'*Are* you Weston?' said Ransom, suddenly turning upon his companion. The persistent mumbling voice, so articulate that you had to listen to it and yet so inarticulate that you had to strain your ears to follow what it said, was beginning to madden him.

'Don't be angry,' said the voice. 'There's no good being angry with me. I thought you might be sorry. My God, Ransom, it's awful. You don't understand. Right down under layers and layers. Buried alive. You try to connect things and can't. They take your head off … and you can't even look back on what life was like in the rind, because you know it never did mean anything even from the beginning.'

'What are you?' cried Ransom. 'How do you know what death is like? God knows, I'd help you if I could. But give me the facts. Where have you been these few days?'

'Hush,' said the other suddenly, 'what's that?'

Ransom listened. Certainly there did seem to be a new element in the great concourse of noises with which they were surrounded. At first he could not define it. The seas were very big now and the wind was strong. All at once his companion reached out his hand and clutched Ransom's arm.

'Oh, my God!' he cried. 'Oh, Ransom, Ransom! We shall be killed. Killed and put back under the rind. Ransom, you promised to help me. Don't let them get me again.'

'Shut up,' said Ransom in disgust, for the creature was wailing and blubbering so that he could hear nothing else: and he wanted very much to identity the deeper note that had mingled with the piping wind and roar of water.

'Breakers,' said Weston, 'breakers, you fool! Can't you hear? There's a country over there! There's a rocky coast. Look there – no, to your right. We shall be smashed into a jelly. Look – O God, here comes the dark!'

And the dark came. Horror of death such as he had never known, horror of the terrified creature at his side, descended upon Ransom: finally, horror with no definite object. In a few minutes he could see through the jet-black night the luminous cloud of foam. From the way in which it shot steeply upward he judged it was breaking on cliffs. Invisible birds, with a shriek and flurry, passed low overhead.

'Are you there, Weston?' he shouted. 'What cheer? Pull yourself together. All that stuff you've been talking is lunacy. Say a child's prayer if you can't say a man's. Repent your sins. Take my hand. There are hundreds of mere boys on Earth facing death this moment. We'll do very well.'

His hand was clutched in the darkness, rather more firmly than he wished. 'I can't bear it, I can't bear it,' came Weston's voice.

'Steady now. None of that,' he shouted back, for Weston had suddenly gripped his arm with both hands.

'I can't bear it,' came the voice again.

'Hi!' said Ransom. 'Let go. What the devil are you doing?' and as he spoke strong arms had plucked him from the saddle, had wrapped him round in a terrible embrace just below his thighs, and, clutching uselessly at the smooth surface of the fish's body, he was dragged down. The waters closed over his head: and still his enemy pulled him down into the warm depth, and down farther yet to where it was no longer warm.

14

'I can't hold my breath any longer,' thought Ransom. 'I can't. I can't.' Cold slimy things slid upwards over his agonised body. He decided to stop holding his breath, to open his mouth and die, but his will did not obey this decision. Not only his chest but his temples felt as if they were going to burst. It was idle to struggle. His arms met no adversary and his legs were pinioned. He became aware that they were moving upwards. But this gave him no hope. The surface was too far away, he could not hold out till they reached it. In the immediate presence of death all ideas of the after life were withdrawn from his mind. The mere abstract proposition, 'This is a man dying' floated before him in an unemotional way. Suddenly a roar of sound rushed back upon his ears – intolerable boomings and clangings. His mouth opened automatically. He was breathing again. In a pitch darkness full of echoes he was clutching what seemed to be gravel and kicking wildly to throw off the grip that still held his legs. Then he was free and fighting once more: a blind struggle half in and half out of the water on what seemed to be a pebbly beach, with sharper rocks here and there that cut his feet and elbows. The blackness was filled with gasping curses, now in his own voice, now in Weston's, with yelps of pain, thudding concussions, and the noise of laboured breath. In the end he was astride of the enemy. He pressed its sides between his knees till its ribs cracked and clasped his hands round its throat. Somehow he was able to resist its fierce tearing at his arms – to keep on pressing. Once before he had had to press like this, but that had been on an artery, to save life, not to kill. It seemed to last for ages. Long after the creature's struggles had ceased he did not dare to relax his grip. Even when he was quite sure that it breathed no longer he retained his seat on its chest and kept his tired hands, though now loosely, on its throat. He was nearly fainting himself, but he counted a thousand before he would shift his posture. Even then he continued to sit on its body. He did not know whether in the last few hours the spirit which had spoken to him was really Weston's or whether he had been the victim of a ruse. Indeed, it made little difference. There was, no doubt, a confusion of persons in damnation: what Pantheists falsely hoped of Heaven bad men really received in Hell. They were melted down into their Master, as a lead soldier slips down and loses his shape in the ladle held over the gas ring. The question whether Satan, or one whom Satan has digested, is acting on any given occasion, has in the long run no clear significance. In the meantime, the great thing was not to be tricked again.

There was nothing to be done, then, except to wait for the morning. From the roar of echoes all about him he concluded that they were in a very narrow bay between cliffs. How they had ever made it was a mystery. The morning must be many hours distant. This was a considerable nuisance. He determined not to leave the body till he had examined it by daylight and perhaps taken further steps to make sure that it could not be re-animated. Till then he must pass the time as best he could. The pebbly beach was not very comfortable, and when he tried to lean back he found a jagged wall. Fortunately he was so tired that for a time the mere fact of sitting still contented him. But this phase passed.

He tried to make the best of it. He determined to give up guessing how the time was going. 'The only safe answer,' he told himself, 'is to think of the earliest hour you can suppose possible, and then assume the real time is two hours earlier than that.' He beguiled himself by recapitulating the whole story of his adventure in Perelandra. He recited all that he could remember of the *Iliad*, the *Odyssey*, the *Æneid*, the *Chanson de Roland*, *Paradise Lost*, the *Kalevala*, the *Hunting of the Snark*, and a rhyme about Germanic sound-laws which he had composed as a freshman. He tried to spend as long as he could hunting for the lines he could not remember. He set himself a chess problem. He tried to rough out a chapter for a book he was writing. But it was all rather a failure.

These things went on, alternating with periods of dogged inactivity, until it seemed to him that he could hardly remember a time before that night. He could scarcely believe that even to a bored and wakeful man twelve hours could appear so long. And the noise – the gritty slipper discomfort! It was very odd, now he came to think of it, that this country should have none of those sweet night breezes which he had met everywhere else in Perelandra. It was odd too (but this thought came to him what seemed hours later) that he had not even the phosphorescent wave-crests to feed his eyes on. Very slowly a possible explanation of both facts dawned upon him: and it would also explain why the darkness lasted so long. The idea was too terrible for any indulgence of fear. Controlling himself, he rose stiffly to his feet and began picking his steps along the beach. His progress was very slow: but presently his outstretched arms touched perpendicular rock. He stood on tiptoe and stretched his hands up as far as he could. They found nothing but rock. 'Don't get the wind up,' he said to himself. He started groping his way back. He came to the Un-man's body, passed it, and went beyond it round the opposite beach. It curved rapidly, and here, before he had gone twenty steps his hands – which he was holding above his head – met, not a wall, but a roof, of rock. A few paces farther and it was lower. Then he had to stoop. A little later and he had to go on his hands and knees. It was obvious that the roof came down and finally met the beach.

Sick with despair he felt his way back to the body and sat down. The truth was now beyond doubt. There was no good waiting for the morning. There would be no morning here till the end of the world, and perhaps he had already waited a night and a day. The clanging echoes, the dead air, the very smell of the place, all confirmed this. He and his enemy when they sank had clearly, by some hundredth chance, been carried through a hole in the cliffs well below water-level and come up on the beach of a cavern. Was it possible to reverse the process? He went down to the water's edge – or rather as he groped his way down to where the shingle was wet, the water came to meet him. It thundered over his head and far up behind him, and then receded with a tug which he only resisted by spread-eagling himself on the beach and gripping the stones. It would be useless to plunge into *that* – he would merely have his ribs broken against the opposite wall of the cave. If one had light, and a high place to dive from, it was just conceivable one might get down to the bottom and strike the exit … but very doubtful. And anyway, one had no light.

Although the air was not very good he supposed that his prison must be supplied with air from somewhere – but whether from any aperture that he could possibly reach was another matter. He turned at once and began exploring the rock behind the beach. At first it seemed hopeless, but the conviction that caves may lead you anywhere dies hard, and after some time his groping hands found a shelf about three feet high. He stepped up on it. He had expected it to be only a few inches deep but his hands could find no wall before him. Very cautiously he took some paces forward. His right foot touched something sharp. He whistled with the pain and went on even more cautiously. Then he found vertical rock – smooth as high as he could reach. He turned to his right and presently lost it. He turned left and began to go forward again and almost at once stubbed his toe. After nursing it for a moment he went down on hands and knees. He seemed to be among boulders, but the way was practicable. For ten minutes or so he made fairly good going, pretty steeply upward, sometimes on slippery shingle, sometimes over the tops of the big stones. Then he came to another cliff. There appeared to be a shelf on this about four feet up, but this time a really shallow one. He got on to it somehow and glued himself to the face, feeling out to left and right for further grips.

When he found one and realised that he was now about to attempt some real climbing, he hesitated. He remembered that what was above him might be a cliff which even in daylight and properly clothed he would never dare to attempt: but hope whispered that it might equally well be only seven feet high and that a few minutes of coolness might bring him into those gently winding passages up into the heart of the mountain which had, by now, won such a firm place in his imagination. He decided to go on. What worried him was not, in fact, the fear of falling, but the fear of cutting himself off from the water. Starvation he thought he could face: not thirst. But he went on. For some minutes he did things which he had never done on Earth. Doubtless he was in one way helped by the darkness: he had no real sensation of height and no giddiness. On the other hand, to work by touch alone made crazy climbing. Doubtless if anyone had seen him he would have appeared at one moment to take mad risks and at another to indulge in excessive caution. He tried to keep out of his mind the possibility that he might be climbing merely towards a roof.

After about quarter of an hour he found himself on a wide horizontal surface – either a much deeper shelf or the top of the precipice. He rested here for a while and licked his cuts. Then he got up and felt his way forwards, expecting every moment to meet another rock wall. When, after about thirty paces, he had not done so, he tried shouting and judged from the sound that he was in a fairly open place. Then he continued. The floor was of small pebble and ascended fairly steeply. There were some larger stones but he had learned to curl up his toes as his foot felt for the next place and he seldom stubbed them now. One minor trouble was that even in this perfect blackness he could not help straining his eyes to see. It gave him a headache and created phantom lights and colours.

This slow uphill trek through darkness lasted so long that he began to fear he was going round in a circle, or that he had blundered into some gallery which ran on for ever beneath the surface of the planet. The steady ascent in some degree reassured him. The starvation for light became very painful. He found himself thinking about light as a hungry man thinks about food – picturing April hillsides with milky clouds racing over them in blue skies or quiet circles of lamplight on tables pleasantly littered with books and pipes. By a curious confusion of mind he found it impossible not to imagine that the slope he walked on was not merely dark, but black in its own right, as if with soot. He felt that his feet and hands must be blackened by touching it. Whenever he pictured himself arriving at any light, he also pictured that light revealing a world of soot all around him.

He struck his head sharply against something and sat down half stunned. When he had collected himself he found by groping that the shingle slope had run up into a roof of smooth rock. His heart was very low as he sat there digesting this discovery. The sound of the waves came up faint and melancholy from below and told him that he was now at a great height. At last, though with very little hope, he began walking to his right, keeping contact with the roof by raising his arms. Presently it receded beyond his reach. A long time after that he heard a sound of water. He went on more slowly in great fear of encountering a waterfall. The shingle began to be wet and finally he stood in a little pool. Turning to his left he found, indeed, a waterfall, but it was a tiny stream with no force of water that could endanger him. He knelt in the rippling pool and drank from the fall and put his aching head and weary shoulders under it. Then, greatly refreshed, he tried to work his way up it.

Though the stones were slippery with some kind of moss and many of the pools were deep, it presented no serious difficulties. In about twenty minutes he had reached the top, and as far as he could judge by shouting and noticing the echo he was now in a very large cave indeed. He took the stream for guidance and proceeded to follow it up. In that featureless dark it was some sort of company. Some real hope – distinct from that mere convention of hope which supports men in desperate situations – began to enter his mind.

It was shortly after this that he began to be worried by the noises. The last faint booming of the sea in the little hole whence he had set out so many hours ago had now died away and the predominant sound was the gentle tinkling of the stream. But he now began to think that he heard other noises mixed with it. Sometimes it would be a dull plump as if something had slipped into one of the pools behind him: sometimes, more mysteriously, a dry rattling sound as if metal were being dragged over the stones. At first he put it down to imagination. Then he stopped once or twice to listen and heard nothing; but each time when he went on it began again. At last, stopping once more, he heard it quite unmistakably. Could it be that the Un-man had after all come to life and was still following him? But that seemed improbable, for its whole plan had been to escape. It was not so easy to dispose of the other possibility – that these caverns might have inhabitants. All his experience, indeed, assured him that if there were such inhabitants they would probably be harmless, but somehow he could not quite believe that anything which lived in such a place would be agreeable, and a little echo of the Un-man's – or was it Weston's – talk came back to him. 'All beautiful on the surface, but down inside – darkness, heat, horror, and stink.' Then it occurred to him that if some creature were following him up the stream it might be well for him to leave its banks and wait till the creature had gone past. But if it were hunting him it would presumably hunt by scent; and in any case he would not risk losing the stream. In the end he went on.

Whether through weakness – for he was now very hungry indeed – or because the noises behind made him involuntarily quicken his pace, he found himself unpleasantly hot, and even the stream did not appear very refreshing when he put his feet in it. He began to think that whether he were pursued or not he must have a short rest – but just at that moment he saw the light. His eyes had been mocked so often before that he would not at first believe it. He shut them while he counted a hundred and looked again. He turned round and sat down for several minutes, praying that it might not be a delusion, and looked again. 'Well,' said Ransom, 'if it is a delusion, it's a pretty stubborn one.' A very dim, tiny, quivering luminosity, slightly red in colour, was before him. It was too weak to illuminate anything else and in that world of blackness he could not tell whether it was five feet or five miles away. He set out at once, with beating heart. Thank Heaven, the stream appeared to be leading him towards it.

While he thought it was still a long way off he found himself almost stepping into it. It was a circle of light lying on the surface of the water, which thereabouts formed a deepish trembling pool. It came from above. Stepping into the pool he looked up. An irregularly shaped patch of light, now quite distinctly red, was immediately above him. This time it was strong enough to show him the objects immediately around it, and when his eyes had mastered them he perceived that he was looking up a funnel or fissure. Its lower aperture lay in the roof of his own cavern which must here be only a few feet above his head: its upper aperture was obviously in the floor of a separate and higher chamber whence the light came. He could see the uneven side of the funnel, dimly illuminated, and clothed with pads and streamers of a jelly-like and rather unpleasing vegetation. Down this water was trickling and falling on his head and shoulders in a warm rain. This warmth, together with the red colour of the light, suggested that the upper cave was illuminated by subterranean fire. It will not be clear to the reader, and it was not clear to Ransom when he thought about it afterwards, why he immediately decided to get into the upper cave if he possibly could. What really moved him, he thinks, was the mere hunger for light. The very first glance at the funnel restored dimensions and perspective to his world, and this in itself was like delivery from prison. It seemed to tell him far more than it actually did of his surroundings: it gave him back that whole frame of spatial directions without which a man seems hardly able to call his body his own. After this, any return to the horrible black vacancy, the world of soot and grime, the world without size or distance, in which he had been wandering, was out of the question. Perhaps also he had some idea that whatever was following him would cease to follow if he could get into the lighted cave.

But it was not easy to do. He could not reach the opening of the funnel. Even when he jumped he only just touched the fringe of its vegetation. At last he hit upon an unlikely plan which was the best he could think of. There was just enough light here for him to see a number of larger stones among the gravel, and he set to work to build up a pile in the centre of the pool. He worked rather feverishly and often had to undo what he had done: and he tried it several times before it was really high enough. When at last it was completed and he stood sweating and shaky on the summit the real hazard was still to be run. He had to grip the vegetation on each side above his head, trusting to luck that it would hold, and half jump, half pull himself up as quickly as he could, since if it held at all it would, he felt sure, not hold for long. Somehow or other he managed it. He got himself wedged into the fissure with his back against one side and his feet against the other, like a mountaineer in what is called a chimney. The thick squashy growth protected his skin, and after a few upward struggles he found the walls of the passage so irregular that it could be climbed in the ordinary way. The heat increased rapidly. 'I'm a fool to have come up here,' said Ransom: but even as he said so, he was at the top.

At first he was blinded by the light. When at last he could take in his surroundings he found himself in a vast hall so filled with firelight that it gave him the impression of being hollowed out of red clay. He was looking along the length of it. The floor sloped down to the left side. On his right it sloped upward to what appeared a cliff edge, beyond which was an abyss of blinding brightness. A broad shallow river was flowing down the middle of the cavern. The roof was so high as to be invisible, but the walls soared up into the darkness with broad curves like the roots of a beech tree.

He staggered to his feet, splashed across the river (which was hot to the touch) and approached the cliff edge. The fire appeared to be thousands of feet below him and he could not see the other side of the pit in which it swelled and roared and writhed. His eyes could only bear it for a second or so, and when he turned away the rest of the cavern seemed dark. The heat of his body was painful. He drew away from the cliff edge and sat down with his back to the fire to collect his thoughts.

They were collected in an unlooked-for way. Suddenly and irresistibly, like an attack by tanks, that whole view of the universe which Weston (if it were Weston) had so lately preached to him, took all but complete possession of his mind. He seemed to see that he had been living all his life in a world of illusion. The ghosts, the damned ghosts, were right. The beauty of Perelandra, the innocence of the Lady, the sufferings of saints, and the kindly affections of men, were all only an appearance and outward show. What he had called the worlds were but the skins of the worlds: a quarter of a mile beneath the surface, and from thence through thousands of miles of dark and silence and infernal fire, to the very heart of each, Reality lived – the meaningless, the unmade, the omnipotent idiocy to which all spirits were irrelevant and before which all efforts were vain. Whatever was following him would come up that wet, dark hole, would presently be excreted by that hideous duct, and then he would die. He fixed his eyes upon the dark opening from which he had himself just emerged. And then – 'I thought as much,' said Ransom.

Slowly, shakily, with unnatural and inhuman movements a human form, scarlet in the firelight, crawled out on to the floor of the cave. It was the Un-man, of course: dragging its broken leg and with its lower jaw sagging open like that of a corpse, it raised itself to a standing position. And then, close behind it, something else came up out of the hole. First came what looked like branches of trees, and then seven or eight spots of light, irregularly grouped like a constellation. Then a tubular mass which reflected the red glow as if it were polished. His heart gave a great leap as the branches suddenly resolved themselves into long wiry feelers and the dotted lights became the many eyes of a shell-helmeted head and the mass that followed it was revealed as a large roughly cylindrical body. Horrible things followed – angular, many jointed legs, and presently, when he thought the whole body was in sight, a second body came following it and after that a third. The thing was in three parts, united only by a kind of wasp's waist structure – three parts that did not seem to be truly aligned and made it look as if it had been trodden on – a huge, many legged, quivering deformity, standing just behind the Un-man so that the horrible shadows of both danced in enormous and united menace on the wall of rock behind them.

'They want to frighten me,' said something in Ransom's brain, and at the same moment he became convinced both that the Un-man had summoned this great earth crawler and also that the evil thoughts which had preceded the appearance of the enemy had been poured into his own mind by the enemy's will. The knowledge that his thoughts could be thus managed from without did not awake terror but rage. Ransom found that he had risen, that he was approaching the Un-man, that he was saying things, perhaps foolish things, in English. 'Do you think I'm going to stand *this*?' he yelled. 'Get out of my brain. It isn't yours, I tell you! get out of it.' As he shouted he had picked up a big, jagged stone from beside the stream. 'Ransom,' croaked the Un-man, 'wait! We're both trapped …' but Ransom was already upon it.

'In the name of the Father and of the Son and of the Holy Ghost, here goes – I mean Amen,' said Ransom, and hurled the stone as hard as he could into the Un-man's face. The Un-man fell as a pencil falls, the face smashed out of all recognition. Ransom did not give it a glance but turned to face the other horror. But where had the horror gone? The creature was there, a curiously shaped creature no doubt, but all the loathing had vanished clean out of his mind, so that neither then nor at any other time could he remember it, nor ever understand again why one should quarrel with an animal for having more legs or eyes than oneself. All that he had felt from childhood about insects and reptiles died that moment: died utterly, as hideous music dies when you switch off the wireless. Apparently it had all, even from the beginning, been a dark enchantment of the enemy's. Once, as he had sat writing near an open window in Cambridge, he had looked up and shuddered to see, as he supposed, a many coloured beetle of unusually hideous shape crawling across his paper. A second glance showed him that it was a dead leaf, moved by the breeze; and instantly the very curves and re-entrants which had made its ugliness turned into its beauties. At this moment he had almost the same sensation. He saw at once that the creature intended him no harm – had indeed no intentions at all. It had been drawn thither by the Un-man, and now stood still, tentatively moving its antennae. Then, apparently not liking its surroundings, it turned laboriously round and began descending into the hole by which it had come. As he saw the last section of its tripartite body wobble on the edge of the aperture, and then finally tip upward with its torpedo-shaped tail in the air, Ransom almost laughed. 'Like an animated corridor train' was his comment.

He turned to the Un-man. It had hardly anything left that you could call a head, but he thought it better to take no risks. He took it by its ankles and lugged it up to the edge of the cliff: then, after resting a few seconds, he shoved it over. He saw its shape black, for a second, against the sea of fire: and then that was the end of it.

He rolled rather than crawled back to the stream and drank deeply. 'This may be the end of me or it may not,' thought Ransom. 'There may be a way out of these caves or there may not. But I won't go another step further today. Not if it was to save my life – not to save my life. That's flat. Glory be to God. I'm tired.' A second later he was asleep.

15

For the rest of the subterranean journey after his long sleep in the firelit cave, Ransom was somewhat light-headed with hunger and fatigue. He remembers lying still after he woke for what seemed many hours and even debating with himself whether it was worth going on. The actual moment of decision has vanished from his mind. Pictures come back in a chaotic, disjointed fashion. There was a long gallery open to the fire-pit on one side and a terrible place where clouds of steam went up for ever and ever. Doubtless one of the many torrents that roared in the neighbourhood here fell into the depth of the fire. Beyond that were great halls still dimly illuminated and full of unknown mineral wealth that sparkled and danced in the light and mocked his eyes as if he were exploring a hall of mirrors by the help of a pocket torch. It seemed to him also, though this may have been delirium, that he came through a vast cathedral space which was more like the work of art than that of Nature, with two great thrones at one end and chairs on either hand too large for human occupants. If the things were real, he never found any explanation of them. There was a dark tunnel in which a wind from Heaven knows where was blowing and drove sand in his face. There was also a place where he himself walked in darkness and looked down through fathom below fathom of shafts and natural arches and winding gulfs on to a smooth floor lit with a cold green light. And as he stood and looked it seemed to him that four of the great earth-beetles, dwarfed by distance to the size of gnats, and crawling two by two, came slowly into sight. And they were drawing behind them a flat car, and on the car, upright, unshaken, stood a mantled form, huge and still and slender. And driving its strange team it passed on with insufferable majesty and went out of sight. Assuredly the inside of this world was not for man. But it was for something. And it appeared to Ransom that there might, if a man could find it, be some way to renew the old Pagan practice of propitiating the local gods of unknown places in such fashion that it was no offence to God Himself but only a prudent and courteous apology for trespass. That thing, that swathed form in its chariot, was no doubt his fellow creature. It did not follow that they were equals or had an equal right in the underland. A long time after this came the drumming – the *boom-ba-ba-ba-boom-boom* out of pitch darkness, distant at first, then all around him, then dying away after endless prolongation of echoes in the black labyrinth. Then came the fountain of cold light – a column, as of water, shining with some radiance of its own, and pulsating, and never any nearer however long he travelled and at last suddenly eclipsed. He did not find what it was. And so, after more strangeness and grandeur and labour than I can tell, there came a moment when his feet slid without warning on clay – a wild grasp – a spasm of terror – and he was spluttering and struggling in deep, swift-flowing water. He thought that even if he escaped being battered to death against the walls of the channel he would presently plunge along with the stream into the pit of fire. But the channel must have been very straight and the current was less violent than he had supposed. At all events he never touched the sides. He lay helpless, in the end, rushing forward through echoing darkness. It lasted a long time.

You will understand that what with expectation of death, and weariness, and the great noise, he was confused in mind. Looking back on the adventure afterwards it seemed to him that he floated out of blackness into greyness and then into an inexplicable chaos of semi-transparent blues and greens and whites. There was a hint of arches above his head and faintly shining columns, but all vague and all obliterating one another as soon as seen. It looked like a cave of ice, but it was too warm for that. And the roof above him seemed to be itself rippling like water, but this was doubtless a reflection. A moment later and he was rushed out into broad daylight and air and warmth, and rolled head over heels, and deposited, dazzled and breathless, in the shallows of a great pool.

He was now almost too weak to move. Something in the air, and the wide silence which made a background to the lonely crying of birds, told him that he was on a high mountain top. He rolled rather than crawled out of the pool on to sweet blue turf. Looking back whence he had come he saw a river pouring from the mouth of a cave, a cave that seemed indeed to be made of ice. Under it the water was spectral blue, but near where he lay it was warm amber. There was mist and freshness and dew all about him. At his side rose a cliff mantled with streamers of bright vegetation, but gleaming like glass where its own surface showed through. But this he heeded little. There were rich clusters of a grape-like fruit glowing under the little pointed leaves, and he could reach them without getting up. Eating passed into sleeping by a transition he could never remember.

At this point it becomes increasingly difficult to give Ransom's experiences in any certain order. How long he lay beside the river at the cavern mouth eating and sleeping and waking only to eat and sleep again, he has no idea. He thinks it was only a day or two, but from the state of his body when this period of convalescence ended I should imagine it must have been more like a fortnight or three weeks. It was a time to be remembered only in dreams as we remember infancy. Indeed it was a second infancy, in which he was breast-fed by the planet Venus herself: unweaned till he moved from that place. Three impressions of this long Sabbath remain. One is the endless sound of rejoicing water. Another is the delicious life that he sucked from the clusters which almost seemed to bow themselves unasked into his upstretched hands. The third is the song. Now high in air above him, now welling up as if from glens and valleys far below, it floated through his sleep and was the first sound at every waking. It was formless as the song of a bird, yet it was not a bird's voice. As a bird's voice is to a flute, so this was to a 'cello: low and ripe and tender, full-bellied, rich and gold-en-brown: passionate too, but not with the passions of men.

Because he was weaned so gradually from this state of rest I cannot give his impressions of the place he lay in, bit by bit, as he came to take it in. But when he was cured and his mind was clear again, this was what he saw. The cliffs out of which his river had broken through the cave were not of ice, but of some kind of translucent rock. Any little splinter broken off them was as transparent as glass, but the cliffs themselves, when you looked at them close, seemed to become opaque about six inches from the surface. If you waded upstream into the cave and then turned back and looked towards the light, the edges of the arch which formed the cave's mouth were distinctly transparent: and everything looked blue inside the cave. He did not know what happened at the top of these cliffs.

Before him the lawn of blue turf continued level for about thirty paces, and then dropped with a steep slope, leading the river down in a series of cataracts. The slope was covered with flowers which shook continually in a light breeze. It went down a long way and ended in a winding and wooded valley which curled out of sight on his right hand round a majestic slope: but beyond that, lower down – so much lower down as to be almost incredible – one caught the point of mountain tops, and beyond that, fainter yet, the hint of still lower valleys, and then a vanishing of everything in golden haze. On the opposite side of this valley the earth leaped up in great sweeps and folds of almost Himalayan height to the red rocks. They were not red like Devonshire cliffs: they were true rose-red, as if they had been painted. Their brightness astonished him, and so did the needle-like sharpness of their spires, until it occurred to him that he was in a young world and that these mountains might, geologically speaking, be in their infancy. Also, they might be farther off than they looked.

To his left and behind him the crystal cliffs shut off his view. To his right they soon ended and beyond them the ground rose to another and nearer peak – a much lower one than those he saw across the valley. The fantastic steepness of all the slopes confirmed his idea that he was on a very young mountain.

Except for the song it was all very still. When he saw birds flying they were usually a long way below him. On the slopes to his right and, less distinctly, on the slope of the great *massif* which faced him, there was a continual rippling effect which he could not account for. It was like water flowing: but since, if it were a stream on the remoter mountain, it would have to be a stream two or three miles wide, this seemed improbable.

In trying to put the completed picture together I have omitted something which, in fact, made it a long job for Ransom to get that picture. The whole place was subject to mist. It kept on vanishing in a veil of saffron or very pale gold and reappearing again – almost as if the golden sky-roof, which looked only a few feet above the mountain-tops, were opening and pouring down riches upon the world.

Day by day as he came to know more of the place, Ransom also came to know more of the state of his own body. For a long time he was too stiff almost to move and even an incautious breath made him wince. It healed, however, surprisingly quickly. But just as a man who has had a fall only discovers the real hurt when the minor bruises and cuts are less painful, so Ransom was nearly well before he detected his most serious injury. It was a wound in his heel. The shape made it quite clear that the wound had been inflicted by human teeth – the nasty, blunt teeth of our own species which crush and grind more than they cut. Oddly enough, he had no recollection of this particular bite in any of his innumerable tussles with the Un-man. It did not look unhealthy, but it was still bleeding. It was not bleeding at all fast, but nothing he could do would stop it. But he worried very little about this. Neither the future nor the past really concerned him at this period. Wishing and fearing were modes of consciousness for which he seemed to have lost the faculty.

Nevertheless there came a day when he felt the need of some activity and yet did not feel ready to leave the little lair between the pool and the cliff which had become like a home. He employed that day in doing something which may appear rather foolish and yet at the time it seemed to him that he could hardly omit it. He had discovered that the substance of the translucent cliffs was not very hard. Now he took a sharp stone of a different kind, and cleared a wide space on the cliff wall of vegetation. Then he made measurements and spaced it all out carefully and after a few hours had produced the following. The language was Old Solar but the letters were Roman.

WITHIN THESE CAVES WAS BURNED

THE BODY OF

EDWARD ROLLES WESTON

A LEARNED HNAU OF THE WORLD WHICH THOSE WHO

INHABIT IT

CALL TELLUS

BUT THE ELDILA THULCANDRA

HE WAS BORN WHEN TELLUS HAD COMPLETED

ONE THOUSAND EIGHT HUNDRED AND NINETY-SIX

REVOLUTIONS

ABOUT ARBOL

SINCE THE TIME WHEN MALELDIL

BLESSED BE HE

WAS BORN AS A HNAU IN THULCANDRA

HE STUDIED THE PROPERTIES OF BODIES

AND FIRST OF THE TELLURIANS TRAVELLED THROUGH DEEP

HEAVEN TO MALACANDRA AND TO PERELANDRA

WHERE HE GAVE UP LEARNED WILL AND REASON TO THE

BENT ELDIL

WHEN TELLUS WAS MAKING

THE ONE THOUSANDTH NINE HUNDREDTH AND FORTY-SECOND

REVOLUTION AFTER THE BIRTH OF MALELDIL

BLESSED BE HE.

'That was a tomfool thing to do,' said Ransom to himself contentedly as he lay down again. "No one will ever read it. But there ought to be some record. He was a great physicist after all. Anyway, it has given me some exercise.' He yawned prodigiously and settled down to yet another twelve hours of sleep.

The next day he was better and began taking little walks, not going down but strolling to and fro on the hillside on each side of the cave. The following day he was better still. But on the third day he was well, and ready for adventures.

He set out very early in the morning and began to follow the watercourse down the hill. The slope was very steep but there were no outcroppings of rock and the turf was soft and springy and to his surprise he found that the descent brought no weariness to his knees. When he had been going about half an hour and the peaks of the opposite mountain were now too high to see and the crystal cliffs behind him were only a distant glare, he came to a new kind of vegetation. He was approaching a forest of little trees whose trunks were only about two and a half feet high; but from the top of each trunk there grew long streamers which did not rise in the air but flowed in the wind downhill and parallel to the ground. Thus, when he went in among them, he found himself wading knee-deep and more in a continually rippling sea of them – a sea which presently tossed all about him as far as his eye could reach. It was blue in colour, but far lighter than the blue of the turf – almost a Cambridge blue at the centre of each streamer, but dying away at their tasselled and feathery edges into a delicacy of bluish grey which it would take the subtlest effects of smoke and cloud to rival in our world. The soft, almost impalpable, caresses of the long thin leaves on his flesh, the low, singing, rustling, whispering music, and the frolic movement all about him, began to set his heart beating with that almost formidable sense of delight which he had felt before in Perelandra. He realised that these dwarf forests – these ripple trees as he now christened them – were the explanation of that water-like movement he had seen on the farther slopes.

When he was tired he sat down and found himself at once in a new world. The streamers now flowed above his head. He was in a forest made for dwarfs, a forest with a blue transparent roof, continually moving and casting an endless dance of lights and shades upon its mossy floor. And presently he saw that it was indeed made for dwarfs. Through the moss, which here was of extraordinary fineness, he saw the hithering and thithering of what at first he took for insects but what proved, on closer inspection, to be tiny mammals. There were many mountain mice, exquisite scale models of those he had seen on the Forbidden Island, each about the size of a bumble bee. There were little miracles of grace which looked more like horses than anything he had yet seen on this world, though they resembled proto-hippos rather than his modern representative.

'How can I avoid treading on thousands of these?' he wondered. But they were not really very numerous and the main crowd of them seemed to be all moving away on his left. When he made to rise he noticed that there were already very few of them in sight.

He continued to wade down through the rippling streamers (it was like a sort of vegetable surf-bathing) for about an hour longer. Then he came into woods and presently to a river with a rocky course flowing across his path to the right. He had, in fact, reached the wooded valley, and knew that the ground which sloped upwards through trees on the far side of the water was the beginning of the great ascent. Here was amber shade and solemn height under the forest roof, and rocks wet with cataracts, and, over all, the noise of that deep singing. It was so loud now and so full of melody that he went downstream, a little out of his way, to look for its origin. This brought him almost at once out of stately aisles and open glades into a different kind of wood. Soon he was pressing his way through thornless thickets, all in bloom. His head was covered with the petals that showered on it, his sides gilded with pollen. Much that his fingers touched was gummy and at each pace his contact with soil and bush appeared to wake new odours that darted into his brain and there begot wild and enormous pleasures. The noise was very loud now and the thicket very dense so that he could not see a yard ahead, when the music stopped suddenly. There was a sound of rustling and broken twigs and he made hastily in that direction, but found nothing. He had almost decided to give up the search when the song began again a little farther away. Once more he made after it; once more the creature stopped singing and evaded him. He must have played thus at hide-and-seek with it for the best part of an hour before his search was rewarded.

Treading delicately during one of the loudest bursts of music he at last saw through the flowery branches a black something. Standing still whenever it stopped singing, and advancing with great caution whenever it began again, he stalked it for ten minutes. At last it was in full view, and singing, and ignorant that it was watched. It sat upright like a dog, black and sleek and shiny, but its shoulders were high above Ransom's head, and the forelegs on which they were pillared were like young trees and the wide soft pads on which they rested were large as those of a camel. The enormous rounded belly was white, and far up above the shoulders the neck rose like that of a horse. The head was in profile from where Ransom stood – the mouth wide open as it sang of joy in thick-coming trills, and the music almost visibly rippled in its glossy throat. He stared in wonder at the wide liquid eyes and the quivering, sensitive nostrils. Then the creatures stopped, saw him, and darted away, and stood, now a few paces distant, on all four legs, not much smaller than a young elephant, swaying a long bushy tail. It was the first thing in Perelandra which seemed to show any fear of man. Yet it was not fear. When he called to it it came nearer. It put its velvet nose into his hand and endured his touch; but almost at once it darted back and, bending its long neck, buried its head in its paws. He could make no headway with it, and when at length it retreated out of sight he did not follow it. To do so would have seemed an injury to its fawn-like shyness, to the yielding softness of its expression, its evident wish to be for ever a sound and only a sound in the thickest centre of untravelled woods. He resumed his journey: a few seconds later the song broke out behind him, louder and lovelier than before, as if in a paean of rejoicing at its recovered privacy.

Ransom now addressed himself seriously to the ascent of the great mountain and in a few minutes emerged from the woods on to its lower slopes. He continued ascending so steeply that he used hands as well as feet for about half an hour and was puzzled to find himself doing it with almost no fatigue. Then he came once more into a region of ripple trees. This time the wind was blowing the streamers not down the mountainside but up it, so that his course had to the eye the astonishing appearance of lying through a wide blue waterfall which flowed the wrong way, curving and foaming towards the heights. Whenever the wind failed for a second or two the extreme ends of the streamers began to curl back under the influence of gravitation, so that it looked as if the heads of the waves were being flung back by a high wind. He continued going up through this for a long time, never feeling any real need for rest but resting occasionally none the less. He was now so high that the crystal cliffs from which he had set out appeared on a level with him as he looked back across the valley. He now saw that the land leaped up beyond them into a whole waste of the same translucent formation which ended in a kind of glassy tableland. Under the naked sun of our own planet this would have been too bright to look at: here, it was a tremulous dazzle changing every moment under the undulations which the Perelandrian sky receives from the ocean. To the left of this tableland were some peaks of greenish rock. He went on. Little by little the peaks and the tableland sank and grew smaller, and presently there arose beyond them an exquisite haze like vaporised amethyst and emerald and gold, and the edge of this haze rose as he rose, and became at last the horizon of the sea, high lifted above the hills. And the sea grew ever larger and the mountains less, and the horizon of the sea rose till the lower mountains behind him seemed to be lying at the bottom of a great bowl of sea; but ahead, the interminable slope, now blue, now violet, now flickering with the smoke-like upward movement of the ripple-trees, soared up and up to the sky. And now the wooded valley in which he had met the singing beast was invisible and the mountain from which he had set out looked no more than a little swell on the slope of the great mountain, and there was not a bird in the air, nor any creature underneath the streamers, and still he went on unwearied, but always bleeding a little from his heel. He was not lonely nor afraid. He had no desires and did not even think about reaching the top nor why he should reach it. To be always climbing this was not, in his present mood, a process but a state, and in that state of life he was content. It did once cross his mind that he had died and felt no weariness because he had no body. The wound in his heel convinced him that this was not so; but if it had been so indeed, and these had been trans-mortal mountains, his journey could hardly have been more great and strange.

That night he lay on the slopes between the stems of the ripple trees with the sweet-scented, wind-proof, delicately-whispering roof above his head, and when morning came he resumed his journey. At first he climbed through dense mists. When these parted, he found himself so high that the concave of the sea seemed to close him in on every side but one: and on that one he saw the rose-red peaks, no longer very distant, and a pass between the two nearest ones through which he caught a glimpse of something soft and flushed. And now he began to feel a strange mixture of sensations – a sense of perfect duty to enter that secret place which the peaks were guarding combined with an equal sense of trespass. He dared not go up that pass: he dared not do otherwise. He looked to see an angel with a flaming sword: he knew that Maleldil bade him go on. 'This is the holiest and the most unholy thing I have ever done,' he thought; but he went on. And now he was right in the pass. The peaks on either hand were not of red rock. Cores of rock they must have had; but what he saw were great matterhorns clothed in flowers – a flower shaped something like a lily but tinted like a rose. And soon the ground on which he trod was carpeted with the same flowers and he must crush them as he walked; and here at last his bleeding left no visible trace.

From the neck between the two peaks he looked a little down, for the top of the mountain was a shallow cup. He saw a valley, a few acres in size, as secret as a valley in the top of a cloud: a valley pure rose-red, with ten or twelve of the glowing peaks about it, and in the centre a pool, married in pure unrippled clearness to the gold of the sky. The lilies came down to its very edge and lined all its bays and headlands. Yielding without resistance to the awe which was gaining upon him, he walked forward with slow paces and bowed head. There was something white near the water's edge. An altar? A patch of white lilies among the red? A tomb? But whose tomb? No, it was not a tomb but a coffin, open and empty, and its lid lying beside it.

Then of course he understood. This thing was own brother to the coffin-like chariot in which the strength of angels had brought him from Earth to Venus. It was prepared for his return. If he had said, 'It is for my burial,' his feelings would not have been very different. And while he thought of this he became gradually aware that there was something odd about the flowers at two places in his immediate neighbourhood. Next, he perceived that the oddity was an oddity in the light; thirdly, that it was in the air as well as on the ground. Then, as the blood pricked his veins and a familiar, yet strange, sense of diminished being possessed him, he knew that he was in the presence of two *eldila*. He stood still. It was not for him to speak.

16

A clear voice like a chime of remote bells, a voice with no blood in it, spoke out of the air and sent a tingling through his frame.

'They have already set foot on the sand and are beginning to ascend,' it said.

'The small one from Thulcandra is already here,' said a second voice.

'Look on him, beloved, and love him,' said the first. 'He is indeed but breathing dust and a careless touch would unmake him. And in his best thoughts there are such things mingled as, if we thought them, our light would perish. But he is in the body of Maleldil and his sins are forgiven. His very name in his own tongue is Elwin, the friend of the *eldila*.'

'How great is your knowledge!' said the second voice.

'I have been down into the air of Thulcandra,' said the first, 'which the small ones call Tellus. A thickened air as full of the Darkened as Deep Heaven is of the Light Ones. I have heard the prisoners there talking in their divided tongues and Elwin has taught me how it is with them.'

From these words Ransom knew the speaker was the Oyarsa of Malacandra, the great archon of Mars. He did not, of course, recognise the voice, for there is no difference between one *eldil*'s voice and another's. It is by art, not nature, that they affect human ear-drums and their words owe nothing to lungs or lips.

'If it is good, Oyarsa,' said Ransom, 'tell me who is this other.'

'It is Oyarsa,' said Oyarsa, 'and here that is not my name. In my own sphere I am Oyarsa. Here I am only Malacandra.'

'I am Perelandra,' said the other voice.

'I do not understand,' said Ransom. 'The Woman told me there were no *eldila* in this world.'

'They have not seen my face till today,' said the second voice, 'except as they see it in the water and the roof heaven, the islands, the caves, and the trees. I was not set to rule them, but while they were young I ruled all else. I rounded this ball when it first arose from Arbol. I spun the air about it and wove the roof. I built the Fixed Island and this, the holy mountain, as Maleldil taught me. The beasts that sing and the beasts that fly and all that swims on my breast and all that creeps and tunnels within me down to the centre has been mine. And today all this is taken from me. Blessed be He.'

'The small one will not understand you,' said the Lord of Malacandra. 'He will think that this is a grievous thing in your eyes.'

'He does not say this, Malacandra.'

'No. That is another strange thing about the children of Adam.'

There was a moment's silence and then Malacandra addressed Ransom. 'You will think of this best if you think of it in the likeness of certain things from your own world.'

'I think I understand,' said Ransom, 'for one of Maleldil's sayers has told us. It is like when the children of a great house come to their full age. Then those who administered all their riches, and whom perhaps they have never seen, come and put all in their hands and give up their keys.'

'You understand well,' said Perelandra. 'Or like when the singing beast leaves the dumb dam who suckled him.'

'The singing beast?' said Ransom. 'I would gladly hear more of this.'

'The beasts of that kind have no milk and always what they bring forth is suckled by the she-beast of another kind. She is great and beautiful and dumb, and till the young singing beast is weaned it is among her whelps and is subject to her. But when it is grown it becomes the most delicate and glorious of all beasts and goes from her. And she wonders at its song.'

'Why has Maleldil made such a thing?' said Ransom.

'That is to ask why Maleldil has made me,' said Perelandra. 'But now it is enough to say that from the habits of these two beasts much wisdom will come into the minds of my King and my Queen and their children. But the hour is upon us, and this is enough.'

'What hour?' asked Ransom.

'Today is the morning day,' said one or other or both the voices. But there was something much more than sound about Ransom and his heart began beating fast.

'The morning … do you mean …?' he asked. 'Is all well? Has the Queen found the King?'

'The world is born today,' said Malacandra. 'Today for the first time two creatures of the low worlds, two images of Maleldil that breathe and breed like the beasts, step up that step at which your parents fell, and sit in the throne of what they were meant to be. It was never seen before. Because it did not happen in your world a greater thing happened, but not this. Because the greater thing happened in Thulcandra, this and not the greater thing happens here.'

'Elwin is falling to the ground,' said the other voice.

'Be comforted,' said Malacandra. 'It is no doing of yours. You are not great, though you could have prevented a thing so great that Deep Heaven sees it with amazement. Be comforted, small one, in your smallness. He lays no merit on you. Receive and be glad. Have no fear, lest your shoulders be bearing this world. Look! it is beneath your head and carries you.'

'Will they come here?' asked Ransom some time later.

'They are already well up the mountain's side,' said Perelandra. 'And our hour is upon us. Let us prepare our shapes. We are hard for them to see while we remain in ourselves.'

'It is very well said,' answered Malacandra. 'But in what form shall we show ourselves to do them honour?'

'Let us appear to the small one here,' said the other. 'For he is a man and can tell us what is pleasing to their senses.'

'I can see – I can see *something* even now,' said Ransom. 'Would you have the King strain his eyes to see those who come to do him honour?' said the archon of Perelandra. 'But look on this and tell us how it deals with you.'

The very faint light – the almost imperceptible alterations in the visual field – which betokens an *eldil* vanished suddenly. The rosy peaks and the calm pool vanished also. A tornado of sheer monstrosities seemed to be pouring over Ransom. Darting pillars filled with eyes, lightning pulsations of flame, talons and beaks and billowy masses of what suggested snow, volleyed through cubes and heptagons into an infinite black void. 'Stop it … stop it,' he yelled, and the scene cleared. He gazed round blinking on the fields of lilies, and presently gave the *eldila* to understand that this kind of appearance was not suited to human sensations. 'Look then on this,' said the voices again. And he looked with some reluctance, and far off between the peaks on the other side of the little valley there came rolling wheels. There was nothing but that – concentric wheels moving with a rather sickening slowness one inside the other. There was nothing terrible about them if you could get used to their appalling size, but there was also nothing significant. He bade them to try yet a third time. And suddenly two human figures stood before him on the opposite side of the lake.

They were taller than the *sorns*, the giants whom he had met in Mars. They were perhaps thirty feet high. They were burning white like white-hot iron. The outline of their bodies when he looked at it steadily against the red landscape seemed to be faintly, swiftly undulating as though the permanence of their shape, like that of waterfalls or flames, co-existed with a rushing movement of the matter it contained. For a fraction of an inch inward from this outline the landscape was just visible through them: beyond that they were opaque.

Whenever he looked straight at them they appeared to be rushing towards him with enormous speed: whenever his eyes took in their surroundings he realised that they were stationary. This may have been due in part to the fact that their long and sparkling hair stood out straight behind them as if in a great wind. But if there were a wind it was not made of air, for no petal of the flowers was shaken. They were not standing quite vertically in relation to the floor of the valley: but to Ransom it appeared (as it had appeared to me on Earth when I saw one) that the *eldil* were vertical. It was the valley – it was the whole world of Perelandra – which was aslant. He remembered the words of Oyarsa long ago in Mars, 'I am not *here* in the same way that you are *here*.' It was borne in upon him that the creatures were really moving, though not moving in relation to him. This planet which inevitably seemed to him while he was in it an unmoving world – the world, in fact – was to them a thing moving through the heavens. In relation to their own celestial frame of reference they were rushing forward to keep abreast of the mountain valley. Had they stood still, they would have flashed past him too quickly for him to see, doubly dropped behind by the planet's spin on its own aids and by its onward march around the Sun.

Their bodies, he said, were white. But a flush of diverse colours began at about the shoulders and streamed up the necks and flickered over face and head and stood out around the head like plumage or a halo. He told me he could in a sense remember these colours – that is, he would know them if he saw them again – but that he cannot by any effort call up a visual image of them nor give them any name. The very few people with whom he and I can discuss these matters all give the same explanation. We think that when creatures of the hypersomatic kind choose to 'appear' to us, they are not in fact affecting our retina at all, but directly manipulating the relevant parts of our brain. If so, it is quite possible that they can produce there the sensations we should have if our eyes were capable of receiving those colours in the spectrum which are actually beyond their range. The 'plumage' or halo of the one *eldil* was extremely different from that of the other. The Oyarsa of Mars shone with cold and morning colours, a little metallic – pure, hard and bracing. The Oyarsa of Venus glowed with a warm splendour, full of the suggestion of teeming vegetable life.

The faces surprised him very much. Nothing less like the 'angel' of popular art could well be imagined. The rich variety, the hint of undeveloped possibilities, which make the interest of human faces, were entirely absent. One single, changeless expression – so clear that it hurt and dazzled him – was stamped on each and there was nothing else there at all. In that sense their faces were as 'primitive', as unnatural, if you like, as those of archaic statues from Aegina. What this one thing was he could not be certain. He concluded in the end that it was charity. But it was terrifyingly different from the expression of human charity, which we always see either blossoming out of, or hastening to descend into, natural affection. Here there was no affection at all: no least lingering memory of it even at ten million years' distance, no germ from which it could spring in any future, however remote. Pure, spiritual, intellectual love shot from their faces like barbed lightning. It was so unlike the love we experience that its expression could easily be mistaken for ferocity.

Both the bodies were naked, and both were free from any sexual characteristics, either primary or secondary. That, one would have expected. But whence came this curious difference between them? He found that he could point to no single feature wherein the difference resided, yet it was impossible to ignore. One could try – Ransom has tried a hundred times – to put it into words. He has said that Malacandra was like rhythm and Perelandra like melody. He has said that Malacandra affected him like a quantitative, Perelandra like an accentual, metre. He thinks that the first held in his hand something like a spear, but the hands of the other were open, with the palms towards him. But I don't know that any of these attempts has helped me much. At all events what Ransom saw at that moment was the real meaning of gender. Everyone must sometimes have wondered why in nearly all tongues certain inanimate objects are masculine and others feminine. what is masculine about a mountain or feminine about certain trees? Ransom has cured me of believing that this is a purely morphological phenomenon, depending on the form of the word. Still less is gender an imaginative extension of sex. Our ancestors did not make mountains masculine because they projected male characteristics into them. The real process is the reverse. Gender is a reality, and a more fundamental reality than sex. Sex is, in fact, merely the adaptation to organic life of a fundamental polarity which divides all created beings. Female sex is simply one of the things that have feminine gender; there are many others, and Masculine and Feminine meet us on planes of reality where male and female would be simply meaningless. Masculine is not attenuated male, nor feminine attenuated female. On the contrary the male and female of organic creatures are rather faint and blurred reflections of masculine and feminine. Their reproductive functions, their differences in strength and size, partly exhibit, but partly also confuse and misrepresent, the real polarity. All this Ransom saw, as it were, with his own eyes. The two white creatures were sexless. But he of Malacandra was masculine (not male); she of Perelandra was feminine (not female). Malacandra seemed to him to have the look of one standing armed, at the ramparts of his own remote archaic world, in ceaseless vigilance, his eyes ever roaming the earthward horizon whence his danger came long ago. 'A sailor's look,' Ransom once said to me; 'you know … eyes that are impregnated with distance.' But the eyes of Perelandra opened, as it were, inward, as if they were the curtained gateway to a world of waves and murmurings and wandering airs, of life that rocked in winds and splashed on mossy stones and descended as the dew and arose sunward in thin-spun delicacy of mist. On Mars the very forests are of stone; in Venus the lands swim. For now he thought of them no more as Malacandra and Perelandra. He called them by their Tellurian names. With deep wonder he thought to himself, 'My eyes have seen Mars and Venus. I have seen Ares and Aphrodite.' He asked them how they were known to the old poets of Tellus. When and from whom had the children of Adam learned that Ares was a man of war and that Aphrodite rose from the sea foam? Earth had been besieged, an enemy-occupied territory, since before history began. The gods have no commerce there. How then do we know of them? It comes, they told him, a long way round and through many stages. There is an environment of minds as well as of space. The universe is one – a spider's web wherein each mind lives along every line, a vast whispering gallery where (save for the direct action of Maleldil) though no news travels unchanged yet no secret can be rigorously kept. In the mind of the fallen Archon under whom our planet groans, the memory of Deep Heaven and the gods with whom he once consorted is still alive. Nay, in the very matter of our world, the traces of the celestial commonwealth are not quite lost. Memory passes through the womb and hovers in the air. The Muse is a real thing. A faint breath, as Virgil says, reaches even the late generations. Our mythology is based on a solider reality than we dream: but it is also at an almost infinite distance from that base. And when they told him this, Ransom at last understood why mythology was what it was – gleams of celestial strength and beauty falling on a jungle of filth and imbecility. His cheeks burned on behalf of our race when he looked on the true Mars and Venus and remembered the follies that have been talked of them on Earth. Then a doubt struck him.

'But do I see you as you really are?' he asked.

'Only Maleldil sees any creature as it really is,' said Mars.

'How do you see one another?' asked Ransom.

'There are no holding places in your mind for an answer to that.'

'Am I then seeing only an appearance? Is it not real at all?'

'You see only an appearance, small one. You have never seen more than an appearance of anything – not of Arbol, nor of a stone, nor of your own body. This appearance is as true as what you see of those.'

'But … there were those other appearances.'

'No. There was only the failure of appearance.'

'I don't understand,' said Ransom. 'Were all those other things – the wheels and the eyes – more real than this or less?'

'There is no meaning in your question,' said Mars. 'You can see a stone, if it is a fit distance from you and if you and it are moving at speeds not too different. But if one throws the stone at your eye, what then is the appearance?'

'I should feel pain and perhaps see splintered light,' said Ransom. 'But I don't know that I should call that an appearance of the stone.'

'Yet it would be the true operation of the stone. And there is your question answered. We are now at the right distance from you.'

'And were you nearer in what I first saw?'

'I do not mean that kind of distance.'

'And then,' said Ransom, still pondering, 'there is what I had thought was your wonted appearance – the very faint light, Oyarsa, as I used to see it in your own world. What of that?'

'That is enough appearance for us to speak to you by. No more was needed between us: no more is needed now. It is to honour the King that we would now appear more. That light is the overflow or echo into the world of your senses of vehicles made for appearance to one another and to the greater *eldila*.'

At this moment Ransom suddenly noticed an increasing disturbance of sound behind his back of uncoordinated sound, husky and pattering noises which broke in on the mountain silence and the crystal voices of the gods with a delicious note of warm animality. He glanced round. Romping, prancing, fluttering, gliding, crawling, waddling, with every kind of movement – in every kind of shape and colour and size – a whole zoo of beasts and birds was pouring into a flowery valley through the passes between the peaks at his back. They came mostly in their pairs, male and female together, fawning upon one another, climbing over one another, diving under one another's bellies, perching upon one another's backs. Flaming plumage, gilded beaks, glossy flanks, liquid eyes, great red caverns of whinneying or of bleating mouths, and thickets of switching tails, surrounded him on every side. 'A regular Noah's Ark!' thought Ransom, and then, with sudden seriousness: 'But there will be no ark needed in this world.'

The song of four singing beasts rose in almost deafening triumph above the restless multitude. The great *eldil* of Perelandra kept back the creatures to the hither side of the pool, leaving the opposite side of the valley empty except for the coffin-like object. Ransom was not clear whether Venus spoke to the beasts or even whether they were conscious of her presence. Her connection with them was perhaps of some subtler kind – quite different from the relations he had observed between them and the Green Lady. Both the *eldila* were now on the same side of the pool with Ransom. He and they and all the beasts were facing in the same direction. The thing began to arrange itself. First, on the very brink of the pool, were the *eldila*, standing: between them, and a little back, was Ransom, still sitting among the lilies. Behind him the four singing beasts, sitting up on their haunches like fire-dogs, and proclaiming joy to all ears. Behind these again, the other animals. The sense of ceremony deepened. The expectation became intense. In our foolish human fashion he asked a question merely for the purpose of breaking it. 'How can they climb to here and go down again and yet be off this island before nightfall?' Nobody answered him. He did not need an answer, for somehow he knew perfectly well that this island had never been forbidden them, and that one purpose in forbidding the other had been to lead them to this their destined throne. Instead of answering, the gods said, 'Be still.'

Ransom's eyes had grown so used to the tinted softness of Perelandrian daylight – and specially since his journey in the dark guts of the mountain – that he had quite ceased to notice its difference from the daylight of our own world. It was, therefore, with a shock of double amazement that he now suddenly saw the peaks on the far side of the valley showing really dark against what seemed a terrestrial dawn. A moment later sharp, well-defined shadows – long, like the shadows at early morning – were streaming back from every beast and every unevenness of the ground and each lily had its light and its dark side. Up and up came the light from the mountain slope. It filled the whole valley. The shadows disappeared again. All was in a pure daylight that seemed to come from nowhere in particular. He knew ever afterwards what is meant by a light 'resting on' or 'overshadowing' a holy thing, but not emanating from it. For as the light reached its perfection and settled itself, as it were, like a lord upon his throne or like wine in a bowl, and filled the whole flowery cup of the mountain top, every cranny, with its purity, the holy thing, Paradise itself in its two Persons, Paradise walking hand in hand, its two bodies shining in the light like emeralds yet not themselves too bright to look at, came in sight in the cleft between two peaks, and stood a moment with its male right hand lifted in regal and pontifical benediction, and then walked down and stood on the far side of the water. And the gods kneeled and bowed their huge bodies before the small forms of that young King and Queen.

17

There was great silence on the mountain top and Ransom also had fallen down before the human pair. When at last he raised his eyes from the four blessed feet, he found himself involuntarily speaking though his voice was broken and his eyes dimmed. 'Do not move away, do not raise me up,' he said. 'I have never before seen a man or a woman. I have lived all my life among shadows and broken images. Oh, my Father and my Mother, my Lord and my Lady, do not move, do not answer me yet. My own father and mother I have never seen. Take me for your son. We have been alone in my world for a great time.'

The eyes of the Queen looked upon him with love and recognition, but it was not of the Queen that he thought most. It was hard to think of anything but the King. And how shall I – I who have not seen him – tell you what he was like? It was hard even for Ransom to tell me of the King's face. But we dare not withhold the truth. It was that face which no man can say he does not know. You might ask how it was possible to look upon it and not to commit idolatry, not to mistake it for that of which it was the likeness. For the resemblance was, in its own fashion, infinite, so that almost you could wonder at finding no sorrows in his brow and no wounds in his hands and feet. Yet there was no danger of mistaking, not one moment of confusion, no least sally of the will towards forbidden reverence. Where likeness was greatest, mistake was least possible. Perhaps this is always so. A clever waxwork can be made so like a man that for a moment it deceives us: the great portrait which is far more deeply like him does not.

Plaster images of The Holy One may before now have drawn to themselves the adoration they were meant to arouse for the reality. But here, where His live image, like Him within and without, made by His own bare hands out of the depth of divine artistry, His masterpiece of self-portraiture coming forth from His workshop to delight all worlds, walked and spoke before Ransom's eyes, it could never be taken for more than an image. Nay, the very beauty of it lay in the certainty that it was a copy, like and not the same, an echo, a rhyme, an exquisite reverberation of the uncreated music prolonged in a created medium.

Ransom was lost for a while in the wonder of these things, So that when he came to himself he found that Perelandra was speaking, and what he heard seemed to be the end of a long oration. 'The floating lands and the firm lands,' she was saying, 'the air and the curtains at the gates of Deep Heaven, the seas and the Holy Mountain, the rivers above and the rivers of under-land, the fire, the fish, the birds, the beasts, and the others of the waves whom yet you know not; all these Maleldil puts into your hand from this day forth as far as you live in time and farther. My word henceforth is nothing: your word is law unchangeable and the very daughter of the Voice. In all that circle which this world runs about Arbol, you are Oyarsa. Enjoy it well. Give names to all creatures, guide all natures to perfection. Strengthen the feebler, lighten the darker, love all. Hail and be glad, oh man and woman, Oyarsa-Perelendri, the Adam, the Crown, Tor and Tinidril, Baru and Baru'ah, Ask and Embla, Yatsur and Yatsurah, dear to Maleldil. Blessed be He!'

When the King spoke in answer, Ransom looked up at him again. He saw that the human pair were now seated on a low bank that rose near the margin of the pool. So great was the light, that they cast clear reflections in the water as they might have done in our own world.

'We give you thanks, fair foster mother,' said the King, 'and specially for this world in which you have laboured for long ages as Maleldil's very hand that all might be ready for us when we woke. We have not known you till today. We have often wondered whose hand it was that we saw in the long waves and the bright islands and whose breath delighted us in the wind at morning. For though we were young then, we saw dimly that to say 'It is Maleldil' was true, but not all the truth. This world we receive: our joy is the greater because we take it by your gift as well as by His. But what does He put into your mind to do henceforward?'

'It lies in your bidding, Tor-Oyarsa,' said Perelandra, 'whether I now converse in Deep Heaven only or also in that part of Deep Heaven which is to you a World.'

'It is very much our will,' said the King, 'that you remain with us, both for the love we bear you and also that you may strengthen us with counsel and even with your operations. Not till we have gone many times about Arbol shall we grow up to the full management of the dominion which Maleldil puts into our hands: nor are we yet ripe to steer the world through Heaven nor to make rain and fair weather upon us. If it seems good to you, remain.'

'I am content,' said Perelandra.

While this dialogue proceeded, it was a wonder that the contrast between the Adam and the *eldil* was not a discord. On the one side, the crystal, bloodless voice, and the immutable expression of the snow-white face; on the other the blood coursing in the veins, the feeling trembling on the lips and sparkling in the eyes, the might of the man's shoulders, the wonder of the woman's breasts, a splendour of virility and richness of womanhood unknown on Earth, a living torrent of perfect animality – yet when these met, the one did not seem rank nor the other spectral. *Animal rationale* – an animal, yet also a reasonable soul: such, he remembered, was the old definition of Man. But he had never till now seen the reality. For now he saw this living Paradise, the Lord and Lady, as the resolution of discords, the bridge that spans what would else be a chasm in creation, the keystone of the whole arch. By entering that mountain valley they had suddenly united the warm multitude of the brutes behind him with the transcorporeal intelligence at his side. They closed the circle, and with their coming all the separate notes of strength or beauty which that assembly had hitherto struck became one music. But now the King was speaking again.

'And as it is not Maleldil's gift simply,' he said, 'but also Maleldil's gift through you, and thereby the richer, so it is not through you only, but through a third, and thereby the richer again. And this is the first word I speak as Tor-Oyarsa-Perelendri; that in our world, as long as it is a world, neither shall morning come nor night but that we and all our children shall speak to Maleldil of Ransom the man of Thulcandra and praise him to one another. And to you, Ransom, I say this, that you have called us Lord and Father, Lady and Mother. And rightly, for this is our name. But in another fashion we call you Lord and Father. For it seems to us that Maleldil sent you into our world at that day when the time of our being young drew to its end, and from it we must now go up or go down, into corruption or into perfection. Maleldil had taken us where He meant us to be: but of Maleldil's instruments in this, you were the chief.'

They made him go across the water to them, wading, for it came only to his knees. He would have fallen at their feet but they would not let him. They rose to meet him and both kissed him, mouth to mouth and heart to heart as equals embrace. They would have made him sit between them, but when they saw that this troubled him they let it be. He went and sat down on the level ground, below them, and a little to the left. From there he faced the assembly – the huge shapes of the gods and the concourse of beasts. And then the Queen spoke.

'As soon as you had taken away the Evil One,' she said, 'and I awoke from sleep, my mind was cleared. It is a wonder to me, Piebald, that for all those days you and I could have been so young. The reason for not yet living on the Fixed Land is now so plain. How could I wish to live there except because it was Fixed? And why should I desire the Fixed except to make sure – to be able on one day to command where I should be the next and what should happen to me? It was to reject the wave – to draw my hands out of Maleldil's, to say to Him, 'Not thus, but thus' to put in our own power what times should roll towards us ... as if you gathered fruits together today for tomorrow's eating instead of taking what came. That would have been cold love and feeble trust. And out of it how could we ever have climbed back into love and trust again?'

'I see it well,' said Ransom. 'Though in my world it would pass for folly. We have been evil so long' – and then he stopped, doubtful of being understood and surprised that he had used a word for *evil* which he had not hitherto known that he knew, and which he had not heard either in Mars or in Venus.

'We know these things now,' said the King, seeing Ransom's hesitation. 'All this, all that happened in your world, Maleldil has put into our mind. We have learned of evil, though not as the Evil One wished us to learn. We have learned better than that, and know it more, for it is waking that understands sleep and not sleep that understands waking. There is an ignorance of evil that comes from being young: there is a darker ignorance that comes from doing it, as men by sleeping lose the knowledge of sleep. You are more ignorant of evil in Thulcandra now than in the days before your Lord and Lady began to do it. But Maleldil has brought us out of the one ignorance, and we have not entered the other. It was by the Evil One himself that he brought us out of the first. Little did that dark mind know the errand on which he really came to Perelandra!'

'Forgive me, my Father, if I speak foolishly,' said Ransom. 'I see how evil has been made known to the Queen, but not how it was made known to you.'

Then unexpectedly the King laughed. His body was very big and his laugh was like an earthquake in it, loud and deep and long, till in the end Ransom laughed too, though he had not seen the joke, and the Queen laughed as well. And the birds began clapping their wings and the beasts wagging their tails, and the light seemed brighter and the pulse of the whole assembly quickened, and new modes of joy that had nothing to do with mirth as we understand it passed into them all, as it were from the very air, or as if there were dancing in Deep Heaven. Some say there always is.

'I know what he is thinking,' said the King, looking upon the Queen. 'He is thinking that you suffered and strove and I have a world for my reward.' Then he turned to Ransom and continued. 'You are right,' he said, 'I know now what they say in your world about justice. And perhaps they say well, for in that world things always fall below justice. But Maleldil always goes above it. All is gift. I am Oyarsa not by His gift alone but by our foster mother's, not by hers alone but by yours, not by yours alone but my wife's – nay, in some sort, by gift of the very beasts and birds. Through many hands, enriched with many different kinds of love and labour, the gift comes to me. It is the Law. The best fruits are plucked for each by some hand that is not his own.'

'That is not the whole of what happened, Piebald,' said the Queen. 'The King has not told you all. Maleldil drove him far away into a green sea where forests grow up from the bottom through the waves ...'

'Its name is Lur,' said the King.

'Its name is Lur,' repeated the *eldila*. And Ransom realised that the King had uttered not an observation but an enactment.

'And there in Lur (it is far hence),' said the Queen, 'strange things befell him.'

'Is it good to ask about these things?' said Ransom.

'There were many things,' said Tor the King. 'For many hours I learned the properties of shapes by drawing lines in the turf of a little island on which I rode. For many hours I learned new things about Maleldil and about His Father and the Third One. We knew little of this while we were young. But after that He showed me in a darkness what was happening to the Queen. And I knew it was possible for her to be undone. And then I saw what had happened in your world, and how your Mother fell and how your Father went with her, doing her no good thereby and bringing the darkness upon all their children. And then it was before me like a thing coming towards my hand ... what I should do in like case. There I learned of evil and good, of anguish and joy.'

Ransom had expected the King to relate his decision, but when the King's voice died away into thoughtful silence he had not the assurance to question him.

'Yes ...' said the King, musing. 'Though a man were to be torn in two halves ... though half of him turned into earth. ... The living half must still follow Maleldil. For if it also lay down and became earth, what hope would there be for the whole? But while one half lived, through it He might send life back into the other.' Here he paused for a long time, and then spoke again somewhat quickly. 'He gave me no assurance. No fixed land. Always one must throw oneself into the wave.' Then he cleared his brow and turned to the *eldil* and spoke in a new voice.

'Certainly, oh foster mother,' he said. 'We have much need of counsel for already we feel that growing up within our bodies which our young wisdom can hardly overtake. They will not always be bodies bound to the low worlds. Hear the second word that I speak as Tor-Oyarsa-Perelendri. While this World goes about Arbol ten thousand times, we shall judge and hearten our people from this throne. Its name is Tai Harendrimar, The Hill of Life.'

'Its name is Tai Harendrimar,' said the *eldila*.

'On the Fixed Land which once was forbidden,' said Tor the King, 'we will make a great place to the splendour of Maleldil. Our sons shall bend the pillars of rock into arches –'

'What are arches?' said Tinidril the Queen.

'Arches,' said Tor the King, 'are when pillars of stone throw out branches like trees and knit their branches together and bear up a great dome as of leafage, but the leaves shall be shaped stones. And there our sons will make images.'

'What are images?' said Tinidril.

'Splendour of Deep Heaven!' cried the King with a great laugh. 'It seems there are too many new words in the air. I had thought these things were coming out of your mind into mine, and lo! you have not thought them at all. Yet I think Maleldil passed them to me through you, none the less. I will show you images, I will show you houses. It may be that in this matter our natures are reversed and it is you who beget and I who bear. But let us speak of plainer matters. We will fill this world with our children. We will know this world to the centre. We will make the nobler of the beasts so wise that they will become *hnau* and speak: their lives shall awake to a new life in us as we awake in Maleldil. When the time is ripe for it and the ten thousand circlings are nearly at an end, we will tear the sky curtain and Deep Heaven shall become familiar to the eyes of our sons as the trees and the waves to ours.'

'And what after this, Tor-Oyarsa?' said Malacandra.

'Then it is Maleldil's purpose to make us free of Deep Heaven. Our bodies will be changed, but not all changed. We shall be as the *eldila*, but not all as the *eldila*. And so will all our sons and daughters be changed in the time of their ripeness, until the number is made up which Maleldil read in His Father's mind before times flowed.'

'And that,' said Ransom, 'will be the end?'

Tor the King stared at him.

'The end?' he said. 'Who spoke of an end?'

'The end of your world, I mean,' said Ransom.

'Splendour of Heaven!' said Tor. 'Your thoughts are unlike ours. About that time we shall be not far from the beginning of all things. But there will be one matter to settle before the beginning rightly begins.'

'What is that?' asked Ransom.

'Your own world,' said Tor, 'Thulcandra. The siege of your world shall be raised, the black spot cleared away, before the real beginning. In those days Maleldil will go to war – in us, and in many who once were *hnau* on your world, and in many from far off and in many *eldila*, and, last of all, in Himself unveiled, He will go down to Thulcandra. Some of us will go before. It is in my mind, Malacandra, that thou and I will be among those. We shall fall upon your moon, wherein there is a secret evil, and which is as the shield of the Dark Lord of Thulcandra – scarred with many a blow. We shall break her. Her light shall be put out. Her fragments shall fall into your world and the seas and the smoke shall arise so that the dwellers in Thulcandra will no longer see the light of Arbol. And as Maleldil Himself draws near, the evil things in your world shall show themselves stripped of disguise so that plagues and horrors shall cover your lands and seas. But in the end all shall be cleansed, and even the memory of your Black Oyarsa blotted out, and your world shall be fair and sweet and reunited to the field of Arbol and its true name shall be heard again. But can it be, Friend, that no rumour of all this is heard in Thulcandra? Do your people think that their Dark Lord will hold his prey for ever?'

'Most of them,' said Ransom, 'have ceased to think of such things at all. Some of us still have the knowledge: but I did not at once see what you were talking of, because what you call the beginning we are accustomed to call the Last Things.'

'I do not call it the beginning,' said Tor the King. 'It is but the wiping out of a false start in order that the world may *then* begin. As when a man lies down to sleep, if he finds a twisted root under his shoulder he will change his place and after that his real sleep begins. Or as a man setting foot on an island, may make a false step. He steadies himself and after that his journey begins. You would not call that steadying of himself a last thing?'

'And is the whole story of my race no more than this?' said Ransom.

'I see no more than beginnings in the history of the Low Worlds,' said Tor the King. 'And in yours a failure to begin. You talk of evenings before the day had dawned. I set forth even now on ten thousand years of preparation – I, the first of my race, my race the first of races, to begin. I tell you that when the last of my children has ripened and ripeness has spread from them to all the Low Worlds, it will be whispered that the morning is at hand.'

'I am full of doubts and ignorance,' said Ransom. 'In our world those who know Maleldil at all believe that His coming down to us and being a man is the central happening of all that happens. If you take that from me, Father, whither will you lead me? Surely not to the enemy's talk which thrusts my world and my race into a remote corner and gives me a universe with no centre at all, but millions of worlds that lead nowhere or (what is worse) to more and more worlds for ever, and comes over me with numbers and empty spaces and repetitions and asks me to bow down before bigness. Or do you make your world the centre? But I am troubled. What of the people of Malacandra? Would they also think that their world was the centre? I do not even see how your world can rightly be called yours. You were made yesterday and it is from old. The most of it is water where you cannot live. And what of the things beneath its crust? And of the great spaces with no world at all? Is the enemy easily answered when He says that all is without plan or meaning? As soon as we think we see one it melts away into nothing, or into some other plan that we never dreamed of, and what was the centre becomes the rim, till we doubt if any shape or plan or pattern was ever more than a trick of our own eyes, cheated with hope, or tired with too much looking. To what is all driving? What is the morning you speak of? What is it the beginning of?'

'The beginning of the Great Game, of the Great Dance, said Tor. 'I know little of it as yet. Let the *eldila* speak.'

The voice that spoke next seemed to be that of Mars, but Ransom was not certain. And who spoke after that, he does not know at all. For in the conversation that followed – if it can be called a conversation – though he believes that he himself was sometimes the speaker, he never knew which words were his or another's, or even whether a man or an *eldil* was talking. The speeches followed one another – if, indeed, they did not all take place at the same time – like the parts of a music into which all five of them had entered as instruments or like a wind blowing through five trees that stand together on a hilltop.

'We would not talk of it like that,' said the first voice. The Great Dance does not wait to be perfect until the peoples of the Low Worlds are gathered into it. We speak not of when it will begin. It has begun from before always. There was no time when we did not rejoice before His face as now. The dance which we dance is at the centre and for the dance all things were made. Blessed be He!'

Another said, 'Never did He make two things the same; never did He utter one word twice. After earths, not better earths but beasts; after beasts, not better beasts but spirits. After a falling, not recovery but a new creation. Out of the the new creation, not a third but the mode of change itself is changed for ever. Blessed be He!'

And another said, 'It is loaded with Justice as a tree bows down with fruit. All is righteousness and there is no equality. Not as when stones lie side by side, but as when stones support and are supported in an arch, such is His order; rule and obedience, begetting and bearing, heat glancing down, life growing up. Blessed be He!'

One said, 'They who add years to years in lumpish aggregation, or miles to miles and galaxies to galaxies, shall not come near His greatness. The day of the fields of Arbol will fade and the days of Deep Heaven itself are numbered. Not thus is He great. He dwells (all of Him dwells) within the seed of the smallest flower and is not cramped: Deep Heaven is inside Him who is inside the seed and does not distend Him. Blessed be He!'

'The edge of each nature borders on that whereof it contains no shadow or similitude. Of many points one line; of many lines one shape; of many shapes one solid body; of many senses and thoughts one person; of three persons, Himself. As in the circle to the sphere, so are the ancient worlds that needed no redemption to that world wherein He was born and died. As is a point to a line, so is that world to the far-off fruits of its redeeming. Blessed be He!'

'Yet the circle is not less round than the sphere, and the sphere is the home and fatherland of circles. Infinite multitudes of circles lie enclosed in every sphere, and if they spoke they would say, For us were spheres created. Let no mouth open to gainsay them. Blessed be He!'

'The peoples of the ancient worlds who never sinned, for whom He never came down, are the peoples for whose sake the Low Worlds were made. For though the healing what was wounded and the straightening what was bent is a new dimension of glory, yet the straight was not made that it might be bent nor the whole that it might be wounded. The ancient peoples are at the centre. Blessed be He!'

'All which is not itself the Great Dance was made in order that He might come down into it. In the Fallen World He prepared for Himself a body and was united with the Dust and made it glorious for ever. This is the end and final cause of all creating, and the sin whereby it came is called Fortunate and the world where this was enacted is the centre of worlds. Blessed be He!'

'The Tree was planted in that world but the fruit has ripened in this. The fountain that sprang with mingled blood and life in the Dark World, flows here with life only. We have passed the first cataracts, and from here onward the stream flows deep and turns in the direction of the sea. This is the Morning Star which He promised to those who conquer; this is the centre of worlds. Till now, all has waited. But now the trumpet has sounded and the army is on the move. Blessed be He!'

'Though men or angels rule them, the worlds are for themselves. The waters you have not floated on, the fruit you have not plucked, the caves into which you have not descended and the fire through which your bodies cannot pass, do not await your coming to put on perfection, though they will obey you when you come. Times without number I have circled Arbol while you were not alive, and those times were not desert. Their own voice was in them, not merely a dreaming of the day when you should awake. They also were at the centre. Be comforted, small immortals. You are not the voice that all things utter, nor is there eternal silence in the places where you cannot come. No feet have walked, nor shall, on the ice of Glund; no eye looked up from beneath on the Ring of Lurga, and Ironplain in Neruval is chaste and empty. Yet it is not for nothing that the gods walked ceaselessly around the fields of Arbol. Blessed be He!'

'That Dust itself which is scattered so rare in Heaven, whereof all worlds, and the bodies that are not worlds, are made, is at the centre. It waits not till created eyes have seen it or hands handled it, to be in itself a strength and splendour of Maleldil. Only the least part has served, or ever shall, a beast, a man or a god. But always, and beyond all distances, before they came and after they are gone and where they never come, it is what it is and utters the heart of the Holy One with its own voice. It is farthest from Him of all things, for it has no life, nor sense, nor reason; it is nearest to Him of all things for without intervening soul, as sparks fly out of fire, He utters in each grain of it the unmixed image of His energy. Each grain, if it spoke, would say, I am at the centre; for me all things were made. Let no mouth open to gainsay it. Blessed be He!'

'Each grain is at the centre. The Dust is at the centre. The Worlds are at the centre. The beasts are at the centre. The ancient peoples are there. The race that sinned is there. Tor and Tinidril are there. The gods are there also. Blessed be He!'

'Where Maleldil is, there is the centre. He is in every place. Not some of Him in one place and some in another, but in each place the whole Maleldil, even in the smallness beyond thought. There is no way out of the centre save into the Bent Will which casts itself into the Nowhere. Blessed be He!'

'Each thing was made for Him. He is the centre. Because we are with Him, each of us is at the centre. It is not as in a city of the Darkened World where they say that each must live for all. In His city all things are made for each. When He died in the Wounded World He died not for me, but for each man. If each man had been the only man made, he would have done no less. Each thing, from the single grain of Dust to the strongest *eldil*, is the end and the final cause of all creation and the mirror in which the beam of His brightness comes to rest and so returns to Him. Blessed be He!'

'In the plan of the Great Dance plans without number interlock, and each movement becomes in its season the breaking into flower of the whole design to which all else had been directed. Thus each is equally at the centre and none are there by being equals, but some by giving place and some by receiving it, the small things by their smallness and the great by their greatness, and all the patterns linked and looped together by the unions of a kneeling with a sceptred love. Blessed be He!'

'He has immeasurable use for each thing that is made, that His love and splendour may flow forth like a strong river which has need of a great watercourse and fills alike the deep pools and the little crannies, that are filled equally and remain unequal; and when it has filled them brim full it flows over and makes new channels. We also have need beyond measure of all that He has made. Love me, my brothers, for I am infinitely necessary to you and for your delight I was made. Blessed be He!'

'He has no need at all of anything that is made. An *eldil* is not more needful to Him than a grain of the Dust: a peopled world nor more needful than a world that is empty: but all needless alike, and what all add to Him is nothing. We also have no need of anything that is made. Love me, my brothers, for I am infinitely superfluous, and your love shall be like His, born neither of your need nor of my deserving, but a plain bounty. Blessed be He!'

'All things are by Him and for Him. He utters Himself also for His own delight and sees that He is good. He is His own begotten and what proceeds from Him is Himself. Blessed be He!'

'All that is made seems planless to the darkened mind, because there are more plans than it looked for. In these seas there are islands where the hairs of the turf are so fine and so closely woven together that unless a man looked long at them he would see neither hairs not weaving at all, but only the same and the flat. So with the Great Dance. Set your eyes on one movement and it will lead you through all patterns and it will seem to you the master movement. But the seeming will be true. Let no mouth open to gainsay it. There seems no plan because it is all plan: there seems no centre because it is all centre. Blessed be He!'

'Yet this seeming also is the end and final cause for which He spreads out Time so long and Heaven so deep; lest if we never met the dark, and the road that leads no-whither, and the question to which no answer is imaginable, we should have in our minds no likeness of the Abyss of the Father, into which if a creature drop down his thoughts for ever he shall hear no echo return to him. Blessed, blessed, blessed be He!'

And now, by a transition which he did not notice, it seemed that what had begun as speech was turned into sight, or into something that can be remembered only as if it were seeing. He thought he saw the Great Dance. It seemed to be woven out of the intertwining undulation of many cords or bands of light, leaping over and under one another and mutually embraced in arabesques and flower-like subtleties. Each figure as he looked at it became the master-figure or focus of the whole spectacle, by means of which his eye disentangled all else and brought it into unity – only to be itself entangled when he looked to what he had taken for mere marginal decorations and found that there also the same hegemony was claimed, and the claim made good, yet the former pattern not thereby dispossessed but finding in its new subordination a significance greater than that which it had abdicated. He could see also (but the word 'seeing' is now plainly inadequate) wherever the ribbons or serpents of light intersected, minute corpuscles of momentary brightness: and he knew somehow that these particles were the secular generalities of which history tells – peoples, institutions, climates of opinion, civilisations, arts, sciences, and the like – ephemeral coruscations that piped their short song and vanished. The ribbons or cords themselves, in which millions of corpuscles lived and died, were things of some different kind. At first he could not say what. But he knew in the end that most of them were individual entities. If so, the time in which the Great Dance proceeds is very unlike time as we know it. Some of the thinner and more delicate cords were beings that we call short-lived: flowers and insects, a fruit or a storm of rain, and once (he thought) a wave of the sea. Others were such things as we also think lasting: crystals, rivers, mountains, or even stars. Far above these in girth and luminosity and flashing with colours from beyond our spectrum were the lines of the personal beings, and yet as different from one another in splendour as all of them from all the previous class. But not all the cords were individuals; some were universal truths or universal qualities. It did not surprise him then to find that these and the persons were both cords and both stood together against the mere atoms of generality which lived and died in the clashing of their streams: but afterwards, when he came back to earth, he wondered. And by now the thing must have passed altogether out of the region of sight as we understand it. For he says that the whole solid figure of these enamoured and inter-inanimated circlings was suddenly revealed as the mere superficies of a far vaster pattern in four dimensions, and that figure as the boundary of yet others in other worlds: till suddenly as the movement grew yet swifter, the interweaving yet more ecstatic, the relevance of all to all yet more intense, as dimension was added to dimension and that part of him which could reason and remember was dropped farther and farther behind that part of him which saw, even then, at the very zenith of complexity, complexity was eaten up and faded, as a thin white cloud fades into the hard blue burning of the sky, and a simplicity beyond all comprehension, ancient and young as spring, illimitable, pellucid, drew him with cords of infinite desire into its own stillness. He went up into such a quietness, a privacy and a freshness that at the very moment when he stood farthest from our ordinary mode of being he had the sense of stripping off encumbrances and awaking from trance, and coming to himself. With a gesture of relaxation he looked about him …

The animals had gone. The two white figures had disappeared. Tor and Tinidril and he were alone, in ordinary Perelandrian daylight, early in the morning.

'Where are the beasts?' said Ransom.

'They have gone about their small affairs,' said Tinidril. 'They have gone to bring up their whelps and lay their eggs, to build their nests and spin their webs and dig their burrows, to sing and play and to eat and drink.'

'They did not wait long,' said Ransom, 'for I feel it is still early in the morning.'

'But not the same morning,' said Tor.

'We have been here long, then?' asked Ransom.

'Yes,' said Tor. 'I did not know it till now. But we have accomplished one whole circle about Arbol since we met on this mountain top.'

'A year?' said Ransom. 'A whole year? O Heavens, what may by now have happened in my own dark world! Did you know, Father, that so much time was passing?'

'I did not feel it pass,' said Tor. 'I believe the waves of time will often change for us henceforward. We are coming to have it in our own choice whether we shall be above them and see many waves together or whether we shall reach them one by one as we used to.'

'It comes into my mind,' said Tinidril, 'that today, now that the year has brought us back to the same place in Heaven, the *eldil* are coming for Piebald to take him back to his own world.'

'You are right, Tinidril,' said Tor. Then he looked at Ransom and said, 'There is a red dew coming up out of your foot, like a little spring.'

Ransom looked down and saw that his heel was still bleeding. 'Yes,' he said, 'it is where the Evil One bit me. The redness is *hrū* [blood].'

'Sit down, friend,' said Tor, 'and let me wash your foot in this pool.' Ransom hesitated but the King compelled him. So presently he sat on the little bank and the King knelt before him in the shallow water and took the injured foot in his hand. He paused as he looked at it.

'So this is *hrū*,' he said at last. 'I have never seen such a fluid before. And this is the substance wherewith Maleldil remade the worlds before any world was made.'

He washed the foot for a long time but the bleeding did not stop. 'Does it mean that Piebald will die?' said Tinidril at last.

'I do not think so,' said Tor. 'I think that any of his race who has breathed the air that he has breathed and drunk the waters that he has drunk since he came to the Holy Mountain will not find it easy to die. Tell me, Friend, was it not so in your world that after they had lost their paradise the men of your race did not learn to die quickly?'

'I had heard,' said Ransom, 'that those first generations were long livers, but most take it for only a Story or a Poetry and I had not thought of the cause.'

'Oh!' said Tinidril suddenly. 'The *eldila* are come to take him.'

Ransom looked round and saw, not the white manlike forms in which he had last seen Mars and Venus, but only the almost invisible lights. The King and Queen apparently recognised the spirits in this guise also: as easily, he thought, as an earthly King would recognise his acquaintance even when they were not in court dress.

The King released Ransom's foot and all three of them went towards the white casket. Its covering lay beside it on the ground. All felt an impulse to delay.

'What is this that we feel, Tor?' said Tinidril.

'I don't know,' said the King. 'One day I will give it a name. This is not a day for making names.'

'It is like a fruit with a very thick shell,' said Tinidril. 'The joy of our meeting when we meet again in the Great Dance is the sweet of it. But the rind is thick – more years thick than I can count.'

'You see now,' said Tor, 'what that Evil One would have done to us. If we listened to him we should now be trying to get at that sweet without biting through the shell.'

'And so it would not be "That sweet" at all,' said Tinidril.

'It is now his time to go,' said the tingling voice of an *eldil*. Ransom found no words to say as he laid himself down in the casket. The sides rose up high above him like walls: beyond them, as if framed in a coffin-shaped window, he saw the golden sky and the faces of Tor and Tinidril. 'You must cover my eyes,' he said presently: and the two human forms went out of sight for a moment and returned. Their arms were full of the rose-red lilies. Both bent down and kissed him. He saw the King's hand lifted in blessing and then never saw anything again in that world. They covered his face with the cool petals till he was blinded in a red sweet-smelling cloud.

'Is it ready?' said the King's voice. 'Farewell, Friend and Saviour, farewell,' said both voices. 'Farewell till we three pass out of the dimensions of time. Speak of us always to Maleldil as we speak always of you. The splendour, the love, and the strength be upon you.'

Then came the great cumbrous noise of the lid being fastened on above him. Then, for a few seconds, noises without, in the world from which he was eternally divided. Then his consciousness was engulfed.

Voyager Classics

The Martian Chronicles

Ray Bradbury

The Martian Chronicles, Ray Bradbury's second book, made his reputation and is still considered by many to be his finest work. These closely interwoven short stories, skilfully linked by recurring images and themes, evoke a beautifully nostalgic sense of loss and isolation.

The book tells the story of humanity's repeated attempts to colonize the red planet. The first men were few. Most succumbed to a disease called the Great Loneliness when they saw their home planet dwindle to the size of a fist. Those who survived found no welcome on Mars. But more rockets arrived from Earth, and more. People brought their old prejudices with them – and their desires and fantasies and tainted dreams. These strange and wonderful tales of man's experiences on Mars are filled with intense images and astonishing visions. As much a work of social criticism as of science fiction, *The Martian Chronicles* is an allegory for the tragic moral blindness of mankind, told in wonderfully evocative prose.

'Bradbury has a remarkable range and intensity of vision'
                                                    Sunday Times

0 00 711962 3

Voyager Classics

The Songs of Distant Earth

Arthur C. Clarke

For many Arthur C. Clarke is the very personification of science fiction. In *The Songs of Distant Earth* he perfectly captures man's longing for the stars in a thoughtful and hauntingly evocative tale of doomsday and beyond that tells of human diversity and the meaning of loss.

Over centuries of knowing the end was at hand humanity launched probes carrying embryos to distant star-systems, relying on machines to incubate the first people of a virgin land under an alien sun. Finally, in the Last Days of Earth, the *Magellan* takes off for the stars carrying a million refugees. They witness the death of Earth as they leave: the Atlantic boils dry, the pyramids disintegrate, the ice of Antarctica melts. Then they sleep. Five hundred years later the *Magellan* must make planetfall for repairs. The voyagers awake to find themselves on the idyllic planet of Thalassa. Curious yet wary, the Thalassans offer their distant cousins a cautious welcome and alien destinies become inextricably entwined in a clash of cultures unlike any before.

'A one-man literary Big Bang, Clarke has originated his own vast and teeming futurist universe' *Sunday Times*

0 00 711586 5

Voyager Classics

The Once and Future King

T H White

Tales of King Arthur and the Round Table have an enduring fascination. T. H. White's glorious retelling of the legend brings to life the major British epic of all time with brillance, grandeur, warmth and charm.

The four volumes that make up *The Once and Future King* (*The Sword in the Stone, the Witch in the Wood, The Ill-Made Knight* and *The Candle in the Wind*) bring into sharp focus the essential tragedy of Arthur's life – his illegitimate birth – which leads to his begetting Mordred upon his half-sister Morgan Le Fay, the Queen of Air and Darkness. The tale begins with the story of a young orphan boy growing up in a castle. His tutor, the magician Merlyn, guards the secret of his true identity until one day the boy comes across a sword stuck fast in a stone. Exquisite comedy offsets the tragedy of Arthur's personal doom and White's own overwhelming nostalgia for a lost land of England.

'Magnificent and tragic, an irresistible mixture of gaiety and pathos'   *Sunday Times*

0 00 711713 2

Voyager Classics

Red Mars

Kim Stanley Robinson

Red Mars is the first volume in Kim Stanley Robinson's monumental *Mars* trilogy, the product of years of dedicated research and the author's fascination with the Red Planet. The result is a timeless masterpiece, the ultimate in future history.

In 2027 one hundred of Earth's finest engineers and scientists make the first mass-landing on Mars. Their mission is to work together to terraform a fozen wasteland with no atmosphere into a new Eden. But before any of the team even sets foot on their new home factions are forming, tensions are rising and violence is brewing. Before they can achieve their dreams the new Martians must struggle against their own self-destructive instincts. *Red Mars* is a gripping study of the human condition and what it takes to create a new world and a brand-new society; a tale steeped in human truths, the development of myth and a love of place that is utterly convincing in its insight into a future that could be ours.

'A complex combination of science fiction and fact, political and social commentary together with strong characterization and a brilliantly conceived plot'   *Time Out*

0 00 711590 3

Voyager Classics

The Fellowship of the Ring

J R R Tolkien

The Fellowship of the Ring is the first part of J.R.R. Tolkien's epic adventure, *The Lord of the Rings*, which has been consistently acclaimed as the most popular and significant book of the twentieth century. With this work Tolkien virtually single-handedly created the fantasy genre, and no other writer has surpassed him.

When *The Fellowship of the Ring* was first published in 1954 its effect on the literary establishment was like a pebble striking still water. Attempting to find words to describe it at the time, reviewers were at a loss; the author, Richard Hughes, said: 'one can't praise the book by comparisons – there is nothing to compare it with. For width of imagination it almost beggars parallel, and it is nearly as remarkable for its vividness and for the narrative skill which carries the reader on, enthralled, for page after page.' C. S. Lewis was equally enthusiastic: 'No imaginary world has been projected which is at once so multifarious and so true to its own inner laws; none so relevant to the actual human situation yet so free from allegory.'

The ripples of its impact continue to be felt today.

0 00 711711 6

Voyager Classics

Fahrenheit 451

Ray Bradbury

Fahrenheit 451 is the classic novel of a post-literate future, a prophetic account of Western civilization's enslavement by the media, drugs and conformity. Bradbury's beautiful, ebullient prose combines with uncanny insight into the potential of technology to create a novel that, almost fifty years since its first publication, still has the power to dazzle and shock.

The hero, Montag, is a fireman. His job is to burn books, which are forbidden, being the source of all discord and unhappiness. Even so Montag is unhappy; there is discord in his marriage. He can't afford the fourth wall-sized television screen his wife, Mildred, wants – for a fuller appreciation of the interactive soaps that occupy her days. An encounter with their new next-door neighbour, Clarisse, further unsettles Montag. The girl has vitality, curiousity, conversation. When Clarisse disappears mysteriously, Montag's melancholy leads his wife to suspect he is keeping books in the house, and reading them.

'*Fahrenheit 451* is the most skilfully drawn of all science fiction's conformist hells'
                                                        KINGSLEY AMIS

0 00 711710 8